A CLARION CALL

RACHAEL C. DUNCAN

A Clarion Call
by Rachael C. Duncan

Published in the United States by Wolfpack Publishing, Las Vegas

CKN Christian Publishing
An Imprint of Wolfpack Publishing
5130 S. Fort Apache Road 215-380
Las Vegas, NV 89148christiankindlenews.com

Paperback ISBN: 978-1-63977-015-1
eBook ISBN: 978-1-63977-014-4
LCCN 2021950980

A CLARION CALL

CHAPTER 1

Julia

Living in poverty was a terrible new experience for Julia.

Her first month of marriage had been eye-opening, to say the least. For one accustomed to endless pillared walkways wrapped in curling tendrils of delicate green ivy, exotic marble archways and elegant cedar panels, blossoming garden courtyards, luxurious ritual baths, enchanting colorful frescoes splashed across the towering walls of wide open spaces, and mesmerizing mosaics swirling elegantly underfoot, the one-room, dirt-floored hovel she now shared with a constantly absent husband threatened to smother the free-spirited Julia in her own thoughts of gloom and despondency.

Oh, how the mighty had fallen! But hadn't she been warned? Didn't Father caution her to rethink her decision to marry Barabbas?

Looking back now, Julia readily acknowledged

her father's wisdom.

But she had been smitten the moment she'd laid eyes on Barabbas. He had possessed a restless energy and an intensity that had left her breathless. His dark, flashing eyes, fierce, handsome features, and broad shoulders atop an extremely muscular form were built to capture maidens' hearts.

Oh, he'd captured Julia's heart, alright. Captured it, then shattered it into a thousand scattered and broken pieces.

Taking up her broom with a dismal sigh, Julia wondered if she'd ever be able to put it back together again.

You can't, beloved. Not by your own strength. But I can. I AM. I am able.

Julia paused mid-sweep, a small smile playing about the corners of her full rosy lips. This was new and exciting – this still small voice that whispered confirmation and encouragement to her broken heart. She now felt God's presence accompany her as she hurried about her daily chores – chores she utterly detested, yet tasks that became bearable when she focused her attentions upon her Heavenly Father, the true Lover of her soul, the One who promised to never leave her or forsake her.

Basking in the warm glow of loving affirmation, Julia drew comfort from the gentle and familiar *swish, swish, swish* of her broom as she swept the floor, careful not to miss any elusive patches or corners of the little house. She still found herself amused at the prospect of sweeping the dirt off the *dirt floor*. But Barabbas insisted she keep an extremely tidy house, often becoming accusatory and confrontational if she neglected one of the household tasks or if her performance didn't meet his expectations.

Well, she'd groveled through the first two months of marriage, learning to do chores she'd never once attempted in her previous life of luxury while living comfortably in her wealthy merchant father's enormous marble villa. With a pang to her heart, Julia often considered the fine luxuries her father had lavished upon her during her golden childhood. Never once had she thanked him for the hard work and sacrifice he had invested in order to provide such things for her, her mother, and her five elder siblings. Though cliché, the phrase was painfully, tragically true: One never truly knew what blessings one possessed until they were gone.

What she wouldn't give to enjoy those comforts and luxuries now! To sleep once more in her luxuriant four-poster canopy bed, to sink into the soft Egyptian sheets and layers of warm blankets! To enjoy her own private chambers, lavishly decorated, rich Babylonian curtains gracing towering arched windows overlooking the lovely, blossoming grounds of her father's villa estate. To soak leisurely in the warm ritual baths and breathe in the heady fragrance of exotic bath salts and rich perfumes! To perch comfortably upon her favorite marble bench encircling the magnificent fountain within the garden courtyard, relishing the soft splashing of the fountain spray as it cascaded into the crystal pool beneath in glorious rainbow-tinted hues.

How Julia longed to run into her father's open arms, to thank him for the blessed childhood he had so lavishly bestowed upon her! How she longed to sit beside him in his enormous office library, asking endless questions about the life-giving truths of the Law she had once despised.

Her father would have the answers to her questions. Her father would know exactly how to instruct her. Unlike the unbearable months preceding her marriage, Julia knew she would eagerly absorb any counsel Simon had to offer. He was such a wise man. Yes, he was an astute and ridiculously successful man of business, but he also possessed a grasp of the Scriptures that was almost uncanny.

How she would welcome such knowledge now!

But Julia hadn't seen her beloved father since the day of her wedding vows. Barabbas had denied her teary requests to visit her childhood home, and her parents were too polite to venture forth where they were clearly not welcome.

Since that fateful day when she had left the protection of her father's house for the promise of love from another, Julia had seen her dear mother only once.

Two weeks after her wedding ceremony – if the pathetic little gathering could even be called a ceremony – one of her father's servants had brought over several trunks containing her elaborate wardrobe and cherished jewelry, along with her elegant little jars of cosmetics. She'd been so ecstatic over the arrival of her belongings that she hadn't noticed the servant's evident concern over her situation.

She received a surprise visit from Iskah several days later. Thankfully, Barabbas was still away with her father's traveling caravan.

In her typically composed manner, Iskah had taken a seat on the splintering little bench at her daughter's kitchen table, accepted the mug of watered wine Julia had offered her, and politely hid her horror at the scarcity and apparent poverty of her daughter's new whereabouts.

Cheeks aflame in shame and embarrassment, Julia had done her best to make her mother comfortable and play the part of impeccable hostess. It wasn't long, however, before Julia found herself enveloped in her mother's warm arms. Sobbing in brokenhearted defeat, Julia had apologized for her rebellion and begged to return home to her father's villa.

Drawing on the inner strength she quietly possessed, Iskah had comforted her grieving daughter, promising to pray for her each day. But she refused to take her daughter away from her husband.

"This is the path you have chosen, my dear Julia," she had whispered softly, stroking back several stray strands of her daughter's prized golden-brown curls. "You must honor God and keep your vows. But know that I love you. I will always, always love you."

These recent memories were painful, but they were also sweet. The long, lonely hours passed more bearably when Julia remembered to count her blessings: She served a faithful God. Her father and mother loved her deeply. They prayed for her.

She had food and shelter, despite the fact that her circumstances left much to be desired. She was healthy and strong.

Julia forced another smile as she continued to sweep the hard-packed earthen floor. She swept beneath the rough wooden table and benches and took special care near the large fireplace, where ashes and soot often gathered in unwanted little piles. Though the two small windows remained open, little light streamed in, and Julia found it difficult to see what she was doing, even with the help of several steadily burning oil lamps.

Having swept the house to the best of her abilities, Julia placed the broom in the small storage room at the back of the home and prepared to kindle a fire in the hearth. She must boil the water first in order to cook the shriveled-looking vegetables she had purchased from a vendor on Small Market Street. Barabbas gave her very little coin to barter with; therefore, she often returned home with old, inferior produce.

She felt an all-too-familiar, unwelcome churning in her stomach, and attempted to push her thoughts aside.

Barabbas made a decent income. Her father paid his salary, for heaven's sake! So where did all that money *go*? He certainly wasn't spending it on *her*. Nor himself, for that matter. He wore the same practical desert garb of a caravan guard day after day. Their home was simple, small, and threadbare. The only furniture they possessed had already been in the house –probably for *centuries*, Julia often thought – when he bought it. He allowed her very little coin for groceries and supplies.

Did Barabbas hoard income, hiding it somewhere in the dark recesses of their little home where she'd never find it? Did he spend it on drink or women – heaven forbid – on his long, arduous treks through Roman provinces?

Julia sighed, silently chiding herself for allowing her thoughts to return down this beaten path again. It only angered her more to think about it. She mustn't dwell on things she could never change.

Bent over a large kettle hanging over sputtering embers, Julia froze, ladle in hand. The faint, soft tingling of bells drifted easily upon the air. The sound was pleasant, light upon the senses, enticing one to venture after the sweetly alluring melody.

Why, Julia was fairly certain the bells were drawing steadily nearer, their high pitch rising in strength and volume in a rather eerie fashion…

KNOCK, KNOCK, KNOCK!

Nearly jumping out of her skin, Julia's heart sprang into her throat at the unexpected raps upon her front door, cutting short the lovely sound of tinkling bells.

With shaking hands, Julia set aside her ladle and padded over to the door. She kept it closed and bolted when Barabbas was away, according to his uncompromising instructions.

Julia swung open the door, totally unprepared for the decadent stranger poised shamelessly on the other side.

CHAPTER 2

"I'm looking for the man of the house."

Julia could hear her own heart hammering loudly in her ears. She was certain this painted woman upon her threshold could hear it, too.

Who on earth was this brazen woman? And why was she standing on Julia's doorstep?

If not for the worldly harshness of the woman's features, she might have been lovely. In another lifetime – before the ravages of life and the cruelties of her profession had taken their ugly toll – perhaps she had been young and attractive. Raven black hair cascaded down her back and shoulders in a billowy cloud of tight, curly tendrils. Her eyes were dark and flashing, rimmed with black kohl and bright paint. Her lips were also generously lined and painted. Bracelets crowned her bare arms. Her ears and throat were graced with gold. She wore no head covering, and her clothing was form-fitting and extremely revealing for a woman of Jewish descent.

"Well?" the woman's tone was harsh, low and breathy. Did men actually consider it seductive?

Julia swallowed hard, her eyes traveling to the intricate golden bells dangling from chunky anklets wrapped about the woman's exposed ankles. Golden bells also jingled from bracelets piled on her delicate wrists. How could such a lovely sound emanate from such a foul source?

Julia had never seen a harlot before – at least not up close. And now, the presence of an immoral woman leaning calmly upon her very own doorpost unnerved her. Why was she here? Surely the woman had mistakenly approached the wrong house!

"Is something the matter? Are you deaf? Dumb? Mute? All of the above?"

Heat coursed through Julia's veins like red hot venom. How dare this wicked creature disrespect her in her own home! It was unthinkable!

Instantly, she found her tongue.

"I believe you have the wrong house. Good day." Julia started to close the door.

Brazenly, the women caught the edge of the door.

Furious, Julia swung the door with all her might. If the woman's long, painted claws and bejeweled fingers were smashed in the door, so be it!

"I come seeking Barabbas of Jerusalem!" the woman rasped. "I was told I would find him here."

Julia froze, releasing her hold on the door, a flood of sickening emotions washing over her like a tidal wave. For a moment, she wondered if she would be sick. If so, she prayed the foul trajectory would spill in this woman's direction.

The woman flashed a racy smile, displaying pearly white teeth. She appeared to be savoring

Julia's discomfort. "Ah, so this *is* the right house."

Julia attempted to calm her racing heart. Angry heat poured into her face, and she could feel the damp sweat beading her forehead.

"My *husband*," she stated emphatically, "is not home. And he wouldn't wish to see you, so please –"

"Oh, but I beg to differ." The woman eyed Julia the way a cat might size up a mouse.

Julia bit back a sharp retort. Taking a deep breath, she forced herself to meet the woman's taunting gaze.

"How do you know my husband?" Julia demanded, her voice shaking angrily.

The woman offered a cat-like smile. "A business transaction."

Julia's eyes narrowed. What kind of *business*?

The woman released a loud, longsuffering sigh. "I see I am not to be invited in. And as you insist upon being disagreeable, I won't overstay my welcome."

Julia's only response was glaring silence.

The woman lifted the hem of her robe, revealing a long, smooth leg. Julia looked away, perturbed. Had this woman not the slightest speck of decency or modesty?

With long, slender fingers, the woman unlashed a dagger strapped to her leg beneath her expensive, flowing robes.

Julia knew a moment of real fear, until she recognized the dagger. It was a stunning piece; a ceremonial dagger Barabbas had acquired – supposedly honestly – on one of his many journeys.

Instantly, her fear gave way to fury. "What are

you doing with my husband's dagger?"

"It was held in surety in exchange for payment. My purchase was delivered this morning, so I am no longer in need of this."

Her *purchase*? Suddenly, the pieces fell into place for Julia. *Her purchase*. Last week, Barabbas had announced he'd found a buyer for the beautiful alabaster jar Iskah had gifted to Julia as a wedding present.

Julia had wept at his announcement. Secretly, she had been praying that Barabbas would be unable to obtain a buyer for something so expensive and exquisite. How could Julia bear to part with it?

Apparently, this painted woman was his buyer. Conveniently, Barabbas had failed to mention the fact that she was a prostitute.

Anger welled up inside Julia. She felt as if her already-fragile heart had been ripped in two. And how was she to know if the sale of her alabaster jar was the only "business" conducted between her husband and this brazen woman? How had they even *met*?

Her thoughts traveled back to her lovely alabaster jar. *Her* alabaster jar! *Hers*! It curdled her gut to even consider the fact that it had been pawned off to this puffed up, immoral ingrate. What would *this* woman even do with something like that? The alabaster jar, filled with the intoxicating essence of nard, was to be used to anoint a husband on one's wedding night.

Julia doubted the woman standing brazenly before her possessed the slightest inclination toward marriage. And furthermore, seriously doubted she'd waste perfume worth an entire year's wages on a...a *client*. Why, a crafty businesswoman like this – she probably planned to sell the lovely jar and make a profit! She wouldn't even appreciate its beauty, its significance.

Life was so unfair.

"Well? Are you going to take this atrocity off my hands, or are you simply going to stand there like a dumb statue?"

Julia was drawn from her silent reverie by the stinging insult. She took the dagger with more force than she intended, slightly tempted to use it.

Amused, the woman planted her hand upon a curvy hip. "Tell your husband I dropped by," she said with an avaricious gleam in her eye.

"And who shall I say you are?" Julia wondered why she cared.

The woman flashed another practiced smile. "Mary. And yours, pet?"

"Julia." *And I'm not your pet,* she huffed silently.

The woman held back a derisive snort. "Julia. A sweet name."

Clenching her jaw at the woman's haughty tone, Julia prepared to shut the door once more.

"Oh, and, Julia?"

Julia hated the sound of her own name on the woman's oiled lips. She acknowledged Mary with a slight lift of her slender brows.

A predatory grin crossed Mary's hard features as she added in a flinty tone, "Your husband is a good-looking man."

Julia writhed inwardly.

"It was a pleasure doing business with him."

Julia slammed the door in the woman's face and pressed her back up against it, breathing heavily. With an angry cry, she flung the dagger across the room. It pinged off the large stone fireplace and landed on the dirt floor with a heavy *thud* and a puff of dust.

It was a pleasure doing business with him!

Just what, exactly, did Mary mean by that? Surely it wasn't what it sounded like. Surely... surely the harlot was a lying witch who relished the suffering of others.

Trembling, Julia drew a shaky hand to her heart, attempting to still its fierce pounding.

What on earth had just happened? Should she question Barabbas about Mary? Should she trust him if he denied anything indecent? Was Barabbas trustworthy? Surely her husband was faithful to her! Surely this was nothing to be concerned about?

Still pressed against the door, Julia uttered a silent prayer and attempted to still her violent trembling.

It is nothing. That woman would like nothing more than to sow dissension within a marriage. Certainly, that's all there is to it. Nothing more. Nothing more at all.

Nevertheless, a seed of doubt – and resentment – had been planted.

CHAPTER 3

Melina

The Upper Agora, with its impressive pillared Greco-Roman arcades surrounding a glistening open court, appeared particularly grandiose – a stark and breathtaking silhouette stamped upon the horizon as dawn's pink and golden hues streaked across a winter sky. The wind had adopted a certain wintry chill, rather unusual for Jerusalem even in the midst of brisk winter months.

Shivering, Melina pulled her shawl closer about her thin ivory stola and picked up her pace, careful to balance her basket of produce as she hastened toward Herod's Jerusalem palace.

The Upper Agora had been rather quiet at this early hour, and she'd had her pick of the day's freshest merchandise. Even so, she had made her selections quickly, eager to return to the warmth of the palace's stone enclosures.

Still, Melina paused, chancing one last glance

behind her.

Elias, the palace cook, continued to send her to the market often, and for that she was grateful. She cherished this small sliver of freedom, this blessed responsibility. Here, she enjoyed weekly meetings with her dear friend, Malchus. Under his knowledgeable tutelage, her own understanding of the holy Scriptures was broadening daily. Therefore, this typically bustling attraction would always hold a special place in her heart.

And yet...she never left the Upper Agora without a sharp twinge of sorrow and regret. For it was here she had met her first and dearest friend, Julia. It was here that their friendship had blossomed and flourished as they shared their secrets and bore each other's burdens. It was here that Julia had schooled her in the ways of the one true God.

And it was here that Julia had forsaken their friendship.

A tremulous sigh escaped Melina's lips as she remembered their last meeting. Malchus had been present as well. It had been a delightful afternoon, as Julia and Malchus recounted stories about heroes of the faith.

A swift and stormy temper had blown over Julia when Melina attempted to offer her counsel concerning Julia's father and the man Julia planned to marry. Julia had been at odds with her father, Simon, at the time, and hadn't appreciated Melina's sympathy for the aging merchant scholar. The young woman had stormed off in a fit of temper.

Melina had not seen her since.

She could only hope that Julia had found the note she had left for her in the barely noticeable crag within one of the colonnaded walls – the special hiding place in which they tucked away secret messages for each other. Melina had returned shortly after leaving the message, to find that her note had vanished.

But many months had passed, and still there was no word from Julia. Melina supposed it was foolish, but she still slipped beneath those massive arcades each time she went to the market – hoping, praying, that perhaps her slender fingers would brush against a welcome message scrawled hastily upon a piece of papyrus.

And, like today, Melina always returned to the palace with a lump in her throat and a heavy heart.

She supposed she must accept the fact that her friendship with Julia had ended months ago. After all, Julia had probably married the man of her dreams by now. Melina doubted that Julia even remembered her. Why would she – the aristocratic and wealthy daughter of the richest merchant in Jerusalem – remember a lowly serving girl like Melina? After all, Julia's wildest dreams had probably come true. She was married. Happy. Determined and headstrong, she had probably succeeded in gaining everything she had ever wanted.

With a quiet sigh of acceptance, Melina drew her shawl tightly about her shivering form and quickened her pace. She was more than ready to escape this wintry chill – not so much the one carried upon the brisk morning breezes as the chill that gripped her heart when she allowed herself to ponder the painful past.

***

Conspicuously situated in the northwest corner of the Upper City, Herod's palace loomed like a massive bird of prey upon an enormous, elevated stone platform. Two massive main structures branched out like wings on either side of the palace compound, sheltering enormous open courtyards and gardens like emerald gems placed within an elaborate golden necklace. Armed sentries stood tall and alert about their posts, swords sheathed at their sides as they leaned upon deadly-looking spears.

Gingerly, Melina picked her way past the layers of bored guards, grateful once she finally found herself within the imposing palace walls.

The Jerusalem palace had remained eerily silent for many months now, as the royal family had taken up residence in Tiberias, and later, at Herod's desert fortress, Machaerus – the easternmost and most forbidding of Herod's palace fortresses. Only a smattering of trustworthy servants remained in Jerusalem to look after the upkeep of the ridiculously garish and overdone palace in Jerusalem.

Basket balanced delicately on one arm, Melina traveled frescoed, pillared walks toward the monumental palace kitchen, wondering when and if the royal family planned to return. She hadn't overheard any recent rumors concerning Herod's plans for the immediate future, despite vigilant attention to palace gossip. Though she refused to participate in it, Melina knew she must always remain one step ahead of her superiors in order to survive in this despotic house of intrigue.

Frankly, she was in no hurry for her master's return. Though beautiful, Herod's stepdaughter, Salome was whiny and demanding. Herodias, Herod's second wife, was pure evil wrapped in human flesh. And despite the fact that Melina was a favorite of Herod Antipas, the man was still unpredictable and dangerous when crossed.

"Back so soon?"

Melina smiled warmly as she passed beneath one of the enormous, beautifully tiled archways that led to the kitchen. "There is a chill in the air," she explained, her voice silvery and sweet.

"If only the rest of the staff were so briskly affected." Elias, a strong, sturdy man despite his age, continued to salt a mammoth slab of meat without bothering to look up. "With Herod so far away, they've spent their days lazing about and lying abed."

Melina noticed the few servants who had remained to serve in the kitchen were nowhere to be seen. Setting aside her shawl and basket of produce, she sidled up to Elias and smiled fondly. "They've left you to work all alone, I see."

"And this is new?" Elias snorted derisively.

"How can I help?"

"Haven't you chores of your own?"

"Plenty, but they'll wait for me to tend to them. They've never been known to do themselves."

Elias snorted again.

Melina hid another smile. She knew the crusty old cook would never admit his deepening affection, but he had proved it time and time again. He alone had stood between Melina and Herod's wicked overseer, Porcius, when the evil man attempted to work the fragile servant girl to death with endless demands and cruel beatings.

Crossing over to an enormous stone fireplace, Melina knelt and began to coax the dying flames back to life. She then added salt to the large kettles situated to boil over the kindling. Reaching for a paring knife, she joined Elias at the massive marble slab at which he worked, and dutifully began paring the fresh vegetables she had purchased at the market.

"If only the others possessed your willing spirit."

Melina glanced up at Elias with large, innocent green eyes, a question in them.

He shook his head. "You never wait to be ordered about. You observe what needs to be done, and you do it. Willingly. Efficiently."

Melina blushed prettily and lowered her gaze to the vegetables she busily pared. "It is my role to serve."

"And you do it gladly."

"As do you, Elias."

"I do it, yes. But gladly, no."

"Have you seen Porcius about lately?" Melina asked, intentionally changing the subject.

Elias lifted the enormous slab of raw meat and slammed it unceremoniously upon the table, salted side down. "Would you believe I have a piece of him right here?"

The chuckle escaped her lips before she could stop it.

"I believe Porcius would prove to be a bit tougher than that tender slab," she quipped, although she immediately regretted voicing the snide comment.

True, Porcius – the steward of Herod's magnificent palace estate – was a wicked man, but he was a lost soul in dire need of repentance. Porcius did not know the one true God as she did. Naturally, his standards would not line up with her own. She knew she must continue to pray for her tormentor. Only God could take a heart of stone like Porcius' and mold it into a tender heart of flesh, sensitive to His will.

"Forgive me," Melina amended, reaching for a fresh onion and a sharper knife. "I should not have spoken about Porcius in such a manner."

"You of all people have every right to speak ill of the man," Elias growled, vigorously salting the other side of meat.

"God is his Judge and my Vindicator," Melina said softly. "I have no right to criticize."

"You say the strangest things." Though Elias had been raised by his father, a Hellenistic Jew, and a Greek mother who worshiped a vast array of pagan deities, he refused to bend his knee to any god, whether Jewish, Greek, or Roman.

"I haven't seen him about in weeks. Do you suppose something has happened to him?"

"One can only hope."

"Elias!"

"Perhaps the man – like Job – has been plagued

by pestilent sores."

"You don't mean that."

"Of course, I don't. I'd rather see him strung up and dangling by his toes as a centerpiece in Herod's gardens."

"Elias."

"Along with the pestilent sores."

Melina shook her head and resumed her chopping.

Elias wasn't finished.

"Perhaps the gods have blessed us, and he's died of severe obesity."

"You don't believe in the gods."

"I'd pledge my allegiance to any god willing to smite him. Perhaps you should pray to your God and ask Him to do so. Doesn't He listen to you?"

"He listens to all of us, Elias."

"Then by the gods ask Him and do it quickly!"

"He doesn't work like that."

"Then I suppose you can see why I have no interest in Him."

Melina touched his arm, her eyes glowing with compassion. "But He is very interested in you."

Elias stiffened slightly at her touch and waved impatiently toward her vegetables. "Get those into the pot. The water's boiling."

Melina simply nodded in obeisance, honoring Elias' silent plea not to press him. He might refuse to discuss his Creator, but he certainly couldn't stop her from praying for him. What a joy it would be if this man would humble himself, becoming her brother in the faith!

Smiling to herself, Melina added her diced vegetables to the vigorously boiling pot, wiping the sweat from her brow as she turned back toward the enormous marble worktable. Despite the cooler weather, the kitchen had warmed up quickly!

"Halt right there!"

Melina's heart sprang into her throat.

An austere man dressed in the elegant Greco-Roman style stood calmly beneath a massive, tiled archway. Tall, lean, and strong, he bore an air of authority despite his graceful posture, soft features, and gently glowing eyes. His was a velvety brown complexion, only a shade or so lighter than that of an Ethiopian's. His head was shaved smooth. Beneath slender, well-shaped brows and a ridge of black lashes, rich chocolate eyes studied the startled pair in the kitchen.

"Kindly state your name and purpose for this intrusion upon my kitchen," Elias barked, bristling like an angry dog.

Melina remained poised near the cooking pots, ready to flee at a moment's notice. How on earth had this man bypassed the layers and layers of armed guards?

Yet despite her rapidly beating heart, Melina found herself curiously drawn to this sophisticated stranger.

His garments were surely impressive...and expensive. His golden robe, chased in elaborate purple and scarlet stitching, draped gracefully about his imposing frame. He wore a pendant of semiprecious stones about his neck. Gold rings glistened upon his fingers. He looked rather like a nobleman from some distant land, and Melina's fears slowly began to evaporate. Something about his composed demeanor set her mind at ease.

Yet despite the fact that this silent intruder appeared to be completely at ease, Melina imagined he was surely one to be reckoned with.

"Pardon the intrusion." The voice, like the stance, possessed both strength and authority.

"You've yet to declare your name and your intent," Elias' tone was brutally uncompromising. For the first time, Melina realized he clenched the largest of the kitchen knives in a white-knuckled fist.

The man wasn't a bit disturbed by the stormy countenance of the fierce palace cook. He offered the slightest trace of a smile.

"My name is Chuza. I am the new steward of Herod's household."

CHAPTER 4

Malchus

"I'm afraid there's very little soup left in the pot." Mara's tone indicated that she was anything but sorry. "And there is no bread. Nor cheese. A bit of watered wine remains."

Malchus retrieved a wooden bowl from a large walk-in pantry, ignoring Mara's feigned sympathy. The shrew had probably disposed of any leftovers worth partaking of. Now she would watch gleefully as he managed to swallow a watery bowl of stone-cold soup.

"I'm terribly sorry," Mara reiterated, crossing the enormous kitchen and reaching for a ladle resting upon the cooking pot dangling over cold embers. She had long since allowed the fire to die out. "You should not have tarried."

A wry look upon his olive-skinned features, Malchus' dark eyes glimmered antagonistically as he took the ladle from Mara's work-worn hand, stating tersely, "I can serve myself."

"Oh, I'm well aware of that."

Malchus glared at Mara sideways. Just what was that supposed to mean? The head cook had once been his closest ally.

Well, the woman was a fool. And a betrayer. Perhaps he'd been too blind to see it, or perhaps her alignment with a foul palace guard had gradually gnawed away at her decency. Regardless, Malchus neither knew nor cared. When Mara had suspected that Malchus may have been entangled with the famous Prophet whom Caiaphas – the treacherous high priest – detested, she had been more than willing to sell him out to their master in order to gain favor with Lucius, the guard she hoped to marry.

Malchus knew her dreams were futile. The man would never marry her. His promises were empty. Though he had convinced her to sell out her friends to a jealous and capricious high priest in exchange for the promise of an eventual union, Lucius simply used her to further his career and gratify his own fleshly lusts. If she was too ignorant to see it or to consider his wise counsel, then let her wallow in her own misery. After all, Malchus had tried to warn her. She had refused to listen.

Attempting to disregard the disturbing thoughts battling for his attention, Malchus fished about the cooking pot with the ladle, hoping to stumble upon a stray lentil or chopped vegetable floating about the watery mess. No such luck.

He'd hoped to evade Mara's presence by waiting until the household help had eaten their fill and retired for the night. He wouldn't make that mistake again. He knew one night on an empty stomach would teach him a lesson. How he loathed his own stubbornness!

Carelessly, Malchus filled his bowl, reached for a spoon, and prepared to leave. He could sense Mara's brown eyes upon him, but he refused to look her direction.

"The master would not approve of you taking those items out of the kitchen."

Malchus stiffened beneath a tiled archway, squeezing his spoon so tightly he wondered if it would snap in two.

"I doubt," Malchus muttered through gritted teeth, "the master will find out." His hackles rising, he turned on his heel to face the woman head-on. "Oh, but silly me. How quickly I forget. That would be your responsibility, would it not? To inform him of my every move."

Mara's large brown eyes flashed in indignation. "You are not being fair!"

"Aren't I? Don't tell me you've already retired from your valuable position as lead informant."

"I am not an informant!"

"No? Then what are you, Mara? A rat? A spy? A traitor? Which venerable title would you prefer? Or should I ask Lucius?"

"Lucius has nothing to do with this!"

"Don't give me that, Mara. You're the only one too blind to see his puppet strings dangling above your head."

"You are completely unreasonable! Can't you see

I am trying to mend things between us?"

"Then perhaps you shouldn't have shattered my trust into a thousand broken and jagged pieces to begin with!"

"Oh, please, Malchus. You were always one for theatrics. You sound like a melodramatic thespian, for heaven's sake!"

Malchus stared at her, drop-jawed, bowl of soup still in hand. He had nothing more to say to her.

"For heaven's sake, Malchus. Sit down!"

Really? She was actually going to order him about.

"I said, *sit*!"

Malchus clenched his teeth, slowly working his lower jaw back and forth. He had no desire to continue conversing with this stubborn woman. And yet something urged him to swallow his pride and take a seat at the large table where the servants often took their hasty meals.

Mara crossed over to the table and placed both hands upon the top of a high-backed wooden chair. "There. Now you're being reasonable."

Malchus despised her parental tone. "Patronize me, Mara, and I'm out that door."

"Why must you take offense at every little thing that I say?"

"It's not what you say, dear Mara, but what you *do*. Which tends to grossly contradict the things you *say* so blithely and easily."

There was a bitter pause. Tentatively, Mara seated herself opposite the younger man who had once greatly admired her. She sighed, appearing to make a study of her own two hands. When she finally spoke, it was so softly that Malchus had to stoop forward in order to catch the words.

"What has happened to us, Malchus?"

Malchus knew she desired sympathy, pity, understanding. Instead, he arched a sardonic brow. "Must you even ask? The fact that you *do* ask proves you bear no repentance, no remorse! You betrayed me – supposedly your dearest friend – for a man who uses you to further his own agenda!"

"Lucius does no such thing!" Mara's eyes blazed. "He loves me!"

Malchus felt his insides trembling with suppressed anger. "Ah, and here we are – yet again – repeating your favorite conversation! Clearly, Mara, we don't see eye to eye on this. So further discussion is a futile waste of time."

"Don't you see I desire to heal our friendship?"

"I desire no friendship with a woman who will gladly turn me over to Caiaphas when it suits her own purposes!"

"I never turned you in!"

"Well, good for you! That would've been rather difficult to do considering the fact that I'm not even a follower of Jesus!"

"But even if you had been, I would not have betrayed you."

"But you would betray others?"

Mara's gaze dropped to her hands once more. "No. Caiaphas simply wishes to stay informed about the goings-on in his household. He won't raise a hand against the followers of that Rabbi."

"Are you truly so foolish?" Malchus' blood was boiling.

"The sect is a threat to the law and the temple," Mara insisted. "I'm sure Caiaphas would desire to turn the followers' hearts back to the true faith. That's his role as shepherd of the people."

A brittle laugh escaped Malchus' lips. "Ah, yes. Caiaphas. The great shepherd of the people."

"Regardless, I would not have told him even if you *were* a follower! You aren't like the others, Malchus. I know you wouldn't wield this new faith as an excuse to breed revolution or uprisings, as Caiaphas fears some may. You wouldn't instigate revolt – why, you'd be the first to run from a fight."

Malchus wasn't sure if he should be relieved or insulted by that assurance.

"You're no threat to Caiaphas' office, and I know that. You can be trusted."

"Ah, if only the same could be said for you."

"You are hateful, Malchus." Mara was fuming. "I wouldn't tell. You should know that."

"I find that rather difficult to believe, considering that unfortunate little conversation I overheard between you and Lucius in the garden."

"I was simply curious!"

"Right."

"I was!"

"You know what, Mara? Just keep lying to yourself. That's about all I've seen you doing lately anyway. You're becoming quite the expert."

"How dare you!"

Malchus didn't hold her fiery gaze. Instead, he

looked away, defeated. Raking his hands through dark abundant hair that curled slightly upon his forehead, Malchus moaned. He hated this – he hated the strife. He'd avoided this woman like the plague for two months, hoping that she'd eventually get the message and leave him alone. He had no desire for confrontation. Only peace.

Yet he couldn't help but wonder how one who'd spent his years diligently seeking peace and avoiding strife should find himself planted right in the middle of ceaseless turmoil.

He'd been sold into Caiaphas' household as a small boy. Mara, a decade older than him, had taken him under her motherly wing. Though he'd done all in his power to erase the dreadful memories, Malchus could still recall the horror of that fateful night when the course of his life had been forever altered. He could see the rabid flames engulfing his small home, feel the stinging heat upon his skin, smell the dark billowing smoke that threatened to choke him. Strong arms had encircled his small, trembling form and delivered him from the ravaging flames.

He couldn't help but wonder...why had he been spared, when his mother and father had perished in the flames?

Malchus winced as fresh memories flooded his tortured mind. The entire house had collapsed upon itself only moments after his deliverance. He remembered hearing his own screams of terror as he'd wept over his inexplicable loss. And then he had given in to the exhaustion and trauma, curled tightly upon his side beneath some shrubby brush, and drifted into a trouble sleep. He had awakened the next morning to a devastating sight. He remembered watching pilfering men as they raked through the charred remains of his childhood home, carelessly kicking aside the bones of his loved ones as they searched for redeemable loot. He had wondered at the time if they were the very men who had set his home ablaze. Consumed with fear, the small boy had fled.

He would never know why his young legs had carried him to the temple. Perhaps it was because his father often spoke to the crowds from Solomon's Porch. Malchus had puzzled over his father's fiery words and the impending fury of the listening crowds many a time. A kindly priest had discovered the small boy, his clothing torn, and his body streaked with ash, soot, and tears.

Shortly after, he'd begun his life as a servant in the home of Caiaphas, the high priest. And since then, he had painstakingly avoided strife of any kind. Had his father kept his controversial thoughts to himself, he might still be alive today. How differently Malchus' circumstances would have been! Surely peace was to be desired above all else.

Malchus tried to remind himself of this as he glared angrily across the table at his former friend. If only she would leave him alone. Neither of them could change the past. They needed to move on – both of them. She was making this so much more difficult than it needed to be.

"You haven't touched your soup." Mara appeared to have composed herself with great effort.

"Funny, I've lost my appetite."

"You should eat to keep up your strength."

"Ah, another command."

"I'm only looking out for you!"

"If that were truly the case, we wouldn't be having this conversation now, would we?"

"You are impossible! You're no longer a child, Malchus! You're a grown man. Grow up!"

Malchus had had enough. The wooden chair legs screeched loudly upon the stone floor as he backed away from the table and propelled himself to his feet. Shoving the wooden bowl of watery soup across the table, he prepared to leave.

"Malchus!"

Malchus paused beneath a gargantuan stone archway, his eyes gleaming menacingly. "I don't need this."

"But your soup?"

"Keep it. I'd rather eat dust."

Mara gasped, insulted.

With a sardonic tip to his mouth, Malchus flung a final insult over his shoulder. "With cooking like that, it's no wonder the man refuses to marry you."

He heard an angry intake of breath as chair legs screeched once more upon the stone floor. He knew instinctively that Mara had sprung to her feet, trembling in rage.

But before she could make another comeback, Malchus slipped under the archway and ducked around a corner, out of sight.

As far as he was concerned, this conversation was over.

CHAPTER 5

Malchus burst into the cool night air, the evening breezes flowing over him like the soothing waters of Caiaphas' lavish ceremonial baths. He paced angrily about a magnificently pillared peristyle within the heart of Caiaphas' mansion. Curling tendrils of bright ivy and breathtaking greenery encircled elegant marble pillars. In the springtime, flowers burst forth in vibrant color, spilling over the sides of the enormous Grecian urns in which they were planted.

Now, in the dead of winter, only the green foliage remained.

Lately Malchus had avoided the palace gardens in the evening hours, as he tired of stumbling upon Mara's secret trysts with Lucius late at night. This peristyle was a magnificent escape. He had come to derive a certain level of peace from this quiet place – a breathtaking, open-ceilinged courtyard surrounded by pillared porticoes on all four sides. Once one escaped the confines of the porticoes, the sky was wide open above them, allowing the evening breezes to filter through the house and stir the tranquil waters of the glistening fishpond in the center of the elaborate affair. Overhead, dozens of dazzling stars winked and glistened from their respective places within a deep sea of black velvet. Underfoot, elegant tiles abounded in a breathtaking display of meandering mosaics – a sea of soft colors and swirling patterns.

Malchus continued to pace like a restless tiger, running his fingers through his dark hair in agitation. Pale moonlight slanted across the verdant courtyard, as elegant and stately as the marble pillars bathed in its light.

Even in his agitation, Malchus was aware of a still small voice buried deep inside him, seeking to be heard.

Forgive, it seemed to whisper softly to his troubled heart. *Forgive.*

But Malchus had no desire to forgive.

Bypassing the curved, polished marble benches arranged gracefully about the fishpond, Malchus dropped heavily to his knees and gazed into the tranquil waters dotted with fresh lily pads and an occasional blooming flower. A gently gurgling fountain bubbled from the depths of the pond, but the spray was so soft and gentle that the waters were barely disturbed.

Even bathed in moonlight, those still waters appeared dark and fathomless, like polished onyx. Malchus gazed into those waters, so peaceful, so serene, and wondered why his life could not be like that.

The Lord is my shepherd; I shall not want. He makes me to lie down in green pastures; He leads me beside the still waters...

Clenching his eyes shut, Malchus allowed the poetic words to roll over his troubled spirit. His mother had painstakingly taught him the Psalm of David. Funny those long-forgotten words should haunt him now. But why? Why now?

Was God speaking to Him? Reminding him of His presence in some way?

Malchus considered a prayer, but quickly dismissed the idea as fanciful and whimsical. Yes, he had acknowledged the God of his fathers – even pledged his allegiance to Him. But Malchus was certain that the Almighty God of the universe had far greater things to worry about than his own grousing complaints. Malchus would not trouble Him over something as trivial as a spat with another household servant.

But was that truly all that was troubling him?

"Well, well. By the gods, it *is* you."

The small bit of peace that had washed over him moments before instantly shattered. Annoyed at being caught off guard, Malchus rose to his full impressive height and turned around.

A tall, well-built man stood within the shadows of a pillared portico. Vaguely, Malchus detected a tall form with broad shoulders, a narrow waist, and strong legs firmly rooted in a confrontational stance.

Though Malchus did not recognize the man ensconced in shadows, something about the form, the voice, was familiar.

"Make yourself known," Malchus ordered, already irritated by this intruder's dramatic entrance. As well as his untimely interruption. Was there absolutely no peace to be had in this place?

What kind of question is that? he thought dryly. Of course, there wasn't.

Malchus drew his focus back to the stranger beneath the portico. Surely this was not a threat. But one never knew for certain.

"Well?" Malchus demanded, on edge.

"So imperious, that tone of yours. I see very little has changed over the years."

Malchus drew back in shock when a familiar figure emerged from the shadows. "Alexander?"

"Surprise."

"What on earth – "

"Just as I thought. You're thrilled to see me."

Malchus despised that dry, condescending tone. He always had. "What are you doing here?"

"I could ask you the same thing."

"How did you get in?" Malchus grit his teeth in restrained anger.

"Ah, I'm overjoyed to see you too, dear cousin."

Cousin! Malchus had supposed he would never see this despicable relative again! Why, oh why, must he make an appearance now?

Relishing Malchus' discomfort, Alexander closed the distance between them, walking with proud, confident strides.

Somehow Malchus found his tongue, his resentment boiling. "And what could have possibly enticed you to forsake your own heathen city to set foot in holy Jerusalem?"

"So I see you've grown religious beneath the tutelage of our revered high priest. No wonder."

"*Our* revered high priest? If I recall, your family bends the knee to stone idols in a Roman atrium!"

"Stone idols that *represent* a far greater power, dear friend." Alexander's mouth curved into a rueful smile.

"You have yet to explain what you're doing here."

Alexander clicked his tongue chidingly, circling him like a predator sizing up its prey. "It has been over a decade since we last met, and yet you hurl questions and insults upon my pitiful, unworthy head. Perhaps we should start over, dear cousin. Put the past behind us, if you will."

"Don't you find it interesting that it is the offender and the tormentor who would so quickly and easily dismiss the past?" Malchus said through gritted teeth.

"So much for your religion. I thought you pious Jews sold the idea of humility and meekness to the masses."

"An eye for an eye," Malchus ground out. "A tooth for a tooth. As our Law dictates."

Alexander laughed harshly.

"And as a child just how many swollen black eyes did I suffer at your hand, Alexander? How many chipped teeth?"

"Boys will be boys, dear Malchus. And boys often scuffle."

"A scuffle is child's play. You waged wars and executed strategized assaults. You – the firstborn –

organized your brothers into an army, turning them against me. You hated my very existence."

"What can I say? I despise stuffy, prudish Jews."

"Have you mentioned that interesting fact to Caiaphas, in whose home you now stand?"

Alexander's lips tipped menacingly, and Malchus recognized that expression all too well. Alexander had a plan, and nothing on earth could stop him from attaining his aspirations.

Alexander stood boldly before Malchus, grinning sardonically. Silvery moonlight bathed his suave, handsome features in a strange, ethereal glow.

Malchus had always resented this cousin of his – resented his strength, resented his stony determination, resented his cursed good looks. The last time Malchus had encountered Alexander, he had been a young boy of six or seven, while Alexander was eagerly breaking down the door to manhood at the age of twelve. Even then, the girls had giggled and swooned over his deceptive charm, suave personality, smooth talk, and good looks. He possessed a masculine grace akin to the likenesses of the Greek and Roman deities, and his jet-black hair, dark brown eyes, and smooth, olive-skinned features often drew the attention of those around him.

Like Alexander, Malchus' mother had been Greek. She had converted to Judaism with enthusiasm and zeal upon her marriage to Malchus' father, a humble potter who sold his wares in Jerusalem's many markets. His mother had always been extremely close to her only sister – Alexander's mother – who had married a wealthy Greek merchant in Tiberias. This aunt and uncle had often visited Malchus' family, their slew of six boys tagging along with them. Malchus quickly grew weary of being bullied and plagued by his intolerant cousins, though his mother insisted he be patient with them and turn the other cheek.

Alexander had always been the ringleader. He had despised his family's journeys to Jerusalem, complaining that the city was a bore compared to his own native Tiberias – an extremely secular city of Galilee boasting the beauty and architecture of Greece along with the pagan idolatry and licentiousness of Rome. Dedicated Jews refused to set foot in the pagan city, as it had been erected by Herod upon ancient burial grounds and would render any observant Jew unclean. To add insult to injury, Herod also built an elaborate pagan temple in Tiberias, filling it with statues of Roman gods and the busts of deified emperors.

Like its founder, the city was a disgrace. And like Rome, Tiberias beckoned to bored, aimless passersby, seducing them to enter and partake of its lewdness and idolatry. Beautiful and alluring, the city possessed a royal grandeur that lured citizens within its golden boundaries, possessing exciting and frightening temptations that later imprisoned them within its walls.

And Alexander was a product of Tiberias. He too, possessed an unusual beauty that drew others to him. But like his great city built upon the unclean, decaying tombs of the ancients, his charms were deceptive, his lure dangerous and self-gratifying.

With great effort, Malchus drew his thoughts back to the present. "I will ask a final time, Alexander: What are you doing here?"

Alexander's dark eyes flashed, and though his smooth features remained veiled, Malchus detected a fierceness in his stance.

"Just who do you think you are, young cousin, to demand anything from me?" He flashed a white smile, daring Malchus to argue with him.

For a moment, neither man spoke as they stood opposite each other, each measuring the other, the gently gurgling fountain the only sound to disturb the taut silence within the peristyle.

The breathless moment seemed to drag on for an eternity. Finally, Alexander broke the silent spell with a brittle laugh. "I see you are no longer the frightened little boy hiding behind your mother's flowing robes. You're a man, and one to be reckoned with, I imagine."

Malchus dismissed Alexander's characteristic flattery. "Do you come bearing news of family?"

Alexander's lips twitched slightly in agitation. "I come as a hireling at the hand of your master."

Malchus's blood froze. "Caiaphas has hired you as a member of his staff?"

An easy smile spread across Alexander's features. A show of confidence to mask any hints of insecurity. "Temporarily, of course. I've fallen upon rather hard times, I'm afraid. And fortunately, I remembered my cousin was employed at this house. Pardon the liberty, but I used your name to gain entrance."

Again, Malchus' blood boiled. "I will offer no

recommendation for your sake!"

"No need." Another slow, predatory smile. "I am already on staff."

"You're a Greek!"

"Yes, but I am also your cousin. Caiaphas assumes the same good old-fashioned Jewish blood flows through my veins."

"Does he know you hail from Tiberias?"

"He knows only what my papers of recommendation proclaim. And the recommendations of a respected Levite priest are as good as gold in Caiaphas' opinion."

Malchus' eyes narrowed suspiciously. "How on earth did you manipulate those circumstances?"

Another sardonic grin. "The temple priests will do anything to protect their precious reputations, or aren't you aware of that? Simply woo the insecure daughter of a proud priest and compromise her reputation, and he'll be groveling at your feet. He'll do anything to shut you up."

Malchus attempted to hide his grimace, sickened at his cousin's base manipulations.

"I've earned this position, to say the least. It took months to orchestrate the circumstances to obtain it."

"How did you know where to find me?"

"The last time we traveled to Jerusalem to visit your mother, we found your old house – well, what was left of it – burnt to the ground. Mother was frantic. She inquired about it and learned that your parents were dead and that you'd been sold into the house of Caiaphas."

Malchus was sickened and disgusted by Alexander's callousness. And it infuriated him to learn that his only known relatives had discovered his sad plight and done nothing to ease his pain.

Alexander's eyes narrowed sardonically. "Oh, I know what you're going to say, Malchus. Why didn't we come for you? Why didn't we rescue you from a life of servitude? Well, Mother was quite right in her assessments – your father was on overly zealous religious fanatic, and your mother was completely entrenched in her new religion. She would have turned over in her grave had we brought you back to Tiberias and defiled her *pure* little boy by our *heathen* ways."

Malchus was weary of that roguish grin. "And your father? Your mother? Where are they now?"

"Dead."

Malchus didn't detect the slightest hint of remorse. "Then as the firstborn son you inherited a sizeable fortune."

"Not sizeable enough, apparently. But I'll recover. I've reformed."

"You blew it all?"

"You sound like my brothers."

"And they were unwilling to help your situation?"

"My brothers are greedy, petty, and jealous – or have you forgotten so soon? They relish my misfortune."

Malchus would have relished his misfortune as well if it didn't mean he'd have to *live* with this impossible relative for the foreseeable future!

"Now have I satisfied your curiosity, or shall I be

subjected to yet another volley of useless questions?"

Malchus caught himself before running his hand through his hair again. He had no desire to display the true depths of his agitation with yet another nervous gesture. "By all means," he said with a dry smile, "go, as you've suffered my presence for the entirety of these five minutes."

"I will go as I please, and I do not need your permission. Nor anyone else's."

"Oh, but have you forgotten so soon? You serve a master now."

"A trifling detail. And there are ways around it."

"We'll see how you feel after one week in service to the high priest."

"Says a man with no will nor mind of his own. I make my own way, choose my own path."

"Ah, yes – a path of a squandered inheritance, poverty, and servitude. You choose well, Alexander. But remind me not to ask you to plan *my* future."

Dark eyes glittering dangerously, Alexander took another step toward Malchus, so close Malchus could smell the scented oils upon his skin. "A warning, dear cousin: cross me, and you'll long for the days when the most you had to suffer were black eyes and broken teeth."

Malchus remained stiff, tall, unbending. He refused to be cowed by the threats of this wicked man.

Eyes blazing, Alexander took several measured steps backward and retreated toward the shadowy entrance from which he had come. Another slow, predatory smile crossed Alexander's striking features as he paused beneath the graceful pillars.

"It is good to see you again, my dear cousin. Very good, indeed."

Flipping his elaborate robes over one arm, he turned on his heel and disappeared once more into the dark recesses of the peristyle as if swallowed up by the grim shadows of the abyss.

CHAPTER 6

Julia

Julia couldn't stop thinking about the woman named Mary.

How on earth had she met Barabbas? What type of relationship did the vile woman share with her husband? Was she simply a chance buyer he had encountered while trying to pawn off her own most prized possession, or something more?

Fuming, Julia went about her evening chores, wondering what was keeping her husband so late.

Probably that vulgar woman. Or one of her wicked friends, she thought snidely, ready to burst in frustration.

Though she'd attempted to push the unwanted episode out of sight and out of mind, Julia continued to worry and fret over the implications of the chance encounter. Married life had proven difficult enough without having to worry about something as shameful as...*this*!

Despite the fact that Barabbas had proven to be anything but a loving, attentive husband, Julia still detested the idea of another woman in his arms.

Her face reddened in anger at the thought, and her insides churned mercilessly like cream being whipped into butter.

Lord God, take these sinful thoughts and stay my mind on You. The only reason I am in this mess is because I refused to heed Your Word. Heaven knows I've learned my lesson, Lord!

Crossing over to the fireplace, Julia inspected the vegetable stew slowly turning to mush in the pot. She doubted it would have tasted much better had Barabbas arrived on time. How she wished she had learned to cook! And now it was too late. Who could teach her now?

The door burst open unceremoniously, and her husband's impressive frame filled the doorway.

Julia's heart lurched at the sight of him. He was so handsome. Devastatingly handsome. It was his striking features and fierce countenance that had drawn her girlish attention to him in the first place. Why, oh why, didn't his character correspond with his pleasing outward appearance?

Your husband is a good-looking man. The words of Mary, the harlot, flashed across her mind for the thousandth time, and Julia clenched her fists, determined not to dwell on them.

Well, he *was* a good-looking man. *Her* good-looking man! Perhaps in time and with God's help, their relationship might grow and flourish –

"What are you cooking? It smells awful."

Or maybe not.

Julia gritted her teeth, determined not to spend another evening engaged in fierce verbal combat. "I'm sure it smelled better several hours ago when it was fresh."

"You know I'm never early."

"A truer statement was never spoken."

"And just what is that supposed to mean?" Barabbas' eyes narrowed dangerously as he dropped his leather satchel on the floor near the entrance and crossed over to a small basin of water placed upon a wooden stand. He proceeded to wash his hands; his eyes fixed menacingly upon his wife.

Julia kept her back turned to him as she stirred the stew and ladled it into wooden bowls. She knew the arrogance of his expression would surely set her off. *Better not to look,* she thought glibly.

"Well?" Barabbas dried his hands and seated himself at the neglected wooden table. "I asked you a question."

"I was simply agreeing with you," Julia responded stiffly, annoyed at his imperious tone. She set the steaming bowl before him, then set her own bowl at her place. Quickly filling two cups with a ladle of water, she placed them at the table before taking her seat on the bench across from her husband.

She no longer asked Barabbas to bless the food, as her father had always done. In his rich, comforting voice, Simon had always offered beautiful prayers of thanksgiving over every meal, thanking God for His loving care and provision.

Barabbas insisted the prayer was a waste of time,

simply allowing the food to get cold. "Pray silently to yourself, if it soothes your conscience," he'd snapped after one too many of Julia's entreaties.

And so Julia did.

Barabbas claimed to be a God-fearer, but Julia had seen little evidence of that in their two months of marriage. She had never seen nor heard him pray. He refused to attend services at the temple or even a local synagogue. He disregarded the Law and most of the commandments, chafing in resentment if she referenced one of them. Nor did he observe the Sabbath, the feasts, or the holy days –

Well, excepting the Feast of Lights last month, Julia thought dryly, annoyed by the sudden recollection.

Apart from the Feast of Purim, the Feast of Lights was the only other of the seven Jewish Feasts instituted by man rather than by God. Beginning on the 25th day of the ninth month – the month of Kislev – it was also called the Feast of Dedication, a popular and patriotic holiday in Jerusalem, as it commemorated the purging of the temple after its complete and utter pollution by Antiochus Epiphanes. The nation celebrated the heroic deeds of Judas Maccabaeus – nearly two hundred years past – for the entire week with feasting, merry fellowship, and much laughter, dancing, and singing. At this time, the homes were brilliantly lit with flickering candles and brightly burning lamps. Jerusalem's streets glimmered and glowed through the long winter nights during the feast, a glorious reminder of the great God of their temple, the God who once said, "Let there be light!"

And there was light. The lights brightly burned during the glorious festival week.

Benevolently, Simon had granted Barabbas the entire week off work, that he might celebrate the joyous festivities with his new wife.

Julia hid her grimace as she remembered that miserable week. She'd seen her husband once, the first day of the feast. After that, he had whiled away his free days in the hills, celebrating the mighty deeds of a long-dead revolutionary with his Zealot friends, drinking until they no longer remembered to whom they proposed toast after toast.

Did he imagine that they, too, would be celebrated one day as the mighty victors and conquerors of Rome?

Julia took a sip of lukewarm water and shook her head in frustration. Surely, they had more sense than that.

So deep in thought was she that she neglected to notice her husband's scathing countenance.

"You're quiet tonight." It was a critique rather than a statement.

Julia bristled but held her tongue. There was safety in silence.

"What's wrong?"

Julia was on guard the moment he asked the question, for those two simple words often opened the argumentative floodgates, releasing a flood of cutting words that resulted in a devastating amount of damage in their rippling wake.

What's wrong? As if he cared to know! Julia knew the moment she began to express her concerns, Barabbas would stiffen, refuse to take responsibility for any wrong, then neatly dump the blame for any and all issues in their marriage squarely upon her shoulders.

Please, Lord, give us peace tonight, she pled silently.

"Again, I asked you a question. Are you too dumb to answer with an intelligent response?"

He was itching for a fight. And Julia was loathe to give him one, though her nerves were fairly bristling at his arrogant manner.

She decided to change the subject.

"I met a very interesting woman today."

Barabbas' eyes narrowed. He sensed something in her voice that tipped him off. Something wasn't right. Already, he was on guard, strapping on his invisible armor. "So?"

"Apparently, she's rather chummy with you, dear husband."

"Where are you going with this?"

Elbows resting lightly on the table, Julia propped her chin up on one closed fist and tilted her head slightly. "Her name was Mary, by the way. Does the name *ring any bells?*"

She knew it was a terrible pun, and she didn't care. She could still hear those loathsome bells tinkling upon her threshold, announcing the arrival of that foul woman. And she wanted to catch Barabbas off guard, to rip the rug out from under him as he had done to her on countless occasions. Let him worry and sputter and make excuses. Let him squirm.

She'd savor his discomfort.

Recognition dawning on his handsome features, Barabbas stiffened momentarily, but he recovered far too quickly. "I suppose she returned my dagger then?" he said as if absolutely nothing was amiss.

"She did, indeed."

"Where is it?"

"On the mantel above the fireplace."

"Why are you looking at me like that?" he demanded.

"Like what?"

Barabbas bristled, his grip tightening on his wooden spoon. "Look, I suggest you wipe that smug look off your face before I help you do it."

Julia wasn't disturbed by his threats, especially when she was too angry to think clearly. His dismissive attitude infuriated her! He should be explaining himself, his actions, to her! He should be groveling at her feet, apologizing! But no, he just sat there like an entitled oaf, daring her to question his unacceptable behavior!

"She seemed rather pleased with her purchase," Julia said with far more calm than she felt.

"She should be. The price was fair, the merchandise good."

"She asked me to tell you that it was a pleasure doing business with you." At this, Julia raised her eyes levelly to her husband's, her cheeks blooming with angry color.

Barabbas drew in a sharp breath, rolling his eyes in frustration. "Is that what's got you all bothered? Come on, Julia. She was talking about the jar."

"Was she?"

Now Barabbas' color reflected her own. "What? You think I'd have any interest in a common whore? If I wanted to be unfaithful, I could have my pick of any beautiful woman I desired – or had you not noticed? Other women notice me, even if you do not. I certainly wouldn't throw out good money for a cheap fling with a diseased harlot."

Trembling, Julia rose from the table and walked away.

"Get back here."

"No."

"By the gods, Julia –"

"Stop yelling!"

"*I'm* not yelling! *You're* yelling!"

"Just leave me alone. Please."

There was a terrible crash as Barabbas' bench turned over backward after he leaped from his seat.

Julia made a beeline for the door, but she wasn't fast enough. Barabbas gripped her by both arms, turning her roughly to face him and glaring down into her face. "What's wrong with you, woman?"

"Why did you ever marry me?" She wept brokenly. "If you have such a vast array of beautiful women waiting at your beck and call, then why marry me?"

Barabbas' eyes softened ever so slightly. "Look, I said that to make you mad. Clearly, it worked."

Julia turned her tear-stained face away from him, shuddering.

"Listen, Julia, I'm not unfaithful."

"Then how did you meet that woman?"

"She's a...um, a *friend* of one of my men. He recommended her when I mentioned the jar. He knew she had the means to purchase it."

Julia had had quite enough trouble at the hands of *his men*. Zealots. For all their glorious claims of fighting for the freedom of their nation, they were a motley crew of lazy men – in her opinion – who lounged about the hills and preyed upon innocent caravans for food and supplies.

Barabbas gazed down at her, his eyes continuing to soften. He stroked her slender arms with strong, well-shaped hands, and Julia knew what he was thinking.

How can his mind switch directions in a split second?! How can he criticize me all evening, then expect me to delight in his love?

Disturbed by what she saw in his eyes, Julia dropped her gaze. Barabbas drew her chin up with one finger, forcing her to look at him.

"Why would I want another woman, Julia? Any man would lose his head just looking at you."

Julia felt her resolve weakening, though she wished it wouldn't. She was so sick of this ridiculous pattern – the insults, the fighting, and the weeping, culminating in the gratification of her husband's desires. How could he possibly expect her to dismiss his cruelties in an instant and gratify his every fleshly impulse?

It wasn't fair. Didn't Barabbas understand how misused and unloved she felt? Couldn't he see that an evening of intimate pleasure could never erase the months of pain he had inflicted?

He was stroking her lush brown hair, then tracing

the delicate features of her face with one finger. He lowered his face to hers and kissed her deeply.

Though her heart was anywhere but here with her husband, Julia remained silent and stifled her protests about the bowls of stew growing cold on the wooden table, forcing herself to appreciate his strong embrace.

If she were to object, she would only create another futile argument.

Better to remain silent and unfeeling than to express her deepest thoughts and suffer emotional wounds that might never heal.

CHAPTER 7

Melina

Chuza proved to be a staunch and efficient overseer.

Despite his calm demeanor and quiet commands, the staff quickly learned that he was not to be argued with. He possessed a quiet strength and an air of humble authority that drove even the most indolent servants to action.

Melina was especially drawn to Joanna, the quiet and unassuming wife of Herod's new house steward. Since she had been assigned to the upkeep of the couple's private quarters, she was granted frequent opportunities to converse with the woman.

Joanna was a serious, enigmatic woman who rarely smiled but possessed a calm delight that incited Melina's curiosity. Her complexion was slightly lighter than her husband's, and her hazel-colored eyes often lit up with a knowing and luminous glow. Though her husband was considered a wealthy man as one of Herod's highest and most highly paid servants, Joanna donned simple but colorful gowns and very little jewelry. She wore her abundant hair in a simple style – a loose bun at the nape of her neck. Exceptionally curly tendrils of stray hair framed her elegant face and forehead. As she strolled calmly about the elegant palace, head high and colorful robes swishing gently, Melina imagined she looked very much like a queen.

But the thing that stood out the most to Melina was a habit of Joanna's that she herself had begun shortly after dedicating her life to God.

Early each morning, Joanna retreated to the palace gardens, settled herself upon a curved marble bench, folded her delicate hands in her lap, and remained quiet and still for quite some time.

Melina couldn't help but wonder...was the woman *praying*? And if so, to whom? Certainly not to one of the Roman deities, who required a temple or lararium containing lifeless stone statues of representation. No, Joanna appeared to beseech a personal God, a God too large to contain within a temple or a shrine constructed by the hands of fallible human beings.

Melina began to contemplate a very real possibility – a possibility so exciting that her eyes sparkled, and her cheeks glowed in anticipation. Could it be possible that she now shared Herod's frightful palace with a fellow sister of the faith?

Perhaps, for the very first time, she was not alone.

But you are not alone, dear one. I will never leave you nor forsake you.

Melina smiled as the unspoken words ministered to her heart – the very words she had often read in the ancient scrolls Malchus smuggled to her when they met at the Upper Market. She had no idea what Herod Antipas – or far worse, his wife, Herodias – might do to her if they ever discovered such scrolls in her possession.

Until now, Melina had served quietly in Herod's palace, drawing comfort from her newfound faith and the God who loved her, cradling her within the palm of His hand. But how wonderful it would be to share this faith with another! To strengthen and encourage each other in the faith and in the mighty Word of God!

Melina sighed wistfully as she arranged a stunning bouquet of flowers upon a marble pedestal in the private quarters of the new house steward and his lovely wife. Such thoughts – of sisterhood and encouragement and shared secrets – always reminded her of Julia. How she missed her dear friend!

Julia was so full of life – so eager to experience all the pleasure and excitement the world had to offer. Melina had often felt rather dull and uninteresting in Julia's presence, but she had never resented the girl's vibrant personality or exquisite beauty. After all, she had read the Psalm of David and understood that God had shaped her and formed her with His own two hands: *I will praise You, for I am fearfully and wonderfully made!* Surely there was a divine purpose in her every feature, her every trait.

Melina paused before an enormous floor-to-ceiling gilded bonze mirror. No, she didn't look like her friend Julia. Julia was voluptuous, lush, and curvy, while Melina possessed a more slender and straighter frame. Julia's rich brown curls cascaded over her shoulders and down her back in billowy waves, while Melina's raven black hair was long and straight. Julia's hazel eyes sparkled playfully; Melina's green eyes glowed with a quiet calm and spirit of acceptance. And while Julia was impulsive, exuberant, and headstrong, Melina was soft-spoken and quiet, happy to love and to serve.

Yes, both women were diametrically different in every single way, but Melina understood that the Lord had a purpose and a plan for both of them. In His mercy and love, He had shaped each of them in their mother's womb and endowed them with the gifting and skills they would need to accomplish His purposes for them. And He would refine them, lovingly pruning them with skillful hands, making them ready and able vessels for His service.

Melina would never stop praying for Julia. She hoped the girl had discovered the happiness she so desperately wanted.

Oh, Julia! Laughing, teasing Julia. How I miss you!

"You appear deep in thought."

Melina stifled a small gasp of surprise at the unexpected voice at her elbow. She had been so lost in thought she had neglected to notice the reflection of the tall woman standing behind her.

Mortified at being caught standing idly before a mirror, Melina's cheeks flushed a deep crimson, and she clasped her hands before her in dismay. "I do apologize, my lady," she fumbled in deep embarrassment. "You must think me terribly idle and vain."

Joanna closed the distance between them, a hint of a smile upon her soft features. She placed a gentle hand upon Melina's shoulder. "I have seen the work you do here. You accomplish the work of ten. One would be a fool to think of you as idle. Or vain. You are among the humblest of women I've been privileged to know."

Melina's heart responded to the earnest compliments of the older woman. She wasn't quite sure what to say.

With the grace and ease of a queen, Joanna glided across the room to examine the exquisite bouquet Melina had patiently and skillfully arranged.

"These are lovely."

"Fresh from the palace gardens, my lady."

"Herod has acquired excellent gardeners."

"He has, my lady."

Joanna caressed a delicate bloom with slender fingers, then bent forward to inhale the lovely scent. She smiled. "God sends the rains upon the earth, and these lovely little flowers spring forth and proclaim the power and glory of their Maker."

Melina froze. *God*, the woman had said. Not *the gods*. God. And she spoke of a Creator God. Perhaps…just perhaps…

Joanna turned her head slowly, her hazel eyes resting knowingly upon Melina. "I can speak of such things with you, Melina, for I believe you understand them. I have seen no amulets on your person. You refuse to engage in idle gossip. And you carry yourself with the grace and confidence of a child of God, a daughter of the King."

Melina closed her eyes and allowed the words to wash over her like a warm and welcome tide. *A child of God. A daughter of the King.* How she loved the sound of it! And yet these incredible titles were truly hers! It was almost unfathomable!

She was a child of God. And she was, indeed, the daughter of the King.

And now she gazed in wonder at the newest member of her spiritual family.

Joanna, the wife of Chuza – daughter of the King.

CHAPTER 8

Malchus

Malchus hastened his steps, his heart pounding a steady beat of anticipation. Soon he would meet Melina under the shaded colonnades at the Upper Market. So intent had he been upon reaching their designated spot at the appointed hour that he'd nearly forgotten to tuck a weathered scroll within the folds of his garment. That precious little scroll was his one and only excuse to continue these regular meetings with the loveliest girl he'd ever met! He would have looked like a fool had he forgotten to bring it with him.

The shade beneath the sturdy marble colonnades was cool and inviting. Malchus caught himself pacing nervously several times after reaching their meeting place, then silently chided himself for his lack of self-possession. Melina would come upon him any moment and wonder why he moved about like a restless animal. Did the lovely young servant have any idea how he really felt about her?

Malchus suppressed a rueful grin. The girl was probably every bit as oblivious about his increasing affection as she was to her own whimsical charm.

How she still affected him! Malchus had been smitten at the first – that fateful moment when he had stumbled upon her in Herod's opulent palace gardens. Unaware of his intrusive presence, she had been singing softly.

How many times had Malchus wished to beg her to sing again? How he longed to hear that sweet, innocent voice praising her Maker in joyful song! Like the woman who claimed it, the voice was soft and enchanting.

Melina possessed a gentleness of heart and peace of spirit that had instantly drawn him to her. She accredited her willing acceptance of her circumstances solely upon her trust in God.

Malchus believed in God. And yet…that perfect peace, that calm acceptance of whatever life might bring, still eluded him. He often pondered the fact, even agonized over it.

Why? What was it that set Melina apart? Like Malchus, she had lost her family at a very young age, sold into a life of service. Her circumstances were anything but pleasant. And yet she went about her duties and performed her daily tasks as if it was her privilege to do so!

How he admired that young woman! How he longed to marry her, to claim her as his own!

Their friendship had blossomed over the months, and Malchus often found himself contemplating the possibility of revealing his true feelings for her. What would she say? Would she laugh? Would she flee in sheer panic? Or would she reciprocate?

"Malchus! It is good to see you, friend."

Annoyed, Malchus realized he had been pacing. Again. His face bloomed with color as a second thought dawned on him – Melina had stumbled upon him in the midst of his forbidden thoughts.

He straightened and looked questioningly at the older woman strolling calmly alongside Melina. The woman was tall, lovely, regal.

Melina must have sensed the question in his eyes, for she smiled brightly and drew the woman affectionately toward Malchus. "Malchus, this is my dear friend, Joanna."

A dear friend? He hadn't heard Melina speak two words about a woman named Joanna in the past! How dear a friend could she be?

Again, Melina sensed Malchus' mounting questions. She offered another smile. "Joanna and her husband, Chuza, have recently joined the palace staff here in Jerusalem. Previously, they oversaw Herod's household in Tiberias."

Tiberias! Fleetingly, Malchus thought of his cousin, Alexander. He quickly dismissed the unwelcome thought. Jerusalem would have proven a better place had Alexander chosen to remain in Tiberias where he belonged!

For Melina's sake, he certainly hoped that this wasn't the case with this woman.

"Joanna is a believer," Melina confided with a warm smile. "The only one I've been privileged to serve alongside in the palace."

Malchus couldn't help but be warmed by Melina's innocent excitement. Even so, he was far less trusting than she. Tiberias was a wicked city.

Joanna sensed Malchus' reservation, but she did not appear offended by it. Instead, she offered the slightest hint of a smile and said quietly, "It is an honor to meet you, Malchus. Melina has told me so much about you."

Now he *really* hoped this woman could be trusted!

"If you will now excuse me," Joanna continued in her gracious tone, "I must attend to some business about the market. I simply accompanied Melina along the way as we sought a common destination."

Malchus attempted to stifle his sigh of relief. He certainly had no desire to share his few precious moments with Melina with this stranger from Tiberias!

"I bid you good day."

Malchus finally found his tongue. "Good day, my lady."

With a queenly nod, Joanna turned and disappeared into the chaotic crowd thronging about the booths and market stalls.

Melina looked to Malchus, a question in her eyes. "You weren't very polite."

Her gentle rebuke felt like a punch in the gut, and Malchus sensed himself bristling despite himself. "Melina, that woman is a complete stranger. And yet you risked bringing her here. Why? No one in the palace knows about our meetings."

Melina's lips parted slightly. Malchus could tell she was about to say something, then thought better of it. Instead, she lowered her gaze and said softly, "She serves our God, Malchus. She can be trusted."

Regretting his own cursed pride, Malchus reached forward and tipped Melina's chin up, forcing her to look directly into his eyes. Her eyes shone with a faint sheen of tears, and he could have gladly kicked himself. "I know you want to trust her, Melina. But trust must be built – not merely doled out to anyone who wishes to claim it."

"Perhaps I am foolish. But I long for a sister, a friend, within the palace."

"I know you do."

"I miss Julia."

"I know you do."

His look was so tender that Melina's insides clenched, and she looked away. "I suppose we should get started on our lesson. We haven't much time."

Malchus sensed her quiet withdrawal. Though he longed to gather her in his arms and comfort her, he knew better. Melina was not like other women. She was cautious. Reserved. He hadn't any idea how long it would take to win her heart.

The one thing he *did* know: he'd wait, no matter how long it took.

Reluctantly, he gratified her desire to change the subject and retrieved the scroll tucked carefully in his robe. "The prophet Isaiah. This passage is said to predict the coming Messiah."

Melina suspected she knew which section they would be reading. She had learned so much about the Word of God over the last few months, eagerly drinking in the facts, the history, the Jewish terms. She knew it was prophesied that the Messiah would set the Jewish people free, casting off the yoke of bondage and establishing an everlasting kingdom.

Would she – a Gentile – be welcome in that kingdom?

Dismissing her concern, Melina settled herself comfortably upon the cool tiles near Malchus' sandaled feet as he unrolled the scroll with a practiced air of dignified solemnity. She laughed at his antics.

Malchus' heart leaped at the sound of it. How he loved that silvery laugh! He didn't like having to look down on her, so he settled himself comfortably beside her – as close as he dared. Their knees were almost touching, but she didn't appear to notice. He felt exhilarated and alive in her presence.

Clearing his throat dramatically, he glanced sideways at Melina. "Are you sure you're ready?"

"Oh, do read, Malchus!"

"But you're *sure* you're ready?"

"Malchus!" She swatted his arm playfully.

"Manners, please," he said, a teasing gleam in his eye. "If you insist, I will begin."

"I insist!"

"All right, then." He cleared his throat once more before diving in. "*He has no form of comeliness; and when we see Him, there is no beauty that we should desire Him. He is despised and rejected by men, a Man of sorrows and acquainted with grief.*"

"The Messiah," Melina asserted softly.

Malchus glanced up over the scroll, always

marveling at her perception. For a woman completely untrained in the holy texts, she possessed
remarkable discernment pertaining to even the
most confusing of passages. "Yes, the Messiah," he
affirmed with an approving nod. "Show off."

Smiling warmly, Melina gestured for him to
continue.

He did so, and his voice was rich and strong.
Melina found herself completely lost within the
wondrous words. Despite the fact that she did not
know the Man described by the prophet Isaiah, the
sadness of the passage pierced her heart as it had the
first time she had read it.

Malchus must have forgotten that he had already
given her a scroll bearing this same passage. They
had discussed it together the following week, but his
heart hadn't been in the discussion. He had seemed
distracted. Restless.

Perhaps he would have more to say about it today.
She forced her attention back to his rhythmic reading.

*"And we hid, as it were, our faces from Him; He
was despised, and we did not esteem Him. Surely
He has borne our griefs and carried our sorrows;
Yet we esteemed Him stricken, smitten by God,
and afflicted. But He was wounded for our transgressions, He was bruised for our iniquities; the
chastisement of our peace was upon Him, and by
His stripes we are healed."*

"By His stripes we are healed," Melina repeated
softly. "Beautiful words, are they not?"

Malchus wasn't terribly impressed. He'd heard
them thousands of times over the years. But he had

no desire to crush Melina's sense of wonder. "Isaiah was quite the poet."

"And a prophet, too!"

"A poetic prophet."

"You do not seem impressed."

"No, no. I am. Very impressed. Shall I continue?"

Melina nodded, and he wondered at the hint of sadness he saw creeping into her eyes. Was she truly touched by the plight of the Man described within the passage? Or had something else disturbed her sensitive spirit?

Troubled, he plunged ahead with the Scripture passage. "*All we like sheep have gone astray; we have turned, everyone, to his own way; and the Lord has laid on Him the iniquity of us all. He was oppressed and He was afflicted, yet He opened not His mouth; He was led as a lamb to the slaughter, and as a sheep before its shearers is silent, so He opened not His mouth. He was taken from prison and from judgment, and who will declare His generation? For He was cut off from the land of the living; for the transgressions of My people He was stricken. And they made His grave with the wicked – but with the rich at His death, because He had done no violence, nor was any deceit in His mouth –* "

"Malchus?"

Malchus paused mid-sentence, surprised by the unusual interruption.

"Tell me what you know about the Messiah."

"The Messiah?"

"Tell me what you know about Him."

Malchus' pulse quickened at the unexpected

query. What did he really know about the Messiah, other than the bits and pieces he had heard discussed among quibbling elders and scribes? Caiaphas seldom spoke of the Messiah. Malchus was convinced the man dreaded the Messiah's coming. After all, his position would no longer be necessary once the Messiah made Himself known. Malchus seriously doubted the power-hungry politico would simply surrender his priestly garments and hand over his coveted position at the Messiah's appearance.

He smirked, amused by the thought. "Well," he mused, stalling for time. "I know He will be a mighty prince, a warrior king of sorts."

Melina tilted her head to one side. "Why do you say that?"

"Because I've heard it discussed in the temple – I've heard debates among those gathered at Solomon's Porch."

Melina didn't look satisfied. "What else do you know?"

"He will demolish the Romans, breaking their bonds and destroying their power over us. The nation will rally after Him, exalting Him as the great king of a united Israel."

"What else?"

"Well…" Malchus fumbled about for the slightest bit of information he might possibly have stored in his mind at some point… *What else did he know?*

"I suppose He will be of a commanding nature, undulating power. The masses will exalt Him. We will no longer answer to Rome. Rome's foul presence will be forever banished."

Melina reached tentatively for the scroll Malchus still held in his hands. "May I?"

"Be my guest."

Taking the scroll, Melina's eyes scanned the ancient writings. "He is despised and rejected by men, a Man of sorrows and acquainted with grief... we did not esteem Him... He was wounded for our transgressions, bruised for our iniquities... He was led as a lamb to the slaughter, cut off from the land of the living..." Melina lowered the scroll, a thoughtful expression crossing her luminous features. "Your Messiah does not sound anything like the Man described in this passage."

Malchus wasn't sure if he should be offended. Was she criticizing his religious knowledge – or lack thereof – or simply seeking another answer to one of her many religious questions?

Malchus shrugged rather indifferently. "I only speak of what I have been told."

"By whom?"

"The religious leaders. The elders. The scribes."

"Do you suppose we should accept their word over the Word of God?"

It was a stunning question, and for a moment, Malchus felt as if the wind had been knocked out of him. He wondered how he could possibly be so dense – he, a man who had been surrounded by the sacred Scriptures his entire life! He had never once considered this.

Why did he simply accept the word of man – even when it blatantly contradicted the Word of God – while Melina, a Gentile who had never known the

Word, could so clearly see the folly of his ways?

Melina touched his arm and he attempted to stifle a soft intake of breath. Her touch sent warm shivers up and down his spine.

"I meant no disrespect, Malchus," she said sincerely. "But the Man I read about in this scroll is not a proud and haughty warrior king. He is humble. Gentle. This scroll tells us that there is nothing particularly stunning about His appearance. The people will despise Him rather than pledge their allegiance to Him. He will be bruised and wounded for our sins – not His own. As other passages seem to indicate, He will be sinless. But He will be oppressed and afflicted – to the point of death, according to this passage – in order to heal us, somehow."

Malchus wasn't sure what to say, but Melina's passionate words ignited a small spark within him – a desire, a longing, that had been put to death years earlier. Was it actually possible to coax those smoldering embers – that tiny spark of hope – back to life?

"I am ashamed to admit this," he began rather slowly, hoping she would not condemn him, "but I have never thought about it in this way. You are right, Melina – this passage does describe a very different Man than the elders and chief priests are promoting."

"Indeed."

"But what of the Romans? Won't He defeat them?"

Melina's brow furrowed as she studied the passage of the prophet Isaiah. "I see nothing about the Romans here."

"Then why do the leaders insist it will be so?"

Again, Melina furrowed her slender brows, deep in thought. "Malchus," she began slowly. "You have shown me that the Jewish nation has been captured and subjected to foreign rule numerous times, yes?"

Malchus wondered where she was going with this. He hoped his dull mind could keep up. "Yes..."

"And I've noticed a pattern: God warned His people every single time. First, the northern kingdom of Israel was conquered by the Assyrians. But God had been warning them, pleading with them to turn from their wickedness and repent. But they refused to repent, and they were conquered. Next, the southern kingdom of Judah was conquered, the inhabitants captured by the Babylonians. God had tried to reach them, too. Then of course there were other nations – Persia, Greece, and now Rome – that succeeded in ruling over them."

"You may have to slow down," Malchus remarked with a self-deprecating grin. "We aren't all as bright as you are."

Melina laughed, a musical sound. "Please, Malchus. You've taught me everything I know."

"Well, I'm flattered. Do go on."

Melina enjoyed his sarcasm and dry humor. Eyes sparkling, she expounded upon her theory, her voice rising along with her excitement, "As long as this nation has existed, God's people have known periods of freedom and prosperity, along with periods of captivity. God allowed the captivity to make them aware of their sin, their need for Him. When the Israelites turned back to the Lord and cried out for help, He always delivered them. Every single time!"

"So you're saying that God punished them for their disobedience and allowed their enemies to conquer them?"

"I'm saying that God *allowed* it to happen because He knew it would draw them closer to Him. A loving God does not desire for His people to continue in sin and rebellion because He knows such sins only harm us and ultimately separate us from Him. Throughout the ages – in His love and mercy – He allowed the suffering and the captivity of His people to open their eyes to their own sin and draw them back into His loving protection. Isn't it far better to be held captive by a foreign power for a season, in order to be released from the captivity of sin for all eternity?"

"And I thought Isaiah was poetic."

"But don't you see it?"

"It does make sense."

"So perhaps…perhaps this is why the prophecy never mentions Rome. Throughout history, God has worked through various world empires to gain the attention of His people, to turn their hearts back to Him. Rome is just one in a long string of them."

"But if the Messiah will not come to break the chains of Rome, then why is He coming?"

"Nations will come and go. Perhaps the Messiah is more interested in something greater than politics, Malchus. After all, this passage speaks of sin."

"I thought you said 'greater than politics'. Are not sin and politics one and the same?"

Melina laughed. "The Scriptures speak of an everlasting kingdom, but no kingdom on this earth is everlasting. But eternal life – that is everlasting. And for those who will not repent, the separation from God will be everlasting. What if the Messiah is more concerned about these kinds of things instead?"

Malchus ran a hand through thick hair, his dark eyes slightly glazed. He hadn't intended to incite a religious debate this afternoon. When would he find the courage to speak to Melina about more personal things? About his feelings for her? His desire for her?

In an attempt to close the current discussion, Malchus decided to agree with her. "I'm sure you're right."

"You don't sound convinced."

Malchus offered a weary smile. "Sometimes I think you are the teacher and I am the student."

Melina sensed his distraction and accepted the fact that – despite her keen disappointment – she had gleaned all the Biblical information available for today. Malchus' mind was clearly on something else. "You seem troubled, Malchus."

Malchus breathed an inward sigh of relief. He welcomed her sympathy and the opportunity to share more of himself with her. "It has been a trying week."

"How so?"

"An unexpected guest arrived at Caiaphas' house this week."

"Oh?"

"My cousin."

Melina clasped her hands together, delighted. "Oh, Malchus! How wonderful!"

Malchus chuckled bitterly. "I wish."

"But it isn't?"

"It might be – if he were not evil incarnate."

Melina's soft green eyes widened. "No relative of yours could be so wicked."

"Oh, no. He can. He's perfected the art, I'm afraid."

"The art?"

"The art of pure, unbridled evil."

Melina touched his shoulder. "Perhaps this is an opportunity from the Lord, Malchus – to lead your cousin to Him."

"I'd rather lead him off a cliff."

"Malchus!"

"You'd have to meet him to understand."

Melina smiled sympathetically. "I am sorry it has been so difficult for you. Did he come to see you?"

"No – worse. He's come to stay and remain under Caiaphas' employ."

"Oh, dear."

"You can say that again."

"Malchus, I will be praying for you. And for your cousin as well. What is his name?"

"Alexander."

"Alexander?"

Malchus detested the sound of it upon her sweet lips. He wished he hadn't told her.

"Like Alexander the Great?" she smiled.

"Like Alexander the Wicked, Alexander the Evil, Alexander the Nasty – "

"Continue to pray for him, Malchus. God often works in mysterious ways."

Malchus realized his fists were clenched angrily

at his sides, and he quickly unclenched them. He imagined there were many factors that had driven his detestable cousin in his direction, but he seriously doubted that *God* was one of those factors.

"To make matters worse, Mara and I are still at odds."

Melina's heart sank like a stone. *Mara?* Who was Mara? Was Malchus involved with a woman among Caiaphas' staff?

Attempting to ignore her rapidly beating pulse, Melina forced a smile and asked casually, "Who is Mara?"

Malchus realized his error and made a mental note to kick himself later. Would Melina trust his belated explanation?

"She is an older woman who works for Caiaphas, the head of the kitchen staff." He hoped he hadn't over-emphasized the world *older*, but he needed Melina to know that Mara was of no romantic interest to him. "She took me under her wing when I first came to the palace as a small boy, and she's mothered me ever since."

Melina breathed a sigh of relief. "She must be very kind."

"I thought so. Needless to say, she's become romantically involved with a Roman guard, and the man has completely corrupted her decency. She and I have been at odds for quite some time now, but she won't leave it alone. She insists on stirring up arguments and strife." It felt good to get his troubles off his chest. Melina was a wonderful listener.

He sucked in a sharp intake of breath when

Melina took his hand tenderly between her own two hands. "She needs prayer, too, Malchus. And I will be praying for her every day. And for you. For peace – and restoration."

Malchus welcomed the peace but had absolutely no desire for restoration. Regardless, he didn't wish to come across as a selfish ingrate to this tender-hearted woman, so he offered her a sincere smile and tried to ignore the fact that she still possessed his tan work-roughened hand.

"Am I interrupting something?"

Both Melina and Malchus jumped a foot at the unexpected inquiry.

Cheeks stained with humiliation, Melina released Malchus' hand and hastened to her feet.

Joanna stood before them, a question in her eyes.

"Of course, you're not an interruption, Joanna. Never! I suppose we must return to the palace. I am afraid I completely lost track of time."

Malchus now disliked this woman more than ever. Who did she think she was to intrude upon this private moment? Didn't she believe in fun? In romance? He took another good look at the woman's severe, austere features and stifled a groan. No, of course she didn't.

The woman was about as soft and cheery as sharpened steel.

Swallowing his frustration, Malchus forced a smile, annoyed that he would not be bidding Melina farewell in private. He supposed he must endure the watchful eyes of Melina's new, self-appointed chaperone.

"Shall we meet again next week?" he asked, his voice sounding a bit strangled in his own ears.

Melina smiled brightly, still flushed. "I would like that."

She started to venture toward Joanna, then paused and offered him the scroll. "I almost forgot I still had it!"

"You may keep it."

"I already have a copy you have given me, but thank you, Malchus."

Malchus felt even more like a fool. Had he actually brought her a copy of a lesson they had already discussed? Why on earth did he continued to behave like a blundering idiot in this woman's presence?

Melina paused, her luminous eyes alive with wonder. "Malchus, perhaps this week we should ponder the things we have learned about the Messiah."

Malchus hoped he would remember to do so. After all, Melina would most certainly bring it up next week. "Of course."

"Did you notice something interesting about this passage, Malchus? Near the end?"

Malchus felt like a dumb ox. He didn't even remember the end. He hadn't gotten that far before Melina had hijacked the scroll and finished reading it silently herself.

Joanna appeared to take an interest, though she remained characteristically silent.

"This passage – it describes a Man who dies for the people. There is no question about it. His death is described in detail – even the fact that He would die among the wicked and be buried with the rich."

Malchus nodded slowly, attempting to track her thoughts. Dumbly, he reached out and accepted the scroll she offered him.

"But at the end, He is clearly very much alive..."

"Alive?"

"Alive! He lives at the end of the passage, despite the fact that He clearly dies in the middle of it. He dies, and yet... He lives!"

Joanna's eyes lit up rather like Melina's, and she nodded her stately head in quiet comprehension.

Melina's features were all aglow. "It is truly something to ponder, is it not?"

Malchus nodded slowly, his throat suddenly dry. For some inexplicable reason, Melina's words filled him with anxiety...and yet, also *hope*.

He dies, and yet... He lives!

Yes, it certainly was something to ponder.

CHAPTER 9

Melina

"Your young man is very handsome."

Melina blushed from the top of her pretty head to the tips of her small, sandaled toes as she drifted alongside Joanna on their return trip to the palace. She fumbled with the woven basket of spices and fresh herbs she had obtained after her meeting with Malchus. "Oh, he isn't *my* young man," she sought to explain, her cheeks a bright crimson.

Joanna's eyes never left the path, though a small smile did touch her lips. "No?"

"He is a dear friend. He knows the Scriptures well. He has been teaching me."

"The Scriptures?"

"Yes."

"And is that all he has been teaching you?"

This coming from the staid Joanna! Melina's color deepened. "Well, of course it is!"

Joanna's lips curved into a rare, full smile this

time. "Good for him. You must know how he feels about you."

"As I mentioned, he is a *friend*."

"Ah, yes. And I am the queen of Rome."

"Joanna!"

"You must assess the situation for what it really is. How else can you seek guidance from the Lord? Do you wish to be caught off guard?"

Melina bit her lower lip, her slender brows drawing together thoughtfully. "No. No, I do not."

"Then be willing to look the situation square in the face for what it really is. The man is in love with you. Take it to the Lord in prayer. What would He have you do should Malchus reveal his feelings to you? Or ask for your hand?"

Melina stifled a surprised gasp. "Oh, but he wouldn't!"

Joanna's confidence unnerved Melina. "He very well might."

The two walked along in companionable silence for several minutes. Melina felt a sense of panic – along with a heady sensation of pleasure – washing over her.

Malchus – in love with *her*? Could it be true? She knew her own feelings for him had grown rapidly over the months, but she had simply dismissed them. Her feelings were impossible, after all. Neither she nor Malchus were free to do as they wished.

Melina tried to ignore the burning heat in her face as she considered such things. How did she truly feel about Malchus? Did she love him? She was certainly drawn to him. She found herself thinking of him often, even dreaming of him on occasion. And yet... she held back. It was as if a still voice within her bid her to wait, to be patient.

But why?

Joanna sensed Melina's unease and gently touched her shoulder as they made steady progress toward the palace. "You mustn't worry. God is in control of your situation."

"I am a servant, little more than a slave. Even if we wished to marry, it would be forbidden."

Joanna's eyes sparkled. "Have you forgotten? I myself am a servant. That didn't stop me from marrying the man I loved."

"But you and your husband are of the highest status, basically free. You come and go as you wish."

"But we weren't always. Certainly not when we married."

"No?"

"You must pray. Seek God's will for your life. Whether His will for you is marriage to this man, to another man, or to no man at all, His will is best."

Melina contemplated Joanna's words of wisdom, wishing she had more faith. It shook her more than she cared to admit to imagine a life without Malchus in it. But she knew she must choose to trust God, despite her feelings.

Joanna steered the conversation to safer topics. "Which passage did you study today?"

"We studied a passage from Isaiah, although Malchus wasn't entirely sure about the interpretation. He knows it foretells events regarding the promised Messiah." In truth, Malchus had presented a scroll bearing the same passage several months prior. Absentmindedly, he had brought the scroll bearing this message which they had already discussed.

Should that concern her? Melina sensed that Malchus wasn't nearly as interested in the Scriptures as she was. If he was, would've he so quickly forgotten the fact that they had already studied this particular prophecy? The thought disturbed her spirit. Surely Malchus treasured the Word of God as she did. Surely it was a crucial aspect of his life.

Squaring her slender shoulders, she followed Joanna, her eyes intent on Herod's magnificent palace fortress.

It was always a chore to reenter the elevated and well-guarded palace of Herod Antipas. The sun was smoldering upon the western plains as Melina and Joanna finally entered the heavily guarded compound.

Melina's thoughts were troubled as she traveled down a pillared, frescoed corridor, Joanna at her elbow.

Joanna sensed the young woman's inner turmoil and touched her shoulder. "The passage you discussed with Malchus today – did you understand it?"

Melina paused to consider the question. No, she didn't fully understand it. Still, the words drew her, whispered to heart. She shook her head to clear the confusion. "Parts of it, I suppose."

"Which parts?"

"I understand the prophet spoke of the Messiah, the Anointed One. And whomever that may be,

He must fulfill the prophecies buried within that difficult passage."

"You are a wise young woman."

Melina smiled wistfully. "And *you* are too kind," she responded with a soft laugh.

Joanna noticed a curved marble bench stationed between two large Grecian urns overflowing with lovely flowers. The seat was situated before an enormous arched window overlooking the city – a calm respite for bustling servants or visiting dignitaries who wearied after traveling the overwhelmingly large palace grounds.

Gracefully, Joanna lowered herself to the bench and patted the empty space beside her. "Melina, sit beside me."

Obediently, Melina did as requested balancing her basket carefully on her lap.

"What else do you know about the Messiah?"

Melina couldn't help but smile. She had asked Malchus the exact same question. "I know there are many prophecies about Him within the Scriptures."

"Yes, there are indeed. For example, we know the Messiah must be born of a virgin in the city of Bethlehem. As a child, He must be called out of Egypt by God Himself. A messenger will prepare the way for Him. He will be a light to the Gentiles and in Galilee."

A light to the Gentiles. How Melina loved the sound of that!

"Then the Messiah will be for all people?" she dared.

"Indeed. All people – for the Jews and Gentiles

alike."

"But...how can we know this?" Melina had no doubt that the God of the Jewish people was also her God. She had no doubt that He loved her. But how was she to know if the Jewish Messiah would be so inclusive? She had heard the Messiah referenced as the Son of God. Did the Son abide by the principles of the Father?

Joanna tucked a stray hair behind Melina's ear tenderly, the way a mother might. Melina couldn't explain why, but the simple gesture brought tears to her eyes. Stubbornly, she blinked, determined to hold them back. She would not cry before this strong woman who had accepted her as a fellow sister in the faith.

"How do I know this?" Joanna repeated, sensitive to Melina's timid reluctance. "God Himself has said it. That is why."

Melina's eyes brightened hopefully. "He has?"

"Many, many times. One of the first examples that comes to mind is when the Lord spoke to the famous patriarch Abraham. You know of him?"

Melina nodded eagerly. How she loved the story of Abraham and Sarah! God had enabled them to bear a son, despite their old age and the fact that Sarah had remained barren all her life.

"When God called Abraham out of Ur of the Chaldeans, He gave him a promise. He promised Abraham that all the families of the earth would be blessed through him. Of course, God was referencing the child, Isaac, who would be born in Abraham's old age; for eventually the promised Messiah would come from this line. This is how every single family on earth would be blessed – through the Messiah, who would come from the seed of Abraham."

Melina stared at Joanna in wonder.

"Obviously, if every single family on earth will be blessed by the Messiah, the Gentiles must be included."

"Thank you for sharing this with me," Melina whispered sincerely.

Joanna squeezed her hand. "The Scriptures tell us many things about the Messiah. But most importantly, we know that He will cleanse us of our sin. We are but filthy rags in comparison to the holiness of God. We cannot reach God on our own, for our sins serve as a barrier between us. This is why we need cleansing. This cleansing will function as a bridge to close the gap between us and the God we love. The Messiah, the Promised One – He is the bridge."

Melina marveled at the impossible words. Her heart yearned for the fulfillment of these wondrous prophetic words, despite the fact that she did not fully understand them.

Joanna leaned in closer, so close that Melina could smell the floral perfume upon her glowing skin. "Melina, I believe the Messiah has come."

Her eyes wide as saucers, Melina stared at Joanna. After a moment of stunned silence, she realized that her mouth was open. She quickly closed it. "Here? Now?"

"Here. Now."

"How can you know this?"

Joanna leaned in even closer, her voice low. "I know this because I have seen Him. I have heard Him speak. In Galilee. I was there when He was baptized. The Holy Spirit descended upon Him like a dove, and a voice thundered from Heaven, declaring boldly, 'This is My beloved Son, in whom I am well pleased. Hear Him!'"

Melina's heart pounded heavily in her chest as Joanna recounted the powerful encounter, her eyes aflame and her voice thick with emotion.

"Now let me ask you," Joanna continued, her eyes sparkling like two gleaming honey-tinted emeralds, "how are we to argue with that?"

Melina could barely speak, so enthralled was she by these staggering possibilities. She realized she was twisting her hands nervously within her lap, nearly upsetting the basket of herbs and produce resting there. Clasping her hands tightly, she attempted to still their trembling. Her eyes darted cautiously about the empty corridor. They were alone. "Do we know," she whispered softly, "if this Man has fulfilled the remaining prophecies about the Messiah?"

"I do not know," Joanna admitted, though her eyes took on a determined shine and she straightened purposefully upon the marble bench. "But you can be sure of this: I certainly intend to find out."

CHAPTER 10

Julia

The morning air was brisk and cool. Julia balanced an aging earthen jar upon one hip as she emerged from her home and crossed the short distance toward the well at the center of the neighborhood compound – an age-old courtyard of timeworn weathered stone. The dilapidated old houses formed a tight pattern about this courtyard. In this way, each house maintained access to the ancient well in the center. Several rough wooden benches were scattered about the compound, but Julia scarcely saw anyone occupying them.

She had learned rather early on that most of these neighbors kept to themselves. The majority of them were elderly. They had been born, raised, and grown old within the limestone walls of these ancient houses.

And rather like these houses in which they dwell, they grow older and more decrepit by the minute,

Julia thought snidely, her frustration mounting.

She stifled a shudder. Was her life to follow suit? Would she, too, grow old while trapped within the confines of this poverty-stricken cluster of hovels in the Lower City? She considered the stately neighborhood in which she had been raised. Towering marble villas graced broad, fashionable avenues. Manicured gardens burst forth with vibrant color as ivy graced elegant marble walls and spring flowers spilled over elegant vats and Grecian urns. Palm trees rose like stately towers and swayed in the early evening breezes. Neighbors often hosted lavish feasts and celebrations. Humdrum everyday occurrences became excuses for extravagant celebrations – the marriage of a son or daughter, the weaning of a child, or a relative's birthday. The feasts and the holy days were observed with great feasting and dancing, celebration and camaraderie, as neighbors, friends, and relatives spilled into festively and lavishly decorated villas, the servants scurrying about in a state of feverish frenzy.

In the Lower City, crumbling houses baked like bricks beneath an unrelenting sun, crammed tightly together like the many seller's booths and stalls on Small Market Street. The unpaved roads were dusty and maddeningly confusing. Julia was convinced that even the most brilliant of navigators would quickly lose himself within the patternless maze of streets and dark alleyways of this pestilent precinct.

Despite the fact that she often found herself desperate to escape the confining walls of her own small home, she rarely ventured forth on her own.

Barabbas had warned her against thieves and robbers that lurked like vultures in dark corners and around concealed bends, waiting to pounce upon their unsuspecting prey.

Adorned in lovely, imported garments from the farthest reaches of the empire and bedecked in her fine jewelry, Julia had realized far too late that she stood out like an exotic peacock strutting about a chicken coop the first time she had ventured to the market across town. The avaricious gleam in the eyes of many ill-clad men about the market had not been lost on her, and her heart had pounded heavily in her own ears on her return trip home.

She'd had no desire to make that mistake again.

That very day, Julia had lovingly folded her sophisticated garments and donned her simplest gown. She would not make herself conspicuous and risk her life for the sake of fashion, though it stung her pride and pained her to the very core to dress like a common poor woman. Despite the fact that he loved to see his wife arrayed in her breathtaking finery, Barabbas had wasted little time in bartering it off piece by piece once everything had been packed away. He'd been eyeing the gowns, jewelry, and cosmetics since their arrival, and Julia had known it was only a matter of time. She supposed she should be grateful for the few plain, simple garments Barabbas had brought home for her in their stead.

In her father's house, she had dressed like a queen. Here, in a nightmare of her own making, she could have easily been mistaken for a common peasant.

And yet, perhaps that's what I am – what I have

become, Julia thought, disheartened. *I am no longer under my father's care. His blessings are no longer mine. I am poor. I am a peasant.*

The realization stung, and Julia dropped heavily upon one of the old benches before the well. Dropping her earthen vessel heedlessly upon the ground, she buried her face in her hands and struggled against tears.

How on earth had she come to this? Why had she been so blind to the blessings lavished so abundantly upon her? Why had she forsaken a beautiful home, a loving family, for a man she scarcely knew? A man who had no love in his heart for her? Her husband cared about one thing, and one thing only – himself. He cared nothing for her. He used her to fulfill his base desires, then discarded her like an old sandal the moment his swift whims were gratified. He left her alone for days and weeks at a time. Though she had expected this concerning his role as a caravan guard, she had assumed his long periods of absence would pertain only to his work. But even when he had opportunity to be home, he abandoned her to seek the company of his Zealot friends in the hill country – sometimes venturing as far as Galilee.

I have made a terrible mistake, and now I will suffer for it for the rest of my life. If only I had waited for a good man, a man who loved God. I could be married to a wonderful man, living in a beautiful home in the Upper City, but no. I had to marry Barabbas.

Julia knew her thoughts were taking her down a dark, despondent path, but she didn't care. She was miserable. She was alone. She knew she needed wisdom, guidance.

But to whom could she to turn?

I AM. I am here. The assurance resonated softly within her heart.

Lord God, You're all I have. And in a way, I am thankful. I was too foolish to recognize how much I needed You until You were my only hope. Lord, I need help. I need wisdom – guidance. All Barabbas and I can do is fight. This isn't what I wanted, Lord. Show me what to do. Show me how to repair the damage I've done – if it's even possible, Lord.

All things are possible with God.

Julia's shoulders shook. She had no idea where the thought had come from, but she sensed it was the Lord's presence with her.

Speak to me, Lord. Show me what to do. If there is any hope for me, please confirm this for me. Give me hope.

For I know the thoughts that I think toward you... thoughts of peace and not of evil, to give you a future and a hope.

A future and a hope...

Julia wept even harder. These were the things she desperately longed for. A future to look forward to, a hope worth clinging to –

Stiffening, Julia drew in a sharp gasp of fear when a gentle arm slid around her shaking shoulders.

Both humiliated and fearful, Julia dabbed at the corners of her wet eyes with her shawl and glanced up. Involved deeply in prayer, she hadn't noticed the kindly neighbor woman slide quietly beside her on the bench.

"At the beginning of your supplications the command went out, and I have come to tell you, for you are greatly beloved."

Wide-eyed, Julia stared at the woman in awe. She recognized the woman's words as the inspired word of God – the very words the angel had spoken to Daniel as he fervently sought the Lord for help, forgiveness, and restoration.

For you are greatly beloved… Julia wondered fleetingly if the Lord had chosen this woman to speak to her on His behalf. After all, this woman didn't know of her secret struggles. How had she known that Julia was beseeching the Lord at that moment? And how had she known exactly what to say?

Had God truly heard her prayer and issued a command on her behalf the moment her petitions reached the Throne Room of Heaven? It was a staggering thought.

A warm smile crossed the woman's round face, and she patted Julia's arm with the tenderness and fondness of a grandmother. "The Lord brought these words to my heart as I swept my house. I hadn't the slightest idea why, until I glanced out the window and saw you seated dejectedly upon this bench, dear one."

Julia didn't know what to say. She wished she could remember this woman's name. She was a kindly, matronly woman with soft gray eyes and pleasant features. She wore her blue shawl swept delicately across one shoulder, though she hadn't veiled her face in Julia's presence.

The woman's eyes never left hers. "May I remind you that God sees you? He hears you. He loves you, dear one."

Julia's eyes filled with tears, but she blinked them back. "How did you know I needed help?"

"Despite the fact that you wept alone on this rickety old bench?" The woman's gray eyes twinkled.

Julia smiled bashfully. "Yes, there was that."

"I have been praying for you, dear. From the moment you moved in next door."

Julia's heart lurched. "But...but why?"

"It's just a burden the Lord has laid upon my heart. If I were a new bride, alone in a strange city, I'd want someone to pray for me. I was there once myself, in fact. I married a sailor. Many nights I'd lie awake, wondering when – or if – he'd come home."

Julia stared at the staid woman in disbelief. "My husband is a caravan guard. His work demands constant travel." She didn't mention that much of his travel was self-imposed and had nothing to do with his occupation.

"Ah. A demanding occupation of treacherous conditions, I imagine. You must worry for him."

Not really, Julia thought glumly. She decided to change the subject. "I will never forget what you did for us the night Barabbas brought me here. You cooked a delicious stew for us, do you recall? I haven't tasted anything so wonderful since."

The woman's brows rose in surprise. "Do you cook?"

"I mostly overcook. And burn. And scorch. Oh, and I also reduce to ashes. I have become rather adept at all those things."

The woman laughed heartily and squeezed Julia's arm. "My dear girl, why did you not seek my counsel?"

"I wouldn't want to impose –"

"Ah, but remember, that's what neighbors are for!"

Julia lowered her eyes, embarrassed. "Please do forgive me, but I fail to remember your name."

"Think nothing of it! My name is Deborah, dear girl. And you are Julia, I recall?"

Julia nodded.

"Well, Julia, cooking lessons shall commence at once! Are you busy this afternoon?"

Julia swallowed the lump in her throat. Her? Busy? That was a laugh! She shook her head.

"Then I'll bring over some supplies and teach you everything you need to know!"

Julia nearly choked on her own words as tears of gratitude poured over her cheeks. "I don't even know how to thank you –"

"Nonsense! It will be a pleasure to be in the company of another woman for a change! You may not have noticed, but we don't live among a particularly friendly or social group." Her eyes twinkled playfully.

Deborah rose slowly, the effort evident in her grimace. "These old bones," she laughed as Julia rose with her. "They creak and groan and put up quite a fuss."

Julia retrieved her earthen jar, which had lain forgotten among the stones and the weeds. "Thank you for coming to me, Deborah. I eagerly await your instruction this afternoon."

"And I eagerly await your company! I'll just be retrieving a few supplies, and then I'll be over shortly."

Julia watched the woman as she strode purposefully toward her own house. She noticed that Deborah had taken great care to keep the house and its grounds in good shape. The shutters were newly replaced, the entrance swept. There wasn't a weed in sight.

Julia glanced at her own rickety little house and felt a pang of conscience. Perhaps there were things she could do to make it a bit more appealing – or at least bearable. Though she kept the inside swept and tidy, she imagined there was much more she could do to improve her situation.

Already, she felt inspired by Deborah's quick action and no-nonsense manner. Perhaps with Deborah's help, she could blossom into a truly capable housewife. Maybe – just maybe – the day would come when she could gladly anticipate mealtime rather than dread it! Julia felt a welcome surge of hope.

Smilingly brightly, she lifted her eyes heavenward and uttered a silent prayer of thanksgiving.

God *did* love her. He *did* hear her.

And He had answered her desperate cry for help.

CHAPTER 11

"Don't you just love the sound of that water boiling over an open flame? It kind of reminds you of home, and all the warm feelings one associates with it!" Deborah bent over Julia's cooking pot, holding her hands above the opening and glorying in the warm steam.

At the rickety old table, Julia smiled as she spread out her meager store of shriveled vegetables for inspection. She had never associated home with menial tasks like cooking. Such mundane jobs had always been doled out to the servants.

"When I think of home, I remember the lovely garden courtyard with the beautiful marble fountain at the center. Sometimes I close my eyes and imagine I can still hear the water falling in silvery sheets upon the glistening pool below. Or I think of the luxurious baths, with the sweet-smelling bath salts and oils and perfumes. Or my father's vast office library, shelves stacked to the ceiling with precious documents and scrolls. I can smell incense burning and see the flicker of many lamps stationed about the chambers."

Deborah arched a brow. "My, you must be missing that place! Common folk like us know nothing of palace life."

Julia laughed. "It wasn't a palace. It was a villa, a house."

"Well, I imagine I could park my entire little house in the foyer of that luxurious home."

Julia smiled to herself. Deborah's statement was true enough.

"It must have been quite a shock moving to the likes of this place."

Julia nodded sadly. "It was."

"And how are you adjusting?"

Julia bit her lower lip, holding back more tears. Could she trust this woman with her deepest secrets? She desperately needed someone in whom she could confide.

She thought of Melina, with her warm smile and luminous green eyes. How she missed that unassuming servant girl. How she longed for her friendship. She wondered how Melina was doing now. Had Malchus finally professed his feelings for her?

She held back a smile. That was doubtful.

Deborah mistook Julia's silent ponderings as a polite refusal in answer to her question. She joined the young woman at the table. "Forgive me, I do not wish to pry –"

"Oh no," Julia quickly amended. "I welcome the conversation. And your wisdom as well."

"Well, what little wisdom I can impart." Deborah smiled ruefully. "Have you adjusted well?"

"Truth be told, I haven't adjusted at all."

"Oh dear."

"I miss my father and mother. I miss my home."

"Time heals, my dear. And you needn't forsake your family. You will simply see less of them."

"How ironic," Julia sighed bitterly. "The moment I truly wish to see more of them, I must see less of them."

"As is often the case with life."

How well I know it! Another sigh.

"Now, let's take a look at those vegetables." Deborah's gaze swept expertly over the shriveled items on the table. "Oh, dear. Where did you find these?"

Julia's cheeks flamed with embarrassment. "At the market."

"Next time, allow me to accompany you to give that crooked merchant a piece of my mind. He cheated you sorely, I'm afraid."

Julia's heart leaped with excitement at the prospect of Deborah accompanying her to the market. "I purchased this produce at bargain price."

"Unless that bargain price was *free*, you were sorely taken advantage of, my dear."

"I suppose I was."

"Well, let's get them in the pot before they shrivel away to nothing. I've brought over a basket of produce from my garden. We'll add it to the stew to enhance the flavor."

"You have a garden?"

"Behind my house. It requires a bit of prayer and patient coaxing, but the little sprouts do eventually push through the rocky soil."

"Growing your own vegetables must save a great deal of money."

"I'll set aside some seeds for you, and we'll plant some together. You can grow your own."

Julia clasped her hands in delight. "Do you really think I could?"

"Of course, you can. All it takes is a little time and patience, a bit of loving care, and a whole lot of prayer!"

Julia suspected that Deborah was referring to more than just the plants in her garden. She turned large pleading eyes toward the older woman. "And does this wise adage apply to other aspects of life as well?"

The woman chopped vegetables quickly and expertly, her eyes fixed upon the produce and the knife. "Well, of course it does!"

"Does it pertain to...to..." Julia's voice trailed off, and she feared she would cry again. Deborah must think her to be the weakest of women!

"To marriage?" Deborah completed the sentence for her.

"How did you know?"

"An educated guess, my dear."

"Deborah, may I be absolutely frank with you?"

"I'd prefer it."

Julia sat heavily at the table, watching Deborah's rapidly chopping knife. She propped herself up on one elbow, forlorn. "I don't know what to do. I've made a terrible mistake."

"And what mistake is that?"

"I've married the wrong man."

Deborah's knife stilled. Thoughtfully, she carried a large pile of chopped vegetables and dropped them in the boiling pot of water mixed with broth, which she had already seasoned with garlic and cumin and sage and thyme. The aroma was already tantalizing.

Oh, please say something! Julia feared she had offended Deborah with her blunt talk.

Once Deborah returned from the cook pot, she settled herself quite comfortably opposite Julia, a small smile playing about the corners of her lips. Allowing her shawl to pool loosely about her shoulders, she asked purposefully, "And what is it that prompts you to state such a claim?"

"My parents warned me. They are wonderful people, but I was too stubborn and blind to see it. They reared me in the Scriptures, but when I met Barabbas…it's as if everything I ever learned vanished from my mind. All I wanted was him. All I cared about was having him. And now…"

"Now it's not quite what you'd hoped it to be?"

Julia lowered her gaze, touched by the understanding in Deborah's eyes. "It is nothing at all like I'd hoped it to be."

Reaching across the table, Deborah took Julia's hand. "My daughter, do you think any situation is beyond God's ability to redeem? *Has the Lord's arm been shortened?*"

Julia smiled faintly, aware that Deborah referenced the Lord's reprimand to Moses when the great patriarch questioned God's ability to fulfill an exceptional promise. "I see where you are going with this, Deborah, but you don't understand."

Deborah arched a brow, her eyes twinkling. "No?"

"I *sinned*. Intentionally. Defiantly. *On purpose*! I shamed and disrespected my parents, blatantly going against their wishes and rebelling against my father's authority. Everyone knew I was making a mistake. God knew. My father and mother knew. And what's worse – even *I* knew! God tried to get my attention again and again. He tried to reach me, to speak to me, but I shut Him out. I behaved like a silly, spoiled child. And that is why I'm in the mess I'm in."

Deborah smiled tenderly. "But what have you learned?"

Julia chewed her lower lip, contemplating the direct question. "I've learned so much," she managed shakily. "God desires our best. His commandments are a hedge of protection about us, but if we choose to disobey, then we wander far from the protection of that hedge. God knows rebellion leads only to misery. This is why He outlines His commandments so clearly – He knows they lead to life and happiness, and that's what He desires for us."

"A true and beautiful assessment."

"I've also learned about the dire consequences of rebellion. I disrespected the authority of my parents. If I could go back, I would treat them so differently than I did. I miss them so much it hurts."

"Anything else?"

"Yes. I had no idea how very blessed I was. I didn't appreciate the privileged lifestyle I led. I was selfish and ungrateful. How I wish I had recognized the blessings I possessed!"

Deborah nodded. "I understand. So it would seem you've learned many valuable lessons through it all."

"Oh, I have!"

"Now let me ask you this: Do you suppose you would have fully grasped such lessons any other way?"

Julia pondered the question. It was a sobering one. "I'm not sure," she answered slowly. "I am so very stubborn at times."

Another understanding smile. "You see, Julia, sometimes the Lord allows His sheep to leave the pasture because He knows there are some hard lessons they must learn. It is often tempting to believe that He is punishing us when we experience the consequences of sin. But on the contrary, we are blessed when He allows us to experience the pain of wrong decisions – this is how we learn not to make the same mistakes again."

"I'm so ashamed. And so afraid."

Deborah squeezed her hand. "Shah, child. Never fear. God is near, and He is your Protector."

"But I disobeyed Him."

"And He sees your repentance just as I do. It would be different were you turning to Him simply to change your undesirable circumstances. But you seek Him in true repentance, humility, and brokenness, yes?"

The tears came then. "Yes. I wish I had done differently. I want to obey God now, Deborah. I really do."

"I know you do, child. And you are forgiven. God will never reject a truly repentant soul."

"Despite the fact that I walked into this mess with my eyes wide open, in blatant rebellion?"

"You have turned from those sins, Julia. And when God forgives, He cleanses us of all unrighteousness. Now, He may not correct your circumstances overnight. He warns us against sin because He knows the consequences are painful and inconvenient. But He can redeem your situation. He has good plans for you, Julia."

"A future and a hope," Julia whispered, her eyes glistening with tears.

"Do you know what I find most beautiful about that passage, Julia?"

She shook her head.

"People are so enthralled by the first part of that verse that they forget the circumstances that led to God's beautiful promise of a future and a hope. You see, the Israelites had rebelled, and the cup of their iniquity had been filled to the brim. As a result, they were captured by their enemies, and they cried out in their affliction. But the Lord heard them. Despite the fact that they deserved their plight. Despite the fact that they had brought this trouble upon themselves. God *still* heard them, forgave their sinful rebellion, and delivered this blessed promise: *For I know the thoughts I think toward you…thoughts of peace and not of evil, to give you a future and a hope. Then you will call upon Me and go and pray to Me, and I will listen to you. And you will seek Me and find Me, when you search for me with all your heart. I will be found by you, says the Lord, and I will bring you back from your captivity.*"

Julia closed her eyes, allowing the promises of God to wash over her like a warm and welcome flood. "That is exactly where I am now, Deborah. My own sins held me captive, and now I must suffer this affliction. I am no better than the Israelites of old."

"But God forgave them, did He not? He has forgiven you, too, child. And He will deliver you of your affliction. Maybe not overnight – but He is working on your behalf. And through this experience, you will draw closer to Him than ever before if you choose to grasp the opportunity."

"Then what must I do?"

"Exactly as you've said. You must obey."

"But I don't know how."

Deborah patted her hand comfortingly. "I believe you do, child. It's never as difficult as we make it out to be. Simply determine to honor God in every single thing that you do. You know the Scriptures. Heed them. In the simple things – the little things – as well as the bigger things. Honor God in the way you clean this house. In the way you prepare your meals. In the way you relate to your neighbors and those you encounter at the market. Honor God in the way you treat your husband – "

Julia's cheeks flamed, and she lowered her head, shamed.

"Ah, a sore subject, I can see."

"He treats me so harshly, Deborah," Julia whispered, her cheeks crimson. "He cuts me down with his words. His tramples all over me. I have tried to reach out to him, but he rejects me every time. He doesn't even attempt to honor me, not in the least."

Now Deborah reached her second hand across the table. She gripped Julia's other hand gently. "And yet the same can be said for each of us, can it not? At some point in our lives, have we not all treated our heavenly Father in such a manner?"

Julia's heart skipped a beat. She considered her decisions and great rebellion leading up to her marriage with Barabbas. All along the way, God had lovingly wooed her, reached for her, called to her. But she had shut her ears to His entreaties and stomped all over His commandments. She hadn't attempted to honor Him. Not in the least.

How was she any different from Barabbas? And yet... God had never once let her go nor stopped loving her. He waited with open arms and cradled her tenderly like a little child when she ran to Him, wounded and bleeding. And what had He done? He had bound her wounded heart, comforting her with His presence and His peace.

"All we ever do is fight." It was a weak excuse, but Julia wasn't sure she was equipped to shower her husband with unconditional love at this point.

Deborah smiled knowingly. "Then perhaps there is another lesson to be learned – the most difficult for all women, I imagine."

Julia studied her, a question in her eyes.

"The art of holding the tongue!"

"But he says the most hateful things!"

"*A soft answer turns away wrath, but a harsh word stirs up anger.*"

"Well, surely my *soft* contribution will matter little – he has enough harsh words for both of us!"

Deborah chuckled. "It is a difficult lesson, but one we can master by the grace of God."

"So what am I to do? When he comes at me like an angry bull, do I simply stand there and take it?"

"I would suggest kindness. Don't let his sharp words and angry barbs unsettle you. Abide in the peace of God, and resort to prayer when the accusations begin."

"And say nothing at all?"

"If the Lord wishes for you to speak, He will provide the soft words – emphasis on *soft*, my dear. But be sure they are His words and not your own."

Julia rubbed her aching head, wondering how on earth she would accomplish the impossible. *By the grace of God*, Deborah had said. Still, she wasn't even sure if this was the proper route to take.

"But, Deborah." Reluctantly, she voiced her concern, her expression troubled. "You say I am to repay my husband with kindness. How am I to do that when I loathe his very existence? Am I not rewarding him for his abominable behavior by showering him with kindness when he behaves like a savage beast?"

Deborah rose to her feet, scooping up more chopped vegetables for the pot. "My! You are very descriptive, my dear." Dumping the vegetables into the pot, she stirred the aromatic brew with a long ladle, her back to Julia. "Let me ask you this – *when* do you suppose would be the proper time to treat your husband with respect?"

"Respect?" Julia was repulsed. Her husband was the most undeserving of men. It sickened her to consider respecting him.

"Yes. Respect. You know the word?"

"Of course, I do! Though my husband hasn't the slightest idea what it means – or how to earn it."

"To earn it, you say. So are you implying that you would respect your husband and treat him with kindness if he earned it with good behavior?"

Julia contemplated her words. "Yes, I suppose so."

"And do you suppose," Deborah continued, returning to the table, "that Barabbas feels the same way about you?"

Julia bristled. "I haven't treated him as wickedly as he has treated me!"

"Do you happily greet him when he returns home at night?"

"I wouldn't have to if he didn't abandon me for days at a time!"

"Do you compliment him about the things you *do* appreciate about him?"

What is there to appreciate? Julia looked away, annoyed.

"Have you thanked him for his provision?"

Julia was aghast. "*Provision*? What provision?"

Deborah smiled, amused. "This house, for example. Food and sustenance."

"My father's storage rooms were larger than this entire house!"

"It's a roof over your head, is it not?"

"And you've just sampled the shriveled 'sustenance' he provides!"

"But you haven't gone hungry."

Julia stared at Deborah in disbelief.

"You have said you neglected to count your blessings while living in your father's house," Deborah reminded her gently. "Yet there are still blessings to be counted. There are many homeless women in this world who would be overjoyed to possess a roof over their heads, however small. And thousands of people go hungry each day, begging at the temple and near the synagogues for their daily bread. Would they appreciate the shriveled vegetables now sizzling over this warm fire?"

Julia lowered her gaze, ashamed. Perhaps she was still a bit more spoiled than she'd realized. *Oh, Lord, please help me. I'm so far from where I need to be...*

"I understand that your husband has left much to be desired," Deborah concluded, her voice compassionate and understanding. "But sometimes a little love and appreciation goes a long way. If you refuse to show love until he lives up to your expectations, and if he refuses to show love until you live up to his..."

Julia knew where she was headed. "Then nothing will ever change."

"Exactly."

"But what if it doesn't work, Deborah?"

"Oh, it won't – not right away. These things take time, and lots of it. But rather like my lovely little sprouts in the garden – given enough time, patience, tender care, and prayer – your marriage can grow. Water it, Julia. Nurture it. Lay aside your selfishness and choose to walk in love."

CHAPTER 12

"What in the world is going on in here?"

Absorbed in her work, Julia glanced up from the fresh spring onion she was carefully slicing. She hadn't heard Barabbas come in, but perhaps that was because she had been absorbed in womanly chatter with her new friend, Deborah.

"Well?"

Julia's eyes flashed at his imperious tone. How dare he greet her with such disrespect before a guest! And he hadn't even bothered to greet their kindly neighbor.

But I suppose I shouldn't be surprised!

In one quick moment, Deborah met Julia's gaze with a calm deliberateness that sent Julia's heart pounding. Julia knew what the woman was silently communicating. *Remember what we spoke about. Choose to walk in love.*

Julia's throat went dry. At this moment, she'd prefer to walk in almost anything but love! But she didn't want to disappoint this wonderful woman who had taken the entire afternoon to teach her cooking tips and tricks, instructing her in the complicated art of cooking. The house was filled with the mouth-watering aroma of fresh vegetable and barley stew. Deborah had sacrificed one of her own expensive golden loaves of barley bread to accompany the meal. Kitchen tools and utensils were strewn across the rough-hewn table, as Deborah had carefully explained the proper usage of each one.

Julia's heart hammered steadily within her chest as another realization dawned on her: she certainly didn't wish to insult this kind woman, but even more than that – she truly *did* desire to please God.

What does the Lord your God require of you, but to fear the Lord your God, to walk in all His ways and to love Him, to serve the Lord your God with all your heart and with all your soul, and to keep the commandments of the Lord and His statutes which I command you today for your good?

For your good. Julia knew the Scriptures. She knew what the Lord required of her. She must walk in *all* His ways – even the inconvenient, seemingly impossible ways.

Though it was a difficult habit to squelch, Julia knew she must forsake dependence upon herself and truly embrace this life-giving truth – God's commandments were for *her good*, as the verse beautifully proclaimed.

For your good. For your good. For your good. The beautiful promise pounded like a steady cadence within her mind along with the rapid beating of her heart.

Taking a deep breath, Julia set aside the knife and

crossed the room to her husband. "Good afternoon – or I suppose I should say *good evening* at this point, my husband." Standing on tiptoe, she planted a gentle kiss along the strong curve of his jawline.

Barabbas stared down at her, mouth agape. But he quickly composed himself. "Have you been drinking?"

His tone was acrid and sarcastic, and Julia wished she could revoke her kiss.

Deborah stepped in and saved the day with a hearty chuckle. "Ah, this one has a sense of humor! Dear boy, I guarantee you nothing of the sort would take place under my watch."

Looking unsure, Barabbas set his leather satchel down and sniffed the air. "Something smells wonderful. Which tells me someone other than Julia has done the cooking."

Julia's insides clenched. How this man galled her!

Again, Deborah saved the day. She smiled. "Then prepare to be pleasantly surprised and amazed. Your wife did indeed prepare this meal: vegetable and barley stew, garnished with fresh thyme and spring onions. I did supply a loaf of bread, which will be absolutely delicious dipped in the stew. Believe me!"

Barabbas eyed Julia suspiciously, clearly unconvinced that she had produced the delicious-smelling stew bubbling in the pot.

Julia sensed his line of thinking and stated humbly, "I had help, and plenty of it. But Deborah is teaching me how to cook. I would like my husband to enjoy his supper rather than dread it from now on."

Her quiet humility unnerved Barabbas. After many nights of bitter arguments and sharp retorts, he clearly remained untrusting.

His suspicious gaze traveled to Deborah. "We needn't your charity. My wife is capable of preparing her own meals."

"That's not what you said last night."

Barabbas' gaze flashed back to Julia, his stance ready. But he saw no malice – only humor – mirrored in her twinkling eyes.

Deborah was fast on her feet. "Believe me, son. This is no charity. I may have an ulterior motive or two up my sleeve."

Barabbas arched a brow. "Such as?"

"One – I miss conversing freely with another woman."

Barabbas glanced uneasily toward Julia. Exactly how *freely* were they conversing?

"And two – " Deborah continued, her eyes gleaming with mischief, "I'd be delighted if Julia would be willing to assist me in the grinding at the millstone. I can't operate the monstrous thing by myself, but I am sick and tired of being overcharged for the baker's bread. And I imagine you are too – I noticed you haven't a millstone of your own. I will gladly continue these cooking lessons if you are willing to spare your wife to help me at the mill. I'll even throw in some freshly milled flour for Julia to take home in exchange for her work."

"I thought the milling was in return for the cooking lessons?"

"You needn't worry that handsome brow of

yours – I wouldn't think of offering charity to the likes of you, my boy." Deborah's eyes sparkled with play. "Have you ever worked a millstone? I thought not. It is hot, sweaty work – believe me! Julia will have well-earned that flour along with the cooking lessons. But if you'd prefer being overcharged by that crafty old baker at the market, be my guest." There was not a hint of malice in Deborah's voice – only business and common sense.

Grudgingly, Barabbas respected the woman's logic. "Julia may assist you as needed."

Julia cringed, annoyed that Barabbas spoke as if he offered Deborah a very great favor.

"I greatly appreciate your generosity."

Barabbas did a double take. Still, he detected no malice in Deborah's features. A bit of mischief, perhaps. Luster. Life. But no malice.

"Now that arrangements have been made, I suppose I should return home to my poor, neglected husband." Deborah grinned. "The aroma of this stew wafting about the neighborhood must be driving him mad."

"Oh, but wait!" Quickly, Julia reached for two wooden bowls and ladled generous portions of stew into each. "You haven't the time to prepare a meal for the two of you now. Take some stew. And thank your husband for sparing you."

Taking the steaming bowls with a smile of gratitude, Deborah grinned at Barabbas. "Thank you, dear one. I myself see no harm in accepting a little charity now and then." She winked at him as he stared at her, speechless.

"Have a blessed and wonderful evening, dear ones," Deborah called blithely over her shoulder. She slipped out the door. "Peace to this house."

Peace to this house. How Julia savored the sound of it. *Peace.* It would seem that Deborah had doused the place in a generous smattering of peace. She wondered if Barabbas could feel it too.

No, Deborah did not bring the peace, Julia amended, warmed to the core. *God supplied it.* Deborah was simply His willing vessel. She delivered the peace her Father supplied.

How Julia longed to serve the Lord in such a way – to fill a room with joy and peace the moment she entered it.

Her gaze came to rest upon her husband, standing awkwardly and uncertainly before her.

She sighed. She supposed she must learn to bring peace to this house first.

O Lord, help me!

"Where do you intend to take our supper, as the table is currently in use?" his tone was brittle.

Julia took a deep breath. "Do not worry, my husband. I will have this cleared away in a moment." Then she set about clearing the table, quickly placing the supplies and utensils in their respective places.

Barabbas watched her, unsettled. He would have preferred her usual snide comeback. That he could work with. But humble acceptance? What was he supposed to do with that?

He noticed the kitchen area had been thoroughly swept, scrubbed, and organized. The women had certainly been busy all afternoon. At least they hadn't wasted the entire day in vain and idle gossip.

He had yet to decide if he appreciated the influence of this Deborah or not.

Only time would tell.

"I've brought something home for you."

Julia's heart did a somersault. Her husband had purchased a gift for her? It was almost too much to believe! She felt her hopes rising, yet at the same time, she quickly suppressed them. She had been disappointed too many times in the recent past. She had no desire for her high hopes to be cruelly squashed – again.

Setting the last item on the shelf, she turned to face her husband, cautious. "You have?"

"Don't look so excited." His tone was dry.

Julia watched as he disappeared out the door. What was that awkward sound? There was a decent amount of shuffling and scraping, then a frightening shriek that sounded rather like a small child in the throes of a full-fledged tantrum...

A moment later Barabbas returned, a long rope in hand –

"Is that a *goat*?"

Maaaaaaaa! Maaaaaaaa!

Julia gasped and drew back against the wall, terrified.

There stood the little horned beast, a rope tied to its neck, its little hooves pawing the ground in indignation, its stony gaze fixed on *her*!

Maaaaaa!

"Barabbas, what on earth –"

Barabbas' eyes flashed angrily. "I should have

known you'd be ungrateful."

"*Ungrateful?*" Julia's eyes were round with fright. "I'm *terrified*!"

"You'll get over it."

"What am I to do with it?"

Maaaaaaaa!

Julia covered her ears, willing the shrill and abominable little beast to disappear.

"It's a goat, Julia – not a monster. Stop cowering in the corner like a child."

"He's staring at me!"

"*She*, Julia. What good would a male goat be?"

"What good is *she?*"

"She will provide milk. Which in turn can produce cheese. She's recently birthed offspring. She has milk."

Perhaps that was why the goat was angry – she had been taken from her kids. Isn't that what baby goats were called – *kids?* Julia hadn't the slightest idea.

"Haven't you ever seen a goat before?"

Julia remained pressed against the wall. "Well, yes. At the temple. And – and in *pens*. Where they belong." *Certainly not in the house!* she wished to declare stoutly. But Deborah's warning remained fresh on her mind. She determined to tame her unruly tongue despite her indignation.

"Well, I can see I will be receiving no accolades on behalf of this gift to my wife."

He had some nerve to declare that wicked, unruly creature a *gift*! And how much *work* would this benevolent *gift* require? Somehow Julia held her tongue.

"Regardless of how you feel about it, she's staying. I'll take her to the pen out back. You will need to feed and water her daily. And she will need to be milked."

More orders. Naturally.

"You can start tomorrow. I'll handle everything tonight."

Well, how kind of you, she wished to retort. Rapidly, she made mental calculations. How easily could one make a goat disappear? If she left the gate open, would the creature wander out? Would Barabbas blame her? Well, of course he would!

After all, everything is always your fault, remember?

It took all the strength she possessed to remain silent as Barabbas led the protesting creature out the door. She shivered when it cast a defiant glance over its shoulder, its beady little eyes boring confrontationally into her own.

Setting the table with trembling hands, Julia wondered if she had just met her arch-nemesis.

When Barabbas returned, his expression was guarded. He seated himself at the table and watched a bit eagerly in spite of himself as Julia placed a steaming bowl of stew before him, followed by a thick chunk of barley bread.

After serving herself also, Julia seated herself across from her husband and inhaled the welcome scent of the warm stew. She noticed that Barabbas was already ripping off large chunks of bread and dipping them in the stew.

"How is it?"

Barabbas swallowed a large chunk of bread saturated in the stew. "Incredible. That woman can cook."

Disappointment washed over Julia. "I helped."

"What did you do? Pass the spoon? Would you like congratulations for that?"

Julia lowered her gaze, her fists clenching angrily in her lap. How she longed to lash out at him, to cut him to the quick the same way he cut her. How would she ever learn to hold her tongue in the presence of this hateful person?

All things are possible with God.

Lord God, help me! Please.

After mopping his bowl clean with chunks of bread, Barabbas slid his bowl across the table.

"I'll take some more."

Then get it yourself. Julia breathed in deeply to calm herself. "I had hoped to save leftovers for several days. Deborah says the stew will keep if –"

"Did Deborah supply the vegetables or purchase the ingredients for that stew? Did she pay for the fireplace or utensils used to cook it?"

Julia stared at her husband, chilled by the hardness of his heart. She considered setting him straight and revealing that Deborah had, in fact, provided much that went into the stew. But she knew it would make no difference. If anything, Barabbas might become indignant and refuse to host the woman at his house again. Though it pained her greatly, she remained silent.

"That's what I thought. And you didn't possess the slightest qualm about dishing out portions of our own sustenance to send over to a couple of complete strangers. So if I want another bowl of stew, I don't need some old neighbor woman dictating whether or not I can have it."

Julia felt the tension building steadily in her chest, but she focused her thoughts on the promise instead. *For your good. For your good. For your good.*

Without a word, she rose and replenished her husband's bowl.

Setting it before him, she proceeded to finish her own supper in silence.

He accepted his seconds grudgingly. "If you really learned so much today," he drawled in an accusatory fashion, "it shouldn't be a problem to make another pot once we finish this one."

And will you supply the coin to purchase the ingredients? Julia wished to retort.

Quietly, Julia lowered her spoon to the bowl. Though supper tasted delicious, Barabbas had sucked the joy right out of the occasion. She wondered why she ever bothered to look forward to anything that included him.

Though she kept her own eyes lowered, she could sense Barabbas' eyes upon her.

"What?"

Julia knew that tone. He was itching for another fight – daring her to take issue with his behavior.

She refused to take the bait. She forced a smile. "This supper is wonderful. Thank you for allowing me to work in exchange for these lessons."

Disarmed, Barabbas lowered his gaze indifferently. Julia could sense his inner turmoil, despite the fact that he wore his disdain like a shield. "Something had to be done. I couldn't stomach your dreadful cooking another week, much less the rest of my life."

The arrow struck its mark as intended, but Julia remained staunch in her mission. "I could not agree with you more, Barabbas." She ignored the bile rising as she spoke the words. "That's why I'm so grateful to have a talented cook like Deborah teach me what she knows."

His nerves taut, Barabbas slammed down his spoon. "What game are you playing, Julia?"

Julia lifted innocent eyes to his. "What do you mean?"

"You are the most abrasive of women, so you can forget about this sweet charade you're playing. We've been married over two months. I know what's under that pretty, composed façade of yours."

Cut to the quick, Julia rose and gathered up her half-eaten supper. She willed her legs to carry her gracefully rather than stomping over to the cook pot, where she emptied the remainder of her stew.

She had completely lost her appetite. But at least there would be more for later...if Barabbas didn't devour it before she had the chance to enjoy it.

Reaching for her shawl, she hurried for the door.

"Where do you think you're going, Julia?"

Another steady breath. "I am feeling faint, a bit dizzy. Perhaps working in the hot kitchen was a bit much for me –"

"Well, heaven forbid you actually have to work for a change."

"I need a bit of fresh air. I won't be long."

"Cover your face," Barabbas hissed as she slipped out the door.

Yes, your majesty. Julia considered a mock curtsy as she shut the door behind her. Leaning up against the doorpost, she allowed the tears to fall.

Lord God, how he hurts me! I hate him, Lord. I hate everything about him.

Be still, and know that I am God.

Pulling her shawl more tightly about her slender shoulders, Julia breathed in the cool night air, glorying in the sight of a trillion glittering stars dazzling in the glorious heavens above.

You are the Creator of every single one of them, Father. You know their names. You know mine.

Maaa! Maaaaaa! MAAAAAA!

Julia stiffened, her heart pounding in terror before remembering the source of that dreadful shrieking. *Oh, it's that silly little goat.*

Striding around the small house, Julia gazed upon the indignant little creature in the pen. Its dark fur blended in with the surrounding night. It looked rather pathetic, all alone in the rickety old pen. *Maaaaaaa!*

Julia hid an amused smile. "Perhaps if you'd stop shrieking so, we could be friends. What do you say to that?"

MAAAAAAAA!

"Haven't you learned any other words, you silly goat?"

Maaa. Maaaaaa!

"We'll work on it, then."

Gazing up toward the heavens, Julia allowed the peace of God to wash over her. Despite her circumstances. Despite her fears. Despite the angry little goat bleating loudly in its pen...

You are the Creator of this abominable little creature, Lord. Yet You have fashioned it for a purpose, as You have done with all things. Even my husband, Lord. You love him. You made him. I must choose to believe You have a plan for him too, if he will only embrace it...

Help me along this difficult road, Lord. You are the only way. I cannot do this on my own.

Only by Your grace.

When Julia returned to the house later that evening, she set aside her shawl and calmly began to clean up from supper, her peace restored, and her thoughts stayed on her Redeemer.

Despite the fact that he said nothing, Julia could sense Barabbas' eyes watching her the rest of the evening as he remained warily silent, deep in thought.

CHAPTER 13

Melina

Jesus.

There was power in the name.

Melina shivered with delightful anticipation as she went about her daily chores, pondering Joanna's testimony.

This wasn't the first time she'd encountered the name of Jesus. Vaguely, Melina recalled a fiery debate between the family of Herod and Pontius Pilate and his wife, Claudia Procula. Herodias had been spewing her venom about the wild prophet who went by John the Baptizer. Claudia Procula had mentioned Jesus in the midst of the discussion. The stately woman's words still rang like a proclamation bell, resounding deeply within Melina's heart.

Claudia Procula had been certain that this Jesus would turn the world upside down.

And now Joanna's testimony appeared to confirm Procula's assessment.

Melina's heart churned with hopeful anticipation as she considered the possibility of witnessing the acts of the Messiah during her own lifetime. What would it be like? What would the Messiah do? Her mind reeled with conflicting thoughts. She knew very little about the Messiah, but she had set her heart on learning.

The thing that troubled her most was that her own discoveries about the Messiah buried within the ancient leaves of Scripture were completely contrary to the facts she gleaned from Malchus, Elias, and the Jewish religious leaders.

He will be a mighty warrior king, Malchus had once proclaimed. *He will deliver a united Israel from the chains of Roman bondage. He will conquer all. He will be invincible, undefeated.*

But what did the prophet Isaiah predict? Melina recalled the words of the ancient prophet from memory. *He was oppressed and He was afflicted, yet He opened not His mouth; He was led as a lamb to the slaughter, and as a sheep before its shearers is silent, so He opened not His mouth.*

Elias' testimony mirrored that of Malchus: *He will rally the people against the Empire of Rome and demolish the power of the emperor. The people will adore and worship Him,* Elias had explained.

But the Scriptures clearly foretold: *He has no form or comeliness; and when we see Him, there is no beauty that we should desire Him. He is despised and rejected by men, a Man of sorrows and acquainted with grief. And we hid, as it were, our faces from Him...*

He will overthrow the Romans, restoring and purifying our Temple, the Pharisees and religious leaders stoutly insisted. *No longer will the Romans stare down their long noses and dictate to us about our religious rites and services. Once again, our ceremonial rituals will be our own.*

But the prophet Isaiah proclaimed that the Messiah would become the ultimate sacrifice: *He was wounded for our transgressions, He was bruised for our iniquities; the chastisement of our peace was upon Him, and by His stripes we are healed.* Would such a tremendous sacrifice occur simply to further the lesser sacrifices of sheep and goats within the temple grounds?

Straightening the soft Egyptian sheets upon the enormous canopy bed in Salome's abandoned chambers, Melina considered another frightening possibility: If the people were deceived by false allusions and the contrary teachings of current religious leaders, would they be blinded to the Messiah's coming? What if they missed it?

What if they were so certain that they knew what the Messiah's coming was going to entail, that they were unwilling to acknowledge it if it happened in a way that contradicted the philosophy they had been taught by the Pharisees and the religious leaders?

Melina shuddered. How was one to know which teachings were true and which were false?

I suppose one must weigh every philosophy against the teachings of God's Word. Since God's Word is true, any idea that contradicts His Word must be false.

After adjusting the plush, freshly washed blankets upon the bed, Melina crossed over to an elegant row of arched windows and attempted to throw open the billowing curtains. She always aired out the chambers even when the fussy young woman to whom they belonged remained absent.

After all, the royal family could return any given day with little to no warning. She must be ready for their appearance at all times.

Rather like the Messiah's coming, she thought, an amused smile touching her lips. *We must be ready at all times. What a tragedy it would be if we missed it!*

And what would be the cost to their souls should they fail to recognize Him?

Melina shuddered. She resolved to corner Joanna the moment their paths crossed. She wanted to learn more about this Man named Jesus. To think that Joanna had seen Him with her own eyes! Heard Him speak with her own ears!

How I envy her! Melina thought, smiling.

Retrieving a damp rag, Melina went about the room, dusting the polished surfaces and numerous gold and silver figurines encrusted with semiprecious stones. It wouldn't do for the mistress to complain of dust or mothballs upon her return. Even as her hands busily worked to complete each task, Melina's mind barreled ahead of her.

I must continue to study the Scriptures, she reasoned, lifting a heavy bronze figurine of some foreign, ill-clad goddess and dusting it carefully. Most likely a souvenir from one of Salome's many travels. Melina detested the gruesome image, but carefully dusted the many cracks and crevices, nonetheless. *If I know the Word like the back of my hand, then I am far less likely to be deceived when the Messiah comes.*

A small smile tipped the corners of Melina's soft lips. She'd best hurry with her chores if she hoped to study one of her precious, weathered scrolls before her exhausted head hit the pillow that night.

***

Malchus

"Have you forsaken the act of eating altogether?"

Malchus glanced up sharply as Mara emerged from the pillared porticoes and entered the peristyle, his sanctuary.

Malchus clenched his teeth along with his fists. Was there no rest for the weary?

"Well?" Mara crossed the distance between them and sat lightly on the other side of his curved marble bench.

"To eat one must set foot in the kitchen," Malchus stated ruefully, "and the company leaves much to be desired."

"Then eat during the rush when the servants storm the kitchen for an evening meal. I'll have little time to *look* at you, much less *speak* to you, at that time."

She hadn't taken the bait. Annoyed, Malchus stared at the crude wooden plate she had brought with her.

"Flatbread with roasted lamb and spring onions. Seasoned with garlic and thyme."

"I must admit it trumps that watery stew you serve us." Even as he delivered the insult, his stomach clenched at the tantalizing aroma of roasted meat and grilled flatbread.

"If you'd swallow your pride as easily as the stew, then you'd appreciate this meal. And our friendship."

"I thought Caiaphas didn't approve of taking such items out of the kitchen."

"You yourself stated stoutly that he'd never find out."

"Ah, but you've forgotten he has eyes and ears everywhere."

"Are we really going to go down that path again?"

"It is the path you have chosen, Mara. And I suggest you leave me out of it."

"Well, if it isn't my dear cousin engaged in his first lover's quarrel."

Their heads came up at the unexpected words emerging from the darkness beyond the pillared porticoes. Alexander emerged with the stealth of a preying serpent; his handsome features bathed in the moonlight slanting across the grounds of the open-air peristyle.

"I am honored to witness this lovely little milestone in your life, dear Malchus."

Malchus rose abruptly to his feet, anger coursing hotly through his veins. "Must you make a grand entrance every time you walk into a room?"

"It is the only way," Alexander smirked, his dark eyes glittering dangerously. He glanced at Mara, her shoulders hunched in a dejected manner, her eyes wet with angry tears. "Is he pestering you, my dear? Shall I do something about it?"

It was evident that Mara noticed Alexander's striking countenance and masculine build. Her eyes traveled up his form, resting upon his flashing eyes as dark as obsidian. "*Cousin*, you say?"

Malchus wished the earth would open up and swallow him. He could see that Alexander would eagerly and readily poison any friendship he himself had cultivated during his years serving in Caiaphas' house. His eyes grazed Mara's dejected form, and a twinge of conscience made him cringe.

It would seem he had successfully poisoned his own friendships. He needed little help from this swarthy cousin.

Mara has herself to blame, he argued silently, his blood boiling. *If she weren't behaving like a desperate fool woman, she would not have fallen prey to Lucius' wicked schemes!*

Alexander took a daring step toward Mara, his eyes traveling boldly over her trembling form. "You work in the kitchen, yes?"

"I do not see how that is any business of yours."

Malchus breathed a deep sigh, relieved, and suppressed a grin. Perhaps Mara would not be fooled by his cousin's empty charm.

How could she? She's already fallen under the spell of another. Malchus' lips formed a grim line.

Alexander laughed, the sound as smooth as oil. "I see you've prepared a delectable feast for your lover, though it appears he isn't the least bit interested."

Mara's lips tightened, and she turned her head away as Alexander seated himself upon the bench.

Malchus' fists clenched. The man had no decency. His broad shoulders grazed Mara's as he reached for the plate in her hands. "I'd be more than happy to accept whatever this fool has rejected."

Mara jerked the plate away. "There is plenty of stew left in the kitchen. You may help yourself."

"I fully intend to."

Startled, Mara looked up and her eyes were met by Alexander's bold gaze. She flushed.

Malchus did not like what he was seeing. What possible use was Mara to this despicable cretin? And why had Alexander felt the need to intrude upon their private conversation?

Mara turned to Malchus, her eyes full of questions. "Is this man your kinsman?"

"Regrettably."

Alexander uttered another smooth laugh. "Malchus has always possessed the most refreshing wit."

"How did you come to be here?"

"Fate, my dear. Fate brought me here."

"Yes, his own two legs had nothing to do with it," Malchus emphasized dryly.

"And now you will work for Caiaphas?"

"It is a privilege I shall not take lightly."

Malchus rolled his eyes.

Mara noticed. "For kinsmen, you appear to be at odds." Her eyes narrowed. "Or perhaps Malchus is simply at odds with everyone in his life, including himself."

"Ah, my dear, you are very astute."

"If you hadn't noticed, Mara and I were in the middle of a discussion."

"Mara – a lovely name. It sings. What does it mean?"

"*Bitter.*" Mara's eyes smoldered with suppressed anger. "And I am fitly named."

Alexander recovered quickly. "If that is the case, you are far more lovely than bitter. Perhaps we can discover the root of such misery, and give you cause for pleasure rather than bitterness."

Mara studied the man in disbelief. "You are too bold."

"And you, my dear, are too innocent."

"Then she's fooled you well," Malchus breathed under his breath.

"But your innocence is refreshing. Alluring, even." Alexander's features were split by a predatory smile.

Malchus' face hardened. "You should go."

Alexander was in no hurry. "So we've clarified the relationship between Malchus and myself. But I do wish to know – what is the relationship between you and my dear cousin, innocent little Mara?"

Mara's eyes flickered. Malchus sensed that her wounded pride was responding to Alexander's flattery, even while her logic cautioned her to be wary.

"We are dear friends," Mara said quietly, her eyes filling with tears.

We were *dear friends,* Malchus wished to retort. And yet he had no desire to further involve his churlish cousin in his own affairs.

"*Friends?* Yes, of course. But why the tears? Do

you long for more?"

Mara's eyes flashed vulnerably. "Heavens, no. I am betrothed!"

Alexander's eyes darkened. "In marriage?"

"Hence the word *betrothed*," Malchus retorted. He considered revealing Mara's mistruth – for the agreement she shared with Lucius was certainly not a legal or binding betrothal – but he thought better of it. Better for Alexander to consider Mara as belonging to another man and therefore off limits.

That is, if he even possesses the decency to consider a betrothed woman as such, he amended wryly.

"And who, may I ask, is the lucky man? Anyone I am privileged to know?"

"Someone who is privileged not to know *you*," Malchus muttered.

"Again, I do not see how that is any of your business," Mara informed him. Though her tone remained firm, she studied the handsome man beside her with veiled interest.

Undaunted by her tone and sensing her silent admiration, Alexander rose slowly, his powerful form appearing to loom over the maidservant seated upon the bench despite her unusual height. "Well, I can see my presence here is making my dear cousin uncomfortable."

Malchus swore if Alexander referred to him as his *dear cousin* one more time, he'd break his aristocratic nose.

"Therefore, I shall take my irritating presence elsewhere."

"Thank you," Malchus stated dryly.

Reaching out a strong hand, Alexander tucked a stray curl behind Mara's ear. She stared at him, wide-eyed and silent. "You may offer my congratulations to the groom."

"Or your condolences," Malchus breathed in annoyance.

Mara failed to hear him, as her eyes were fixed on Alexander.

"Until we meet again –"

"Should we be so unfortunate," Malchus groaned through gritted teeth.

"– I bid you both farewell."

Alexander turned and, taking powerful, confident strides, disappeared into the shadowy alcoves, melting into the darkness as he was prone to do.

Openmouthed, Malchus and Mara stared after him, both disturbed and unsettled for entirely different reasons. Mara battled her own attraction toward this interesting and exciting newcomer, while Malchus' conscience warned against the hatred he harbored against his kinsman. After all, Alexander was a close relative, the son of his mother's beloved sister.

Hadn't Melina advised him to pray for Alexander? Should he not be concerned for the welfare and spiritual state of his own relative – his kinsman?

True, blood was thicker than water. The problem was Malchus possessed no qualm whatsoever that Alexander would gladly slit his throat and spill every ounce of his thick blood if it would further his own insatiable greed and selfish ambition.

CHAPTER 14

Julia

The dreary winter month of Tevet rolled into Shevat, though the typically slow and sluggish wintry days were more or less a blur for Julia.

Though her husband remained aloof and often absent, Julia found solace in her daily walk with the Lord and in her flourishing friendship with Deborah. Her cooking lessons were yielding excellent results, and she was beginning to feel confident as she moved about the kitchen preparing the daily meals.

Under Deborah's skilled tutelage, Julia learned many tips and tricks concerning the art of cooking and housekeeping. She had learned to mill flour and bake fresh bread. Deborah had also shown her how to milk the little goat and prepare deliciously crumbly goat cheese. She now possessed a vast arsenal of recipes from which to choose when supper time approached. And she took pride in keeping her home neat and tidy, despite the fact that it was nothing like her father's gleaming marble villa in the sophisticated Upper City.

Deborah had helped her sand and polish the wooden furniture in her tiny home. The table, benches, and shelving gleamed beneath flickering oil lamps. Each cooking utensil and cooking pot beckoned from their organized spots on the shelves, and supplies were stacked neatly in the small storage room. Julia had even learned to make minor repairs on the home, sealing gaping cracks with stucco and realigning the sagging shutters.

One would have never guessed, upon first glance, that Deborah was so handy with tools nor skilled in workmanship. Julia supposed that Deborah had been forced to learn many masculine skills when her husband, Isaac, became an invalid. The old sailor still possessed a barrel chest, a lusty voice, and a large sense of humor, but he had nearly lost the use of his legs after a tragic accident. They hung limp and shriveled with disuse when the big man sat in his chair. It saddened Julia to see such a jovial and compassionate man in such a condition, though his misfortune certainly hadn't dampened his spirits. In his own words, he clung to his faith in God and refused to waste his life wallowing in self-pity.

Julia rounded the corner of the house and the small animal pen loomed before her. Even this rickety old pen had been reinforced and repaired due to Deborah's careful instruction. If Barabbas had noticed their diligence and hard work, he certainly hadn't taken the time to compliment them.

Balancing an earthen jar upon her hip, Julia carried it toward the pen. She no longer feared for her life when replenishing the water or feeding trough. The little female goat pranced happily about the pen, especially now that Barabbas had supplied a male goat to join her in captivity. He hoped they would produce litters of kids, which he would no doubt sell for a profit. Though his business ventures were many, Julia seldom saw the resulting coin and wondered where the money could possibly be going. She had also wondered where Barabbas had obtained the animals, but he had eluded her questions when she had dared to voice them. She certainly hoped he had obtained the animals by honest means – especially as rumors abounded throughout Judea and Galilee.

The Zealots were becoming far more daring in their exploits. Whereas they had once proudly attacked Roman legions in sparse desert regions or raided Roman caravans, distributing the loot among the struggling nation's many poor, their antics were becoming far less benevolent. While the raids increased in regularity and ferocity, the loot often vanished, never to be seen again – and certainly not by the nation's many poor. Even more astonishing was the fact that the Zealots now attacked the caravans of their own Jewish neighbors. At first, the people justified the Zealots' actions by rationalizing that the revolutionaries only struck the caravans of those who groveled at the feet of Roman power, paying substantial tribute and paying homage to the emperor. But soon even this weak excuse was refuted, as the Zealots descended upon their own people with a vengeance – breaking into homes and businesses, looting Jewish traveling caravans, robbing shepherds in the distant hillsides of their sheep and goats.

Julia couldn't help but wonder...were her father's caravans in imminent danger? And what of the men who guarded them?

She suppressed a faint shudder as she emptied the jar of water into the trough.

Another astonishing question assaulted her troubled mind. While guarding her father's traveling caravan, was Barabbas in danger at the hands of the very men to whom he claimed allegiance? How would he respond should her father's caravan be attacked? Would he defend Simon's merchandise and the lives of his men against the fierce Zealots to whom he claimed allegiance? Or would he allow the Zealots to loot, to wound, and to plunder, unwilling to bear the sword against his Zealot brethren?

Julia shook her head to clear the confusion. It was all so terribly frustrating and confusing. When Barabbas had joined the Zealot cause, he had promised her that he would never lift a hand against a neighbor. He had sworn that he would remain loyal to her father's post and continue to work under his stead. He had pledged to drive out the Romans, to set their nation free from the cruel heel of Roman oppression. It had sounded so honorable, so noble, at the time.

But now, as rumors abounded and the villagers grew warier and even more discontent, Julia began to wonder. Were the rumors true? Had her husband participated in any of the local raids that had the people in an uproar?

She hoped with all her heart and soul that he had not.

Maaaaa!

The bleating demands of the residents within the pen drew her attention back to the present. The goats pranced about the pen, bounding like frolicking children, bleating playfully. Julia couldn't help but chuckle at their antics. They were certainly amusing – when observed from the safety of their pen.

She supposed she should name them. After all, they had been in residence for over a month, and it didn't appear that they would be going anywhere soon.

"But what shall I call you?" she mused, watching in amusement as they gamboled lithely about the pen.

Maaaa! Maaaa!

MAAAAAAAAAA!

They called to each other as they romped happily about despite their confinement. They pranced upon nimble hooves as if they hadn't a care in the world.

"That's what I'll call you!" Julia exclaimed, delighted. "Adam and Eve. I imagine they were every bit as blithe and carefree before they rebelled against God and were expelled from their garden paradise. You will be Adam and Eve from now on!"

Maaaaaa!

Based on that response, Julia wasn't sure if they approved. But she had already settled the matter in her mind.

Adam and Eve it would be.

Satisfied with her decision, Julia set aside the earthen vessel and hurried toward Deborah's house. They had planned to mill flour today, and she didn't wish to be late.

When Julia ducked beneath the low hanging doorframe, she found Isaac with his shriveled legs propped up on a stool, Deborah beside him applying a damp cloth to his forehead. Julia saw the beads of sweat dotting his brow, and despite the fever, he shivered miserably beneath a wool blanket.

Frightened, Julia rushed to his side. "Deborah! What has happened?"

Isaac coughed hoarsely, motioning for her to step back. "It might be catching," he managed around a painful spasm of harsh coughs.

Julia's eyes widened in horror. "Deborah? How long has he been like this?"

Deborah offered a weary smile. "He awoke with chills early this morning. I've been trying to keep the fever down."

"Why didn't you send for help?"

"No point in troubling you, dear. What else could be done?"

"You could certainly take a rest and allow me to nurse your husband and prepare a meal for you both."

Laying aside her shawl, Julia hurried toward the kitchen. Selecting several vegetables, she carried them to the table and began to chop diligently.

Deborah chuckled. "Shah, child! You have your own home to care for."

"Not once has that stopped you from helping me! Now it is my turn." Slicing several cucumbers and onions, Julia wrapped the vegetables neatly in slivers of flatbread and doused them with a generous sprinkling of goat cheese.

Wringing out the damp cloth in a full bucket, Deborah accepted the wooden plate Julia offered her and seated herself heavily upon a stool.

When Julia offered a plate to Isaac, he waved it aside with a forced smile. "This fever's eaten up my appetite but thank you kindly nonetheless."

Julia was firm. "You must eat to keep up your strength."

"But I –"

"Isaac!" There was no arguing when Deborah used that tone. "Eat!"

Isaac glanced up at Julia, his eyes twinkling despite his discomfort. "Don't mind if I do."

Smiling fondly, Julia reached for the wet rag, submerged it in the cool water, wrung it out, and pressed it gently against Isaac's brow. She had grown to love these two older neighbors, considering them rather like the grandparents she had never known.

Lord God, protect this man. Drive the fever far from him. For Deborah's, sake, Lord, and for mine!

Setting aside her empty plate, Deborah sensed Julia's distress. "You mustn't worry, child. These bouts of chills and fever have come upon him rather suddenly ever since the accident. Whether or not they are related to the incident, we haven't the slightest idea."

"I am sorry to hear that." Julia meant it with all

her heart. Hadn't Isaac endured enough without having to suffer through miserable bouts of ravaging fever and cold sweats?

"Quite frankly, it isn't the fever that worries me."

Julia looked to Deborah in question, disturbed by her urgent tone.

"We received word this morning from relatives in Capernaum. It's Isaac's sister."

The humor died in Isaac's eyes. "She isn't expected to make it. Her sickness has steadily progressed."

Still holding the cold compress firmly in place, Julia covered Isaac's large, gnarled hand with her own. "I am so sorry."

"She is at peace. Her heart belongs to God, so she needn't fear. It is those of us left to mourn her passing who will suffer most." Isaac's poignant observation was cut short by another terrible coughing spasm.

Julia patted his back, the concern clear in her eyes.

"We must go to her," Isaac managed, recovering from the painful spasm.

Deborah murmured, "But how are we to travel when you are in this condition? It is difficult enough under normal circumstances." Her eyes came to rest upon her husband's dysfunctional legs.

Julia's eyes grew round. "Is it safe for him to travel in this condition?"

"I must see my sister. God has confirmed this in my heart."

Deborah threw her hands in the air. "He insists."

"Perhaps the Lord desires for us to minister to her in her last days. Or perhaps there is another reason. We cannot understand the ways of God."

Julia knelt before him, her eyes pleading. "But what of your health?"

"Perhaps I, too, will join my sister in her peaceful rest."

"Isaac!"

Isaac's eyes danced despite his misery. "I'm sure she has missed me greatly."

"Unfortunately, your wife still has need of you here!"

Isaac reached for Deborah's hand and squeezed it gently. "The Lord will carry us."

All the way to Capernaum? Julia wished to voice her concerns, but she knew it was not her place. Surely the grueling trip would be too difficult for Isaac in his feverish condition. He must stay home! He simply must.

Deborah sighed. "We will need your prayers more than ever, Julia."

Julia didn't like the defeat she detected in the woman's tone. Instantly, she was seized by a moment of sheer panic as the awful truth of it registered in her mind: Deborah was *leaving*! For Capernaum!

How long would she be away? And how would she ever manage without Deborah's calming presence and the peace that followed wherever she went?

Deborah sensed the girl's tension and took her hand. "We will stay only as long as necessary – and by the sound of it, it won't be long, though it grieves us to say it."

"Oh, Deborah, I'll miss you so much."

"And I will miss you as well."

Julia attempted to blink back her tears, but they

spilled over her cheeks anyway. "I am glad you have been given opportunity to comfort your relative, but I don't know what I'll do without you."

"I know exactly what you'll do, dear one – the same thing you've been doing all along."

Julia stared at her, the questions written all over her lovely face.

"You will lean on God and depend on Him. He is the one who guides you through each day – not I. He is your rock, your fortress, your place of safety. Trust in Him, Julia, and He will see you through."

Julia nodded through her tears. Of course, Deborah was right. Though she would greatly miss Deborah's physical presence within her house, the Lord's invisible presence was no less certain. He would be there with her through the long, lonely days, comforting her heart. He was faithful. She could trust Him.

And she was certain that Isaac and Deborah could trust Him as well. If they believed they were called to Capernaum, then the Lord would see them there safely.

Squeezing Deborah's hand, Julia set aside the damp cloth and took Isaac's hand as well. "Let us pray for your journey."

CHAPTER 15

The door banged open and slammed against the wall. Barabbas burst into the small house with the force of an angry bull.

Suppressing a frightened cry, Julia glanced up from the golden loaves she was in the process of removing from the small bread oven. She cried out in anger when Barabbas grabbed her by the shoulders, sending her loaves flying.

"Barabbas! What on earth –"

"Quiet!" Barabbas hissed, grabbing her wrists and pulling her toward the storage room.

Shocked and frightened, Julia struggled against his iron grasp. "What are you doing – "

"Shhhh!" Barabbas clamped a strong hand over her mouth and dragged her toward the storage closet. "Get in there and wait until I summon you. Don't make a sound. Understand?"

Julia's heart pounded in fear. "Barabbas, what is happening?"

"Our leader has returned with me. He cannot know of you."

Julia balked, anger washing over her. "Why –"

Half-crazed, Barabbas' eyes darted toward the door. "They're coming. Not a word." Shoving her into the storage closet, he nearly closed the door. Only a very slight crack allowed any light to pass through.

Kneeling upon the dirt floor, Julia shook in her fury and fear. How dare her husband barge into their home and treat her like a pet animal! Shoving her into the storage closet and ordering her to remain silent! The nerve! His actions shook her to the very core.

Something was wrong. Terribly wrong.

Our leader has returned with me...our leader... to whom was Barabbas referring?

Julia sucked in a sharp intake of breath as realization struck her, for there was only one leader to whom her husband could possibly be referring: the leader of his band of Zealots!

Julia's heart churned, and for a brief moment, she wondered if she would be sick. Forcing herself to take slow, steady breaths, she remained kneeling on the dirt floor, her hand pressed lightly upon the doorpost for support.

The front door banged open once again, and Julia heard the gruff voices of coarse men. "Nice little shack you have here, Barabbas. No wonder you abandon your men every night."

Not every night, Julia thought, annoyed by the stranger's condescending tone. Despite her annoyance, she shivered deep inside. Something about the way that man spoke – she could sense the wickedness in him. His voice alone conveyed a dark and sinister character, a man one dared not challenge.

"It's a worthy investment, nothing more." Julia wondered at the subservient tone her husband used. Never once had she heard him speak in such a manner. Her anger boiled.

Had the men in the hills no idea that Barabbas was a married man?

Julia clenched her fists. How she wished to banish that wicked Zealot from her little *shack*.

Julia heard the creaking of the benches around the table as the men took their seats.

"You keep a tidy house." The tone was mocking and tinged with suspicion.

"The elderly woman next door serves as housekeeper."

"Did the woman next door bake those loaves as well?"

"She often cooks for me."

"Perhaps we should recruit her up in the hills."

Julia's insides clenched in anger. She hoped the hills would split and the earth would open up to swallow that vile, arrogant man.

Despite her better judgment, Julia's curiosity got the best of her. Rocking forward on her heels, she dared a peek through the narrow crack in the door.

Barabbas' broad back faced her from his seat at the table with the leader of his band. The looks of the man made her skin crawl.

He was not tall in stature, but he was a bulky man hard-packed with muscle. A wide striped band was tied around his head, revealing unkempt, greasy black hair. His beard was equally ragged and unkempt. His clothing was soiled, and Julia wondered if he had ever bathed, as filth crusted his hairy arms and legs. She cringed at the thought of all that dirt and grime in such close proximity to her kitchen and her table.

There was nothing commendable about the appearance of this man. Nothing whatsoever. But even worse was the sense of unrest that emanated from his form. He reminded Julia of a raging panther, its muscles tensed and ready to strike at the first available opportunity.

Julia was also surprised to see another man – a familiar face – seated at her table near her husband. Barabbas had brought him to their home shortly after their marriage. She remembered his name only because he shared a common name with her beloved father – Simon.

Why, Simon knew Barabbas was a married man! She had served him supper – or at least, the semblance of a supper – the night Barabbas had brought him into their home. Her eye traveled to the rough-looking leader seated across from her husband. Would Simon keep silent about her? Could he be trusted?

Clearly, Barabbas feared for her safety in the presence of his leader. But why?

"I sought this respite because our men our growing lazy and fat," the leader was saying, his mouth full of her freshly baked bread.

Have you taken a good look at yourself lately? Julia wished to retort. It galled her to watch that ungrateful man devouring the loaves she had intended for herself and her husband.

She derived the slightest measure of comfort knowing the golden loaves had probably received a generous coating of dirt when they rolled across the floor. But then again, the miserable cretin didn't appear to be bothered by a bit of filth. She doubted it would have disturbed him in the least to eat directly off the dirt floor! Barabbas must have gathered the loaves back up again before the men's grand entrance into her home.

"What would you have us do?" It was Simon who spoke. His tone betrayed confidence and a bit of annoyance as well.

"It's not looking good for our cause. The people are turning against us. And our own are growing indolent." This from the leader.

"The people demand results. They see none."

Julia was surprised by Simon's boldness. While her husband appeared to show reverence toward this leader, Simon simply put up with him.

"And what do you expect when I command a band of worthless and sluggardly fools?" the filthy man seated at Julia's table sneered.

"Perhaps if we were to cease the raids upon the locals –"

"How, then, are we to sustain ourselves?" The leader nearly exploded, interrupting Simon's logical suggestion. "The worthless fools pay tribute to the puppet priests and the Romans alike, and yet they balk at the scant tribute we collect from them? We are the ones fighting for them. We are the ones taking the hits, making the sacrifices.

They should gladly offer up food and supplies to support the cause."

"And if they do not, we simply take it, yes?" Simon observed coolly. "I see that's how it works under your watch."

It was a bold statement, and Julia cringed. She sensed the rabid Zealot leader would not take kindly to resistance of any kind.

"We are willing to act, Amraphel," Barabbas interceded. "We simply await your command."

Ah, yes, Julia thought with disdain. *Your wish is my command, Master.* She surmised this fierce leader must be called Amraphel. Why on earth had Barabbas aligned himself with a man as crude and despicable as this?

"I am devising a plan, but there are risks. Before I move forward and involve the other men, I need to know if you're with me." Amraphel's eyes narrowed as he studied the two men seated at the table with him.

"To the end," Barabbas responded without hesitation.

Julia rolled her eyes in frustration. If only her husband would pledge such loyalty to his own wife!

Simon remained broodingly silent. His green eyes studied Amraphel with an air of disdain. "What is it this time?"

"Watch your tone."

"And you – watch your back. You've made many enemies in your recklessness, and you've drawn your men into the midst of it." Simon's eyes flashed fiercely.

"I will tolerate no disrespect!"

"Neither will your men," Simon declared forcefully. "They are on the edge of revolt, or haven't you noticed? They follow your orders. They plunder and steal, laying it all at your feet. And yet they seldom see hide nor hare of the plunder after that. They grow more restless by the day, wearying of your grand proclamations of a united Israel. A united Israel? When? How exactly do you expect to obtain that when the extent of our feats of courage and bravery consist of robbing elderly shepherds and plaguing the caravans of our brothers? What do you intend to do to seal their loyalty?"

Amraphel's face was mottled with rage and growing redder by the minute. Julia was disturbed by the sight of the blue veins bulging in his face and neck. "You speak too freely. I still possess allies – allies who would not hesitate to slit the throat of a dissenter."

Barabbas was sweating, clearly eager to end the discussion. "Amraphel, what are your orders?"

"What the people need is a show of courage and patriotism."

"And that is all it will be – a *show*."

"Shut up and listen for once, Simon, you fool. A band of Roman officers will be traveling along the Damascus Road within the week, bearing the royal standard and escorting some pompous dignitary from some equally pompous nation. You know as well as I the barren stretches of land they will encounter. We will bury ourselves within the rocky crags, springing to life in the moment of ambush.

They won't see anything coming. If we take them down – or at least scatter them and send them running with their tails tucked – we'll be heroes once again in the sight of the people."

"If only it were that simple," Simon countered, shaking his head in disgust.

"Even if the people require a bit more convincing, it will satiate our lust for Roman blood." A low chuckle rumbled from somewhere deep within Amraphel's throat.

"And what of your men?" Simon argued vehemently. "How many do you suppose you will send to their deaths?"

"My men knew when they enlisted, they must one day pay the price. The price may very well be their lives."

Julia was shocked and sickened by Amraphel's callousness and lust for evil. It chilled her to the very core to imagine her husband in league with this man.

Simon leaned forward, his strong arms crossed upon the table's smooth surface. "There is talk of a new Rabbi, and many claim He is the Messiah."

It was as if the air had been sucked out of the room. The silence that followed Simon's declaration was both swift and deadly.

Amraphel's hands visibly clenched into fists as he leaned over the table, his body tense. "What, pray tell, does this have to do with us?"

"For decades the Zealots have gained rapport because the people expect us to overthrow a foreign power as Judas Maccabaeus overthrew Antiochus

Epiphanes. Legends abound, depicting the Messiah as a mighty warrior king, a raging and powerful Zealot, who will break the bonds of Roman captivity and release our nation from her slavery."

"That was a lovely little speech, but still, I fail to see any correlation."

"If the people rally around this Man whom they believe to be the Messiah, our cause is null and void. The sliver of support we have maintained will be permanently severed."

Amraphel slammed his fist upon the tabletop, rattling the utensils and overturning a bowl of fruit. "I dare this Man to challenge our cause! A Messiah? *We* are Messiah! We will set our people free. We will be the deliverers."

Julia rocked back on her heels, clenching her churning stomach. The longer she observed, the clearer it became.

This wicked man – Amraphel – had no intentions of setting his people free. He had no love in his heart for anyone but himself. He relished his position, ordering men about and feasting like a king upon the plunder his cronies lay at his feet.

But never would this man bring peace to Israel. Despite his grandiose claims, he cared nothing for his nation or his people. He cared only about himself. He relished the power he wielded with a fat, iron fist. He was a cruel dictator and a selfish glutton. He savored the power and control he exercised over well-meaning men, and he instigated bloody skirmishes to satisfy his own twisted cravings for violence.

It sickened Julia to look at him, to listen to his angry rants, to know that such men even existed.

Clearly, the meeting was drawing to a close. The legs of a bench screeched as Amraphel gracelessly threw himself to his feet. "It is decided then. We will commence with the raid. Barabbas, you're my man in charge for this one."

It took every ounce of strength Julia possessed not to throw open the door and fly at that wicked devil, pummeling him with her fists. How dare he place her husband in that dangerous and precarious position, involving Barabbas in his own wicked schemes!

Amraphel crossed over to the door, ignoring the dark stares of Simon. Stretching his meaty arms, he yawned contentedly. "Thanks for the refreshment. And you can thank that *elderly neighbor* of yours for me as well."

Barabbas visibly stiffened. "She is a gifted cook and a kind woman."

"Oh, I'm sure she is. And probably forty years younger than you claim, and gorgeous, too. But I see how it is – you are unwilling to share your enticing little mistress."

Amraphel's voice grew fainter as the men left the house. Julia's insides churned violently, and she clutched her roiling stomach with shaking hands. She had known her husband was involved with disreputable men, but she hadn't had the slightest clue about the full extent of their depravity.

The conversation she had just witnessed shook her to the very core.

Oh, merciful Father, help me. Help my husband. Pluck him from the grasp of that wicked man, Father.

Covering her head with her shawl, Julia buried her face in the dirt floor and wept as if her heart would break.

CHAPTER 16

"Julia!" Barabbas reentered their home, tense and trembling with suppressed rage. He had been belittled before a fellow brother *and* his unseen wife. Though he had hated his capitulation to Amraphel's imperious demands, he knew the man possessed both the resources and the cruelty to make his life miserable...or worse. He had joined the Zealots not for the freedom of his country, but rather for vengeance upon Rome. And he needed Amraphel and his men in order to fulfill such ambitions. After all, what was one lone man against the might and power of an empire?

Initially, he had been convinced that the men were capable of destroying the Romans one by one like the Maccabees against their foes. Amraphel had wooed him with brute force, a commanding air, and an all-consuming hatred against the Romans. The prospect of vengeance had seemed so promising at first.

But now...now he wasn't so sure. Yet he knew the fate of one who abandoned the cause – a swift and merciless death was sure to follow.

"Julia! Come out."

Kneeling on the floor in the storage shed, Julia buried her face within the soft folds of her blue shawl. She had no desire to see her husband. No desire at all.

He was supposed to be her protector, and yet he had brought a dangerous and bloodthirsty man into their home.

First, she had suffered that awkward encounter with the prostitute named Mary. That humiliating incident alone had been enough to completely shatter a wife's trust. And now this?

What was she to do with *this*?

The storage room door jerked open forcefully, the ancient hinges squealing in protest.

Barabbas found his wife huddled on the dirt floor, her shawl draped protectively over her head, her forehead touching the ground.

"By the gods, Julia!" Barabbas reached for her arm, but she stiffened, pulling away from him.

"Julia! They're gone. It's safe."

"Safe?" Julia's voice was little more than a muffled sob. "Safe!"

"Julia –" Hissing angrily through his teeth, Barabbas reached for Julia's chin and tilted it upward, forcing her to look at him. Tears streaked through the dust clinging to her fair cheeks.

"You're a mess. What's gotten into you?"

"I could ask you the same question!"

Barabbas withdrew, taken aback. Over the last few weeks, he had noticed a subtle change in her.

A quietness, an acceptance. There were moments when he knew she wished to burn him with a scathing retort, and yet she had held her tongue.

Why was she falling apart now?

"You will have to bake more bread. The men devoured it."

Oh, the nerve of this man! The gall! Waves of fury swept over Julia, and she struggled to press them down. She could not be carried away by the powerful flood of her emotions. She had to remain calm.

She forced herself to her feet, though the entire room spun about her as dizziness engulfed her being. Reaching for the doorpost, she steadied herself and glared at her husband's broad retreating back. "Who was that man?"

Barabbas stiffened, strapping on his invisible armor. He was ready for a fight. "Amraphel."

"He is your leader?"

"You take issue with him?"

"You don't?"

Barabbas' dark eyes flashed. "He is a good leader. He is zealous for the peace of Jerusalem."

Appalled, Julia laughed aloud. "Peace? Peace! That rogue wouldn't know the first thing about peace!"

"Watch yourself, Julia."

"I am not intimidated by your threats!"

Barabbas looked into the eyes of his wife and saw brokenness and despair. He also saw himself reflected within those lovely hazel pools. Instinctively, he knew he had inflicted much pain. In a flash, he saw himself, bowing in unwilling subservience before Amraphel and his endless demands.

Did Julia loathe him the way he despised his own cruel taskmaster?

Taking a steadying breath, he dropped onto a bench and rubbed the back of his neck, defeated. He knew he'd gone too far. A faint flicker of conscience remained, though he had seared most of it by years of anger, rebellion, and defiance.

Sensing his defeat, Julia drew near and placed a hand upon his shoulder. She felt his muscles tense beneath her gentle touch, but she did not remove her hand.

"How is it you have become entangled with these men?"

"We seek a common goal."

"And what is that?"

Peace for Jerusalem. A united Israel. Freedom from Roman oppression. Freedom from fear. He could have satisfied her prying questions with any number of poignant platitudes. But one look into her perceptive eyes and he knew she would see right through his web of lies.

"I shouldn't be discussing this with you."

"And why not? Barabbas, I am your wife. You are my husband. When will we begin to behave as such?"

His moods were as variable as the morning mists that faded and fled. Reaching for her, he pulled her onto his lap and buried his face in her hair. He loved the scent of it. "We behave as such every time I take you into my arms and show you how much I love you."

Julia blushed deeply, both in anger and embarrassment. Why, oh why, did he equate physical oneness with sacrificial love? Yes, marital intimacy was meant to unite, but only if it was accompanied by trust, commitment, and love demonstrated by one's actions.

She knew if she allowed Barabbas to have his way in this moment, she would never obtain the answers she so desperately needed – even as her heart responded to his strong arms around her and the rare profession of his love for her.

Perhaps he was simply trying to distract her. If so, it was working. She steeled herself, determined to find answers.

"Barabbas, why are you in league with a man whom you fear? You couldn't even tell him about your wife. Why is that?"

Barabbas' arms stiffened around her waist. "It was a precaution. Nothing more."

"You didn't take that same precaution when you brought Simon into our home."

"Simon is different. He respects other men."

"And Amraphel does not?"

"Amraphel is fierce, a born warrior. He destroys his enemies with the brute force of a battering ram. But these traits are required if he is to be a warrior, a leader of men."

It angered Julia to hear Barabbas defending him. How could he defend a man whom he knew to be capable of assaulting his own wife? "Many great men of old were warriors and leaders of men – Abraham, Joseph, and King David among them. And yet none of them possessed the crudeness and vulgarity of that man. They strove to protect the women of their clans rather than violate their purity."

"Have you forgotten about David and Bathsheba?"

"That was one moment of weakness for which David repented in sorrow and in tears. Amraphel is a snake wrapped in human flesh."

"You've met him but once and already you are determined to cast judgment."

"Actually, I did not *meet* him, as you deemed it unsafe to do so."

His passion long since waned, Barabbas gave Julia an unwelcome little shove and she climbed off his lap.

"You wouldn't understand."

"Oh, Barabbas, I want to try! Please, forsake these wicked men."

"It's not that simple."

"Simply walk away!"

"I can't."

"And why not?"

"Death is the only release."

Julia froze, her mouth open. Her eyes narrowed as fear coursed through her entire body. "What do you mean?"

"The penalty for desertion is death. Death is a Zealot's only release."

Julia's entire body went cold. "You mean...there's no way out?"

"No easy way."

Julia's legs felt like jelly, and they buckled beneath her weight. Barabbas caught her in his arms before she went down, gently lowering her to the floor like a sleeping child. She felt like a rag doll in his arms.

"Julia?"

Her eyes were still and wet with tears. For the first time since their marriage, it pained him to know he was the cause of those tears.

"Julia."

"There's no way out. What will we do? There's no way out."

"You needn't worry, Julia. I can take care of myself."

"But do you want this, Barabbas? A life of thievery, of violence? Is this really what you want?"

"I want vengeance. This is the only way."

"Oh, Barabbas. Vengeance belongs to the Lord."

"Hush." Barabbas flinched as if he'd been struck. *Vengeance belongs to the Lord.* He didn't want to hear about the Lord. The Lord had done absolutely nothing to avenge his loss.

Had the Lord avenged the death of his father? His brothers? Had the Lord intervened and stilled the Roman sword that slashed through his weeping mother as she scrambled to shelter her sons from Roman legions? Had He rescued his father from the cruel and torturous death of public execution by crucifixion?

No, He had done none of those things.

Rome would suffer for all the trouble she had caused him. Rome would suffer for the death of his loved ones. He knew he could not allow them to die in vain. Their blood must be avenged.

Surely, he was doing right by them. It must be so!

Still, a quiet voice within urged him to pause. To

be still. To evaluate his thoughts and actions.

If he was doing right, why this constant doubt and affliction? Why this never-ending battle within himself?

Nothing felt right. Nothing was right. He would never be right again.

Barabbas realized he still cradled his trembling wife in his arms. Impulsively, he bent down and kissed her. He was sure he loved her, despite himself. He often wondered if he would lose her, too. Perhaps that's why he held her at arms' length, refusing to let her in. It wouldn't hurt so much when she left. Even so, he was overcome by a fierce desire to protect her.

He thought of the Roman threat and shut his eyes tightly to drown out the sight of his mother falling beneath a Roman's glistening sword.

He would protect his wife from the power of Rome.

And how exactly do you plan to protect her from yourself, Barabbas? It was a staggering thought, and Barabbas wondered where it had come from.

Amraphel's mocking laughter filled his head, and Barabbas considered the dire consequences that would surely ensue if the man ever discovered his secret. Or – far worse – if he ever suspected that Barabbas had considered desertion. Amraphel would not hesitate to use Julia like a pawn against Barabbas. He would not hesitate to teach Barabbas a lesson he would never forget – a lesson that his innocent young wife would likely not survive.

No, Amraphel must never learn about Julia. Never.

Rome. Amraphel. He, himself. Who was the true enemy?

***

Julia lay awake on their small sleeping pallet, restless and nearly paralyzed with fear after the day's troubling events. Barabbas slept soundly beside her, overcome with exhaustion.

Pushing herself up on her elbows, she rose slowly and crossed the dark house toward the window overlooking the neighborhood courtyard.

All was calm. All was quiet. The tranquil scene was bathed in moonlight as the world slept.

As I should be doing, she thought glumly, resting her elbows upon the windowsill. But sleep eluded her. In her present state, she wondered if she would ever sleep again.

No way out. No way out. No way out, pounded like a steady drumbeat within her troubled mind. *No way out. No way out. No way out.*

Whatever should she do? She knew she could not seek help. To reveal Barabbas' alliance with the Zealots could very well result in his execution. And one thing she knew for certain: her husband was not right with God. She knew he wasn't ready to meet his Maker.

Amraphel. She writhed inwardly as the face of that vulgar man emerged in her mind. Oh, how she loathed the man, for he represented everything that bound her husband more securely than chains or fetters. If not for Amraphel, could her husband peaceably abandon the cause? Amraphel was their leader, the only barrier standing in the way.

Fleetingly, she wondered if there were some way to get rid of the man. He was evil incarnate. The world certainly wouldn't miss him. If she hadn't known the Lord, she might even consider putting an end to the man herself! Had she no code of conduct by which she lived, she might be sorely tempted to slip a little something into Amraphel's drink the next time Barabbas brought him under her roof! Let the miserable wretch die choking on his own poison!

Julia shuddered, overcome that such flagrantly wicked thoughts had even crossed her mind! Had she truly entertained the thought of poisoning a man – even though she knew she would never go through with it? Her mind was in such a state of havoc that she scarcely recognized her own ludicrous thoughts.

Oh, but dear Lord, I know that's no excuse. My mind is also vile, impure. Though I've never killed a man, I just murdered one in my mind! Oh Lord, help me, help me, please! There's no way out. Oh Lord, there's no way out.

Her harried thoughts were interrupted by the most sensational sense of calm. She quieted, resting in the peace that was steadily washing over her.

I am the Lord, your Holy One, the Creator of Israel, your King. Thus says the Lord who makes a way in the sea and a path through the mighty waters… Do not remember the former things, nor consider the things

of old. Behold, I will do a new thing, now it shall spring forth; shall you not know it? I will even make a road in the wilderness and rivers in the desert.

Resting her head upon her folded arms propped upon the windowsill, Julia wept. The promises of her loving Father washed over her like a flood, and she clung to such promises with all her might. She recognized the verses penned by the great prophet Isaiah, but she knew it was the Lord Himself who ministered to her heart with words of hope tonight.

I believe you, Lord. I believe you, Father. You will make a way. I don't know how You will do it, but still I believe.

The words of Simon the Zealot flashed through her mind, unexpected and unbidden: *"There is talk of a new Rabbi, and many claim He is the Messiah."*

Behold, I will do a new thing...

Somehow, Julia sensed that the two were connected, related, somehow. The Lord was at work. The same God who made a way in the sea and a path through the mighty waters would indeed make a way for her.

"Thank You, Lord. Please forgive my wicked thoughts and unbelief."

Julia left the shutters open, comforted by the slanted beams of silver moonlight spilling into the house. She knew the Creator of that moon. She felt closer to Him, washed in the lovely light of creation's shining countenance.

As she knelt once more upon her sleeping pallet, she placed a gentle hand upon her husband's shoulder.

"Lord God, I commit this man to You. Shake him up, Lord. Light a fire inside him. Make him a worthy vessel for Your use. Take his heart of stone and shape it into a tender heart of flesh, sensitive to Your will."

Closing her eyes, Julia knew sleep would now come. The Lord had made His promise, and He would make it good.

Behold, I will do a new thing... I will even make a road in the wilderness...

If God could make a road in the wilderness and split a path through the raging seas, then He could certainly make a way for her, His beloved child.

She smiled despite her pain as wonderful realization dawned.

In truth, God Himself *was* the way. The only way.

CHAPTER 17

Melina

"And Joanna believes this simple carpenter of Nazareth to be the Messiah?"

Melina studied Malchus' handsome yet skeptical features. His expression was almost comical. "It's too early to know for sure, but she has been investigating this possibility since the Man's baptism in the Jordan River."

"Ah, yes. That infamous baptism." Caiaphas had been furious when he had learned of it, dismissing it as fanciful gossip fabricated by coarse and unsophisticated Galileans.

"You don't believe it happened?"

The two strolled side by side along one of the elevated pillared walkways overlooking the bustling Upper Market, enjoying the small sliver of freedom they shared each week.

Pausing, Malchus leaned upon a limestone barricade and studied the harried shoppers conducting business among the many booths and market stalls below. A group of well-dressed, wealthy men were engaged in a heated debate beneath the shade of one of the pillared colonnades. Merchants called loudly to the passersby, attempting to draw attention to their wares.

"Malchus?"

Drawn back to the present, Malchus forced what he hoped was a smile. "I apologize. I was lost in thought."

"So I gathered." Melina's eyes twinkled pleasantly. She touched his arm.

Terribly aware of her touch, Malchus attempted to remain composed. "I must ask, Melina, only because I care about you –"

Melina blushed prettily and lowered her gaze.

"– but why are you so willing to take the word of this new servant Joanna? You know next to nothing about her."

Melina's emerald eyes were filled with understanding rather than condemnation. She smiled. "Because I have witnessed her zeal for the Lord. She demonstrates her love for God in the way she honors her husband, in the way she sees to her duties with diligence and without complaint, in the way she treats the other servants."

"I am not arguing that she is a good woman. But what if she is misguided?"

"Misguided?"

"About these grandiose claims."

Melina smiled her understanding. "She hasn't proclaimed this Man to be the Messiah as of yet,

Malchus. She simply believes it to be a very real possibility. And we must do our part to investigate such claims and to be prepared."

Prepared for what *exactly?* Malchus decided not to voice his skepticism.

"You never answered my question," Melina reminded him, her eyes smiling.

Malchus had never been fond of questions. "Which one?"

"Do you doubt the baptism of Jesus which Joanna described?"

"Oh, I don't doubt it happened – although the *details* of the event are highly disputed. Caiaphas was informed shortly after it occurred. The man was livid."

Melina glanced up at him with questioning eyes. "Livid? Why?"

"Let's just say he doesn't appreciate the competition."

"Competition?"

"Caiaphas is first and foremost a politico. He plays the part of priest only when absolutely necessary. This Man they call Jesus has gained quite a bit of attention, and apparently His teachings are a bit, shall we say, controversial? It's no secret this new Rabbi doesn't think very highly of the priestly class."

This was news to Melina. "But why not?"

Malchus' lips tipped in a wry grin. "Let's just say men like Caiaphas invest a lot of time and money to buy a reputation with which to wield power over poor, ignorant common folk like us. They impose countless ceremonial laws upon the masses, while making every effort to appear as if they themselves follow these impossible principles. All the while, they recline on their fat rumps and feast off the coin they've siphoned from widows and orphans, indulging in every fleshly comfort and luxury one could possibly imagine – however vile, base, or corrupt. This Man they call Jesus simply doesn't hesitate to point this out."

Melina's eyes widened in astonishment. "The *priests* behave as such?"

"My dear little Melina, you have much to learn."

"Aren't the priests called to set an example for the people? To lead them to God?"

"To be *called* is a very different thing than to *obey*."

Melina pondered Malchus' words, unsettled. "Your words," she said quietly, her expression solemn, "are so very true, Malchus."

"Well, that's unusual."

Melina acknowledged his dry humor with a soft smile. "Truly, God calls every single one of us. But so few of us will choose to heed the call and respond in obedience. We must pray, Malchus. We must pray that we will always respond to the call of God in swift and cheerful obedience."

Sometimes Malchus was blown away by the depth of this woman's character. She often uttered profound statements that took poets hours to pen. The difference between Melina and the poets of the day, however, was that Melina believed the words with all her heart and sought to incorporate the truth of them into her daily life.

"Do you know another reason why I believe

Joanna's testimony?"

Malchus was growing weary of discussing Joanna. He arched a brow in question.

"Because she was there."

"Where?" Malchus hoped his tone did not reveal his boredom with the subject.

"At the River Jordan. She was there when Jesus was baptized."

This unwelcome bit of news gave Malchus pause. He had yet to meet an eyewitness of the hotly debated event.

"She saw it all with her own eyes," Melina explained, her silvery voice rising in her excitement.

"What does she say?"

"She said it happened just as the rumors pronounce. At the time, Joanna and her husband Chuza were serving Herod Antipas in Tiberias. Apparently, the rumors were circulating even more so in Galilee than here in Jerusalem. Herod sent her and her husband to investigate John the Baptist. It was that day by the River Jordan that Jesus approached John."

Malchus remained doubtful. "And?"

"Joanna says that John made a rather grand statement as Jesus approached: 'Behold! The Lamb of God who takes away the sin of the world!'"

"The Lamb of God? A rather odd title for a man reputed to be a fighter possessing the strength and ferocity of the warrior king David."

"An odd title?" Melina repeated, her head tilted to one side. "But is it?"

"Evidently, you think not."

"Remember the messianic prophecy you taught

me? *He was led as a lamb to the slaughter, and as a sheep before its shearers is silent, so He opened not His mouth.*"

"Well, I'm sure that passage is figurative in some way."

"Is it?"

"Melina, I'm no Bible scholar."

Yes, this is becoming increasingly evident. Melina was surprised by her own irritation. Rarely was she irritated by anyone or anything. Why did Malchus' lack of zeal for the Scriptures irk her so?

After her confidential conversation with Joanna on their way home from the market, Melina had honestly evaluated her feelings for this handsome young man. She could not deny that she had developed feelings for him – feelings that far surpassed that of friendship. Perhaps this was why Malchus' lack of enthusiasm for the Word of God disturbed her.

She realized she did indeed desire a future with Malchus. But – despite his confession of faith – would she be unequally yoked if they were to marry? Was his walk with the Lord as real as he professed?

For both their sakes, she certainly hoped so. She knew she could not disobey God by joining herself with a man who did not love her Lord with all his heart and soul.

The thought greatly troubled her spirit.

She blushed deeply, realizing the direction in which her thoughts had taken her. Why, not once had Malchus expressed marriage as his intent! For all she knew, he viewed her as a pleasant diversion and nothing more. Perhaps he had no desire to marry. His duties to one of the most powerful men in Judea encompassed most of his time. Did he even have the time or ability to pursue a wife, much less marry one and support her?

"Well, *now* look who's lost in thought."

Malchus' wry comment dragged Melina's attention back to the present.

Cheeks aflame, Melina prayed he didn't suspect the deeply personal course her thoughts had taken. Smiling sheepishly, she glanced up at him through dark lashes. "I suppose my thoughts ran away with me," she confessed.

"Where to?" his grin was impish and slightly roguish. "Perhaps I'd like to accompany them."

Melina swatted at his arm playfully. "Stop it."

Though spring was right around the corner, the afternoon air was still a bit cool. Pulling her shawl tightly about her shoulders, Melina resumed her walking, enjoying the gentle breezes caressing her face and hair.

Spinning on his heel, Malchus followed and strolled alongside her, both charmed and disquieted by Melina's thoughtful mood. He sensed she was deeply disturbed by something. Perhaps she sensed his annoyance with her new favorite topic: a Messiah.

Malchus understood that the concept was new and exciting for her – a converted Gentile – but he'd endured the telling and retelling of exaggerated legends about the Messiah his entire life. His father had been certain the Messiah's coming was near... as had his grandfather, and his great-grandfather, and his great-great grandfather. For centuries, Jews had trumped that grand proclamation from the housetops – *the Messiah is coming soon*! And yet, generation after generation, the promise remained empty, and the hopes of the people had died along with them. The Messiah had not come.

Perhaps his people had misread or misinterpreted the Scriptures. Or perhaps the kingdom of Heaven was something far less mystical and profound. Perhaps it was simply a state of mind. He neither knew nor cared.

After all, he'd made his peace with God. Wasn't that all that mattered? He hadn't the slightest interest in poring over dull scrolls for hours and days on end in a futile attempt to unveil secrets that his ancestors had supposedly missed.

In his opinion, such ventures were best left to the scholars and the scribes.

"I suppose I should finish Joanna's account."

Ah, yes. More divine enlightenment from the sagacious Joanna. He'd thought they had avoided that conversation. Apparently not.

"Jesus waded into the river and spoke with John, asking John to baptize him. John insisted that *he* needed to be baptized by *Jesus*, not the other way around!"

How touching. Malchus held his boredom in check.

"But Jesus insisted, and when He came up out of the water, the heavens burst open and the Spirit of God descended upon Him in the form of a dove, alighting upon Him."

"And how can one be certain this phantom bird of sorts was the Spirit of God and not an evil spirit or simply a clever trick?"

"Because immediately a voice mightier than thunder possessing the power of the crashing ocean waves resounded from Heaven!"

"Ah. And what did it say?"

"'This is My beloved Son, in whom I am well pleased.'"

From somewhere deep inside, Malchus trembled, his skepticism silenced. Something about those few words invoked an unexplainable response within his soul. He sensed an unfamiliar, unfathomable power in the words, and even greater power by Him who spoke such words.

Troubled, he shook his head to clear the fog. "One must admit the tale is fanciful, to say the least."

"There were eyewitnesses, Malchus. Joanna estimates there were at least fifty bystanders, perhaps more. She and her husband interviewed as many as were willing to speak. Every single one of the testimonies agreed."

Malchus' logical and skeptical mind grasped for any possible holes in the argument. "Yes, but *you* have not spoken with these witnesses. You have spoken with only one woman, who *claims* she has spoken with all these witnesses."

Shivering slightly despite the shawl draped over her shoulders, Melina lowered her gaze as they traversed a broad stone staircase that would take them to the ground level. "There is more."

Well, of course there is! Malchus wished to retort.

Instead, he said as lightly as possible, "Do tell."

"This Jesus is a direct descendant of King David. This also is a sign of the Messiah."

"And how can this be corroborated?"

"Careful research. Joanna's husband, Chuza, spoke with villagers of Nazareth – Jesus' hometown."

"Aha! The Messiah is to be born in Bethlehem – not Nazareth."

"Yes. At first, we found this to be problematic as well. But Chuza is a very wise man and an astute keeper of records according to his occupation."

Well, good for Chuza.

"Before Tiberias assumed the throne, his predecessor Caesar Augustus issued a decree that all must be registered. This decree was promulgated at the time of this Man's birth. His mother was heavy with child when she and her husband received the emperor's orders. Because this man's father Joseph was of the line of King David, where do you suppose he and his wife Mary were forced to travel in order to fulfill not only the emperor's decree but the ancient prophecy as well?"

Malchus paled, his heart hammering in his chest. Surely not! It was too neat. Too tidy. Too *perfect*!

Melina's eyes glowed with exuberance. "Where would they have to go to register, Malchus?"

Swallowing hard, Malchus attempted to ignore the discomfort of his own sweaty palms. He attempted to sound confident despite his mounting uneasiness. "Bethlehem, of course."

"Bethlehem, the city of David. And the birthplace

of the Messiah, by the mouth of the prophets."

Malchus' head was spinning, for already Melina had laid a mounting pile of evidence at his feet – evidence he wasn't quite ready to confront. "And how do you know all this?"

"Joanna has worked tirelessly to learn these things."

"Joanna is a worthy investigator." Malchus wondered why the thought disturbed him. "Perhaps she has missed her life's calling."

Melina's eyes filled with tears, though she tried to hide it.

Pained that he might have initiated those tears, Malchus reached for her arm and drew her down to the steps with him. Seated on the step beside her, he tucked a stray strand of raven black hair behind her ear and offered his most pacifying smile. "You're upset."

"Yes."

He hid another smile. She was too honest to deny it. He adored her innocence, her purity. A startling thought occurred to him. If not for her complete devotion to God, she would not possess such qualities. Why, then, did he shirk from her animated conversation pertaining to spiritual things?

"Tell me why you're upset."

Melina searched his face with tearful eyes. Clearly, she was trying to decide whether or not to share her heart.

"You can trust me with anything, Melina. I won't be angry."

She exhaled softly before speaking. "You don't

seem the least bit interested, Malchus."

Oh, I am interested. More interested than you could possibly know! I am interested in YOU, Melina! You!

But Malchus knew such grand proclamations would only succeed in further distancing her from him. "What do you mean?"

"You haven't the slightest interest in the Scriptures, the Word of God. In the prospect of the Messiah's coming. In the testimony I long to share with you about all these exciting possibilities."

"I do care."

Melina's eyes narrowed in disbelief.

"Really, I do. I've just had so much on my mind. Life has been unpredictable lately, to say the least. But that is no excuse to hurt you, Melina. I never, ever want to hurt you."

But it's not about hurting me! Melina wanted to cry out. *It's about your own walk with the Lord! Your soul! Eternity!*

Somehow, Melina knew now was not the time to delve into another deep discussion. Both of them had masters awaiting their arrival. They had tarried at the Upper Market long enough.

"Perhaps," Malchus continued, his expression grim, "I am also contemplating the complications we would encounter, should this Man prove to be the Messiah."

Melina's stomach flopped. There was a very real possibility that the Messiah walked among them even now, and he was worried about *complications*?

"I serve in the house of the high priest. I can

guarantee you that Caiaphas will not welcome this Messiah with open arms. Already he has his eye on anyone proclaiming to be a follower of this new sect. And you – you serve Herod Antipas. Do you imagine he will eagerly relinquish his self-proclaimed title and welcome a new king? We are both in equally dangerous and precarious positions, Melina – Caiaphas is the final religious authority, and Herod the ultimate political authority. To pledge allegiance to any man other than our own masters could very well cost us our lives."

Melina's heart pounded in her chest. She wondered if Malchus could hear it. Never once had she considered the fact that Herod, the man to whom she was legally bound to serve, might decide to crush the followers of another leader. Fleetingly, she recalled witnessing one of Herod's rages after Herodias had accused him of being a weak ruler capable of allowing another to usurp his power.

Herod had made it clear in no uncertain terms that any threat to his rule would be obliterated. Swiftly. Without mercy.

And Malchus faced a very similar predicament. If Malchus' words regarding his master could be trusted, Caiaphas was a suspicious and merciless ruler. He would not take kindly to one of his most trusted servants joining any cause other than his own.

Malchus relaxed slightly, seeing that Melina acknowledged the reasoning behind his argument.

"I suppose…" Melina's voice caught in her throat, and she attempted to slow her rapidly beating heart. "I suppose it is as you said –"

"Impossible? Yes."

"No," Melina corrected, and the strength returned to her voice. Straightening, she took Malchus' hands in her own.

Heart pounding, Malchus gazed into those emerald eyes and forced himself to focus on whatever she might say.

"In your very own words, Malchus: To be *called* is a very different thing than to *obey*."

Malchus could have kicked himself for providing the necessary fuel for her rebuttal. *It figures – the one smart thing I have to say is twisted and used against me!*

"If indeed the time has come for the Messiah to be revealed, then the call goes forth to all of us. But to be called is a very different thing than to obey. All are called, but few obey. Few accept the call. But will *we*? Will we obey? We must make a decision, Malchus. We must take a stand, make a choice."

Malchus wondered at the peace that emanated from Melina's fragile form. She had never appeared lovelier to him than now as her eyes fairly glowed with hope, her gentle features transformed by courage and conviction.

"There may come a time when we are faced with a decision, for we cannot serve two masters. Which will we serve?" Melina's eyes were no longer fixed on him. She gazed steadily ahead as if foreseeing a frightening and unknown future. "Will we avoid the pain of death in this life, and cleave unto a worldly master? Or will we cling to the promises of God and proclaim Him to be our Master, despite the cost?"

Malchus swallowed hard, unsettled. The pain of death didn't sound the least bit appealing to him.

"Either way, we must choose. And we must choose now, Malchus. Choose this day whom you will serve." Melina's eyes were alight with a glowing intensity and the kind of peace that surpassed human understanding. "One thing I know for sure: eternal life – an eternity of perfection with God – is far more valuable than anything we could possibly lose on this earth, including our lives."

Malchus stared at her in disbelief. Wasn't she aware of the fact that an alliance with a controversial Rabbi would obliterate the chances of the peaceful life he had hoped to share with her? Above all else, he desired peace.

But trouble seemed to follow this controversial new Rabbi wherever He went!

If this Jesus did indeed turn out to be the Messiah, if they chose to pledge allegiance to Him, would trouble follow them as well?

CHAPTER 18

Julia

The twelfth and final month of Adar swept in like an unrelenting storm.

Isaac and Deborah still had not returned from Capernaum, and Julia began to wonder if she would ever see them again. How had Isaac fared on the difficult journey to Galilee? Had he made a full recovery? Had they reached their relatives in time to comfort his dying sister? She certainly hoped so.

How she missed Deborah's staid and calming presence, her cheerful countenance and her wise counsel! Julia felt as if she were starving for sound counsel.

She hadn't the slightest idea what to do about Barabbas. She was convinced the man was at war with himself.

One moment, he would burst through the front door, declaring he was finished with Amraphel and his endless demands. He would find a way out, even if he had to kill the man. But always within a day or two, he'd be packing his leather bag and setting out for the hills, eager for another exhilarating and life-threatening assignment.

The past few weeks had proven more difficult than Julia had been prepared to handle. Barabbas' temper remained at a steady simmer, and the slightest little thing sent that simmer to a full-fledged boil. He remained silent, pensive, brooding. Julia suspected he was beginning to regret his hasty decision concerning the Zealot cause. As he himself had aptly stated, there was no way out.

Despite his misgivings, Julia also sensed that Barabbas was deeply conflicted. His conscience was beginning to awaken after a long and dormant sleep. The demands of a wicked leader could not be reconciled with his conscience or his upbringing.

And yet his heart cried out for vengeance. He viewed the Zealots as the only way.

Julia often wondered if Barabbas had initially sympathized with the Zealots because their frenetic activity and vicious ambushes enabled him to vent the rage that always lurked just beneath the surface.

Oh, Barabbas! I see the realization dawning. You know you're doing wrong. Repent! Turn to God! Forsake this dangerous path you have chosen!

Julia often found herself guessing and reflecting about whatever dreadful course of events could have possibly led to her husband's intense hatred of anything Roman. Her sympathetic inquiries only further piqued his rage.

She supposed she would never know.

Oh, Lord, what must I do? Should I go to Father or Mother? Should I seek help? Should I wait and pray? Lord, I don't know what I'm supposed to do.

Desperate to escape the confines of her small house, Julia reached for her shawl and slipped outdoors, eager to breathe in the fresh night air.

Lamps burned brightly within the neatly ordered houses, casting a faint glow and slanted beams of light that fell across the dusty street. Even in this unfriendly and poverty-stricken precinct, merry laughter and festive music spilled into the streets as the residents feasted and celebrated the patriotic holiday called Purim.

At first, Julia enjoyed the merriment, listening as friends called to one another and smiling as children scampered and skipped about like spring lambs. She noticed several neighbors bearing large gift baskets and knew they would be delivering them to their friends. Initially, the tradition of Purim entailed delivering gifts to the poor. In more recent years, the poor had become more of an afterthought as the rich attempted to outdo their wealthy neighbors with extravagant gifts.

As a child, Julia had balked when her father dismissed the holiday so easily. Her peers raved about the extravagant banquets and feasts they enjoyed in honor of Purim. But Simon had insisted Purim was a man-made festival rather than a God-given mandate that had simply become an excuse for excessive drinking and gluttony.

Julia understood his line of thinking now. She saw many neighbors staggering about and drew back in revulsion. One man lay sprawled near the road, poorly clad and completely oblivious in a state of drunken stupor.

Still, the laughter and the merrymaking continued all around her.

Rather suddenly, a heavy cloud of depression settled over Julia, and she wondered if she could bear the sharp stabs of loneliness that pierced her heart. Once again, her husband had deserted her for the company of Zealots. She tried not to think about the drunkenness and depravity of her husband's surroundings. She remembered the immoral woman named Mary and wondered if women were permitted in the camp.

Clenching her fists, Julia turned and hurried back to her own little house. Her heart fluttered like a caged bird, and she felt faint. Even the poorest in Jerusalem reveled in gaiety this night, and yet she must endure it alone.

If Deborah were here, she would have welcomed me into her home with open arms for this holiday, Julia thought, tears streaming down her face. She was certain that to be alone was one of life's cruelest fates.

Several young children skipped past her, giggling and bearing parcels wrapped in lovely fabric. Obviously, they were delighted to deliver their gifts.

Oh, Lord, where are You? I'm so alone. I'm sick of this. I'm sick of being alone. Where are You, Lord? Julia stumbled along the dusty road, blinded by tears. She wondered if the passersby suspected she had indulged in a few too many celebratory toasts in honor of Queen Esther and her cousin Mordecai.

Instinctively, Julia knew she herself was to blame for her lonely state. She had walked into this marriage with her eyes wide open and her ears completely closed to godly counsel. She cried even harder, realizing the question she had silently posed to the Lord had been a thinly veiled accusation.

Oh Lord, I'm so sorry. Please forgive me. My own disobedience led me here. You tried to spare me, Lord. But, please, Lord, make Your presence so very real to me tonight. I need You, Lord. I feel so alone.

Julia was so intent in her silent pleadings that she nearly stumbled past her own house. Though her eyes still swam with tears, she noticed an oddly shaped object before her front door.

That's odd, Julia thought, attempting to dry her tears with the soft corners of her shawl.

It was a beautifully woven gift basket! Julia traced the smooth lines of the finely weaved basket with one finger, amazed by the overflowing contents. It occurred to her that she must get the heavy basket inside as soon as possible. It wouldn't do to examine all the lovely items out in the open, where greedy and drunken revelers might consider her easy prey. Reaching for the handle, Julia attempted to lift it.

It was heavy! She pushed open her front door and its ancient hinges groaned in protest. Julia opted to drag the heavy basket into the house, for it was far too heavy for her to lift alone. She pulled the heavy basket across the room, leaving it near the table, then hurriedly slammed her front door and bolted it.

Her enthusiasm nearly bubbled over as she knelt

before the basket and gingerly removed the note tucked within the overflowing items. She held it toward the light with trembling fingers, instantly recognizing the lovely, flowing hand:

To our dear daughter Julia and our son Barabbas,
Happy Purim! May you be reminded of the love and deliverance of our Lord on this night of remembrance.
Much love,
Simon and Iskah

Julia's eyes filled with tears as she clutched the note to her heart. She missed her parents desperately. There was once a time when she was sure her life would be better without them. She wondered how she could have possibly been so misguided!

She shook her head in awe. Despite the pain Barabbas had caused them, they still lovingly addressed him as their son. How did they do it? If she had been in their position, she doubted she would possess the same selfless love for the man who had whisked away her cherished daughter. He had made it blatantly obvious that he hadn't the faintest desire to involve Simon and Iskah in their lives.

The thought angered Julia even more, and for the umpteenth time, she wondered how she could have possibly been so foolish.

Enough of this, Julia thought, annoyed that Barabbas had intruded upon even this unexpected happiness. *I won't think of him. I will thank God for His goodness. I will be thankful for this special blessing. Thank You, Lord. You knew I needed this encouragement. Despite my poor attitude, You have still showered me with undeserved kindness. Thank You, Father. I love You.*

Determined to enjoy this moment, Julia plunged eager hands deep within the contents of the basket.

She discovered heavy clusters of fresh grapes, ripe, heavenly scented peaches, sweet dates and figs, and several golden loaves of freshly baked bread. Several jars of milled flour were also tucked carefully within the basket, along with accompanying vials of olive oil. Julia rejoiced, for it had been weeks since she had last milled flour with Deborah. The flour was desperately needed.

To her great delight, she also discovered a lovely pair of amphora-shaped sapphire-studded silver earrings for her, and a golden wristband for Barabbas. Julia quickly tucked away the earrings, fearful that Barabbas might pawn them off and lay the proceeds at the ungrateful feet of Amraphel. It was becoming increasingly obvious that a great deal of Barabbas' income was dispersed among the Zealots, many of whom refused to work to earn a living. Let him sell his own wristband if he so desired, but she would not part with the lovely earrings.

She lifted a unique pottery jar, skillfully painted by a local artisan. Charmed, Julia placed the jar upon a shelf and delighted in the burst of color it brought to her otherwise bland surroundings.

But what delighted her the most were the weathered scrolls tucked in the corner of the enormous gift basket. Tears sprang to her eyes as she lifted them reverently from the basket, for she recognized that these had come from her dear father's cherished library.

Carefully, she unfurled the first scroll and instantly recognized the text as the book of Esther. A fitting gift for the Feast of Purim! Julia could hardly wait to curl up with the scroll by the light of many lamps and lose herself within the story of a simple Jewish girl who became queen of Persia.

The other scrolls contained the ancient words of the prophets Isaiah and Jeremiah, along with the sage musings of the famous King Solomon and the Psalms of his father David.

Julia knew a wealth of treasures were to be found within the yellowing pages of the ancient scrolls.

Lord God, You are far too good to me. Please speak to me through Your Word.

Settling down upon her sleeping pallet, Julia unfurled the scroll containing the captivating story of Queen Esther.

In a small way, she felt as if she could relate to the Jewish queen. After all, Esther had been married to an impulsive man as well – a man who did not fear God, a man with a will of steel and a reckless nature.

And yet God had still used Esther to do great things.

True, Esther had not married Xerxes, also known as Ahasuerus, by choice. Julia recognized that her circumstances differed slightly, for hers was a misery of her own making. Still, she believed in the mercy and the redemption of her loving Father.

Even if Barabbas never made a decision for God, she herself was His precious daughter. Her salvation was not dependent on Barabbas, just as Esther's was not dependent upon the whims of a capricious pagan ruler.

A small smile crossed Julia's lovely features as her eyes scanned the neat lines upon the scroll:

Now it came to pass in the days of Ahasuerus (this was the Ahasuerus who reigned over one hundred and twenty-seven provinces, from India to Ethiopia), in those days when King Ahasuerus sat on the throne of his kingdom, which was in Shushan the citadel, that in the third year of his reign he made a feast for all his officials and servants...

Julia reveled in the beauty of the tale late into the night, thanking God profusely for the unimaginable privilege of possessing her very own scrolls which bore the life-changing power of the Word of God.

She had no doubt such words would bring great comfort in the lonely nights to come.

CHAPTER 19

It was an unusually warm day for early spring. Julia balanced a heavy earthen jar upon one hip, weary of heart and soul.

Shortly after the Feast of Purim, Barabbas had left for another long journey with her father's traveling caravan. As usual, he had forbidden her to stay with her parents during his absence.

How she loathed him for his stubborn selfishness! What exactly was she supposed to do while he traveled the known world protecting her father's expensive wares? Isaac and Deborah had still not returned from Capernaum. And with her husband on the road for weeks on end, she found herself completely alone.

No, she reminded herself firmly. *Are you as foolish and stubborn as the Israelites of old? Have you already forgotten the promises of God? You are not alone. You are never alone.*

There were days when the Lord's presence felt so thick Julia could almost feel it like a warm blanket wrapped around her entire being. Then other days, like today, she felt so very alone. Bereft. It took great effort to remember that the Lord's presence was not dependent upon her feelings. He was there, whether His presence was blatantly apparent or not.

Having drawn the water necessary to complete the day's tasks, Julia turned back toward her own house. It felt more like a suffocating prison of her own making rather than a loving home these days.

Pensively, Julia wondered if Barabbas would return before the Passover commenced two weeks hence.

Not that it matters, she thought glumly. *I will be alone regardless, as he will abandon me for those gluttonous wolves in the hill country.*

The thought set her blood to boiling. The uncouth and disgusting rogues didn't possess a religious bone in their body! And yet they eagerly awaited the arrival of Jewish feast days, for it was simply another excuse to indulge in a night of gluttonous and drunken revelry. How it angered her!

Vividly, Julia recalled the events of the last Passover she had shared with her family. Could it truly have been less than a year ago? It seemed as if an entire lifetime had slipped through her delicate fingers since then, but she remembered the celebration well. The servants had bustled about in a state of frantic and constant motion, for there were countless preparations to be made in order to observe the Passover. Her siblings had converged upon the family villa with spouses and children in tow. Her typically staid mother had been nearly beside herself with joy in the presence of her many children and grandchildren.

Truly, Iskah had outdone herself, overseeing the servants as they prepared the customary and symbolic dishes pertaining to the festival, as well as a sumptuous feast to accompany it. Rich delicacies were piled high upon the banquet table, which stretched out like an endless sea of savory cuisine. The gold and silver goblets and platters had glistened and gleamed in the flickering lamplight as the heady fragrance of incense had filled the enormous triclinium-style banquet hall.

The scene was rather entrancing, and despite her inner turmoil at the time, Julia had been impressed. She remembered reclining listlessly at the table, thankful that her siblings had left her alone in her dark mood. Though her father's Passover speech had been riveting, she had listened to very little of it and remembered even less. Her mind had been completely consumed by one thing and one thing only: Barabbas.

How foolish she had been! She remembered fantasizing about the day when Barabbas would accompany her to her father's exquisite religious feasts. She had imagined they would lounge side by side, delighting in the rich delicacies while feasting their eyes upon each other.

How very wrong she had been! Though she certainly planned to obtain Barabbas' permission to attend her father's Passover feast this year, she doubted her husband would have any interest in accompanying her. After all, the gluttons in the hill country possessed far more appeal to him than a romantic evening spent with his wife.

The big lout. Why had she ever married him?

Sinking deeper and deeper in the mire of self-pity, Julia had nearly reached her front door when the creaking of a rickety old wagon met her ears.

Instinctively, Julia turned her head toward the street.

Yes, a wagon was indeed approaching, led by a tired old mule.

Julia's heart stood still, for even at this distance, she recognized the stoic form seated at the helm, the donkey's reins firmly in her grasp.

Deborah! Deborah had returned! Frantic with joy, Julia's hand flew to her heart. Oh, how she had missed her! How she had longed for her return!

Another thought occurred to her. A disturbing thought.

Where is Isaac?

Julia's heart nearly stopped, for Deborah was the only figure in the wagon. Choking on a sob, Julia's heart pounded ferociously in her chest. She remembered Isaac shivering upon his wooden chair, his withered legs propped up on a stool, the day before they left for Capernaum. She could almost hear his wheezing cough. She could see the sweat upon his feverish brow. She remembered her great concern for him, deeming it completely unsafe for him to travel in that condition, ravaged by fever and chills.

And now...now Deborah returned alone.

Oh, dear God, what has happened to Isaac?

For the first time, Julia noticed a sturdy man leading the donkey at the front of Deborah's wagon.

Tears clouded Julia's eyes as she hiked up her robe with her free hand, and, water jug in tow, rushed toward Deborah.

A relative seeing Deborah safely back to Jerusalem could only mean one thing: Isaac had not survived the journey.

Julia heard herself crying as she rushed for Deborah's wagon, the water jug immensely heavy but unnoticed even as water sloshed about and trickled down her sleeve and soaked the front of her gown.

"Julia, our dear girl! Slow down, beloved, before you break your neck! We're nearly upon you!"

Julia froze in the middle of the road, cold sweat dotting her forehead and trickling down her back. Her entire world swayed as her earthen jar crashed to the ground, punching a dent in the dirt road with a resounding *thud*. Shaking all over, Julia clasped both hands to her heart and attempted to still her violent trembling, to no avail.

She knew that lusty voice – the full-bodied tone of a sailor, a voice capable of contending with the roar of the high seas. And yet…yet the one who spoke to her was the powerfully built and sturdy man leading the mule at the head of Deborah's wagon…

Skillfully, the man leading the mule steered the wagon to the side of road and reached for Deborah. Planting her hands upon the sturdy shoulders, Deborah allowed the man to sweep her off the wagon and place her steadily upon the road. Her small, sandaled feet had scarcely touched the dirt road before she rushed at Julia, arms outstretched, tears streaming down her weathered face.

"Julia, my dear! How I've missed you!"

Julia couldn't move. She couldn't breathe. For the man behind Deborah who strode confidently upon two sturdy and powerful legs was without a doubt the same man who had left Jerusalem with two useless and withered limbs.

Deborah caught Julia up in her arms and squeezed her fiercely, but Julia scarcely noticed.

Dazed and trembling, Julia drew back from Deborah's embrace and stared at Isaac, her eyes round in wonderment and fear.

Laughing lustily, Isaac clamped a firm hand upon her shoulder. "You look a mite surprised, dear one."

"But – but – Isaac…your legs –"

"I couldn't have picked out a better pair myself."

"But…what happened?"

"I was *healed*, that's what happened!"

"Healed?" Julia looked from Isaac to Deborah, her eyes wild as the blood drained from her face. She swayed.

"Heavens, child!" Deborah steadied Julia, gripping her firmly by the arm. She looked to her husband, concerned. "I don't suppose we considered what a huge shock this might prove to be! She's paler than death."

Another lusty laugh from Isaac. "She looks worse than I did when we left for Capernaum!"

Tenderly, Deborah took Julia by the shoulders and steered her in the direction of their homes. "Come, dear girl. Let's get you a cup of cold water and a chair. You look as if you might drop at any given moment. We can talk inside."

Julia nodded dumbly, unable to take her eyes off the sailor who stood before her – completely whole.

"Isaac, see to it that her jar is retrieved and refilled with water. She's lost all of it on the road, and down her front too, I'm seeing."

Isaac shared a knowing smile. "You see to Julia, and I'll be in shortly."

"Do hurry. She'll want to hear all about this from you!"

"And I anticipate the telling." With twinkling eyes, Isaac stooped to retrieve Julia's earthen jar as Deborah led her gently toward the home she had shared with a disabled husband for more than twenty years.

CHAPTER 20

"We were heartsick. We had just lost Shoshanna, after several grueling weeks of caretaking and witnessing her daily decline. It is terrible to watch the life slowly slip away from someone you love." There were tears in Deborah's eyes as she recalled the grief and bereavement of recent weeks.

Isaac placed a strong hand upon his wife's shoulder. She was seated upon a stool in their home, but Isaac – enjoying his newfound limbs – remained standing behind her, despite just returning from a long and rigorous trip. "But my dear sister was ready. There was no struggle – only a simple faith and a calm acceptance on her part when the time came. She went to sleep peacefully, like a child content in the arms of her father."

"And that's exactly where she is and always will be – in the arms of her loving Father," Deborah added with conviction. "The Almighty cradles every single one of us in the palm of His hand. One day, when that mighty trumpet sounds, both the living and those who sleep will be transformed in but a moment! And we will dwell with the Lord forever."

Julia was seated across from the happy couple, her arms wrapped about her slender frame as if to still her inner trembling. She still could not believe her own eyes as she studied the confident man towering over Deborah. Even his countenance appeared transformed, younger, brighter, somehow. His eyes danced with warmth and vibrant life. The lines of worry that had once shadowed his worn face had disappeared. It was as if she gazed upon a brand-new man!

"Are you sure that our Isaac has not been transformed without us?" Julia managed a shaky smile.

"Transformed, I am! Transformed, indeed! I am a living, breathing, walking – *walking*! – miracle, dear Julia! A miracle, indeed."

Julia could not argue with his assessment. "But how?"

Husband and wife exchanged meaningful glances, their eyes knowing and tender.

"We had recently buried Shoshanna. Our hearts were heavy. Yet the city was abuzz with rumors of a traveling Teacher – a Man reputed to exceed even the religious leaders in His knowledge and zeal for the Scriptures."

"And He was said to preach with great and undeniable authority – unlike any man before Him."

"We were curious about what He had to say, and frankly, the men were rather desperate for distraction. Our sorrow was fresh."

"So my brothers loaded me upon a rudely constructed litter and we set out for the location in which He was rumored to be teaching."

"It was Isaac's idea. He was downright insistent, in fact. At the time, I would have preferred to remain in seclusion and in mourning."

"But isn't that just like our Lord?" Isaac's eyes fairly danced. "*For I will turn their mourning to joy, will comfort them, and make them rejoice rather than sorrow!*"

"But…earlier you mentioned it was a Man who healed you. And now you speak as if it was the Lord?"

Again, Isaac and Deborah exchanged knowing smiles.

"And therein lies the question." Isaac's brows rose cryptically, and his smile stretched across his joy-filled features. "A Man possessing the power to heal…what might we call such a Man? A great Prophet? A Teacher?"

"Or the Messiah?"

Julia's attention snapped back to Deborah. Her heart hammered rapidly at such an astounding claim. "The Messiah?"

"Oh, Julia, if only you could have heard Him speak! With such power and authority – unlike anyone I've ever heard in all my years of living! But also with such tenderness, gentleness, and humility… We have never known a Man like this."

Julia's mind reeled at Deborah's description, for she had heard another described in the exact same way. A memory long forgotten emerged at the forefront of her mind, and she was suddenly transported back in time, back to her father's lovely garden courtyard as the torches flickered and sputtered and the late-night breezes whispered their way through swaying palm fronds.

A respected member of the Sanhedrin had paid a visit to her father that night – a man by the name of Nicodemus. And he had described a meeting with a Man very much like the one Deborah and Isaac now described. A Man of resounding authority and undulating power, yet gentle and humble of heart.

Julia even remembered her father commenting about the Man's unusual combination of traits.

Could this possibly be the same Man of whom Isaac and Deborah now spoke about? Why, her father had buried himself within his scrolls that night, determined to learn the truth about the Messiah. And his words had frightened her at the time, for Simon – an astute and able scholar – had not dismissed the possibility that this Man could, in fact, be the long-awaited Messiah.

"My brothers had quite a time hoisting me up that hill!"

Isaac's chuckle drew Julia back to the present. She realized she was nervously fingering the folds of her shawl, so she clasped her hands tightly in her lap and forced her attention back to Isaac.

"I'd never seen so many throngs of people converging upon one lonely little hilltop. Hundreds and hundreds of them, possibly even thousands. I was still sick and miserable, shivering despite the warmer weather as my brothers dutifully carried me upon my litter, Deborah trailing sorrowfully behind us."

"I must admit I nearly stumbled several times, for

the terrain was rough and my eyes were blinded by fresh tears every time I thought about Shoshanna no longer with us."

"Oh, and the jostling! The pushing and the shoving. I was certain I'd be thrown off the litter and go rolling down the hill like a falling log."

"But it was a beautiful scene, once we reached the top. Oh, Julia, I can't begin to tell you how many times I wished you were there. I do believe that hilltop is one of the most breathtaking and enchanting places on this earth!"

"And this happened in Capernaum?" Julia found herself wishing she, too, had been present.

"Near Capernaum," Isaac interrupted with the logic of a captain. "Overlooking the northwestern shores of the Sea of Galilee. Just beyond the sea one could clearly distinguish the slanting cliffs of Gaulanitis."

"It was a truly breathtaking sight I can tell you that. The Sea of Galilee glittered like a sparkling gem as the sun shimmered upon its smooth, deep blue surface, and little waves rippled happily upon the shores as fishermen's boats bobbed about in the gentle waters. We could smell the salt air and listen to the gulls as they soared majestically in open skies, calling to one another as if announcing the arrival of a very great thing."

Julia closed her eyes, hungry for the salt air and gently lapping waters of a sea she had never known. She imagined the sun upon her face, the sand beneath her bare feet. What she wouldn't give to escape to such a place!

"We couldn't get close to Him, and I feared our difficult trek up the hillside had been for naught," Deborah continued, her eyes reflecting the discouragement she had experienced in that moment. "But in the distance, at the highest point of the hill, we could see Him. He was perched upon a tall outcropping of rock, and throngs of people surrounded Him from all sides."

"What did He look like?" Julia couldn't help herself.

Both Isaac and Deborah grew quiet, reflective, as if seeking just the right words to describe this magnificent Person.

It was Deborah who responded first. "It was not so much His appearance that drew one's notice," she said slowly, thoughtfully. "His looks were ordinary in every way. He was of an average build, though He possessed the agile and muscled arms of a carpenter. There was nothing showy about Him whatsoever. Nothing showy at all."

"He wore traditional garb, like all the rest of us common folk. His clothing was simple and practical," Isaac added approvingly.

"Quite frankly, He would have blended in with the crowd had He not been seated where He was, at the highest point for all to see. His coloring was like ours – an olive-skinned complexion with dark hair and a beard, as can be expected. But His eyes…" Deborah's voice trailed off, and Julia was surprised to notice tears in the woman's own eyes as she appeared to relive the recent past. "I've never known such eyes. Such tenderness. Such warmth. As if He could see into my very soul, read my thoughts, know my heart, and – remarkably, unexplainably – love me in spite of all He saw."

Isaac squeezed his wife's shoulder, understanding her emotion. "Shall we tell her what He said?"

"Oh, do tell her, Isaac. His words were beautiful."

"My brothers had lowered my litter to the ground, and I could see nothing above the hundreds of heads that blocked the Teacher from view. But even from my lowly vantage point, I was certain we had come in vain. We wouldn't be able to hear a word He said from our great distance."

"I considered asking Isaac if we should turn back," Deborah admitted. "But then… He *spoke*."

"He spoke, and His voice rang out over the hillside like the blast of a mighty trumpet. Even those scattered about the hill far behind us were silenced and drawn by the mighty voice of Him who spoke. Like the sounding of the shofar announcing our Sabbaths and holy days, His voice was a call to something great. A call not only to *listen*, but to *hear*. To respond. To act. Do you see what I mean?"

Mesmerized by Isaac's words, Julia gave one slow nod. She believed she understood. Was it possible that she sensed that call even now, miles and miles removed from that lovely hilltop scene?

"I will never forget what He said, for I've never heard such speech. He said *blessed are the poor in spirit, for theirs is the kingdom of Heaven. Blessed are those who mourn, for they shall be comforted*."

"We were in deep mourning, distressed in our souls. And even as He spoke these words, we were comforted."

"The pain dimmed as the Spirit of God hovered above that hillside, anointing the countenance of the young Teacher who spoke, and comforting the hearts of all who were present. He went on to say, *Blessed are the meek, for they shall inherit the earth. Blessed are those who hunger and thirst for righteousness, for they shall be filled. Blessed are the merciful, for they shall obtain mercy. Blessed are the pure in heart, for they shall see God.*"

Julia was swept away by the words of the Teacher on the mount, for they resounded within her soul. Instinctively, she sensed the truth of them despite their contradictory nature.

She wondered if she herself could be included in any of the blessed categories spoken of by this great Teacher. Blessed are the poor in spirit, those who mourn. Her marriage to Barabbas had certainly rendered her poor, and she wondered if that meant she, too, was poor in spirit. She also spent her days in mourning over her husband's painful decisions. Could she, too, be considered a mourner? But what about the following categories? Blessed are the meek, those who hunger and thirst for righteousness, the merciful, the pure in heart...

She winced, considering the thoughts she often harbored against her husband and his band of Zealots. Such thoughts surpassed righteous indignation and bordered upon outright hatred. Surely, she could not be considered pure of heart.

Mentally, she inventoried her own strengths and weaknesses in accordance with the Rabbi's teaching. Was she meek? She may have learned to hold her tongue with far more success than at the beginning of her marriage, but she knew she was still far from meek. And what of mercy? Was she merciful? She bit her lower lip and lowered her gaze.

It was as if this unknown Man upon the hilltop held up a mirror by which she could gaze into her very soul. And she was disturbed by what she saw reflected in that soul-searching glass.

Despite her disturbing thoughts, Julia realized that Isaac had not completed his recitation of the Man's discourse, and, with great effort, pulled her attention back to the present. She was eager to learn what else this controversial new Teacher had to say.

"*Blessed are the peacemakers, for they shall be called sons of God. Blessed are those who are persecuted for righteousness' sake, for theirs is the kingdom of Heaven. Blessed are you when they revile and persecute you and say all kinds of evil against you falsely for My sake. Rejoice and be exceedingly glad, for great is your reward in Heaven, for so they persecuted the prophets who were before you.*"

Nothing that Isaac had to say should have caused Julia to weep. And yet the tears sprang to her eyes even as he spoke.

Blessed are you when they revile and persecute you and say all kinds of evil against you falsely for My sake... Julia's heart ached as arguments she'd had with Barabbas surfaced in her troubled mind. Barabbas was often very cruel, cutting her to the quick with his angry accusations. He often felt threatened by her growing convictions and was quick to cut her down when her own deeds magnified his misdeeds.

But, Lord, if these words be true, then I am blessed. Even if Barabbas does not understand why I love You, why I read Your Word and commune with You, even when he harasses me and criticizes me and tells me I shouldn't bother trying because I am such a failure, I am blessed. Oh, Lord, am I truly blessed?

"Jesus shared many other things as well, and each new teaching was every bit as profound."

Julia's heart sprang into her throat, quaking as the memory swept over her. *Jesus!* She knew that name!

Nicodemus had spoken of Jesus! They were, in fact, the same Person!

"I have heard of Jesus – before I left my father's villa."

Isaac and Deborah looked to Julia in surprise.

"One of my father's closest friends, Nicodemus, met with Him here in Jerusalem. Nicodemus was convinced this Man is the Son of God."

The air fairly crackled with intensity as the three within the small house contemplated the power behind the words.

"I must say I tend to agree with his assessment," Isaac stated slowly, his eyes burning with intensity. "I was captivated by His words, but it was His touch that set me free."

Julia was astounded to see tears reflected in the eyes of the powerful old captain. To see a man of his strength and build brought to tears nearly overwhelmed her, and she wondered if she would humiliate herself and dissolve in tears before her friends.

"Eagerly, we drank in every word He had to say," Isaac managed after allowing himself a moment to regain his composure. "We knew instinctively when His time with us had drawn to a close. He rose, several men along with Him, and began to pass through the crowd. Amazingly enough, the people respected His wishes and did not clamor after Him. Several seated upon the ground reached forth to touch the hem of His garment. And then... He was right there. Before me. Gazing into my face." Here, Isaac bit his lower lip and paused, his jaw working back and forth as he attempted to compose himself once more. "He knelt before me, and I was ashamed. I lay there upon the hard ground like a worthless sack of potatoes."

"Isaac."

"I was humiliated by my own brokenness, and – what was worse – my own sin, for I saw my own vile sins more clearly than I ever had before. I recognized my need for cleansing, my need for redemption. He looked into my eyes. He knew me. There is no doubt about that. He knew everything about me – my past, my present, my future. My pain. My misgivings. My fear. He knew it all. And He loved me. His eyes spoke for Him. I knew it beyond any shadow of doubt. He stretched out His hand. He touched me. And power – mighty, awesome, fearsome power – coursed through my entire body."

Deborah was crying softly, remembering the awesome sight.

Reaching for her hand, Isaac continued. "I could feel my legs! I could feel the muscle, the sinew, the strength of the bones – none of which had been there seconds before. I sprang to my feet, and Deborah cried out –"

"'Be healed,' Jesus said! His features reflected Isaac's joy. Isaac reached for Him, but He was already walking away."

"I praised God, and I started to hurry after Jesus, but a small voice from within bid me to let Him be. He had many works to do – God-ordained works. I knew this as Jesus continued to move about the crowds, touching others and healing them. I've never seen anything like it, nor will I ever again. I was desperate to express my gratitude. But what could I do? How could I do it? And then the words of the psalmist David burst forth in my mind with such shining clarity that I knew what I had to do: *You have turned for me my mourning into dancing; You have put off my sackcloth and clothed me with gladness, to the end that my glory may sing praise to You and not be silent. O Lord my God, I will give thanks to You forever.*"

Julia's eyes never left his. "But what must you do?"

"Exactly what the psalmist did! Jesus turned my mourning into dancing – in the most literal sense, dear one! I can leap and dance and pump these two strong legs as if they'd never been destroyed in that fierce and mighty gale upon the sea! The psalmist proclaimed that God had replaced his sackcloth and clothed him with gladness *to the end that he might sing praises to God and not be silenced.* And I will not be silenced. I am a living, breathing testimony to the power of God through this Man, Jesus! Not only will I give thanks to Him forever – I will spread His name far and wide. Of those who knew of my crippled state, who can stand against the evidence of the power and might of God through this Man?"

"The Messiah," Deborah echoed softly, her expression filled with awe. "He is finally here. And in our lifetime – just imagine!"

Isaac chuckled softly. "Yes, just imagine. Imagine what awesome events are about to unfold. Imagine what we shall be privileged to witness, to experience! The longings of a nation of thousands upon thousands of years is about to be fulfilled – before our very eyes."

Julia was captivated, completely mesmerized. Her heart cried out for the healing touch of a Man she knew next to nothing about. Could this Man named Jesus heal her wounded heart as easily as Isaac's injured legs? What of her broken dreams? Could a touch from the Teacher restore her marriage? Her home? Her peace?

"We returned to the hill day after day, eager to hear Jesus speak," Deborah interrupted Julia's hidden thoughts, her eyes alight. "He explained the Scriptures so clearly I wondered how I could have possibly been confused by them in the first place. He said He came not to destroy the Law or the Prophets, but to *fulfill*. What do you suppose He meant by that, Isaac?"

Isaac stroked his cropped beard thoughtfully. "Our entire religion is based upon the sacrificial system for the covering of one's sins. We observe many ceremonial and religious laws to this end.

But we know these things are but a shadow of what is to come. Jesus says He Himself is the fulfillment of those laws, the realization of all that the prophets foretold. I suppose we must watch and pray, seeking God on a daily basis and asking for discernment concerning the signs of these times in which we now live."

Julia's heart swelled within her as she contemplated the gravity of these unfolding events – events she herself might be privileged to witness. Silently, she thanked the Lord that she could now eagerly await the fulfillment of the Messiah's coming. She remembered the fear that had swept over her as Nicodemus had recounted the words of Jesus. At the time, she hadn't been ready. She had feared that Messiah's coming might interfere with the plans she had made for her own life.

With a wry smile, she wondered how she could have possibly been so foolish.

Now, a year later, Julia could anticipate the Messiah's coming with joy and gladness. And now, more than ever, she needed to see her father. Not only did she long to share all she had learned today, but she was also certain that Simon could easily refresh her memory regarding that late night discussion with Nicodemus concerning the words of Jesus.

One particular phrase she had overheard that night remained with her, and she pondered its meaning.

Born again.

She looked at Isaac – his eyes aglow, his body

whole. There was no doubt in her mind that Isaac had experienced that powerful phenomenon.

Born again.

Her heart fluttered like a caged bird as she considered the glory and the wealth of learning that must be in store for her – for all of them.

In that moment, she made a decision.

I will find a way to speak with Father, and Melina too. Her heart ached at the thought of the cheerful servant girl who had been so eager to find God. How she missed her dearest friend! *Melina would want to know about Jesus. Not only that, she deserves to know! I simply must speak with them – both Father and Melina. No matter what it takes, I will find a way. Lord God, please make a way!*

CHAPTER 21

Melina

Despite the fact that Herod Antipas had already entered the gates of Jerusalem, the palace remained in a relatively peaceful state.

Melina could hardly comprehend the difference. When Porcius had overseen the Jerusalem estate, he had bullied and threatened the frightened servants into compliance, forcing each one to accomplish the tasks of ten, then flogging them if they did not meet his harsh demands. His unjust management only intensified when it was known that Herod ventured toward his Jerusalem abode.

Chuza was of an entirely different breed. Early on, he had established allies within the palace walls and quickly learned which of the men could be trusted. A born leader of men, he had then established a chain of command in which worthy servants were placed over the others in order to direct and supervise the allotted tasks.

Based on information she had gleaned from Joanna over the months, Melina knew Chuza's life had not been an easy one. His father had been a tribal chief in a land neighboring Ethiopia, but as a young boy their village had been raided and pillaged. He had witnessed the murder of his father before his village was torched, then he was cruelly plucked from all he had ever known by ruthless slave traders, destined to sail across the Mediterranean in the bowels of a foul ship bound for the heart of the empire. Joanna had been among the young female villagers gathered to be sold as prostitutes and slaves, and she, too, had endured the miserable voyage. She once told Melina she had spent the entire voyage praying to any god who would listen that she would be sold as a slave rather than a temple prostitute forced to perform all manner of terrifying obscenities and foul rituals in a Roman temple.

Though Joanna had been ignorant at the time, she had instinctively known that Someone with great power had heard and answered her prayer, for she was purchased at a slave auction by a kindly heiress who treated her slaves well. Though the wealthy woman owned several notable estates, Joanna was designated to serve in the woman's stately compound in Tiberias. Chuza had been sold into this same household. Over the course of several years, they had fallen in love, and the older woman had permitted them to marry shortly before her death.

The heiress had possessed many friends in high

places. It was from her that Herod Antipas had learned of Chuza's incredible gifting as an overseer.

Melina supposed that the trials Chuza had faced had simply strengthened the uncanny leadership ability with which God had gifted him. Faith in the one true God fueled his desire to excel in all he that did – even if that meant serving in the palace of a half-crazed ruler in a defeated region swallowed up by the most ruthless empire that had ever existed.

God had a plan. Though Chuza rarely spoke or voiced his own opinion, this was one statement he never hesitated to proclaim.

Meticulously, Melina prepared Salome's chambers for her arrival as she pondered such thoughts. She wondered what it would be like to have the princess in residence again.

It will certainly liven things up a bit, Melina thought with a slight smile, remembering Salome's frequent outbursts, fits of temper, and imperious demands. *Oh Lord, grant me the strength to serve!*

Rumor had it that Pontius Pilate and his lovely wife, Claudia Procula, would arrive shortly after Herod Antipas. Melina didn't doubt it. Both the tetrarch and the governor were expected to be in residence for the Passover week. Even with the two uncompromising rulers breathing down their necks, the celebrants often grew rowdy and boisterous. Pontius Pilate and Herod Antipas were well aware of the fact that revolt was most likely to occur while the city brewed in a feverish state of religious and patriotic fervor.

Already the ancient city was bloated with thousands upon thousands of pilgrims who crowded within Jerusalem's age-old walls. Passover loomed just upon the horizon, for the day would be upon them in less than a week!

Carefully spreading the freshly washed Egyptian sheets upon Salome's enormous, four-poster canopy bed, Melina hummed happily to herself, for this was indeed a special time of year.

She remembered the events of the previous Passover season vividly. Of course, the royal family had been in residence at that time as well. Herodias had fumed about the gall of the prophet named John the Baptist, even as Herod secretly admired the man. Salome, of course, had sided with her diabolical mother.

It was then that Melina had determined to seek the one true God, whoever He might be. And it was then that the one true God lovingly began to reveal Himself to her. It had been an exciting journey – one she would not trade for anything in the world. And daily, her journey continued. Her walk with the Lord was strengthened. Her knowledge of the Scriptures grew. And her passion for the Lord increased with every beat of her heart.

Smiling, Melina spread luxurious, imported blankets upon the bed, careful to fluff the pillows and arrange them in a pleasing fashion at the head of the bed. For now, she must focus on the preparations necessary for the arrival of the royal family.

Perhaps tonight, there would be time to contemplate all the wonderful things the Lord had already accomplished in her life.

In light of the magnificent events Joanna had witnessed in Galilee, Melina had no doubt that even greater things were in store – not for her alone, but for all the watching world.

***

"I see that Jerusalem is the same dusty, rebel-breeding rat hole it was when last we left."

Seated ramrod straight before her enormous, gilded vanity, Salome gazed at her own reflection in the expensive oval mirror. With luxurious black hair cascading down her back, exquisite emerald eyes, and expertly applied makeup, she appeared rather queenly in her elaborate robes and glittering jewelry, her arms resting lightly upon the curved armrests of her handcrafted chair overlaid in gold.

Melina wasn't sure if she was expected to comment, but there was safety in silence. She offered a polite smile as she fluttered about Salome's chambers and began to draw the billowing Babylonian curtains for the night.

She had been abundantly grateful that Chuza had not assigned her to serve with the kitchen staff upon the royal family's arrival. That first supper was always excruciating. Always, Herod would lounge, stiff and brooding, upon his couch. Though he appeared outwardly relaxed, his body emanated the restless energy of a preying tiger, poised to strike a killing blow with deadly accuracy at the slightest provocation.

Herodias would try her husband's patience, of course. She would badger and whine, complaining about the quality of the wine or the toughness of the meat.

And Salome would follow suit, carping about anything and everything while she studied the palace guards beneath long, veiled lashes.

Melina had always assumed the girl was simply sizing up her prey. Her most recent conquest – a salacious palace guard by the name of Gallus – had taken to moonlight trysts with one of the serving girls in her absence. Melina wondered if Salome would simply dismiss him, feigning complete lack of interest, or welcome the competition.

Salome interrupted Melina's meandering thoughts with her usual imperious demands. "How long does it take to close a few curtains? Come over here and braid my hair. You know it tangles too easily if I leave it down all night."

Forcing a pleasant smile, Melina drew the final curtain closed and crossed the room to Salome's vanity. Reaching for a lovely ivory hairbrush chased in gold, she stood behind her young mistress and began to brush with long, delicate strokes. She knew better than to rush through the task, tugging at Salome's prized raven black locks. She took careful, gentle strokes, fully aware of the fact that others had suffered lashings for far less than pulling the mistress' long hair. Salome would not hesitate to order a servant punished for even the smallest offense. Like her mother, Herodias, Salome's moods were dark, her temper swift.

Melina sensed that something was amiss as she set aside the ivory brush and delicately began to separate Salome's thick hair into three separate sections. The rigid set of Salome's delicate shoulders, the firm set of her contoured jaw, the avarice gleaming in her jade-colored eyes – all these signs warned Melina to tread carefully. Something had greatly disturbed Salome – something far beyond her typically petty annoyances.

Stomach churning, Melina offered a silent prayer to the Lord for guidance – and protection.

Salome remained uncharacteristically silent, studying her own reflection with grim approval and…something else. Was it sorrow? Regret? Fear?

Growing uneasy in the mounting silence and sensing the apprehension which fairly crackled in its intensity, Melina wondered if she should say something.

She didn't have to wonder long.

With no warning whatsoever, Salome slammed a fist upon her vanity's surface, rattling the delicate glass jars of perfumes and cosmetics upon the table.

"I'm too young and beautiful to marry a dull old man! I won't do it! I won't!"

Melina gasped, startled by Salome's violent and unexpected outburst. Though she had sensed something was terribly wrong, this news was a shock. She was taken completely by surprise. Salome was betrothed in marriage? When? And to whom? Clearly, it was not to someone of her choosing.

Uncertain and fearful she might say the wrong thing, Melina drew a shaky breath before resuming the braiding of her mistress' hair.

Salome remained seated in her chair, rigid and

fierce.

"How can I help, my lady? What troubles you so?"

Salome arched a sharp, slender brow. "Have you no ears in that worthless head of yours? What did I just say?"

Melina swallowed nervously. "You refuse to marry a dull old man?" She hoped the dull old man – whoever he was – was not within earshot of Salome's violent tantrum. What if he, too, resided in the palace? Herod the Great had designed the massive structure to comfortably accommodate hundreds of guests at a time, and Herod Antipas frequently invited honored dignitaries and politicians to enjoy the luxurious guestrooms, meandering garden pathways, and lush baths.

"I won't do it," Salome insisted forcefully. "I won't. They cannot force me to do anything."

"Who, my lady?"

"My mother. And Herod. I bow to no one."

How well I know it, Melina thought ruefully. Though her mind was brimming with a thousand questions, she knew she must tread carefully in this situation. Her first duty, of course, was to calm her mistress' frazzled nerves.

"Here, my lady," Melina said gently, as if soothing a recalcitrant child. "Let me help you to bed, mistress."

"To bed? How could I possibly sleep? I'll never sleep again – and certainly not in the bed of that foul old goat!"

Coloring in embarrassment, Melina gently took Salome's elbow and helped her rise from her chair.

"You mustn't sleep if you do not wish to, my lady, but let me help you to your bed nonetheless. I shall serve you something warm to drink to soothe your spirit, if you desire. That will help you relax."

"I don't want to relax." Even as she whined her protest, Salome allowed Melina to lead her toward her enormous canopy bed.

Once Melina had drawn the covers to the young girl's chin, she fluffed the pillows behind her and touched her arm soothingly. "I shall return with something soothing to drink," she promised.

"Move quickly then, and hurry! I hate to be alone right now."

Melina offered what she hoped to be a reassuring smile, then slipped from Salome's chambers and hurried down the confusing labyrinth of corridors toward the kitchen. Elias would concoct a relaxing brew for Salome – not for the sake of the spoiled princess, whom he detested, but for Melina's sake. After all, she would be forced to suffer through the difficult night along with the overwrought young woman.

Over the past year, Melina had prayed constantly for her young, demanding mistress. Though she possessed no natural affection toward Herod's difficult stepdaughter, Melina prayed that the Lord would supply the love she lacked, and He was faithful. It was certainly difficult to rouse any feelings of fondness for Salome, but Melina was certain that God had called her to serve the girl in humility and love.

And Melina had certainly done so, to the best of her abilities.

Salome was a like a wildfire – bright and beautiful yet dangerous, raging and devouring anything that stood in its way. Her longing for excitement and romance often led her down forbidden paths. Desperately, she sought fulfillment everywhere except where she would actually find it.

Melina pitied her. Despite the fact that she herself was a servant forced to serve in a dangerous and unpredictable household, Melina sensed that she herself was far freer than Salome would ever be. Salome was enslaved by her own passions and selfish desires.

Nearing the kitchen, Melina could hear Elias' clanging pots and pans as he made preparations for the following day. Even as she hurried along dark, torch lit corridors used by the servants, she prayed for her young mistress.

Lord, only You can heal Salome's brokenness. Please turn her heart toward You. Use me however you wish, Lord, to guide her to Your truth.

CHAPTER 22

"Here, my lady. Drink. It will help you relax." Melina sat on the edge of Salome's bed and the girl reluctantly accepted the steaming mug Melina offered her.

She eyed the brew suspiciously, sitting up in bed. "What is it?"

"Spiced wine with some herbs to help your body relax. Elias has prepared it especially for you."

"I don't like him."

Then the feeling is mutual, Melina thought with a hidden smile. Instead, she replied, "He is a genius in the kitchen. This brew is guaranteed to calm your nerves and help you rest."

Salome continued to eye the brew suspiciously.

With delicate fingers, Melina tipped the bottom of the mug, and the brim touched Salome's full lips. "Drink, my lady. You will feel much better."

Surprisingly, Salome did as she was bidden. After a long draught, she cradled the mug between trembling hands. "I don't know what to do."

Melina sensed that Salome needed to confide in

someone. She hoped she would not regret lending a listening ear. "About your betrothal, my lady?"

"Don't say that! I am not betrothed yet. Perhaps the gods will strike him dead before it happens!"

Melina was horrified by Salome's violent speech. "Surely you don't mean it, my lady."

"Oh, but I do! I hate him. I want nothing to do with him!"

"With who, my lady?"

"The man they want me to marry! May the gods curse him with pestilent sores!"

Melina wondered how Herod would receive such talk. She simply must help Salome see reason. Perhaps Herod had selected a good man for her to wed. Perhaps this was God's plan for Salome's life. Maybe an older, mature husband could teach Salome to tame her restless spirit and settle into a sensible, responsible lifestyle.

"Who is this man you are to wed?"

"Philip!"

Melina recoiled. "Your father?"

"No, you fool! Another Philip – my father's half-brother, my uncle! It's sickening, that's what it is! I shall be forced to wed my own uncle, a man as old – possibly even older – than my own father!"

Melina knew immediately to whom Salome was referring. Why, the entire region knew of him! The son of the notorious Herod the Great and his fifth wife, Cleopatra of Jerusalem, Philip was raised in Rome, receiving the finest education imaginable. He had inherited a notable kingdom upon the death of his father, including the well-known regions of Iturea, Trachonitis, Gaulanitis, and Paneas. Even more famous was his construction of the great Roman city, Caesarea Philippi, near the base of Mount Hermon. Several years prior, he had sparked an outrage among observant Jews by minting a coin bearing the emperor's image, commemorating the establishment of his great city. Despite this offense, Melina had overheard many positive reports concerning the leadership and abilities of Philip the Tetrarch.

"My lady, Philip is an able ruler."

Salome stared at Melina, wide-eyed and furious. "Well, he should be! He began ruling the region *twenty years* before I was even born, so he's had plenty of experience."

Twenty years was a slight exaggeration, but Melina wisely held her tongue.

"He's nearly four decades older than I am! He's older than time itself! I can't bear the thought of marrying him. I won't do it!"

Melina longed to comfort her distraught mistress, but she wasn't sure what to say. It was a well-known tradition of the Herodian dynasty to intermarry with close relatives such as first cousins and uncles. Still, the practice made her rather uncomfortable, although she knew it had been done for centuries – especially among royal families. Herod the Great had been notorious about arranging familial marriages in order to maintain control and dominance by keeping the family in power.

Despite this uncomfortable fact, Melina also knew that Salome lusted after beautiful, well-formed young men. In Salome's opinion, good looks and a desirable build were paramount. How would she feel about a lifetime commitment to a man old enough to be her father, possibly even her grandfather?

Oh, my! This revelation triggered another thought. *A lifetime commitment?* To Salome, the term alone would be daunting, possibly even terrifying. Salome grew disinterested in her lovers with alarming speed. She would capture the heart of one, only to tire of her conquest and grow restless for another hunt within a matter of months, sometimes even weeks!

How would Salome react to a lifetime of commitment to one man – and a much older man, at that? A man unlike any she had ever pursued.

And what if the girl grew restless under her aging husband's authority? What if she sought male attention elsewhere? How would Philip respond to Salome's infidelity? Her life would be in danger. The results could be disastrous for everyone involved.

Oh Lord, may Your will be done for Salome.

"Mother says I shouldn't fight it. Philip is a powerful man, she says. She says it is a smart alliance." Although Salome adored her mother, it was obvious the two remained in complete disagreement concerning this matter. The doubt was written all over Salome's face.

"I am sure your mother is only trying to do what is best for you, my lady," Melina tried to comfort her.

"Best for me? *Best for me!* She's only going along with the whim of that pompous windbag she married. He probably plans to pawn me off for his own benefit, whatever that might be."

"Surely your mother and stepfather desire your good."

"Herod desires his own good, and Mother is foolish enough to listen to him."

"Have you met this Philip?"

"Oh, yes. Many times. As a *child*! I had no idea at the time that they would force me to marry the decrepit old man!"

"Perhaps he is kind and fair."

"Kind and fair," Salome nearly spat. "Those traits will set my blood afire with passion, alright. You are worse than Mother."

"He is a relative and he will treat you well, my lady."

"I'd rather he forget I even existed."

"But he wishes to marry you. He must care for you, my lady."

"He doesn't even know me. I am merely a tool to further his own ambitions."

"We do not know that, mistress."

"All rulers are alike, or haven't you learned that by now? Well, of course you haven't. You are far too naïve and innocent.

Melina hid her smile. She would take that as a compliment considering the fact that it was Salome who spoke.

"I hate him. I wish he were dead! And to think, he rules the region of Baal Gad! Well, so much for luck. I have the worst luck of all!"

Melina hid another smile. The region which Philip ruled was rumored by the superstitious to be the land of Baal Gad – Master Luck, the god of fortune later associated with the Greek god Pan. Superstitious residents treaded carefully about the numerous ancient shrines erected in honor of the pagan entity.

If Salome hoped to obtain luck by the hand of a fickle pagan god, she was to be sorely disappointed. Happiness could only be found in the one true God of heaven and earth, and Salome had absolutely no interest in discussing Him. She was far more interested in the adventurous and scandalous escapades of the fabled Greek and Roman entities – fanciful characters created by the imaginative minds of playwrights and poets. She would glean no help from them. Nor would she discover the peace and fulfillment she so desperately craved pursuing the immoral, rapacious lifestyle they represented.

"I will take your mug if you have finished, my lady."

Her lips drawn in a typical pout, Salome relinquished the empty mug.

"Thank you, my lady. I hope you will sleep well now."

"I haven't slept well since Mother told me about Philip." Salome's slanted eyelids drooped sleepily even as she protested, and she nestled snugly beneath the plush covers. "But you were right – that bizarre concoction did help."

"I will serve it every night if it induces a peaceful sleep, my lady."

"Do it," Salome ordered tersely. "I'm desperate for rest."

"It shall be as you say."

"I suppose now I must devise a plan. No matter what it takes, I will find a way out of this marriage – even if I have to poison the man myself."

Melina recoiled. "Oh, mistress, please don't say such things. What if Herod were to find out?"

"Let him find out, then! I wish he were dead, too! He's brought nothing but misery to Mother and me."

"Your mother loves him."

"You're such a child, Melina. Don't let her fool you. My mother is a wise woman. She uses Herod to her own advantage."

Such frank talk disturbed Melina's spirit. *Oh, Lord, will they ever learn Your ways?*

Salome noticed the distress reflected in Melina's pale green eyes. Annoyed that a servant would dare question her morality, Salome was quick to retaliate. She knew how to cut anyone to the quick, and her tenderhearted maidservant was an easy target.

Curling up on her side, Salome did not bother turning her head to glimpse Melina's expression. Like a poison dart, she knew her venomous words would strike their mark. "Well, despite this present struggle, at least one problem has been resolved – that raving fool they call John the Baptist has been arrested. He is rotting in a miserable dungeon at Machaerus even as we speak."

Having just risen from Salome's bed, Melina froze, gripping one of the long wooden posts for support. *John the Baptist – arrested?* She felt as if she'd been punched in the gut.

The great and mighty prophet John, the man who

so boldly professed the Messiah's coming, urging people to repent and prepare their hearts for him – imprisoned? And at Machaerus, no less – often called the Black Fortress – the most horrific and foreboding prison in the region.

Nestled comfortably within the folds of her lush, billowing blankets, Salome cast a smug glance over her shoulder. Melina was pale and trembling. The princess grinned, pleased.

"Ah, you remember hearing of him? He was a pestilent nuisance. It will be good riddance when Herod finally slits his worthless throat."

"Will he – will he do that?" Melina's voice sounded strangled in her own ears, despite her great effort to appear normal and unaffected.

"In time. He will have to allow the people time to forget about the crazy desert rat first – after all, they were terribly upset when John was arrested. But trust me – they'll forget about him, and it won't take long. People are fickle. They'll move on to someone more interesting and forget all about that raving lunatic." Her eyes narrowed with malevolent intent. "And then Herod can do as he pleases. I beseech every god that ever existed – may Philip the Tetrarch suffer the same fate as that filthy so-called prophet."

Trembling, Melina turned and prepared to escape her mistress' chambers. She could no longer stomach Salome's violent musings, nor her wicked lust for the blood of innocent men. Salome was just like her mother, who in turn was very much like Rome – beautiful and alluring, though dark and dangerous. The external beauty was simply a façade – a veil that masked the startling level of wickedness and depravity within.

"I hope I haven't upset you with that bit of news," Salome called after Melina smugly, "although I haven't the slightest idea why you would care. You haven't even met the man."

And now I never shall, Melina thought, overcome with sorrow. How would she ever tell Joanna? She could barely grasp the news herself.

Oh God, protect that man. He is Your servant, but You know this. Send Your angels roundabout him, Father. Do not allow him to fall prey to the schemes of this wicked family.

"Goodnight, my lady." Melina closed the enormous double doors behind her. Nausea swept over her, and her legs felt like jelly under her weight. She pressed her back against the door's cool surface and drew a ragged breath.

How could anyone be so wicked, so cruel?

Overcome, Melina buried her face in her hands and wept.

CHAPTER 23

Mara

"Do you understand what I am saying? Leah spoke with an eyewitness last night. This Man is *healing* people!"

Lucius studied Mara with the practiced eye of one trained to detect subterfuge. "Leah works in the kitchen with you?"

Guilt-ridden, Mara bit her lower lip and looked away.

Sensing her uncertainty, Lucius reached out and stroked her cheek tenderly. "There is no danger to your friend, Mara. I simply must gather all the information I can."

"Leah herself is not a follower. She has never even heard the Man preach. But a relative of hers has just arrived from Galilee for the Passover festivities. He is the one who witnessed these…these *healings*."

Lowering his hand to the hilt of his Roman gladius, Lucius' eyes hardened. "You sound rather impressed."

Mara was growing impatient. Day after day, Lucius hounded her for more information about the followers of this controversial new Teacher. And day after day, she obliged. But he had yet to fulfill his promise of marriage. If his mission was truly providing a bountiful stream of fresh income, then why hadn't he made the arrangements for an official betrothal? Why did he tarry?

Seating herself upon one of many curved marble benches of the lovely terrace overlooking the radiant temple compound, Mara shook her head to clear its confusion. Malchus' dire warnings vied for her attention, but it was simply too painful to consider them. Surely Lucius loved her! He had sought her company for years. He had promised to marry her. And he trusted her to assist in this mission that was so crucial to his career. Surely that was something!

"Well?"

Lucius' impatient question drew Mara's attention back to the present. She sighed. "I do apologize, Lucius. I suppose I was lost in thought."

"So I gathered. When you decide to acknowledge our existence here in the present, do let me know."

His imperious tone angered Mara. She felt angrier and angrier all the time. But why? Shouldn't she be happy? Her wildest dreams were finally within reach. Lucius had promised to marry her – eventually. Shouldn't she be ecstatic?

"I am listening, Lucius." Her voice sounded tired in her own ears.

"I simply stated that you seem rather impressed

with this miracle-working rebel rouser."

"Perhaps you should be, too. Can *you* heal people?" Mara rarely challenged Lucius, but she wearied of these endless interrogations.

"Your friend has only met someone who claims the Man heals."

"An eyewitness."

"People say what they want others to believe."

"And of what possible benefit would it be to fabricate such a tale?"

Lucius' mouth formed a grim line. He hadn't the slightest idea, but he certainly intended to find out.

"Lucius?"

The ex-soldier turned to her with an air of impatience and longsuffering.

Mara sighed. Years ago, Lucius had gazed upon her with a look akin to awe. Now he studied her the way a stray dog sized up a piece of meat. At times he approached her hungrily, ravenous to fulfill his own desires. But in those moments, there was no tenderness in his touch. He seldom spoke her name. He sought her out seeking instant gratification, and she performed.

Rather like a trained animal, Mara thought grimly, her mouth tipping in disgust. *Will he ever marry me?*

"This relative of Leah's –" Lucius' harsh tone broke through her silent reverie. "Does he have a name?"

"Well, I suppose he does, unless his mother failed to christen him at birth."

Lucius' features hardened and his knuckles

whitened upon the hilt of his gladius. "I see you are in no mood to be of help. Let me know when your disposition improves."

Mara turned on her bench, her fists clenching in anger as Lucius stalked away. "Perhaps my disposition will improve when you fulfill your promises to me!" she shouted after him, too angry to care if anyone heard them.

Lucius froze mid-step, his entire body stiffening. He glared at her. "And how exactly am I supposed to do that when you make it impossible for me to fulfill my mission?"

"Oh, I'm sorry but I was under the impression that Caiaphas assigned *you* to this mission – not I!"

"You agreed to assist."

"And I do! Every day!"

"Not well enough."

Mara stared at him, openmouthed and trembling. "What more shall I do, Lucius? Take to the streets and interrogate every single person about Jerusalem?"

"Enough! You are an entitled and ungrateful woman."

"And you are a liar."

Lucius' features were taut with rage. "I refuse to stand here listening to your groundless accusations."

"Groundless? You make promises until you're blue in the face, but even after all these years you refuse to marry me!"

"Ah, I assure you, the prospect of marriage is tempting, my dear. Especially in light of your delicate speech and sweet disposition."

Mara studied the palace guard she thought she loved as he stood aloof on the opposite side of the terrace. His fist rested upon the hilt of his gladius as he cradled his plumed helmet with his free hand. He looked fierce and magnificent with his armor gleaming in the early morning sun. He was the embodiment of all the Roman army represented – the deadliest war machine the world had ever known.

Why had she ever been drawn to him in the first place? And why did she tremble in fear at the thought of walking away from him? Was it simply fear of being alone?

Mara had never considered herself lovely. Her features were plain. She was too tall, in her opinion, and too straight. As for feminine charm, she supposed she was lacking in every way. She was a simple woman, straightforward and direct. Men had never flocked about her as they did with other maidservants in Caiaphas' house. Lucius was the first man to display the slightest interest in her.

Mara longed for a family, for the joy of children. But she wasn't getting any younger, and Lucius appeared to be her only candidate. She was certain there would never be anyone else if she were to end her relationship with Lucius.

Fear began to take root, crowding out her rage. She gazed at Lucius with frightened eyes. "We mustn't quarrel, Lucius. Please forgive my sharp speech."

"Ah, easily spoken by the initiator. And shall I forgive your blatant disrespect and sour disposition as well?"

Shamed, Mara lowered her gaze.

Shaking his head in disdain, Lucius left the terrace.

Hurt and confused, Mara twisted her hands nervously in her lap and gazed into the distance, scarcely noticing the glorious temple compound bathed in brilliant sunlight, its towering marble walls reflecting the blinding light. Pilgrims visiting Jerusalem on pilgrimage were awestruck by the majesty of the Jewish Temple, but Mara was no longer impressed. It was simply another feature of the city landscape – one she saw many times a day.

Situated on the eastern edge of the Upper City, Caiaphas' palatial mansion provided an excellent view of the Temple Mount and compound. This was simply one of three magnificent terraces overlooking the famous city. The elaborate structure spilled over the side of an elevated cliff face, and some of the massive rooms were carved into the rock itself. The home was an architectural marvel. But this, too, failed to impress Mara. She knew the man who resided within the house and presided over the temple compound. His religion was a farce. She wanted no part of it.

"Ah, sweet Mara. You look dejected, my dear."

Mara's head came up in surprise. Her heart pounded rapidly in her chest as Alexander strolled casually across the elevated terrace, a smug grin splitting his handsome features.

Mara's pulse quickened. "I agree with Malchus – you have a terrible habit."

"Well, at least the two of you agree on one point."

"Are you always on the prowl?"

"No, at times I skulk in the shadows as well."

"As you were just now?" Mara could feel the heat creeping into her face. Had Alexander overheard her spat with Lucius? Oh, how she loathed him! Curse his good looks and deceptive charm!

A slow, easy smile crossed Alexander's swarthy features, and he studied her boldly. "You needn't worry, my dear. I won't share your secret."

"I have no secrets."

"No?"

Biting her lower lip, Mara looked away. She couldn't bear the intensity in Alexander's eyes. How much had he overheard?

"Call me ignorant as to the customs of these prudish Judeans, but is it not forbidden for a Jewess to marry a Gentile?"

At this, Mara met Alexander's gaze head on. "I am a Jewess in name only. And besides that, the Law does allow for intermarriage if the man converts to Judaism."

"Ah, I'm sure that Roman fellow – Lucius, is it? – is more than eager to undergo that lovely little ceremony you Jews like to call circumcision. If I'm not mistaken, it's required at the point of conversion, yes?"

Mara hoped her loathing was accurately conveyed in the glare she offered him. "It is."

"And you Jews call us Gentiles barbarian!"

"In my opinion, it's too kind a word for you."

Laughing softly, Alexander paced before the picturesque scene of the temple compound.

Mara hated to admit the fact that the man was

rather picturesque himself. He carried himself with confidence, poise, and masculine grace. Annoyed, she looked away.

"Despite your cutting remarks at present, I must disagree with Lucius. You have an excellent disposition."

"You mock me."

Alexander paused, one dark brow arched in question. "Have you so little confidence in your own worth?"

"I haven't the slightest idea what you're talking about."

"I think you do."

Mara met his gaze and trembled at the intensity of those dark eyes. "What do you seek?"

"I simply despise that foul cretin for taking advantage of you the way he does."

"Now you sound like Malchus."

"Funny, that. I hadn't realized we had anything in common."

"Perhaps you have more in common than you think," Mara observed, noting Alexander's dry humor and charisma.

"And is this what has created the rift in your friendship? Malchus' disapproval of that diplomatic gentleman?"

"That is none of your business."

"You like that phrase, don't you?"

"By all means do explain how my personal affairs are of any possible use or interest to you! You know nothing about me. You do not know me at all."

"I'd like to."

"Whatever for?"

"You are a lovely and intelligent woman."

This gave Mara pause. If Malchus disapproved of Lucius, what on earth would he have to say about Alexander's interest? The thought was so comical she nearly smiled.

But despite Alexander's charm and carefully polished demeanor, Mara didn't trust him. Clearly, Malchus despised him – and Mara had known Malchus long enough to know he was a good judge of character. Perhaps that was why he had turned against her. He sensed her true heart, her many weaknesses...

"I must admit, you are the first woman I've ever met who did not find me irresistible," Alexander acknowledged ruefully.

Mara lifted slender brows. Therein lay the answer to her unasked question. Alexander pursued her because he could not have her. The moment she succumbed to his charm, she would simply become one of a long string of meaningless conquests. The thought infuriated her. "Your humility is moving."

"Isn't it? I amaze myself at times."

"Then you are easily impressed."

Alexander paused, studying her enigmatically. "No, actually. Very little impresses me." Unexpectedly, he knelt before her, taking her hand in a firm grip. "But you, my dear – you impress me greatly."

Horrified, Mara snatched her hand away and rose to her feet. She turned her back to the bold young man before her, troubled.

Alexander rose gracefully and followed her.

"Name one good reason as to why I should no longer seek your company."

"I am betrothed!"

"And I am the Emperor Tiberius! Spare the blatant lies, please."

"Well, I will be betrothed. Soon."

"Ah, yes. Your conversation with Lucius this morning was extremely promising."

Anger coursed through Mara's entire being, and she was sorely tempted to wipe that smug look right off Alexander's face. "If you will excuse me, I have chores to attend to."

"Am I so easily dismissed?"

"I wish you were! And yet every time I turn around, there you are!"

"The other maidservants would be thrilled."

"Then by all means, go thrill them!" Trembling in anger and confusion, Mara spun on her heel and stalked toward one of the pillared entrances.

"Mara."

Her back still turned Mara paused. Her stomach clenched, for she was struck by the urgency in Alexander's tone.

"Your man's a fool. I'd marry you in a heartbeat."

Her pulse pounded furiously in her temples as tears slipped down her cheeks. Clenching her fists, Mara ducked into the house without looking back.

CHAPTER 24

Julia

"Passover arrives within the week."

"Am I supposed to be impressed?" Barabbas glared indolently across the table, his body tense and rigid.

Julia's initial response was wrath, but she uttered a silent prayer and forced herself to remain calm. Anger would only fuel her husband's defiance. If she were to obtain his permission to celebrate the Passover with her family, she must tread carefully.

Your will, Lord, she prayed silently. *But please move him to grant me this one small request!*

Rising gracefully, Julia gathered the supper dishes and turned toward the hearth. She could sense Barabbas' eyes upon her slender back as starkly as if he were boring holes into her. Setting aside the dishes, she turned and offered a pacifying smile.

"As a child, I loved celebrating the Passover with my family. There was always food and family and fellowship!"

"Some of us were not so fortunate as to enjoy a golden childhood."

His response rankled, but she held her peace. Deborah's words whispered softly through her mind: *Choose to walk in love...*

Biting back a sharp retort, Julia chose love. Crossing the room, she seated herself upon the bench beside her husband and took his hand. "I know very little of your childhood, Barabbas. But the pain I see in your eyes makes my heart ache."

Barabbas stiffened. "What do you want?"

"What do you mean?" His words stung.

"You know exactly what I mean. Here you are – all cozied up to me, your words dripping honey. It can mean only one thing."

Julia's pulse quickened along with her frustration. "I am simply trying to comfort you!"

"Then you can honestly say you have nothing to ask me?"

Julia's face reddened in anger. "I am kind to you regardless of whether or not I have a request."

"So you *do* want something."

Julia rose to her feet, trembling in fierce anger. "If I were only kind to you when you granted my requests, then you'd never know a kind moment from me!"

Barabbas jumped to his feet so abruptly his bench toppled over behind him. "And what is that supposed to mean?"

"Exactly what it sounds like – you don't care about what's important to me!"

"And what's important to you, Julia? Going to your father's house to waste an entire week in sheer boredom, watching your family go through the meaningless rituals of a faith they refuse to act upon?"

Tears stung Julia's face even as she wondered how he had known her request before she had voiced it. "That is the most ridiculous accusation that has ever proceeded forth from your mouth! My parents are wonderful, God-honoring people. You have treated them like a sack of dirt, and yet they pray for you and treat you kindly!"

"I do not need nor want their kindness!"

"Fine, reject their kindness then. But you could certainly use their prayers!"

"We're not going to their house for Passover, Julia."

"Fine. I'll go alone."

"You will do no such thing!"

"Won't I?"

"By the gods, Julia, don't test me!"

Choose to walk in love... Julia stood panting near the hearth, one hand placed protectively over her rapidly beating heart. *Choose to walk in love...*

Why, Lord? Why? Barabbas hasn't walked in love a day in his life! And it isn't working! I bend over backward to be kind to him, to hold my tongue, to keep my peace – and see how he treats me? I cannot do it, Lord. I can't...

All things are possible with God.

Groaning, Julia covered her face with her hands. The room was silent. Utterly silent. And still. So still, she could hear her husband's labored breathing across the room.

It took all her strength to meet his gaze without a trace of malice. "I will not defy you. If you do not wish to celebrate with my family, then I will accept that."

Barabbas eyed her suspiciously. "Your capitulation is surprisingly uncharacteristic."

Julia lowered her gaze. "I have asked the Lord to help me respect you."

Barabbas rolled his eyes and rubbed the back of his neck. "Why must you bring God into everything? I can't even relieve myself without you trying to turn it into some profound spiritual lesson!"

"God *is* involved in everything, Barabbas. Without Him we cannot draw another breath. Why would we try to force Him aside when He is our all?"

"I might almost accept your sincerity had I not witnessed your fit of temper just moments earlier."

Barabbas knew exactly how to ignite her fury! She offered another silent plea for peace and clarity. "I should not have responded in anger, but God is merciful." *Even if you, Barabbas, are not,* she added silently, peeved. "He forgives our failures when we repent."

"And I suppose you see my poor, unworthy soul in dire need of repentance?"

His derision stung. Folding her hands before her to still their trembling, Julia lowered her gaze. "We are all in need of forgiveness, Barabbas."

"You are quite the evangelist. Perhaps one day you will practice what you preach."

"The Lord helps me grow in my walk with Him each day. I don't doubt that He will continue to shape me and mold me."

"If He doesn't weary of your unbending stubbornness and refusal to comply."

Julia remained silent.

"Have you nothing more to say?"

"Will you celebrate the Passover with me, Barabbas? Here at home?"

Barabbas' eyes narrowed. "You know I don't observe meaningless religious rituals."

"It is a command."

"It is also a command to obey your husband, but you don't seem to be in any rush to comply."

"Have I not submitted to your will tonight, despite the fact that it pains me greatly? If you will provide the coin, I can purchase the lamb and prepare the feast. We can –"

"I'll think about it."

"Please, Barabbas –"

"I said I will think about it. Don't push me."

Sighing in defeat, Julia turned to wash the dishes and store the leftover meal. She knew she must find some way to observe the Passover, despite her husband's obstinance. True, a wife was expected to honor her husband, but she also knew that obedience to God must supersede that command.

I suppose I shall join Deborah and Simon for Passover if Barabbas refuses to participate this year, she thought glumly. Barabbas never forbade her to see Deborah.

Shamed, she remembered all the years she had

been free to enjoy the special feast with her family. At the time, it had seemed like a chore, and she had resented it. What she wouldn't do for that same privilege now!

Dear Lord, forgive me for being so foolish. You blessed me with the freedom to worship exactly as I chose, and yet I was far too self-absorbed to recognize it as a blessing.

Julia had nearly finished sweeping near the hearth when she heard the door open and close. Barabbas had left, possibly to check on the goats, Adam and Eve. She didn't really care why he had left. If anything, she was relieved to be rid of his smoldering presence.

Though it was still rather early, Julia unrolled their sleeping pallet and retrieved several thin blankets. She was soul-weary. Perhaps she would feel rejuvenated after a good night's rest.

Stretching out upon the uncomfortable pallet, Julia stared at the low ceiling, mesmerized by writhing shadows cast by the flickering oil lamps.

Memories from the previous Passover flooded her mind, bringing a pang to her heart. The Passover was a celebration of the wondrous works the Lord had wrought while delivering His chosen people from a cruel, relentless taskmaster. Enslaved by the Egyptian pharaoh, the Israelites had toiled and labored from dawn until dusk. In desperation they had cried out to God, and God had heard them. He raised up Moses to be a mighty deliverer to lead His people out of bondage and into freedom.

The more she pondered the significance of the

event, the more she recognized the symbolism behind it. She, too, was the victim of a cruel taskmaster – the enemy of her soul. But despite the fact that he did all in his power to keep her in bondage, her God was greater. The almighty God of the Passover had set her free.

But there was more to the story than that...there had to be more... She sensed it with her entire being. Furrowing her brows, Julia attempted to recall every detail of the Passover story.

Something seemed to be missing.

Words from the sacred text of Deuteronomy sprang to her mind as she contemplated the matter – words her father had taught her, words she had long since forgotten, prophetic words which Moses had spoken to the Israelites many centuries ago...

"And the Lord said to me... 'I will raise up for them a Prophet like you from among their brethren, and will put My words in His mouth, and He shall speak to them all that I command Him. And it shall be that whoever will not hear My words, which He speaks in My name, I will require it of Him...'"

Curled up on her side and enjoying the tranquility of the evening, Julia contemplated the testimonies of Deborah, Isaac, and Nicodemus. They spoke of a great prophet named Jesus, One who claimed to speak the words of God and possessed the power to heal men.

Did He possess the power to heal the souls of men as well?

The blood of the Passover lamb was a symbol of God's covering, His protection. But a symbol was a mere representation. Of what, then, did the blood of a pure and spotless Passover lamb upon those wooden beams represent?

Somehow, Julia accepted the fact that this powerful new Prophet possessed the answers. What she wouldn't give to hear Him speak!

Another thought occurred to her – if this Jesus was a devoted Jew, then He would be in Jerusalem for the Passover this week, residing in her city! Perhaps her wildest dreams were not out of reach...perhaps she could find a way to meet Jesus.

Oh, Lord, if He is truly who He claims to be – if He is truly Your Son – make a way. Open the doors for me. Grant me the privilege to hear the words He speaks, for His words would be Your words, Lord. What a joy that would be!

Beside herself with anticipation, Julia attempted to calm her excitement and leave her request in the hands of her faithful Lord. But even as she attempted to sleep, her mind raced ahead of her. Sleep was elusive.

She remembered the blood her father had slashed upon the elaborate doorpost of the banquet hall Passover night – exactly one year ago. She had cringed along with the others when Simon had dipped the hyssop branch in the blood-colored paint, striking the doorposts and the lentil with swift, sure strokes. For some reason, the fact that the blood-spattered doorframe appeared both vertically and horizontally had stood out to young Julia despite her boredom.

Though Iskah had held her tongue at the time,

Julia had overheard a hushed conversation between her parents the following day.

"I have asked Jacob to repair the doorway in the Triclinium," Iskah had informed her husband.

"Are you referring to the blood upon the door-post?" Simon had asked quietly.

"Yes. What else?"

"Leave it, my dear. I'll speak with Jacob."

Iskah had visibly recoiled. "Must it remain forever?"

Simon had remained uncharacteristically rigid. "It's not coming down."

"But why not?"

"We must remember."

"Remember! Simon, it's gruesome."

"Our *sin* is gruesome. The blood upon that door-post is a reminder that we must not grow comfortable with our sin. We must remember that our sins must be offered to God on a daily basis. We must ask Him to take it away."

Tears slipped down Julia's cheeks as she remembered the words of her parents. How she longed to sit beside her father and ask him all about the significance of the Passover feast. He would have so much wisdom to impart!

Jolted from her silent reverie, Julia heard the door open and close once more as Barabbas returned for the night. His presence dampened her spirit. She shut her eyes tightly, hoping he would not disturb her or insist upon intimacy tonight. She hadn't the heart to embrace him – not after the hurtful things he had said.

She could feel his body heat as he lowered himself to their sleeping pallet without a word. He must have assumed she was already asleep, and she did not open her eyes to contradict his assumption. She was simply too weary to risk igniting yet another disagreement.

Lord God, she silently prayed, *redeem my foolish mistakes. As my father pointed out, sin is gruesome. My sin is gruesome. Please take it away, Lord. Make me clean as only You can do.*

Julia drifted off to sleep, dreaming of the same tender, unassuming Shepherd who had called to her in her dreams the night before her wedding.

CHAPTER 25

Melina

Serving Salome had never been pleasant, but the past few days had proven nearly unbearable.

Sensing her handmaiden's discomfort with the subject, Salome gloated over the imprisonment of John the Baptist, sorely testing Melina's patience and self-control. She seemed to derive great satisfaction in Melina's silent suffering.

Perhaps her cruelty simply distracts her from her own fear regarding her upcoming betrothal, Melina attempted to justify Salome's behavior as she stood behind her young mistress, arranging her hair in an elaborate Roman design.

Salome had requested the impossible hairstyle, insisting that Melina weave her finest pearls into the hair arrangement. Pontius Pilate and Claudia Procula would be arriving within the hour, and Salome couldn't resist another opportunity to flaunt her wealth and beauty.

Salome's antagonism toward Claudia Procula amused Melina. Though Procula had never given the girl cause for her acute distaste, Salome detested the woman fiercely. Perhaps she simply sensed her mother's keen dislike for the soft-spoken wife of the prelate. Salome was constantly tossed about by the ever-changing whims of her wicked mother.

"Melina, a word."

Deep in thought, Melina had not noticed Chuza standing regally beneath an arched entryway. He appeared grim and austere in his elegant robes and fine jewelry.

Salome's head spun around, despite the fact that Melina's fingers were intertwined in her lush black hair. "Imbecile!" she spat, and Melina cringed at her disrespect. "Can't you see the girl is styling my hair?"

Chuza remained calm, unmoving. Not even a flicker dimmed his soft eyes.

"Go away," Salome ordered imperiously. "You can speak with my maidservant when I am done with her."

Chuza remained rooted in place. "Your mother has instructed me to speak with your servant, my lady, and so I shall."

Salome's face reddened, her pride smarting. She would not dare to defy her mother's orders.

"Melina? A word?"

Obediently, Melina crossed over to Chuza, who stood with his arms crossed in front of his broad chest. He towered over her like an unbending, mighty oak.

Leaning toward her ear, Chuza lowered his voice.

"The prelate has arrived with his wife, an entourage of slaves, and his personal staff."

Salome, who had been eavesdropping, stared at Chuza in alarm. "They're here? Melina, get over here! Hurry up and fix my hair!"

Chuza held up an authoritative finger. "A moment." He lowered his voice even further. "Procula's personal maid has succumbed to a severe fever. Attendants are attempting to revive her, and naturally Procula is concerned for her."

"What can we do for her, my lord?" Melina's eyes conveyed her deep concern.

"Very little, I'm afraid," Chuza answered honestly. "But Herodias insists upon replacing the girl, as Procula depends heavily upon her service. You are expected to report to Claudia Procula within the hour. You shall serve her during her stay in Jerusalem."

At this, Salome sprang to her feet, her half-styled hair drooping pitifully to one side. "This is an outrage! Melina is *my* servant! She belongs to *me*! You can't just pass her around to anyone who wants to use her!"

"Your mother's orders, miss. Not mine."

"Tell her to find someone else!"

"Perhaps you would wish to volunteer your services?"

Salome's eyes flashed violently. "How dare you!"

Chuza remained cool, composed. "Then I suggest we adhere to the orders of Lady Herodias. Melina, you may finish styling Salome's hair, and then gather whatever belongings you deem necessary for the following week. You will be staying in the opposite wing serving Claudia Procula until her maid revives and regains her strength."

"Are you blind? Procula's wicked little slave is feigning illness to get out of work!" Salome fumed, shaking in her rage. "How dare you take my servant when Procula has an entire fleet of her own!"

"You may take that up with your mother," Chuza responded, unmoved.

"I hate you!" Salome shrieked as Chuza left the room without another word. "I hope you drop dead of the same illness!"

Alarmed by Salome's blatant outburst, Melina went to her and took her hands. "My lady, it will be alright. You must calm down."

Salome shook free of Melina's grasp and paced the room like an angry tiger, her hair drooping as the pins clattered to the floor. "How dare they offer you up to that witch! She has an entire fleet of servants to care for her! But what do I have?" She spun on her heel, facing Melina head-on. "*What do I have?*"

"Look around you, my lady," Melina dared softly. "You have much to be thankful for." Totally unprepared, she slammed against an elaborate wooden dresser when Salome slapped her across the face.

Reeling from the blow, Melina drew a trembling hand to her face. It stung terribly.

"That'll teach you not to speak out of turn!" Salome hissed, her eyes fierce. "You have no right to lecture me!"

"I – I meant no disrespect –"

"Shut up and fix my hair before they take you from me!" Salome slammed herself down in front of her vanity, tears of self-pity pooling in her green eyes. "Just start over. My hair is ruined! Ruined!"

Shaking, Melina prayed silently as she approached her mistress. Carefully, she removed the remaining pins and the string of expensive pearls.

"We will fix it, my lady, and it will look lovely like always."

Salome remained silent, her back rigid and her eyes glittering in rage.

Melina prayed for the strength to show love to this hateful young woman. How easy it would be to despise her! Even so, she knew that was not her Lord's way.

In recent days, Salome had begun to frighten her. The entitled young woman had always been willful and selfish. But Melina sensed something dark and malevolent brooding within the young woman now – something that hadn't been there before. It was as if Salome's stubborn refusal to turn from her wickedness had kicked the door wide open for evil to preside within her. And moments like this, when Salome glared at her with angry, glittering eyes, it was as if a darker, more sinister presence peered out from beneath those deceptively lovely emerald pools.

Attempting to still her shuddering, Melina completed the hairstyle in record time. She had no desire to remain in the chamber with Salome a moment longer than necessary.

***

Claudia Procula was a tall, regal woman with clear brown eyes and a creamy complexion.

Despite Procula's calm smile and kind eyes, Melina trembled at the mere thought of serving her. Procula was royalty – and not the kind of royalty by which Herod's family could boast. No, Procula was not the descendant of a rugged Hasmonean dynasty within the realms of a defeated empire like the Herodians were. Rather, she was the grand-daughter of Rome's mighty Caesar Augustus – the infamous man who had preceded Emperor Tiberius. Royal blood flowed through her veins, and she possessed the power of life and death in her delicate hand.

Melina had long suspected that this fact alone had permanently turned Herodias against the elegant lady. After all, Herodias craved the power and the bloodline of women like Claudia Procula. Herodias was bitter with jealousy toward the stately woman.

Pausing before the enormous double doors of Procula's private suite in the opposing wing, Melina attempted to still her trembling and uttered a silent prayer.

Lord, I know very little about this famous woman I am to serve. Please grant me favor in her sight.

Calmed by the knowledge of her Lord's presence, Melina gave two soft raps on the door.

A haughty slave girl opened the door, eyeing Melina with open disdain. "What do you want?"

"I am Melina. I have arrived to present myself to the Lady Procula to offer –"

"The Lady Procula has no slave by that name," the girl retorted, preparing to slam the door.

"But –"

"Melina! Do come in. A messenger informed me of your coming." The voice was soft and smooth as golden oil, though Melina detected a hint of authority behind the soft-spoken words. "Miriam, step aside and let her in."

Miriam, the haughty slave, did as she was told, be it grudgingly. Timid, Melina stepped inside the luxuriant chambers. Herod had not spared a single shekel in the elaborate furnishings, elegant design, and grand architecture.

Procula glided across the room with an outstretched hand. "Melina! You have served me on multiple occasions during my luncheons with Lady Herodias and Lady Salome. You have always served us well."

Flattered, Melina suspected that Procula spoke not only for her benefit but for that of the haughty slave at the door as well.

"I am honored that you remember me, my lady."

"How could I forget? I am delighted Herodias has sent you to assist me."

"I am delighted as well, my lady."

Procula leaned forward conspiratorially. "I do believe you will find it rather dull and uninteresting over here as opposed to the flurry and excitement in the household of the tetrarch this Passover week."

Melina looked to the regal woman, a question in her eyes.

"You see, my husband detests Jerusalem this time

of year. Well, I suppose he detests it year-round," she amended with a mischievous gleam in her lovely eyes. "But he particularly despises the city during the feasts and holy days. His presence is required, of course, to keep the peace. But he refuses to observe the Jewish customs, which naturally includes the Jewish Passover. So while the rest of the city remains in an uproar, I tend to barricade myself within these protective walls and wait out the chaos that is sure to ensue. It seems rather selfish of me, I suppose, but my husband would have it no other way."

Melina offered an understanding smile. Procula was no more a Jew than her husband, Pontius Pilate. She would not understand the significance of the Passover celebration. Melina had gladly anticipated the Passover this year, for she had hoped to watch and observe in order to learn more about the sacred holiday. Despite her disappointment, she knew she had entrusted herself into the hands of her Creator, and clearly, this was where He had placed her today. She would choose to be content, as well as thankful that she would avoid the frantic flurry and frenzy of the Passover preparations. A faint smile played about the corners of her lips as she thought of Elias working madly in the kitchen. How he would miss her helping hands! She prayed that the other servants would pitch in and help carry the load.

Oh dear! For the first time, Melina remembered the day. She was supposed to meet Malchus at the Upper Market within the hour. This sudden turn of events had rendered her unable to meet him or even warn him about her absence.

I suppose we both understand that there will be times when we cannot escape our duties and are unable to send word, she thought glumly. Was it selfish to pray that the Lord would make a way for her to meet with Malchus, despite her duties to Lady Procula?

No, I suppose it is impossible, she thought, attempting to mask her disappointment. It wouldn't do for her to serve this lovely lady with a doleful expression. *Even if I were to pray, I am to meet Malchus within the hour. There's absolutely no way –*

"Melina, I do hate to ask this of you, but I am afraid I must make a rather inconvenient request: I must ask you to make a trip to the Upper Market."

Melina's heart sprang to her throat. She stared questioningly at Procula, stunned. The Upper Market? Now? Why, it was too perfect to fathom!

"I know the city is overrun with pilgrims and revelers, but I am so terribly worried for Domitia. You have heard she's fallen ill? She is often susceptible to bouts of fever and chills, but our physician in Caesarea often prescribes hot pepper along with a mustard paste, and we heed his suggestions. I have already inquired of the man in charge of Herod's kitchen, and he was terribly sorry to inform me that he didn't have any such ingredients on hand, but he mentioned that you often make trips to the market for him. He explained that you are entirely trustworthy, and I believe him."

Elias – bless his crusty old heart! Melina knew he was now aware of her weekly meetings with

Malchus. She must remember to thank him when she returned to Herod's wing.

Melina lowered her head, for tears stung her eyes and she did not wish for this kindly woman to see them. She was shamed by her lack of faith, for she hadn't even bothered to pray over this small matter, and yet God had made a way. She was also overwhelmed that the Lord had answered a prayer she had failed to ask Him. In His loving watch, care and provision, He had known of her need before she had even spoken of it! And He had met her need, despite the fact that she did not deserve it.

Thank you, Lord, she prayed silently, her heart full. *Please forgive my lack of faith.*

Crossing over to a stately table near an elegant window, Procula seated herself gracefully and began to scribble a hurried list of necessary groceries. She glanced up and smiled, embarrassed. "I suppose I should have asked – can you read, dear one?"

Melina was warmed by the woman's familiar tone. "I can, my lady."

"Excellent! You are a very intelligent girl, Melina." Procula finished her list with a flourish, then rose from her seat and presented it to her newest servant. "I can't begin to tell you how much this means to me. I am terribly concerned for Domitia. Thank you for your willingness to help a servant girl you've never even met."

Melina's eyes clouded with tears. In all her years of service, she had never been thanked for performing a task. Procula's humility was touching.

"It is an honor to serve you and your handmaiden Domitia, my lady," Melina said with a tremulous smile.

Accepting the coins Lady Procula offered her and tucking the list within the hidden pocket sewn in her garment, Melina slipped out the door past Miriam, making haste for the Upper Market.

CHAPTER 26

The crowds were thick and roiling as Melina attempted to navigate her way through the throng of shoppers making last-minute purchases for their Passover celebrations. The sea of people seemed to be alive and moving as one massive, powerful, roiling ocean, the undulating waves both angry and turbulent.

Now she understood the reason for Procula's apology.

Melina had never experienced the city in the midst of a religious festival. Her heart thudded frantically in her chest as she located the booth that would provide the medical remedies she sought. She was astounded at the price the merchant demanded and assumed he was simply taking advantage of the rapidly approaching festival. Prices always skyrocketed before the sacred feasts and holy days.

Understanding how desperately Procula desired the natural remedies, Melina paid the man without a qualm.

Burrowing her way through the deafening crowd, Melina's eyes scanned the sea of humanity, seeking out her friend.

Malchus emerged from the pillared colonnades and raised a fist.

Frightened and unsettled by the roiling crowd, Melina quickly traveled the distance between them and rushed into his arms.

Malchus attempted to hide his surprise as he wrapped his arms gently about her trembling frame. "You're shaking."

"I'm terrified!"

The corners of Malchus' mouth tipped ruefully. "Ah, your first visit to the Upper Market during a festival season."

"I've never seen so many people in my entire life!"

"You haven't missed anything."

With a jolt, Melina realized Malchus' arms still encircled her. Shocked and embarrassed, she pressed her hands against his chest, freeing herself, and took several steps back.

Malchus attempted to hide his disappointment. "I'd like to tell you these suffocating crowds will let up after Passover, but it would be a blatant lie."

Melina stared up at him with wide eyes. "How long will the city be like this?" She had to raise her voice in order to be heard.

Malchus' eyes scanned the overflowing perimeter of the compound as he spoke, tense and on the alert. "Seven weeks, at least. They will remain until Shavuot – the Feast of Weeks – seven weeks after the Passover. Many of these pilgrims have traveled hundreds if not thousands of miles to reach Jerusalem in time for the great feast. It would make little sense for them to turn back, since the men are required to remain within Jerusalem's borders for both the Passover and Pentecost."

Wrapping her arms about her shivering frame, Melina observed the cacophony all about her. The Upper Market appeared to be bursting at the seams, swollen with the raging sea of humanity. The air fairly crackled with tension and suppressed energy.

Attempting to calm her racing heart, Melina glanced up at Malchus. "Perhaps we should wait to meet again until all this blows over seven weeks hence."

"Absolutely not."

Melina was taken aback by the decisiveness of Malchus' tone. "But why not?"

"I cannot stomach the thought."

"The thought of what?"

"Being apart from you for seven weeks."

Her cheeks blooming with color, Melina lowered her gaze to the medicinal contents in the small basket balanced upon one arm.

Closing the distance between them, Malchus brushed her cheek lightly with the back of his knuckles and smiled down at her.

Heart pounding and stomach clenching, Melina took another step back.

Hurt crept into Malchus' eyes. "Why do you distance yourself from me?" he asked softly.

If she were perfectly honest with herself, Melina wasn't entirely sure. Malchus was a kind young man. He claimed to serve her God.

And yet, a quiet voice within urged her to wait. To be still.

But why, when her own heart so desperately longed to be joined to this man? She loved him – perhaps too much. Her love for him grew steadily by the day. Her desire for him plagued her thoughts by day and her dreams by night.

Oh, Lord, why must I hold back?

Sensing her inner struggle, Malchus tweaked her shoulder, allowing his hand to glide easily down her slender arm. "Talk to me, Melina. What can I do to set your mind at ease?"

Melina gazed into the face of the man she loved. The tenderness and desire she saw reflected in his eyes nearly unnerved her. Why was he voicing his feelings now – in the midst of all this chaos and tumult? She wished she could disappear into the raging crowd even while she longed to melt into Malchus' strong arms. She knew he would hold her close and whisper words of love to her. She knew how he felt.

She also knew there would be no turning back from that point.

Oh, Lord, give me direction. Give me peace. Don't let me hurt this man, Lord! I love him too much.

"Melina?"

"Oh, Malchus."

"I love the way you say my name. I always have."

"You are so very dear to me, Malchus."

Cupping her face in one strong hand, Malchus forced her to look into his eyes. "I want to be with you."

"I don't know –"

"I want to marry you, Melina."

Alarmed, Melina stared into his soft brown eyes, her heart racing. "But how?"

"I will find a way. I can make arrangements with Caiaphas."

"Herod will not release me."

"I will find a way."

The determination in his tone both thrilled and frightened her.

Tipping her chin up, Malchus gazed intently into her eyes. "Why do you hesitate?"

Tears moistened Melina's eyes. "The Lord always gives me peace when I remain in His will..."

"And?"

"When we discuss these things, I have no peace."

Malchus looked as if he'd been punched in the gut. Melina wanted to weep.

"But why?"

"Oh, Malchus, I wish I knew."

"How can I change your mind?"

"Only God can do that. I must walk in His will."

"And His will does not include me?"

Closing her eyes, Melina prayed fervently. For one heady moment, the chaos and the noise were silenced. In that instant, Melina was only aware of one thing: her Father's instruction. The answer came to her so clearly that she knew it had to be from the Lord.

"*He has made everything beautiful in its time,*" she murmured, drawing comfort from the Scripture the Lord had spoken to her heart. "The timing isn't right, Malchus. The Lord is asking me to wait." Didn't the wise King Solomon caution young men and women not to awaken or stir up love until the proper time? She would wait on the Lord's direction and guidance, despite her deep inner struggle. She could only pray that, in time, the Lord would allow them to come together.

Malchus visibly relaxed. "Melina, I will wait as long as it takes."

Oh, Lord, don't let it take too long! I can't bear it!

Reaching out, Malchus smoothed her long black hair. "I am prepared to wait for you, Melina." He smiled, and his voice grew hoarse. "But I must admit, I hope it won't be long."

Melina's entire being grew warm. Never in her life had she experienced such raging, contrary emotions. But she knew she was doing right by heeding the voice of the Lord. He knew what was best for her – and for Malchus.

"I must return to the palace."

Her voice was nearly swallowed by the chaos and tumult of the market. Malchus had to stoop to catch her softly spoken words. "We haven't had our lesson."

"I know, and I desperately wish we could study today, Malchus. But I have been designated to serve Lady Procula during her stay here in Jerusalem –"

Malchus' brows rose in surprise. "The wife of Pontius Pilate?"

"She's a very kind woman. It is a pleasure to serve her. But her maid has become very ill, and she is in great need of these medicinal remedies. I am afraid I have tarried far too long already."

Malchus smiled faintly. Melina had always considered the needs of others above her own. He loved her for it, though at times like this the endearing trait proved to be rather inconvenient.

"I want to see you again next week, festival or not."

Melina's cheeks grew warm. "Is it safe? It is said the chaos grows worse and worse by the day."

Feasting upon the sight of her, he drew her closer to him. His eyes were soft. "We'll meet somewhere else. Somewhere quiet, more private. Deserted. There we will avoid the crowds as well as the danger."

Melina knew instinctively that to knowingly place herself in an isolated area with this desirable young man would be far more dangerous than braving the crowds. "Considering our feelings for each other, Malchus, I'm not sure that's a wise idea."

"Why not?" His disappointment was evident.

"If we were to meet in a deserted place, we would be entirely alone."

Malchus' mouth tipped in a teasing grin. "That was rather the point."

Melina looked away from his compelling eyes, her stomach churning. "We must be wise, Malchus. We need accountability."

Malchus' brows rose in surprise. "I swear to you I would never take advantage of you, Melina."

Melina bit her lower lip in consternation. "You wouldn't have to."

Malchus' brows rose at her honest implication. She had rendered him speechless.

Offering a comforting smile, Melina touched his arm. "Do you understand my concern, Malchus?"

"I'd like to think we have more control than that." Even as he spoke the words, he knew better.

"As would I, but what does the Lord instruct us concerning our purity? We are to flee temptation."

"Well, I am rather tempting."

"Stop it." Melina's pale green eyes shone merrily.

"Shall we meet here then and suffer the presence of these ridiculous crowds?"

Melina smiled, her eyes alight. "I suppose we shall."

"I shall await that day with bated breath – despite the jostling crowds and the miserable noise."

Laughing aloud, Melina nodded her agreement. "I shall miss you."

"Not nearly as much as I will miss you." Leaning into her, Malchus kissed her forehead lightly.

Attempting to ignore the pleasant little tingles that skittered down her spine, Melina offered her warmest smile and forced herself to turn on her heel and work her way through the thronging crowds again. She didn't look back. She feared if she did, she would not be able to resist the urge to turn and run back into Malchus' arms.

Yelping in shock, Melina drew back when a solid form collided heavily into her. Two strong hands gripped her forearms, steadying her. She gazed up into cold, dark eyes.

"I do beg your pardon, my lovely lady."

The face that gazed down at her was swarthy and strikingly handsome. The man's jet-black hair paired nicely with smooth olive-toned skin. He carried himself with the air of a prince. But those eyes – she'd never seen such cold eyes.

Unsettled, Melina mumbled a weak apology and hurried away from him as fast as her two feet could carry her. When she chanced a glance over her shoulder, the princely young man remained firmly rooted in place even as hundreds of harried people weaved their way around him. But there he stood – tall, proud, unbending, his arms crossed, and his mouth tipped in a sardonic smile of amusement.

A strange, unpleasant feeling settled in the pit of Melina's stomach. Somehow, she sensed that this unsettling stranger had been watching her far longer than she had suspected.

CHAPTER 27

Julia

"Open this door or I swear I'll break it to the ground!"

Julia awakened with a start, her heart pounding furiously in her chest. A single oil lamp burned feverishly from the kitchen table. Other than that, the house was engulfed in utter darkness.

Barabbas was springing to his feet, uttering angry words she was thankful she could not understand in her half-conscious state.

Someone pounded heavily and relentlessly upon the barred door, continuing to shout angrily.

"I said open this door!"

Wide-eyed and frightened, Julia pulled herself up on two wobbly legs as her husband threw open the front door.

A young man of fifteen or sixteen barged in, the power of his emotions crackling in the air. The boy's fury was equally matched and met head-on by Barabbas.

"Dan! What is the meaning of this?"

"Amraphel. He has lost his mind!"

"You could have fooled me – I would swear it's *you* who has lost his mind!"

"We need to talk."

"It's the middle of the night!"

"We need to talk. Now."

"And who are you to order me about?"

Trembling near the hearth, Julia lowered her gaze. She had no desire to witness a brutal beating, and the boy was asking for one.

The two fierce Zealots stood toe-to-toe, measuring one another, both tense and rigid in their fury.

Then, for the first time, the young man named Dan seemed to notice the trembling young woman at the opposite end of the room, her golden-brown curls cascading over her shoulders, her lovely eyes wide with fright. He looked to Barabbas in question.

"My wife," Barabbas conceded. "Amraphel must not know about her."

Julia exhaled tremulously. At least Barabbas considered this young man worthy of his trust.

Dan nodded respectfully and directed his next statement toward Julia. "I apologize for the intrusion."

Julia nodded dumbly.

"Julia, fetch some water for our guest."

Julia was too frightened to be insulted by Barabbas' curt orders. Fumbling for a wooden cup, she poured a long draught of water from the pitcher and carried it to the table, where Barabbas and Dan had seated themselves before the flickering lamp.

"Light the lamps, Julia. It's black as night in here."

That's because it is *night,* she thought in annoyance as she turned to do his bidding.

"No lamps."

Barabbas glared at the young man who dared to rescind his orders.

"This lone lamp is sufficient," Dan continued calmly. He turned to Barabbas. "Do you wish to alert the entire neighborhood to my arrival?"

"As you undoubtedly already did when you attempted to beat down my door a few minutes ago?"

Dan acknowledged Barabbas' logic with a wry half-smile. "If you didn't sleep like a rock, such measures would not have proven necessary."

Uncomfortable with the prospect of returning to her sleeping pallet in the presence of this stranger, Julia seated herself upon a stool and drew her blanket about her shivering form. She was curious about what this daring teenage boy had to say to her husband.

"Simon has deserted the cause. Eight of our men followed suit tonight."

Barabbas stared at him in disbelief. "You're sure of this?"

"Simon told me he would do it. I failed to believe him."

"But why?"

"He claims Amraphel is a preying wolf dressed in sheepskins – claiming to shepherd the people of Israel even as he devours them one by one."

Simon is a smart man, Julia thought ruefully. Even so, she wondered what might happen to him. Would Amraphel have him hunted down like a dog because he had forsaken the cause? She liked Simon and admired his boldness. Silently, she uttered a prayer for his protection.

"Besides that," Dan continued, leaning forward on the table, "Simon claims he has met another Man whom he believes to be the Messiah. He wants to follow Him. He has forsaken Amraphel."

"Amraphel will murder him."

"My thoughts exactly."

Barabbas exhaled softly, his arms folded thoughtfully as he studied the young man across the table.

"Does Amraphel know?"

"He learned of it this night."

"Simon's participation is crucial for our –" he paused midsentence when he noticed Julia hungrily absorbing every word he said. "His participation is crucial for our...our *venture*, tomorrow night."

Julia's entire body went cold. Was Barabbas to participate in another raid? On the *Passover*? Her entire being recoiled at the thought, at the blatant sacrilege of her husband's actions! Now she understood why he had refused to provide the coin for the purchase of the Passover lamb and the necessities by which to observe the sacred feast. He had no intention of being home for the celebration! He would be off with his Zealot friends wreaking havoc upon some unsuspecting squad of Roman soldiers. Robbing. Looting. Pillaging...

Oh, God, please don't let him kill anyone! I couldn't live with it. I couldn't!

"Amraphel demands we follow through with it – with or without Simon and the rest."

"It's impossible."

"Tell Amraphel that."

"I will!"

"So did the rest of us. It won't do you a bit of good. Amraphel won't budge. He insists the soldiers will be totally unprepared for an attack outside the city walls the night of Passover, as every Jewish man is required to remain within Jerusalem for the entirety of the feast."

"He's right."

"He's right about *that*. But he's wrong to send his men straight into an ambush."

"The Roman swine won't suspect a thing."

"But they will be equipped to combat us. We've lost nine men – all crucial to this mission. How on earth do you expect us to pull this off?"

"Amraphel knows what he's doing. He's been raiding and ambushing since before you were born."

A comforting thought, Julia thought, sickened.

"It's a death trap."

"Amraphel wouldn't order us to our deaths."

"Wouldn't he? Amraphel doesn't care about us, Barabbas. When will you open your eyes to see it? He's *using* us to inflict vengeance upon his enemies and to supply his daily bread!"

"His enemies are also ours, or have you forgotten?"

"And what are we truly accomplishing, Barabbas? The Roman Empire dominates the entire earth. We can't even scratch the surface. We are an annoyance, at the most – a pesky little fly buzzing about the face of the most ferocious beast the world has ever known. We can't crush her, Barabbas. We cannot crush the might of Rome."

"You sound like Simon."

"I'll take that as a compliment. Simon possessed the sense and the courage to walk away."

"He will pay for it. Amraphel will see to it."

"I wouldn't be so sure."

"And why not?"

"Simon plans to place himself beneath the protection of a Man claiming to be the Son of God."

"Anyone could make that claim."

"Can anyone heal the sick? Restore sight to the blind? Cleanse the leper?"

Barabbas studied Dan coldly.

"All of these things He has been reputed to do."

"You believe these groundless rumors? I'm disappointed in you, Dan."

"Then allow me to disappoint you once again. We cannot go through with the ambush tomorrow night."

Barabbas slammed his fist against the table loudly and nearly snarled. "You're a coward."

"A living coward is better than a dead hero, in my opinion."

"Spoken like a true coward."

"Look, Barabbas, there's a fine line between bravery and stupidity. Don't cross it."

Barabbas lurched to his feet, his face mottled with rage. "Don't cross *me*, Dan. Have you so swiftly forgotten your place?"

Unflinching, Dan remained seated. He studied Barabbas with an expression of grim amusement. "Are you prepared to lay down your life at the whim of a rabid leader who cares nothing for the lives of his men?"

Julia gasped. She couldn't help it.

Barabbas glowered menacingly at the young man, who rose slowly from the table and eyed him levelly. "You are frightening my wife."

"Perhaps she ought to know what she can expect."

Julia stared at the two men, shaking deep inside.

"I'll come out of this stronger than before."

"For her sake, I hope you do."

"Leave my house."

Dan allowed his gaze to rest sympathetically upon the beautiful young woman trembling on the bench. He smiled softly.

In that moment, Julia knew she must do everything in her power to convince Barabbas to reconsider. She feared for him. She feared for Dan. She feared for the other men who would blindly follow their crazed leader into an inescapable death trap upon the morrow.

"Look at my wife that way again, and I'll crush your skull."

Dan paused at the door, undaunted by Barabbas' threats. "You have so much to live for, Barabbas. Don't throw it all away."

"Get out!"

"For once in your life, Barabbas, swallow your pride and do the sensible thing. If you go through with this, men are going to die. You will take the fall. Their blood will be upon your hands."

Without another word, Dan slipped out the door and disappeared into the night.

CHAPTER 28

Malchus

The temple was like a living, breathing, roiling sea of frantic human activity.

Gazing out upon the glittering expanse of the temple compound, Malchus grimly observed the chaos from his vantage point at the sheltered portico of the Royal Colonnade – a magnificent Romanized structure overlooking the entire temple compound. The Royal Colonnade served as the hub of all commercial activities related to the temple and its courts. Here, sacrificial animals were purchased while greedy moneychangers exchanged the prohibited image-bearing coins of foreigners for acceptable currency. Though Caiaphas preferred the ancient Chamber of Hewn stone, the hallowed halls of the Royal Colonnade had also become the seat of the Jewish Sanhedrin.

Devout Jews detested the presence of the magnificent structure, considering it terribly sacrilegious to house the center of commercial activity in such close proximity to their sacred temple. In Malchus' opinion, it was simply a bridge built by the late Herod the Great to seal the gap between the political, the commercial, and the religious aspects of Jewish life.

Strolling along a massive walkway graced by breathtaking Corinthian pillars, Malchus watched in amusement as thousands upon thousands of pilgrims poured into the temple compound, each dedicated worshiper careful not to surpass their designated place. The compound was meticulously divided into various segments, and the people fully understood that crossing the boundaries would result in certain death. Temple guards stood vigilantly at each post, their pointed spears dissuading even the rowdiest of revelers from attempting to cross the line.

The first and most inclusive court within the temple compound was known as the Court of the Gentiles. Foreigners were permitted to enter this court and bask in the beauty and majesty of the Jewish Temple. Even so, this court was separated from the courts intended for the Jewish populace by a sturdy stone wall nearly five feet high. The message was clear, for evenly spaced pillars bore a clear warning to any Gentile tempted to pass into the courts intended for God's chosen race: *No foreigner is to go beyond the balustrade and the plaza of the Temple zone. Whoever is caught doing so will have himself to blame for his death which will follow.*

Nothing like a warm welcome, Malchus thought smugly, recalling the threatening messages carved laboriously into the pillars below.

The temple grounds were elevated with each new court, as if emphasizing the importance of those permitted to pass from one court to the next. Immediately after the first court was the Court of Women, elevated eight feet higher than the court designated for lowly Gentiles. Following the Court of Women was the Court of the Israelites, where Jewish men were permitted to worship. This court was elevated an additional ten feet. Beyond that segment rose the prestigious Court of the Priests, an additional three feet in height. And beyond the Court of the Priests towered the temple floor, rising nearly thirty feet above the initial Court of the Gentiles.

Rising majestically from the midst of the elaborate pillared courts was the great temple itself. Boasting of three stunning varieties of marble and crowned with gold, the breathtaking temple housed the most sacred rooms of the entire compound – the Holy Place and the Most Holy Place. Only the priests were permitted to enter the Holy Place, and the Most Holy Place was an entirely different matter.

The Most Holy Place had once housed the sacred Ark of the Covenant, containing Moses' stone tablets bearing the Ten Commandments, Aaron's blossoming rod, and a pot of manna from the Israelites' sojourn in the wilderness. Here, in the Most Holy Place, the high priest would have sprinkled the blood of atonement upon the mercy seat. As the ark was no longer in residence, the priest simply sprinkled the blood into the empty place where the glorified Ark of gold had once presided.

Malchus had always been disturbed by the exclusiveness of the Most Holy Place. An enormous curtain hung from floor to ceiling, jealously guarding the Most Holy Place and the presence of God within. Gracing the front of that imposing curtain were towering cherubim. Though Malchus had never personally seen the cherubim of the curtain, he imagined they must appear somewhat like the cherubim brandishing flaming swords stationed at the entrance of the Tree of Life in the garden of Eden. When Adam and Eve chose to rebel against God, they were banished from His presence in the garden and from the Tree of Life. That divisive curtain within the Most Holy Place stood as a stark and painful reminder that the cherubim still kept vigilant watch. Sinful man was not permitted to enjoy communion with a holy God.

For this reason, the Most Holy Place disturbed and troubled Malchus' spirit. It always had.

Ah, the Most Holy Place, Malchus thought, his expression grim. *Reserved explicitly for worthy men like Caiaphas, our humble and pious high priest.*

There was a time when the title of high priest had meant something. Now it was little more than an office designated to the highest bidder. Caiaphas was simply rich enough and shrewd enough to maintain the esteemed position.

On more than one occasion, Malchus had wondered why God had not struck Caiaphas dead on the Day of Atonement – the one day each year the high priest was permitted to enter the Most Holy Place to make atonement for the sins of the people.

Perhaps the Lord had simply wearied of the priests' hypocrisy and abandoned the temple altogether.

Malchus certainly would not blame Him for it. He was sorely tempted to do the exact same thing.

In fact, he would prefer to be anywhere but here at the temple compound, awaiting the slaying of the Passover lambs.

In the past, he had disregarded the sacrifices, repulsed by the blood and the bleating of frightened animals.

But as the Passover approached this year, Malchus had sensed the need for atonement for the first time since childhood. He could no longer deny the existence of God. The God of His fathers was very real indeed. Not only was He real – He was holy. And Malchus knew he was in need of cleansing.

He would offer a sacrifice, even if it meant being jostled about the Royal Colonnade overflowing with revelers eager to exchange their pagan coins for temple currency.

Beneath the Royal Colonnade, streams of worshipers poured into the temple compound by means of the main entrance, the Huldah Gate. Malchus' head swam as he considered the vast number of devoted worshipers.

It was no surprise the Romans feared revolt during the Jewish festivals and holy days. The people came together like a mighty force, and their numbers were staggering. Their presence was frighteningly intimidating. Rather like the Roman war machine, the religious worshipers of Jerusalem moved about the city as one unified and powerful force.

The sights and sounds and smells that assaulted Malchus' senses were nearly overwhelming. The uproar was deafening, and his insides quaked as the cacophony continued to rise in both volume and intensity.

The badgering cries of merchants hawking their wares intermingled with the bleating of frightened sheep, the laughter and chatter of celebrators, and the endless chanting of the Temple priests as the Levites continued their dramatic recitation of the *Hallel*, accompanied by the mournful dirge of brass instruments, timbrels, lyres, and harps. Their mesmerizing vocals rose in pitch as their feverish recitation continued, pounding out the same steady cadence of Malchus' rapidly beating heart.

"Praise the Lord! Praise, O servants of the Lord, praise the name of the Lord! Blessed be the name of the Lord from this time forth and forevermore! From the rising of the sun to its going down the Lord's name is to be praised. The Lord is high above all nations, His glory above the heavens. Who is like the Lord our God, who dwells on high, who humbles Himself to behold the things that are in the heavens and in the earth?"

From the elevated southwestern corner of the Royal Colonnade, the piercing cry of the shofar rent the air, tearing through the deafening din of a hundred thousand voices, silencing the bleating of two hundred and fifty thousand frightened animals, and halting the eerie chants of the decorated priests.

The shofar's mournful call resounded loud and clear, reverberating off the stone walls and bouncing off the distant hills.

Malchus realized his palms were sweating. His mouth was dry, his heart hammering mercilessly within his chest. That lone dismal cry pierced him to the very core. Melina had unwittingly spoken words that haunted him, and now they floated upon the air along with the shofar's resounding plea…

"If indeed the time has come for the Messiah to be revealed, then the call goes forth to all of us… All are called, but few obey. Few accept the call. Will we?"

The hairs rose on the back of Malchus' neck as the eerily insistent call of the ancient shofar pierced the air yet again, silencing a city of one hundred thousand revelers.

The slaughtering of the Passover lamb had begun.

CHAPTER 29

Julia

"Blessed be Thou, the Eternal, our God, the King of the world, who hast sanctified us by Thy commands, and has ordained that we should eat the Passover." Pronouncing the expected benediction before the commencement of the feast, Isaac beamed upon the two women who shared his table. As he poured the watered wine into cups, he pronounced a special blessing upon it. Then he passed the brimming cups to his wife and the lovely young woman at her side.

This Passover Julia shared with Isaac and Deborah was far simpler than the feast of which she had partaken at her father's fabulous villa the year before. Simon's professional cooks had prepared a feast fit for a king, while the household staff scurried about in frenetic activity, readying the sprawling banquet hall. Julia had lounged upon a plush couch of her own during the feast as servants waited upon her, refilling goblets and removing empty trays. Her entire family had been present – brothers, sisters, in-laws, nieces, and nephews. The house had become a din of humming activity and scarcely-contained energy as children laughed, chattered, and played while their parents engaged in polite conversation and servants rushed about, franticly completing their tasks before the feast commenced.

Here, in Isaac's humble abode, three lone figures reverently partook of the feast, which was spread upon a rickety wooden table. Rather than reclining upon a beautifully upholstered couch, Julia sat upon a hard bench. Last year, she had drunk the very best wine from a goblet of gold. Tonight, she sipped old, watered wine from a wooden cup. There were no servants to attend them, nor to refill empty cups or dispose of empty trays. Rather than jubilant laughter and excited chatter, the room was hushed and still.

Despite these drastic differences, Julia recognized that this feast was no less beautiful, no less sacred, than the extravagant affair in which she had participated the year before.

Oh, how her family must be celebrating the occasion! It pained her to even consider it. What explanation had her father provided her other siblings, who faithfully attended the Passover celebration at his villa year after year? *Your sister married a heathen who refuses to observe the holy days? She is locked away in a miserable little hovel in the Lower City, and we may never see her again?*

Julia winced. She was thankful she was not present to witness her father's explanation regarding her absence.

Tasting the bitter herbs, Julia wrinkled her nose and decided that they aptly represented the bitterness of slavery. The Israelites were bound by the Egyptian pharaoh, a wicked and cruel taskmaster.

She herself was bound by the consequences of her own rebellion.

Last year, Julia had resented the entire Passover celebration. Her mind had been completely clouded with thoughts about Barabbas. She had done all in her power to drown out her father's teaching and stay her mind on the man with whom she had fallen madly in love.

This year, however, she longed to think of anything but Barabbas. Desperately, she attempted to focus on Isaac's meaningful remarks concerning that first Passover thirteen hundred years before, but wayward thoughts sunk eager talons into her troubled mind, causing her attention to wander.

The night before, she had done everything in her power to dissuade Barabbas from his intent. She had begged, pled, and wept – all to no avail.

Barabbas was determined to carry out the ambush Amraphel had assigned. Despite the fact that he had too few men. Despite the fact that the most able and capable men had deserted the cause. Despite the fact that his actions were anything but pleasing to God.

Julia's insides quaked when she considered the gravity of her husband's deeds. She did not wish to know what he was capable of. She was afraid to know.

Forcing a small smile, she folded her hands atop the rickety old table and attempted to focus as Isaac continued to expound upon that very first Passover.

His words were not nearly as eloquent or polished as her father's had been, but the power of the tale resonated deep within her heart.

Oh God, I am like those Israelites – enslaved by my own sin! I followed my heart rather than Your Law, and now I am in this mess! What should I do, Father? What should I do?

Julia realized she had never felt more torn in all her life. For while she sat in the cozy lamplight in the company of dear friends, her husband was out there somewhere...raiding, pillaging, inflicting violence. What if he was injured? What if he never came home? Dan had warned him that he was walking straight into a death trap.

Was he?

Julia had to force herself to partake of the feast, for her stomach was in knots. She feared she might lose the bit of food she had managed to swallow.

Oh, God, what have I done? How could I marry a man like Barabbas? How could I be so deceived? Waves of guilt swept over her, for she felt partially responsible for her husband's wicked deeds. *I should have tried even harder to dissuade him! But what could have I done?* She had lain awake all night long, wondering if she should tell someone about the raid. What if men were killed? What if someone was hurt? Her own silence might result in her husband's demise.

She supposed she could confide in Isaac and Deborah, but what could they do about it? She didn't even know where the skirmish was to occur. Barabbas had remained tight-lipped and silent regarding any and all details. She had considered fleeing to her father's villa in the Upper City, but what if Simon felt honor-bound to alert the authorities? Barabbas and all his men would be crucified.

Could she live with herself knowing she had instigated the death of so many men? Then again, weren't they deserving of death? They were criminals. Even so, she couldn't imagine sentencing her own husband to a slow, torturous death upon a Roman cross.

Oh, Lord God, I don't know what to do! If I speak, then men will die. But if I keep silent, men will very likely also die. And if they were to die tonight, or even weeks from now on a Roman cross in retribution for their deeds, they are not ready to meet You, Father. Oh God, how did I ever get into such a mess? I don't know what to do. Oh God, I don't know what to do!

Julia's cheeks flamed when she realized that Isaac and Deborah had already begun the recitation of the *Hallel!* How long had she been completely lost in thought, oblivious to her surroundings? Embarrassed, Julia clasped her hands in her lap and joined in the recitation, but her voice shook.

"*When Israel went out of Egypt, the house of Jacob from a people of strange language, Judah became His sanctuary, and Israel His dominion. The sea saw it and fled; Jordan turned back. The mountains skipped like rams, the little hills like lambs. What ails you, O sea, that you fled? O Jordan, that you turned back? O mountains, that you skipped like rams? O little hills, like lambs? Tremble, O earth, at the presence of the Lord, at the presence of the God of Jacob who turned the rock into a pool of water, the flint into a fountain of waters..."*

Julia closed her eyes, losing herself in the beauty and power of the Scriptures. Her heart cried out to the Almighty God who parted the Red Sea and stopped the River Jordan, who shook the entire earth in the awesome might of His presence.

"Not unto us, O Lord, not unto us, but to Your name give glory, because of Your mercy, because of Your truth. Why should the Gentiles say, 'So where is their God?' But our God is in heaven; He does whatever He pleases..."

Oh God, Julia's heart cried, *You are God. You are mighty! Set me free this night as You did on Passover a thousand years ago for Your beloved. Set me free, Father. Set me free!*

"Their idols are silver and gold," the three reverently continued in their somber yet joyful recitation. *"The work of men's hands. They have mouths, but they do not speak; eyes they have, but they do not see; they have ears, but they do not hear; noses they have, but they do not smell; they have hands, but they do not handle; feet they have, but they do not walk; nor do they mutter through their throat. Those who make them are like them; so is everyone who trusts in them."*

Lord God, Julia's heart pleaded in silence, *Barabbas is like them. He has a mouth, but refuses to speak Your name; eyes, and yet he cannot see Your marvelous works nor the wonderful plan You have for him; ears, but he covers them with his hands in anger and defiance, refusing to hear You. The hands You have blessed with strength he uses to rob and to steal. His sturdy feet carry him down forbidden paths. Oh Father, turn him away from the path of destruction! Lead Him to the green pastures and the still waters of Your peace and presence, Father!*

"O Israel, trust in the Lord; He is their help and their shield. O house of Aaron, trust in the Lord; He is their help and their shield. You who fear the Lord, trust in the Lord; He is their help and their shield!"

Be still, beloved; trust in Me. I AM your help and your shield.

Julia's heart stirred as tears streamed down her cheeks. She clung to the promises of God, whispering the sacred Scriptures, deriving strength and comfort as she spoke them aloud with her dear friends.

"The Lord has been mindful of us; He will bless us; He will bless the house of Israel; He will bless the house of Aaron. He will bless those who fear the Lord, both small and great..."

O Lord God, I know You are mindful of me. What a wonder it is. I love You, Lord. I love You, Father...

"We will bless the Lord from this time forth and forevermore. Praise the Lord!"

Later that evening, Julia's hands shook as she helped Deborah clear the table and tend to the dishes and serving utensils.

Taking a stack of wooden plates from Julia, Deborah set them aside and reached for Julia's shaking hands. "Alright, child. Speak up. What's troubling you?"

From her peripheral vision, Julia noticed Isaac's head come up as he lounged comfortably before the fire burning in the hearth.

Her eyes filled with tears at Deborah's frank concern. Lowering her gaze, she shook her head, her voice caught in her throat.

"I know you, child. Something weighs heavily upon your heart. What are friends for if not to bear one another's burdens?"

But this is a burden to great to bear, Julia thought, tears coursing down her cheeks. *There is nothing you can do.*

Tenderly, Deborah led Julia by the hand toward the crackling hearth.

Obediently, Julia seated herself next to Isaac. Deborah stood before her, clasping her hands.

"It's Barabbas," Julia said weakly, frightened she might say too much.

"Ah, you are disturbed he has chosen not to observe the feast."

If only it were that simple!

"Is that it?"

Julia nodded, dashing away her tears with an impatient hand. She was so tired of crying! "But it's more than that, Deborah. He has no fear of God at all. I am afraid about what he might do."

Isaac leaned forward on his stool, his eyes intense. "Does he hurt you, Julia?"

Julia shook her head, weeping. "Not in the way you mean. He hasn't physically beaten me, but he breaks my heart every day."

Deborah stroked Julia's soft hair, understanding

glowing upon her staid features. "We must continue to pray for him, Julia. The Lord will do all in His power to gain Barabbas' attention."

"Barabbas will not listen."

Isaac chuckled knowingly. "The Lord has a way of getting our attention, beloved. It may not be pleasant. It may be downright painful. But He has His ways, and He knows how to do it."

"Still, Barabbas must make a choice. And I am afraid. I fear he has hardened his heart for too long."

"I don't know your husband well, Julia," Deborah said quietly. "But when I look into his eyes, I see despair. He is searching for answers, and I imagine he isn't thrilled about his findings. But we must be patient. The Lord will continue to work on his heart. We mustn't lose hope."

Julia lowered her gaze, distraught. "You don't understand, Deborah. He is a thief. He does terrible things."

"Why wouldn't he? He has not accepted the Word of God, so why would he obey it?"

"I fear for him."

Kneeling beside Julia, Deborah draped an arm around her shoulders. "Then we shall pray for him together. Right now."

Rising from his stool, Isaac knelt beside his wife upon sturdy legs. Julia followed suit, kneeling across from him so the three formed a close circle. Draping their arms about each other's shoulders, the three believers bowed their heads and sought the presence of the only One capable of mending their brokenness.

"Oh gracious Father, Lord of the Passover and Healer of human hearts, we beseech Thee," Isaac began in his booming sailor's tone. "Guard the heart and the mind of our dear brother, Barabbas. He is hastening down the path of destruction, but Lord, we pray that You intervene. Throughout Your Word, we see how aptly You gain the attention of Your chosen ones. Father, do so with Barabbas, Your child, this night. Stop him dead in his tracks. On this night of sacrifice, stun Him with the power of Your love. Sacrifice is but proof of love, and obedience swiftly follows. Pour out the power of Your love and with it the knowledge of true sacrifice upon our brother, Barabbas, this night. Bring him to his knees, Father. Whatever it takes, whatever the cost, lead him in the way everlasting..."

CHAPTER 30

Barabbas

It was a treacherous stretch of land, with jagged cliffs rising like crooked sentries and towering into the black depths of an inky night sky.

But, naturally, Amraphel would have known that. Barabbas had no doubt that the man had chosen this particular location for that very purpose.

Below the ridged outcroppings of rocky cliffs and hidden ledges, a small cook fire burned. Here, a lonely contingent of Roman soldiers had set up camp.

The narrow valley encircled by a rugged outcropping of jagged rocks was made for ambush.

Barabbas was stunned that the soldiers had chosen to bed here for the night. But Amraphel had insisted that they would. Somehow, he had known. He had sources the other men knew nothing about.

Barabbas' chest tightened, and his breath came out in short puffs. Warily, he attempted to silence his own sporadic breathing. He had waited like this, poised for attack, awaiting just the right moment to swoop upon an unsuspecting caravan or a band of weary travelers, more times than he cared to recount. He knew what to do. He had spent hours beyond number training his hands for battle, conditioning his body for warfare. He was prepared.

But he had never taken a life. By some miracle, it had never been required of him. Others in the band had not been so fortunate. He knew Amraphel had taken over a dozen lives without remorse since Barabbas had joined the cause.

Instinctively, he knew tonight would be different. This was not a poorly guarded caravan or a lone pair of legionnaires traveling a deserted stretch of road.

This was a contingent of well-trained and highly specialized Roman soldiers, however small.

Amraphel's message had been clear: Kill them. One by one. As many as you possibly can. And flee the moment the tide turns in their favor.

Zealots were notorious for sneaking up on unsuspecting troops, showering them with rocks or flaming arrows, then disappearing into the night the moment the soldiers recovered and regrouped.

It was cowardly, in Barabbas' way of thinking. But how else were they to destroy the morale of the Roman war machine? They would have to bide their time, striking their victims down one by one.

Did the other men recognize how bleak their situation? How dire the consequences? If any of them were captured, they would be crucified. To be swiftly dispatched would be a mercy, but Barabbas knew Roman soldiers possessed not a shred of mercy.

This could very well be his last night on earth.

What would happen to him if he perished? Did he have a soul, as the Word of God stoutly proclaimed? Would he go to hell? Or float unknowingly upon a sea of nothingness for all of eternity?

Breaking out in a cold sweat, Barabbas watched from his hidden perch in a rocky crag as the soldiers bedded down for the night. They were expecting a quiet evening, no doubt, as the rowdies and revelers were tightly sealed within the city walls for the remainder of the Passover celebration.

Several alert guards stationed themselves about the narrow perimeter of the small encampment. Barabbas knew the invisible eyes of his comrades gauged the soldiers' every move, from their hidden positions among the cliffs.

Soon, he would give the signal. Reaching for his bow, he carefully and silently fitted the arrow in place. He touched the sharp point and winced, then turned his attention back to the guard stationed directly beneath him. He would be the first to die.

Palms sweating, Barabbas wondered why his conscience suddenly battled for his attention. He had prepared himself for this raid. He was ready to lay down his life for the cause.

Wasn't he?

***

Isaac, Deborah, and Julia remained kneeling in prayer, even as the fire sputtered in the hearth and the lamplight began to dim. Fervently, they beseeched Almighty God on behalf of their lost brother, Barabbas.

"Father," Isaac pled, his voice steady and strong, "remind our brother of Your goodness. Chase away the hatred and the bitterness that consumes him. Shock him by a glaring and undeniable example of Your unfailing love, dear God. Remind him that there is a way that seems right to man, but ultimately leads to death."

"Speak to him, Father," Deborah interceded, her grip tightening upon Isaac's and Julia's shoulders. "Turn him from his sin and guide him by Your truth. Remind him that sin crouches at his door, Father, and its desire is for him. Show him that he must rule over it, Father. He *must* rule over it."

***

With precision and stealth, Barabbas drew his bow-string. Squinting, he took careful aim.

Why are you angry?

Barabbas paused, his forehead breaking out in another cold sweat.

Why has your countenance fallen?

Barabbas grit his teeth. He had no time to battle his own conscience! A very real battle lay before him now. He hadn't the slightest idea that the greatest battle had already been waged against him. The enemy warred violently within his own mind and heart.

If you do well, will you not be accepted?

Was he insane? Was he hearing voices? Or was his mind playing tricks on him now that his life was on the line?

Sin lies at your door. And its desire is for you, but you should rule over it.

A vivid recollection of one year earlier came rushing back. Barabbas remembered another night, another Passover. He had lain beneath a sheet of glittering stars, thankful to have escaped the chaos of Jerusalem during the festival season.

These very Scriptures had assaulted his mind then, as well.

Was it possible that God was trying to get his attention?

Shaking his head violently, Barabbas cleared his mind of the thought. It was useless. It was futile. God had long since deserted him. Why would He bother reaching out now?

Even in the midst of his own mental argument, Barabbas knew he was not being fair. But he didn't care. He was too involved now. Too lost. Bent on vengeance. Thirsting for the blood of his adversaries.

He knew the Lord's way. God spoke of love and mercy and faithfulness.

No, thank you. Not for me. He had no desire to show love or mercy toward the men who had murdered his family.

An eye for an eye, a tooth for a tooth. Romans destroyed. They in turn deserved to be destroyed.

Perhaps what he was doing wasn't so wrong after all.

Sin lies at your door...

Gritting his teeth, Barabbas drew his bowstring, sweat streaking down his face and trickling down his back.

Its desire is for you...

Barabbas' fingers tensed, taut like the string that would release his deadly arrow upon an unsuspecting human being below.

You must rule over it.

With a savage cry, Barabbas released his arrow, thereby giving a signal to the Zealots hidden within the rocky crags encircling the Roman camp.

In a split instant, a sea of arrows rained down heavily upon the unsuspecting soldiers below. Shouts of alarm and screams of pain rent the air, and Barabbas heard the metallic sound of swords drawn.

The soldiers were readying themselves for battle.

Barabbas fitted another arrow to the bow. Dust billowed about the campsite as the soldiers sprang into action and arrows continued to rain upon the camp. It was then that Barabbas saw a Roman soldier charging up the incline directly toward the hidden crevice in the craggy rock, shield raised, sword outstretched.

Barabbas knew his life was about to end.

***

Rocking gently back and forth on her knees, Julia derived strength from the prayers of her faithful neighbors.

With a pang to her heart, Julia sensed that her husband's life was in jeopardy at that very moment. "Oh, dear God," she wept brokenly, "protect my husband. He is not ready to die, but he is in great danger."

If Deborah or Isaac had questions about Julia's confession, they held their tongues, joining her in her desperate prayer. There would be time for questions later.

"Spare his life, Father, I beseech You. Protect him and shield him. Be his place of refuge. Don't let him pass from this life until he has given his soul to You."

***

Unable to give the distress signal, Barabbas prepared to face the Roman soldier head on, praying desperately to any god that might listen. His men must retreat. The soldiers were too prepared, and the Zealots were outnumbered.

How many lives would be lost because he had refused to defy Amraphel's impossible orders?

Praying for an opening, Barabbas fitted another arrow to his bow. Raising the bow, he awaited the soldier's approach.

How on earth would his arrow meet its mark with that impenetrable Roman shield masking the soldier's body?

Barabbas prepared to release the arrow, knowing it would not meet its mark. Lowering the bow, he withdrew the dagger at his side instead.

What were his chances against this highly trained soldier clad in the best armor and outfitted with the deadliest weapons?

Rocks and boulders began to crash down the sides of the cliff face, and Barabbas knew the Zealots overhead had resorted to phase two of the ambush. More cries of fury and pain rent the air as heavy rocks and boulders crashed upon the legionnaires below.

The night air was thick with dust. Barabbas crouched, readying himself for impact.

The soldier uttered a fierce battle cry of rage as he descended upon Barabbas, his hobnailed boots pounding upon the rocky floor. He was so close that Barabbas could see the hatred glittering in his cruel eyes.

And then something happened.

The flash of a man's tattered robe filled his vision, coming between him and the arced sword of his opponent. Fingers of steel clamped around Barabbas' arm, nearly wrenching it out of joint, and he was hurtled into the side of a limestone wall.

The flash of the sword glistened in the moonlight, then came down with a fierce and mighty blow.

A gasp of pain was followed by a scream of sheer terror.

Sprawled across the cavern floor, Barabbas raised his head in time to see the Roman soldier tip over the side of the cliff face.

Instinctively, Barabbas knew the soldier would not survive the long, hard fall. Had the soldier lost his footing when assaulted by the force that had come between Barabbas and certain death?

Dazed, Barabbas pushed himself up on one arm. Searing pain shot through his shoulder all the way down to his wrist and fingers. But he had to move.

What had come between him and the deadly Roman sword?

Gritting his teeth against the pain, he pushed himself up to a sitting position. For the first time, he noticed a still form sprawled unnaturally near the mouth of his miniature cavern.

Heart pounding, Barabbas held his injured arm with his right hand and rushed toward the still form.

The boy lay upon his back, his eyes hazy and his tunic smeared with blood. He wasn't moving.

Fear unlike anything he had ever experienced coursed through Barabbas' entire being. Dropping to his knees like a heavy sack of grain, Barabbas gathered the limp form into his arms. Shaking violently, he buried his face in the boy's chest and began to sob.

Dan.

CHAPTER 31

Julia

It was almost noon when the door banged open, and Barabbas threw himself into the small house with the force of an angry bull.

An entire day had lapsed since the Passover feast Julia had shared with Isaac and Deborah.

She had been near panic.

Barabbas looked at his wife. It was obvious she had not slept in two days. Kneeling in prayer upon her sleeping pallet, she sprang to her feet and rushed her husband.

"Oh, Barabbas, you're alive! I was so frightened –"

Barabbas grasped her wrist and dragged her toward the open door. "Come with me. Now."

Julia balked, frightened and angry. She hadn't slept in two days. Her hair was a tangled mess, and she still wore the thin robe in which she slept. "I cannot leave the house in this state."

"Stop talking. You need to come. Now!"

Julia froze, the color draining from her face. Her eyes traveled down the front of her husband's tunic, stained with blood. "You're hurt!"

Barabbas' face contorted in grief and rage. "It's not my blood. Come, Julia, now! Or I swear I'll throw you over my shoulder like a sack of grain and carry you out."

Alarmed, Julia balked. Fear coursed through her veins. Something was terribly wrong.

It's not my *blood,* he had said.

Oh, God, what has he done?

Barabbas' eyes shone with pent up fury. "By all the gods of the universe, Julia, if you believe your God has any power at all, then come with me! I need you to pray over him."

Julia began to quake. "Over whom? Why?"

Barabbas gripped her arm and jerked her toward the door. "Let's go. We'll talk on the way."

***

The city was alive and seething with chaotic activity as thousands upon thousands of pilgrims remained within Jerusalem's walls for the Feast of Unleavened Bread, the week following that first Passover night.

Julia had never experienced her native Jerusalem in such a state. In the past, she had remained safely sheltered within the towering marble walls of her father's villa during the great feast.

The tight streets, open-air markets, and elegant bazaars overflowed with people – some of them pilgrims and tourists seeking affordable souvenirs, others devout Jews hoping to obtain what was necessary to celebrate the feast according to the dictates of the religious leaders. Temporary pens housing bleating sheep, goats, and even cattle were scattered all over the narrow streets, where greedy merchants sold them at ridiculous prices. Crates were piled here and there, haphazardly stacked one atop the other, overflowing with cooing sacrificial doves.

The frightened cries of the sacrificial animals filled Julia's entire being with a sense of dread. These poor creatures were to be placed upon an altar, burnt as an offering and reduced to ashes. Could they possibly comprehend their fate?

Her eyes rested upon her husband's broad shoulders as he pushed his way roughly through the crowd ahead of them. He gripped her firmly by the hand and she trailed behind him, frightened and helpless.

Didn't Barabbas understand that, at this point, his fate was no better than that of these poor, doomed animals? He had no excuse, for he knew the Scriptures. Those who hardened their hearts against the Lord were destined to become ashes as well.

For dust you are, and to dust you shall return. Once sin entered the world, all men were destined to die. Whether or not they suffered the second death was entirely up to them.

Had Barabbas no fear of God at all?

Swallowing her tears, Julia struggled to keep up with her husband. His purposeful strides matched the look of steely determination on his handsome face.

Julia yelped when a careless pedestrian plowed

into her shoulder. She wondered if she would have any toes left when this was all over, for she had lost track of how many times they had been stepped on.

She had no idea that the city was capable of housing so many people at once.

Dingy stalls lined the already narrow streets, and merchants shouted loudly to the various passersby, struggling to be heard above the deafening noise of the crowds. Wine, oil, and spices were flying off the wooden shelves despite exorbitant pricing. The merchants were taking full advantage of the festival season. Some merchants had even set up crudely built ovens to sell to the populace, aware of the fact that the ovens were needed for roasting and to prepare meals for the overwhelming number of relatives flooding the homes of Jerusalem.

Potters had also set up booths, displaying their glazed pots and pans and clay dishware and utensils. People flocked to their stalls as well, despite the fact that their merchandise was also blatantly overpriced.

Julia also noticed people exchanging foreign currency for the acceptable Temple shekel. She wondered how much profit the greedy moneychangers were pocketing on a day like this.

Women screamed shrilly at willful children, merchants shouted out their wares, and men called to one another above the noise, drowning out her troubled thoughts. Babies wailed and animals bleated their protests. The air was heavy with smoke from thousands of sacrifices. The smell of roasting meat and exotic spices assaulted Julia's senses.

Perhaps the atmosphere was even more chaotic since today was Friday – Preparation Day. The Sabbath would arrive the following day, and everyone was eager to make their preparations and return home for a day of rest and worship.

As Barabbas dragged her through the suffocating crowds of people, Julia doubted they would return home unscathed.

Despite her great curiosity regarding her whereabouts, she had never been so frightened in all her life. The immense crowds and deafening noise certainly contributed to her fear, but it was the source of the sick feeling curling within the pit of her stomach that frightened her the most.

Where were they going in such a hurry? She had demanded an explanation from Barabbas but received little in response. It had been necessary for him to shout in order to be heard above the crowds. He supplied her with the briefest of explanations, and she doubted he would even be able to hear her own questions above the roaring din. So she remained silent, beseeching the Lord in prayer and steeling herself for the horror that was surely to come.

She knew someone was hurt. How badly? Would he live? What if he died? She knew Barabbas expected her to pray over the injured man.

What did he think she was? A miracle-worker? How on earth did he expect her prayers to reverse the consequences of his own rebellion?

Julia glanced sideways at her husband as they joined the sea of humanity flowing toward the impressive healing pools of Jerusalem. Had Barabbas left his dying friend at the mercy of the healing pools? Did he actually believe the troubled waters possessed any real power?

Julia had heard many stories about the mystical waters, of course. Everyone in Jerusalem knew about the Pool of Bethesda. It was often a dying man's final resort – his last attempt to find healing when all else had failed and physicians had proven unable to help him.

Located below the imposing Antonia Fortress built by Herod the Great, the Pool of Bethesda was an enormous spring-fed pool boasting five elaborate porches just north of the Temple Mount. Clearly visible, the northern temple wall rose like a majestic sheet of gold, glistening in the late afternoon sun. Above the wall, the spectacular Temple of God appeared to float majestically above the city like a gleaming, heavenly beacon.

Julia was rather surprised that Barabbas had brought his friend here rather than taking him to the pagan healing pools east of this one. While the well-known pagan healing sanctuaries were dedicated to the Greek gods of Asklepios and Fortuna, the Pool of Bethesda was rumored to gain its power by an angel of God.

The pagan healing pools would have certainly proven to be far quieter, Julia thought ruefully, for they were located beyond the city walls. Established by the Roman garrison of the Antonia Fortress, the heathen sanctuary was also under the garrison's protection. Though the Jews detested the pagan presence so close to their holy city, the fact that it was constructed outside the city walls rendered its existence permissible.

Julia would have expected Barabbas to seek help from a pagan deity before he dared show his face at a site supposedly consecrated by the God he had forsaken.

Julia's stomach lurched once they entered the area sheltered by impressive colonnades surrounding one of the rectangular pools. She had been totally unprepared for the sights and smells that assaulted her senses.

Scattered about the stone steps were countless sick and infirm, many of them dying. While despondent relatives hovered about a few of the unfortunate, the vast majority of the sick were alone. A few moaned in pain, while others wept. Others coughed violently, while still others shivered uncontrollably, ravaged by fever. Most were dressed in soiled, threadbare garments. Very few possessed even a blanket or mantle to cover them.

Julia drew in a sharp breath when her sandal brushed against a stiff form at her feet. Terrified, she averted her eyes, recognizing that she had stumbled upon the recently deceased. Further sickened, she clenched her fists and struggled against the nausea. According to the Law, she was now rendered ritually unclean. Unknowingly, she had touched a dead body.

How long must she bathe in order to cleanse herself of her impurity? Tears welled in her eyes, more for the still form of the disease-ravaged corpse than for herself.

Healthy men and women – seemingly oblivious to the suffering souls surrounding the pools – had also gathered at the pool to bathe or wash clothing. Children splashed in the tepid water and shouted to one another, while their young mothers chided them, and their fathers laughed and debated with friends.

Julia wondered how the healthy gathered at the Pool of Bethesda could so easily dismiss the apparent suffering of those scattered near the pool or placed in various locations upon the ancient stone steps. Never in her young life had Julia witnessed such abject suffering.

It sickened her.

Ignoring the pleading cries of those at their feet, Barabbas drew Julia toward one corner of the large pool, where layers of stone steps descended into the cloudy water.

Julia's heart swelled with pity when she noticed a very young man lying at the edge of the pool, covered almost reverently with a thick mantle. As Barabbas led her closer to that motionless form, her heart skipped a beat. She recognized the mantle. It belonged to her husband.

This must be the injured Zealot Barabbas had brought her to pray for.

Kneeling respectfully beside the young man, Julia drew back the mantle and recoiled. It was apparent he had suffered a terrible wound, for dried blood covered the front of his garment.

She felt rather than saw her husband beside her, for the depth and ferocity of his emotions was like the presence of a dangerous and malevolent being. The air about them crackled with tension.

Barabbas stared dully at the still form of his friend, the muscles in his jaw clenched. "He's gone," he stated abruptly.

Kneeling at the boy's side, Julia wondered if she would be doubly unclean for touching the garment of yet another dead person. Her insides clenched painfully, and her heart hammered with such force she was certain it would stop.

Despite her dread, she forced herself to look into the face of the deceased.

The face of the young man was white and still, his eyes closed. His features were smooth and relaxed, as if he were simply enjoying an afternoon rest. But it was the soft tip of his mouth that most unsettled Julia. Why would a dying man attempt a gentle smile?

Her heart wrenched violently in her chest as recollection hit her with the force of a battering ram.

She knew this young man. She recognized the gentle tilt of his lips. He had smiled so kindly upon her the night before the raid...the night he had warned Barabbas not to follow through with it.

Men are going to die. You will take the fall. Their blood will be upon your hands. Even now, his final words rang loudly in Julia's ears.

Barabbas had been warned, and yet he had stubbornly refused logic and reason.

And Dan – a boy scarcely past his sixteenth birthday, so vital, so full of restless energy and life – had taken the fall.

Julia turned demanding eyes toward her husband. Dan's blood was indeed upon his hands. Never before had she experienced such powerful feelings of complete and utter loathing.

"What happened to him?"

Standing beside his wife's trembling form as she knelt beside his dead friend, Barabbas' eyes hardened. "He died."

"That," Julia said with a dangerous calm, "is quite evident. How did he die?"

An expression crossed her husband's face that chilled her to the very core. She had never seen a look so savage, so full of deadly vengeance, upon the face of another human being. "They will pay for this. Dan's blood will be avenged."

Julia rose to her feet and met her husband's gaze, unflinching. "Have you failed to notice that the more blood you attempt to *avenge*, the more blood is in need of avenging?"

Barabbas eyed her coldly.

"Where does it end, Barabbas?"

Barabbas gripped her by the arm, his fingers digging into her flesh. "Enough. You're drawing attention."

"Perhaps that's exactly what you need!"

"Shut up, Julia, or by the gods –"

"I am sick of your threats. You are the one who shall have the almighty God to reckon with. Have you no fear at all?"

Barabbas' eyes hardened, and his grip tightened. "Clearly, you do not."

"Oh, I've fear aplenty, Barabbas. I fear for the state

of your soul."

Barabbas stared at his wife, his expression taut. "Perhaps if you'd arrived here at the pool sooner –"

"Don't put this on me, Barabbas. You walked into that death trap with your eyes wide open. I begged you not to do it. I tried to warn you." Tears filled her eyes as she motioned toward the young man at their feet. "*He* tried to warn you!"

"Enough." Barabbas' voice was low, threatening.

Covering her face with her hands, Julia attempted to still her weeping. "Oh, the cost of our sins to the innocent," she whispered bitterly. "What have you done, Barabbas? What have you done?"

Gripping her by the elbow, Barabbas jerked her down to the stone steps. Stiffly, Julia sat beside him, her eyes brimming with tears.

"Nothing more can be done," Barabbas said sharply. "Today," he added menacingly.

"What do you mean by that?"

"You know exactly what I mean."

"And if ten other men are murdered during your next attempt at *vengeance*, then what? Shall you engage in yet another battle and instigate the death of ten more?"

"Lower your voice, woman. Would you wish to have me crucified?"

Straightening, Julia turned and met her husband's gaze. "Perhaps that is what you deserve."

The silence between them was nearly as deafening as the uproar all around them, the tension so thick it suffocated.

The impact of Julia's words was far more detrimental than the slice of a Roman sword. His emotions raw, Barabbas acknowledged the truth of his wife's words, though he hated her for voicing them aloud. *He* deserved to die, not Dan. Barabbas considered the fact that Dan had stepped between him and certain death. Selflessly, he had stepped between Barabbas and the sword of his attacker. Knowingly, willingly, Dan had taken the killing blow meant for him.

But why?

Barabbas recalled the words of his dying friend as he had attempted to relocate him to this healing pool. In a rasping tone, Dan had struggled to assure Barabbas that he was ready to die.

The morning of the raid, Dan had heard a Man speak.

Later that night, Dan had refused to participate in the raid. Yet fearful for the soul of his friend, Barabbas, he had watched from the sidelines.

And he had sacrificed his life to spare Barabbas'.

Barabbas had begged to know why. In his last hours, Dan had struggled to speak, but Barabbas had caught one phrase the dying boy had repeated several times: "You weren't ready."

What had he meant by that?

Barabbas possessed a sneaking suspicion that perhaps he *did* understand: He himself was not ready to die.

But Dan had insisted that he was ready to leave this earth behind.

Why?

Trembling with suppressed rage, Barabbas

glanced sideways at his wife. She sat rigidly beside him, her fists clenched, her face white.

He longed to discuss these things with her, but his anger would not permit it. He suspected she could provide some answers for him.

Answers he did not wish to hear.

CHAPTER 32

Reverently, Julia covered Dan's face with her husband's blood-stained mantle. She couldn't bear to look at him any longer.

How could a boy who had suffered a violent, deadly wound bear the mark of peace and serenity upon his features?

Julia knew absolutely nothing about this boy. Did he have a family? Was his mother worried sick about him, wondering why he hadn't come home? In that moment, Julia determined she would find out. If Dan did have a family, they deserved closure. Though the truth would hurt, surely it would be better than the agony of uncertainty. It pained Julia to imagine an aching mother clinging to a false hope that her son might return day after day, year after year.

Julia hadn't the slightest idea how long she had been sitting in silence beside the corpse of her husband's friend. Barabbas had long since abandoned her, furious that she refused to walk home with him.

She just couldn't stomach the thought of being alone with her husband. And frankly, she realized she was rather afraid of him.

Barabbas had led an ambush, fully aware of the fact that men could die.

Was his deep hatred reserved only for the Romans? Or like Amraphel, was her husband a ruthless man who camouflaged his lust for violence in the name of patriotism? How could she possibly know?

Fleetingly, she wondered if the death of his dear friend would force Barabbas to consider the grave consequences of his bitterness and rage.

She sighed in dismal defeat. She had seen the fire in his eyes, the determined set of his jaw. The venom in his tone had been unmistakable.

Barabbas sought vengeance, not repentance. Dan's death had further fanned the flames of Barabbas' hatred and animosity. Rather than accepting responsibility for his own careless deeds, Barabbas conveniently placed the blame at the feet of the Roman legions.

Overhead, the sun's steady light began to wax and wane. Evening was swiftly approaching.

Julia found it rather odd that the occupants of the pools were clearing out so quickly. Soon, she would be surrounded by the sick, the maimed, and the dying. Why were all the others in such a hurry to return home?

Julia realized she should probably follow suit. She considered traveling the distance to her father's villa but decided against it. If she were to return to the safety of her childhood home, her parents would expect a worthy explanation. And if she told the truth, men's lives would be at stake.

Oh, Lord, I just don't know what to do. I'm so afraid.

Gazing into the gently lapping waters of the mysterious healing pool, it occurred to Julia that she was still ritually unclean. According to the Law, one must bathe after coming into contact with a dead body. But for how long? Was she to be in seclusion for a time? She couldn't remember. The details regarding the ritual were as hazy to her as the murky waters of the so-called healing pool before her.

Oh, God, forgive me, but I don't even remember what to do. Gazing furtively about her, Julia rose upon shaky legs and descended upon the first step of the healing pool. Tepid water lapped against her ankles.

Repulsed, Julia descended more stone steps and waded into the cloudy water. She writhed inwardly at the thought of sharing the murky waters with disease-ravaged people. Were their conditions contagious?

Covering her mouth and nose, Julia submerged herself beneath the tepid water, nearly panicking when the darkness closed over her head. Gasping for air, she came up out of the water, feeling rather like the scandalous Greek depictions of willowy mermaids she had glimpsed as a child.

Standing in the midst of the mystical healing pool, tears mingling with water, Julia covered her face and wept. She felt every bit as filthy as she had before stepping into the pool. Not only did she feel physically dirty and unkempt – she knew the thoughts of her heart were not clean. Her motives and her intents were often self-seeking. Even now, she despised her own husband with a ferocity that both startled and frightened her.

Weeping, she recognized that she was in need of a cleansing that these troubled waters could never provide.

In that moment, the deep, mournful cry of the shofar rent the air.

Julia's insides clenched in horror as recognition dawned: the shofar ushered in the arrival of the Sabbath. Two more successive blasts would soon follow the first.

Oh, Lord, forgive me. I was so absorbed in my fear and my concern that I completely forgot about Your holy day. May I observe it in a manner pleasing to You, despite these dreadful circumstances...

Glancing about her dismal surroundings, Julia vaguely remembered that the Pharisees forbid a person to travel beyond a certain distance on the Sabbath. She had been so distracted on the journey toward Bethesda's healing pools. Had she traveled further than the 2,000 cubits permitted on a Sabbath? And if so, would she be breaking the Law if she attempted to return home?

Oh, Lord, what do I do?

A shiver of dread wracked Julia's spine as the solemn sound of the shofar floated upon the air. It sounded so close...as if she could reach out and touch the priest who blew the ancient horn from his pedestal at the southwestern corner of the Royal Colonnade overlooking the temple compound.

Shivering, Julia wrapped her arms about her

chilled body and waded toward the stone steps that would deliver her from the unwelcome waters of the healing pool. Her thin robe clung to her slender form as she emerged, dripping, from the steps. She blushed, aware of the fact that she had neglected to bring a mantle or even a head covering in her haste to accompany her husband to the pools. She had nothing to cover herself as her drenched robe clung to her slender frame.

Embarrassed, Julia stepped past several invalids stretched out upon the ground, careful not to let her soaked garments drip on them. She found a quiet corner beneath the shelter of a pillared colonnade and huddled against the stone wall, shivering from cold. Drawing her knees to her chin, she wrapped her arms about her small frame. Though the prospect of spending the night in a public bath overflowing with the sick and the maimed frightened her, the prospect of facing her husband was even more disturbing. Perhaps in her sodden and bedraggled state she would simply blend in with the pathetic sea of diseased humanity seeking healing from the troubled waters of the Pool of Bethesda.

Besides, the Sabbath has arrived, Julia remembered, almost thankful that the holy day of rest had sneaked up on her unawares. It was a fitting excuse to avoid returning home to a husband she feared and detested.

Lord God, protect me tonight.

The words of the psalmist David whispered comfort to her heart as she turned on her side and attempted to succumb to her exhaustion:

Whenever I am afraid, I will trust in You... You number my wanderings; put my tears in Your bottle; are they not in Your book? When I cry out to You, then my enemies will turn back; this I know, because God is for me.

"God is for me," Julia whispered, determined to rest in the promises of her Lord. "God is for me."

"God," a gravelly voice spat, startling her from her peaceful reverie. "God has forsaken us."

Sitting up swiftly, Julia's heart hammered rapidly in her chest. She had not noticed the limp old man lying a few feet away from her. He was stretched out on a rotting sleeping mat. A thin blanket riddled with holes was draped carelessly over his form. Despite his violent outburst, he remained eerily still.

The sun was setting swiftly, casting eerie shadows over the still forms of the sick remaining by the pools. The man who had spoken was nearly covered in the gloomy evening shadows. Just as Julia was wondering if she should respond or simply ignore his unwanted intrusion, the man spoke again.

"Thirty-eight years. That's how long I've been waiting for my miracle. Thirty-eight years I've been paralyzed, unable to move so much as a finger."

Fleetingly, Julia wished he were unable to move his lips as well. Would she be forced to endure the tragic regaling of a bitter old man when all she longed to do was lose herself in a state of oblivious slumber?

"Now if God be for us, surely He would have intervened by now," the gravelly voice continued. "But here I am – a shame to my family, a burden to society. My relatives – they brought me here claiming it was an act of mercy. You know what they were doing? Unloading me. Leaving me to beg and scrape for a living. They don't care if I'm healed or if I'm left to rot another thirty-eight years, as long as my troubles don't inconvenience them nor infringe upon their own fragile happiness."

The man's tone was so full of bitterness and loathing that Julia found it rather difficult to muster up any sympathy for him. Especially when he spoke of the Lord in such a callous and disrespectful manner. Still, she shuddered at the prospect of spending one night alone in this place reeking of sickness and death. How might she feel if she had been lying alone, completely paralyzed, at the mercy of the goodwill of others, for nearly forty years?

Oh, Lord, comfort him, for I cannot.

"You're new around here."

Julia nodded, only to realize that he could not turn his head in order to see her nodding in response. He must have noticed her slip past him after emerging from the pool. How had he known she had bedded down several feet behind him? Perhaps his senses were sharper considering the vegetative state of his physical body.

"What ails you?"

"My heart." It was a true enough answer. She had no doubt her heart was every bit as broken as the body of the paralyzed man.

"Ah, the heart, is it? I had a relative with a weak heart. Dropped dead like a rock in the middle of the street."

How encouraging, Julia thought, miffed.

"Might as well resign yourself to fate, girl," the older man continued, his voice grating. "There's no hope for the likes of us. No hope at all."

"*Why are you cast down, O my soul?*" The Scriptures bubbled over Julia's lips before she was even aware she had spoken them. "*And why are you disquieted within me? Hope in God, for I shall yet praise Him for the help of His countenance.*"

"The help of His countenance?" the man spat again. "What help?"

"God has good plans for us – plans to give us a future and a hope."

"I'm an old man. I have no future."

"Perhaps you have no future because you have no faith."

There was a stilted pause. Clearly, the older man had not appreciated her direct speech. "You're a bold one, girl. And religious, too."

Julia bit her lip. Perhaps she had said too much. "I am."

The man remained perfectly still, his threadbare blanket rustling in the soft evening breezes. "Well, if you are forced to endure even half the suffering I've known, you'll get over it."

"If you have no hope at all, why do you remain beside the healing pools?"

"What am I to do? Simply take up my bed and walk?"

Julia's cheeks flamed at her own insensitivity. The paralyzed man could not leave even if he wished to do so! She should have held her tongue. Why was she even arguing with an embittered old man who had long since forsaken his faith?

"Besides," the aging man continued, "even if I wished to wade into the healing pools, I could not. I tried for years. Someone always got into the water before me. I have no one – absolutely no one – to help me into the pool."

Julia sighed, defeated. She hadn't any more encouragement to offer this man.

Lord God, if the rumors are true and it's really You at work, stir the waters for this man. Set him free, Father.

Behold, I will do a new thing...

Julia's heart stirred in response to the gentle impression deep within her spirit. Despite the pain and suffering on all sides, the Lord was at work.

Stir the waters, Lord. Stir them up!

Despite the fact that her cold, wet garments clung to her body in the most unpleasant way, Julia felt warmed from deep within. It was as if she could sense the presence of the Lord burning brightly beside her with the warmth, comfort, and intensity of a roaring fire in the hearth on a chilly night.

She curled up on her side, drawing warmth from the words she had memorized from the scrolls her father had sent for her...

Is this not the fast I have chosen; to loose the bonds of wickedness, to undo heavy burdens, to let the oppressed go free, and that you break every yoke? Is it not to share your bread with the hungry, and that you bring to your house the poor who are cast out; when you see the naked, that you cover him, and not hide yourself from your own flesh?

Then your light shall break forth like the morning, your healing shall spring forth speedily, and your righteousness shall go before you; the glory of the Lord shall be your rear guard. Then you shall call, and the Lord will answer; you shall cry, and He will say, "Here I am." If you take away the yoke from your midst, the pointing of the finger, and speaking wickedness, if you extend your soul to the hungry and satisfy the afflicted soul, then your light shall dawn in the darkness, and your darkness shall be as the noonday. The Lord will guide you continually, and satisfy your soul in drought, and strengthen your bones; you shall be like a watered garden, and like a spring of water, whose waters do not fail...

Fleetingly, Julia glanced at the gently lapping waters of the healing pool. The multitude of suffering and dying people roundabout its perimeter was proof enough that those waters had failed. But the Lord promised that those who walked in His statutes would flourish and thrive like a watered garden, a place in which the healing waters failed not...

Oh Lord, I want to be like that. But how? What had the ancient verses prescribed? Wrinkling her brow, Julia mentally skimmed over the passage. Share your bread with the hungry. Bring to your house the poor and the outcasts. When you see the naked, cover him. Extend your soul to the hungry and satisfy the afflicted soul...

Sitting up once more, Julia's eyes traveled the vast perimeter of the massive structure in which she had taken refuge. So many sick. So many dying. So many poor.

Share your bread with the hungry.

Julia's eyes traveled to the lonely invalid upon his sleeping mat a few feet from her own resting place. When was the last time he had eaten? What about the others scattered about the pool? By choice, she had not eaten that day, and now her stomach churned in painful protest. She colored, realizing that she always had plenty to eat, despite the fact that her circumstances left much to be desired. But what about these people? The hunger she was currently experiencing was not even worthy to be compared with the starvation of the gaunt and sickly forms around her.

Impulsively, she considered traveling the distance to her home in order to gather bread for them. She could not feed them all, but she could certainly meet the needs of some.

But no. Today is the Sabbath. The priests forbid us to travel so far on God's holy day.

Something stirred within her spirit. Did the Scriptures themselves forbid walking on the Sabbath? Were the priests' teachings in line with God's Word? Would the Lord prefer she acknowledge the dictates of man on the Sabbath day, or would He urge her to meet the desperate needs before her eyes?

She did not know.

Lord, I am so ignorant. Teach me how to honor You.

When you see the naked, cover him.

Without her own assent, Julia's eyes rested upon the pathetic form of the paralyzed man. Whoever had left him at the pool had not even bothered to place him beneath the shelter of the pillared colonnades. How often had he shivered beneath a drenching rain or an icy wind? The threadbare blanket thrown carelessly over him had caught in the gentle breeze and nearly fluttered away.

When you see the naked, cover him.

Trembling with apprehension, Julia rose slowly and crept over to the man.

He was still awake. He gazed up at her with glazed eyes, a look akin to fear springing into them.

Without a word, Julia bent and tucked the flimsy blanket beneath him the way a mother might gently tuck in a child before bed.

"The Lord has not forsaken you," she whispered gently. "He loves you still."

Without another word, Julia returned to her sheltered place under the colonnades and curled up on one side.

But she could not sleep for the weeping of a lonely, paralyzed man.

CHAPTER 33

"Julia, Julia!"

Julia's eyelids fluttered slightly, and she moaned. Why did her bones ache? And why this terrible, splitting headache?

"Oh, Julia, for the love of all that is good and just, *please* wake up!"

Julia crinkled her brow, confused. Someone was shaking her and speaking her name. Rather impatiently, too.

It was a man's voice, but it wasn't her husband.

"Julia!"

Painfully, Julia squinted against the bright sunlight pouring over her face. Where was she? Why was her gown stiff and uncomfortable? And had she neglected to lay out her sleeping mat the night before? The ground was harder than stone...

"*Julia!*"

Julia sat up as though she had been struck, the memories rushing back. She was at the Pool of Bethesda. She had remained through the night.

Startled, she realized a handsome man with a

dark complexion and gentle eyes knelt before her. He held her by the shoulders. "Oh, thank God!" he breathed. "What on earth would I have told Melina had you been dead?"

Julia stared at the young man, wide-eyed. "Malchus?"

"So you do remember me."

Grimacing, Julia sat up straighter and rubbed the back of her neck. "Not by choice," she murmured, miffed. She and Malchus had gotten off to a rather rocky start. Melina had been their only common ground at the time.

Oh, *Melina*!

Julia's eyes widened and she gripped Malchus by the shoulder. "How is Melina?" she gasped.

"I'm doing well, thanks for asking. I'm glad you care."

"Malchus!" Julia was desperate for information about her friend and in no mood to deal with his sarcasm.

"She is well. She misses you, although I can't say I understand why."

Julia's brows knit together in frustration, although she recognized the fact that she could no longer treat Melina's friend with disdain. She had given her life to the Lord since their last encounter, and her entire code of conduct had been turned upside down.

Malchus studied her soberly, his eyes sympathetic. "How the mighty have fallen."

Julia glared at him. "What do you mean by that?"

Malchus rocked back on his heels and studied

her intently. His eyes betrayed not the slightest hint of admiration. Perhaps he was even disgusted with her.

She blushed, mortified. What a sight she must be in her bedraggled state with tangled, uncombed hair and dark circles rimming her eyes. She realized she still donned the thin, simple robe in which she often slept, and her cheeks flushed with further humiliation.

"What happened to you? Did your father disinherit you after you fell for that caravan guard?"

"Disinherit me? Heavens, no!"

Malchus tipped a skeptical brow. "No?"

"No! He would never do that."

"Ah, so you simply sleep in the open streets and beg in filthy garments because you enjoy the change in scenery as opposed to your father's magnificent palace?"

Julia's temper boiled. This *servant* had some nerve! Shamed, she realized that her own status no longer rivaled his. Once, she had been the pampered and spoiled daughter of Jerusalem's wealthiest merchant prince. Today, she was the wife of a poverty-stricken outlaw, the scum of society. As a favored attendant of the high priest, Malchus' status now far surpassed her own.

The realization stung. Even more so the knowledge that she had once looked down upon those she considered "beneath her".

Forgive me, Lord! This has been a "rude awakening" in the most literal sense, but I intend to learn from it!

Clearly, Malchus expected a response. He watched her, bemused.

"You are enjoying my humiliation," Julia observed, attempting to curb her impatience.

"Ever so slightly," Malchus confessed with a mischievous smile. Softening, he touched her arm. "In all seriousness, what has happened to you? Melina has never stopped praying for you. You simply fell off the face of the earth, and now here you are. Dressed like a pauper and sleeping beside the Pool of Bethesda."

Julia sighed. "It's a terribly long story."

"Terrible? Or long?"

"Both, I'm afraid."

"It's the Sabbath, and Caiaphas' servants are forbidden to work. I have nothing but time."

"I married Barabbas."

"Ah."

"Don't sound so smug. We all make mistakes."

"I tried to warn you."

"Remind me to kiss your feet."

"I doubt your husband would approve."

"Do you think I care?"

"You're still your same old self, I see."

Malchus' words halted her in the midst of her frustrated banter. Her same old self? Oh, she certainly hoped not! And yet here she was, behaving in the same haughty manner in which she had once conducted herself.

It saddened her to realize that Malchus hadn't detected the slightest change in her.

"Oh, Malchus. Forgive me. I pray to God I am

not the same woman you met a year ago."

Malchus' eyes grew serious. "Has it been that bad?"

"Oh, worse. I've made a terrible mistake. I should have listened to my father."

"And to me, of course."

Julia bit her tongue to silence a snide retort.

"Can you return to your father's villa?"

"Not without breaking my vows."

Malchus' eyes narrowed dangerously. "Does he harm you?"

Julia sighed, "Not physically." Emotionally, he had torn her to shreds.

"But you are unhappy."

Tears welled in Julia's eyes, threatening to spill over her cheeks. She attempted to hold them back. "I've learned so much, Malchus. Melina was right. The Lord doesn't give us commandments simply to control us or to curb our enjoyment. He knows what is best for us, and He truly wishes to save us from pain. I rejected God's way and chose to walk in my own will. Unfortunately, I've had this entire year to pay for my rebellion."

"Why are you here rather than at home with your husband?"

Covering her mouth, Julia attempted to hold back her tears.

"You can talk to me, Julia."

The genuine care in Malchus' tone released the floodgate of her tears. And she told him *everything*. About her husband's anger and bitterness toward Rome. About his decision to join the Zealots. About their life of poverty in the Lower City and her many nights alone. Even about the terrible ambush and the death of her husband's friend, Dan.

"He's right over there," Julia whispered, choking back another sob. "I didn't know what to do, but I couldn't leave him. I don't know what to do with the body."

Malchus touched her shoulder comfortingly, his eyes betraying his concern. "I'll take care of it. There are those designated to remove the deceased, and I know how to notify them. Obviously, we can't just leave them to rot by the pool. And besides that, it's not reassuring to come to Bethesda seeking healing, only to be greeted by a multitude of the dead. The priests have a reputation to uphold, you know."

Julia acknowledged his logic with a weak nod.

"So don't let that worry you anymore. I'll take care of it."

"I can't even tell you how much I appreciate this, Malchus."

"I'm not doing it for you," he said, his eyes betraying his humor. "I'm doing it for the fair Melina. For some reason unbeknownst to me, she likes you."

Julia smiled. "Did you ever find the courage to tell her how you feel?"

"She says we must wait on God's timing."

"In other words, she turned you down."

"Ah, another rancorous taunt."

"I'm sorry, I couldn't resist teasing you."

"If you weren't in such dire straits, I'd beat you at your own game."

"I want to see Melina again. Can you arrange it?"

Malchus studied her seriously. "Julia, you hurt

her terribly when you walked out of her life. How am I to know that you won't do it again?"

His accusation stung, but Julia realized she deserved it. She had done nothing to arrange a meeting with Melina since her marriage. She had used her husband's dominance as an excuse. Perhaps pride had played a partial role in holding her back. She was ashamed of herself and her circumstance. Even now, she cringed when she considered the report Malchus was sure to deliver.

"My husband has been very difficult. He does not like me to leave the house."

"A weak excuse."

"Perhaps. But I know he will be traveling with a caravan after Passover. I can meet her then, when he is away. I cannot promise I will be able to meet often, but I will do everything I can to see her when my husband is away."

Malchus' mouth formed a grim line. Clearly, he was uncertain about making the arrangements. "I'll see what I can do."

"Oh, Malchus, thank you!"

"I didn't say I could definitely make it happen."

"But you will try?"

"I'll try."

"That's all I ask!"

Malchus' mouth tipped teasingly. "At least you're *asking* now. There was a time when you simply made demands."

"I'm afraid you're right."

"Humble, too? What did that man do to you?"

Julia managed a shaky smile. "It wasn't Barabbas.

I've committed my life to God, and He is teaching me to walk in His ways." Remembering the life-giving words that had sprung from her heart the night before, Julia was reassured. Unlike the troubled waters of the Pool of Bethesda, the Scriptures were not vague and mystical. God's commandments were plainly written. This did not make it any easier to obey difficult commands, but she knew the Lord would enable her to do His will.

Scanning her surroundings, Julia realized that the sun was rising steadily in the sky and people were flocking into the colonnaded confines of the pools. Were these Gentiles who did not observe the Sabbath day, or simply people who lived nearby?

Malchus met her gaze and forced a smile. "Shall I walk you home?"

Julia's stomach clenched in fear. She could only imagine her jealous husband's response if this handsome stranger brought her home after a long night of absence! "I appreciate your offer more than you know, but I don't think it would be wise."

Malchus' eyes darkened. "Barabbas?"

"Yes."

"It might be fun to see the look on his face."

"The last look either of us would ever see, I'm afraid."

Malchus sobered. "You're in a terrible place."

"Don't you think I know it?" Sighing, she pressed delicate fingertips against her temples, attempting to shut out the pain.

"I'm sorry."

"Not as sorry as I am."

Gently, Malchus helped her to her feet. She grimaced.

"This terrible headache!"

"Don't tell me he's driven you to drink."

"Of course not!" Julia hissed, looking sharply about to make sure no one had overheard Malchus' ridiculous insinuation.

A crowd had gathered within the colonnades. Julia was astounded by the vast number of people that had spilled in unnoticed. She looked to Malchus, confused. "Where did they all come from?"

Stern-faced, Malchus folded his arms and studied the crowd with grim amusement. Noting the dark tasseled religious garb of both Pharisees and Sadducees, Malchus snorted. "From the pit of hell, if you ask me."

"Hush, they'll hear you."

"They're far too involved in some worthless debate to take note of anything I say."

"Why are they here?"

"I haven't the slightest idea."

Julia covered her ears, intimidated. The volume of the crowd had risen drastically, and the pandemonium was disturbing. "It's like they appeared out of thin air!"

"I wish they'd disappear just as easily."

Wrapping her arms about her slender frame, Julia watched the frenzied crowd nervously. Clearly, they were worked up about something. Throngs of commoners, scribes, priests, Pharisees, and Sadducees clustered tightly about something or someone. "Perhaps we should leave."

"My thoughts exactly."

Someone broke through the ranks of roiling humanity and strode purposefully toward the colonnades. As one, the crowd turned their heads to mark the lone Man's progress.

"Malchus." Weakly, Julia gripped his arm.

Malchus stared down at her, confused. "What is it?"

Julia's heart pounded unrelentingly within her chest as her eyes followed the simple form of a Man dressed in a clean white tunic and a soft blue cloak.

She'd seen this Man before. The night before her wedding. He had called to her, inviting her to follow Him. She'd know Him anywhere, absolutely anywhere.

The tender Shepherd from her dream now walked among them.

One by one, the pieces were falling into place in her mind.

The Lord is my Shepherd, I shall not want...

The Lord. My Shepherd.

She needn't ask His name, for she knew what it would be.

Jesus – the One they called Messiah. The Son of God.

CHAPTER 34

Like a vast living, breathing, human sea, the crowd began to move as one toward the Man who carried Himself with grace, ease, and humble confidence.

Though Deborah had warned her about the simplicity of this Man, Julia was taken aback. There was absolutely nothing spectacular about His appearance. And yet there was something about *Him* that drew her. Her soul was drawn to Him. Her entire being longed for Him. Her spirit yearned for Him.

Who was this Man that so powerfully emanated the peace of God?

Taking her by the arm, Malchus attempted to steer Julia away. "We should leave."

"Malchus, wait. I want to stay."

"Are you crazy?"

"I know Him."

"Who?"

"That Man."

Malchus raised a cynical brow as he examined the vast crowd pressing into every colonnaded corner. "I'm sorry, but you're going to have to be a bit more specific."

Julia looked up at him, her lips parted in surprise. Surely Jesus had stood out to him as well! His presence was far too overwhelming to simply blend in with the crowd!

"We should go." Malchus sounded nervous as people began to press in on them from all sides.

"You go. I'm staying."

Malchus grit his teeth in frustration. "And what shall I tell Melina when her best friend is trampled to death at the Pool of Bethesda?"

"If I'm trampled to death, then throw me in the healing pool and perhaps I'll be resurrected," Julia said blithely. Her spirits soared as she watched the graceful movements of the powerful Miracle-worker.

"Can you swim?" Malchus ground out through clenched teeth. "It would do you little good to be resurrected just to drown moments later. And I'm not jumping in after you."

Julia caught her breath as Jesus walked with ease in their direction. The crowd parted for Him like the Red Sea, and it was an awesome sight to behold.

Then, Jesus did something unexpected. He knelt beside the paralyzed man she had met the night before.

Consumed with curiosity, Julia stood on tiptoe to see over the crowd that had formed like a solid wall between her, Jesus, and the paralyzed man. He was so close, and yet she could scarcely see or hear Him above the crowd!

She saw His lips moving, so she knew He must be speaking.

"Oh, Malchus, can you tell what He's saying?"

"Who?" Malchus sounded annoyed.

"Jesus!"

"Who is Jesus?"

Julia glanced at him sideways. "Don't you know Him?"

Malchus appeared to be mulling it over. "It's a common enough name. Although it does have a familiar ring to it –"

"He is the Man kneeling beside the paralytic. Many claim He is the Son of God. He healed my next-door neighbor's withered legs. Isaac walks about as if he'd never been lame."

Malchus stared at her, the color draining from his face. "That's *Him*?"

"It must be Him! I've seen Him in my dreams."

"You said the same about Barabbas and look how that turned out!"

"Hush! This is different. What is He saying?"

Malchus still appeared rather pale, but he was a good deal taller than Julia and had a far better vantage point. "I think He asked that cripple if he wants to be made well. What is He doing? Taunting him?"

Julia stared at him, openmouthed.

"Well? Some might call it harsh to mock a paralyzed old man."

Julia stared at him in disbelief. "Malchus, He possesses the power to heal."

"Melina says the same."

"He healed my neighbor, Isaac!"

"How can you be sure it's Him?"

"I just know!" Irritated, Julia pushed through the ranks, leaving Malchus standing wide-eyed and openmouthed behind her. She received several choice words and hard shoves, but she didn't care. She just had to get closer to Jesus.

Drawing as close as she dared, Julia craned her neck to see above the tall men standing in front of her.

Jesus still knelt beside the withered man, His eyes brimming with compassion and understanding.

Those eyes! Julia wanted to weep at the sight of them. Never had she seen such love in the eyes of another human being. It was overwhelming. Breathtaking. Compelling. All-encompassing. Surpassing human understanding.

It took her a moment to realize that the paralytic was speaking. He appeared frightened and clearly mortified to be surrounded by a gawking crowd in his wretched state. Julia's heart went out to him.

The paralyzed man was still speaking. His voice shook. She could barely detect his words.

"...I have no man to put me into the pool when the water is stirred up; but while I am coming, another steps down before me..."

Julia was tempted to roll her eyes. He'd regaled her with the same pitiful story last night! Didn't he know who he was talking to? Even so, Julia recalled her prayer of the night before, and her heart leaped into her throat as compassion for the paralyzed man gripped her once more.

Stir the waters for Him, Lord! she reiterated passionately. *Stir them up!*

Jesus' eyes filled with warmth and something akin to joyous anticipation. He touched the man's withered shoulder. "Rise, take up your bed and walk!"

Julia had never heard a voice like His. Like the blast of a mighty trumpet calling the people to action! Like a clap of fearsome thunder or the crashing ocean waves. Full of absolute power and authority, and yet gentle, resounding with humility.

Even so, the impossibility of His command hung heavily in the air, and Julia heard many among the crowd snickering and laughing in shameless derision.

Indignation welled up in Julia at their blatant disrespect, but before she could burst with the intensity of her own emotions, the paralyzed man gave a triumphant shout and sprang from his mat!

"What on earth –"

Julia wheeled around to find Malchus at her elbow. She raised a triumphant brow. "See?"

"He healed him?"

"And you wanted to leave!"

"He *healed* him?" Malchus' dark eyes were like two round saucers, his face completely drained of color.

Julia was giddy with joy and excitement. "I'm surprised you haven't tried to convince me that the whole thing was a setup."

Malchus stared at her, his expression enigmatic. "Julia, I've known of these pools since I was a small child…"

Julia gazed up at him, expectant.

"That man has lain here paralyzed since before I was born. A setup? Impossible. Not even I could argue that."

Awed, Julia gazed upon the man who had lain paralyzed moments earlier. He had scooped up his mat in a hurry and now danced at the feet of Jesus, his expression overflowing with joy as tears spilled down his weathered cheeks. Amazed, Julia realized that this was a miracle no one could dare argue with. Surely everyone present had witnessed this man's paralyzed state, as he had lain shriveled and immobile for nearly forty years.

The crowd rippled with shock and awe. A few fell to their knees in worship. Some shouted and cried out *hallelujah!* Messiah! Savior!

But just as swiftly a dark wave of hostility swept over the entire crowd. Julia was both startled and numbed by it. A powerful force swept over the sea of people like an evil tidal wave, washing away the joy and ecstasy that had reigned moments earlier.

Puzzled and deeply unsettled, Julia looked around. What was happening?

The whispers of the onlookers grew menacing. Julia noticed a wide ring of men dressed in the dark religious garb of the Pharisees and the Sadducees flanking the outer circle of the crowd. They swept their striped prayer shawls over their foreheads and turned to each other, their eyes dark and menacing, their bodies tense and poised to strike. Like dark angels in a sea of unsuspecting human beings, their bitterness touched the crowd of gawkers like a contagious disease.

Whispers began to circulate among the crowd, and Julia strained to catch the murmured words of the people closest to her.

"He has healed a man on the Sabbath…"

"And commanded the man to *carry* his bed!"

"On the Sabbath? An outrage!"

Jostled about by the roiling crowd, Julia looked to Malchus, alarmed. "What is happening? Why are they turning against Him?"

"It would seem the religious leaders are stirring things up again. Their venom spreads swifter than a contagious disease."

"I've never known anything like it. He *healed* a man, Malchus, and yet they're angry!"

"They're envious. The religious leaders are worse than a pack of petty and jealous concubines."

Afraid for Him, Julia's eyes searched the crowd frantically for Jesus. The place where He had stood just moments before was empty. He was nowhere to be seen.

"Malchus, where is He?"

"Gone, just as we should be!"

"But, Malchus –"

"Let's go. Now." Taking her arm in a vise-like grip, Malchus drew Julia through the rough throngs of onlookers. He had no intention of allowing her to escape this time.

As they reached the hem of the crowd, a grim-faced line of Sadducees flanked the perimeter, busily engaged in a hushed discussion. "This is an outrage. He all but commanded that poor man to break the Law…"

With little thought to the consequences, Julia glared up at the Sadducee who had spoken so haughtily. "He *healed* a man," she declared in disgust, "and yet you dare take issue with Him?"

Malchus' face drained of color. "Julia, come."

"Where in the *sacred texts* does it forbid a man to carry his bed on the Sabbath day? How, then, was the man encouraged to break the Law?"

Julia met the Sadducees' stony gaze and looked into the coldest pair of eyes she had ever seen.

"Now, Julia!" Malchus dragged her away, praying neither of them would be stoned.

Once they emerged from the arched mouth of the entrance to the healing pools, Malchus shook her arm in frustration. "Don't ever do that again!"

"Their behavior was petty and childish!"

"Yes, and I haven't the slightest desire to be caught in the middle of one of their tantrums."

"They stirred up the people against Him!"

"Of course, they did. He is a threat to them."

"I detest them!"

"You wouldn't be the first." Calmly, Malchus drew her aside as people poured out of the magnificent structure housing the healing pools. "Listen, the religious leaders are childish, yes, but they're also dangerous. You need to understand that."

Julia's expression sobered.

"Don't cross them. It isn't wise."

"What will they do? *Kill me*?"

Malchus' expression was grim. "They will do whatever is necessary to preserve their reputations and abolish any threat to their power."

Julia's stomach turned. "Jesus is a threat to their power. What if they seek to destroy Him?"

Malchus' mouth formed a taut, grim line. "I'm afraid it has already begun."

CHAPTER 35

It was a long walk home, and Julia was in no hurry. After all, the streets were quieter on the Sabbath Day. The shops and businesses dotting the streets and alleyways were shuttered and closed until the following day. Today, she would not be assaulted by the sharp, badgering cries of merchants and shopkeepers determined to sell their wares.

Julia was not the least bit eager to return home. Malchus had bidden her farewell outside the Pool of Bethesda, and now she traveled alone, savoring the solitude and basking in the glory of the miracle she had just witnessed.

Jesus was the *Messiah*! The Son of God.

No one could convince her otherwise.

It was not merely the mind-numbing and awesome power of the miracle she had encountered that day. There was something about the mysterious Rabbi named Jesus that whispered of Heaven. Despite the confining quarters, the flocks of disease-ravaged humanity, and the pressing crowds, Jesus had carried Himself with a knowing sense of peace and humble confidence. The determination in His step bespoke the urgency of His mission.

Jesus was here for a purpose. He knew what He was about.

With all her heart, Julia longed to know what that was.

Quickening her pace, she determined that she would find out. She would read every single line within the weathered scrolls her father had sent her, scrutinizing them for the slightest hints pertaining to the Messiah. What exactly was His mission? His purpose? She knew the Messiah was all about the salvation of mankind, but how would He go about accomplishing such an impossible and insurmountable task?

What did it truly mean to be saved?

Did His plans include revolt, or were His intentions less political? Would He reign over a powerful and united Israel like His forefather David, ushering in peace and safety for all eternity? Or was there more to it than that?

Deep in her heart, Julia sensed that the Messiah's mission had little do with earthly things.

Today, she had witnessed the impossible. And she had no doubt that Jesus could accomplish anything His Father sent Him to do.

Behold, I will do a new thing...

Clearly, God was at work. He was, in fact, working mighty wonders through His humble servant, Jesus.

Weary and hungry, Julia allowed herself a moment to rest upon a fountain ledge in the midst of a quiet courtyard. She supposed this refuge was designed specifically for pilgrims who traveled to Jerusalem for feast days. Despite the fact that the Feast of Unleavened Bread continued, this small refuge remained deserted. Limestone walls rose on three sides, and several stone benches were scattered about the small, unimpressive fountain.

With a pang to her heart, Julia remembered the beautiful marble fountain gracing her father's magnificent garden courtyard. How she would love to take refuge there now, enjoying the lovely scenery and the tranquility of the morning!

I really should be walking, she thought with a sigh. *Barabbas will be furious if I tarry any longer.* She cringed inwardly as she imagined the reception she would receive from him after staying away all night.

The guilt that had plagued her the night before when she had considered the possibility of walking home on the Sabbath no longer disturbed Julia's conscience. As far as she could remember, there was no written law in the Scriptures that forbade a person to walk any given distance on the Sabbath.

Rather, the same men who forced this unwritten law upon their people also condemned Jesus for *healing* a man on the Sabbath.

Seated upon the bench, her hands clenched in her lap, Julia recalled the fury in the eyes of the Pharisees and Sadducees gathered around Jesus and the paralyzed man. Why were they so threatened by a Man whose very existence was the embodiment of heavenly peace?

Fleetingly, Julia remembered a conversation she had shared with her father, Simon, in his enormous library shortly after he had spoken with Nicodemus. She and her father had argued about the characteristics and traits the Messiah would possess. Coloring slightly, she recognized that her father had been right about that, as well.

Sadly, she wondered how she could have possibly been so blinded to his wisdom at the time.

Simon had also mentioned the religious leaders that night, claiming they relied more heavily upon the traditions of their ancestors than the truth of the Scriptures. They confused the people by enforcing hundreds of "laws" that were nowhere to be found in the Scriptures. And many of the laws they had created actually contradicted the true laws found in the Word of God.

Furrowing her delicate brows, Julia attempted to recall the words of wisdom her father had bestowed upon her unlistening and unwilling ears that night.

"God was so specific, so careful to give us His commandments and preserve them throughout history so that we would know how to live. Those laws are spelled out in black and white, and they are indisputable. And yet, our religious teachers have taken those laws and expounded upon them, tweaking them a little here and a little there, until they are scarcely recognizable... Take the fourth commandment, for example. God is quite clear: we are to keep the Sabbath day holy, refraining from any and all work on that day. The seventh day is to be a day of rest and holy convocation before God.

But look at what the scribes and Pharisees have done with that commandment! They've taken a very simple commandment and rendered it so complicated that the people haven't the faintest idea of how to observe it. The Pharisees say it is not acceptable to lift a stone – however small – on the Sabbath day, for that would be considered work. But if we lift a child in whose hand is a stone, it is acceptable, for we ourselves are not lifting the stone! Do you see how laughable it has become?"

Julia crossed her arms, deep in thought. Her father had made a very good point, though she hadn't comprehended his wisdom at the time.

But today, she had seen firsthand exactly what Simon had spoken about. Recalling the fierce malice in the eyes of the Pharisee with whom she had locked eyes at the Pool of Bethesda, she shuddered. These men claimed to be special men, set apart by God to instruct the people. Instead, they wielded their power over others, controlling them with both fear and intimidation.

And, sadly, we allow the religious leaders to manipulate and control us because we do not know what the Word of God actually says, Julia realized, alarmed. *If we but took the time to study and learn the Scriptures, then we would know exactly what was acceptable and pleasing in the sight of God. Instead, we exhaust ourselves by desperately attempting to live up to the standards of men who have twisted the Word of God to meet their own agenda.*

It was an enlightening and groundbreaking thought! With a sense of purpose and enthusiasm rushing over her entire being, Julia resolved to diligently study the Word of God for herself. Above all else, she wanted to please her Maker. And she wanted to be ready for the salvation the Messiah would bestow upon all who were looking for Him.

After all, if the people neglected to study what the Scriptures had to say about Him, it was very likely that they would completely overlook His coming. With hearts and minds filled with the fanciful teachings of the priests and religious leaders of their day, God's chosen people would fail to recognize a Messiah contrary to the popular teachings of the day.

Julia had absolutely no desire to fall into that category. When the Messiah moved, she intended to be among the first prepared to usher Him into His kingdom.

Rising thoughtfully from the bench, Julia resumed her journey home. Silently thanking the Lord for the tranquility of the Sabbath morning, she pondered the words she had recently committed to memory from the prophet Isaiah...

If you turn away your foot from the Sabbath, from doing your pleasure on My holy day, and call the Sabbath a delight, the holy day of the Lord honorable, and shall honor Him, not doing your own ways, nor finding your own pleasure, nor speaking your own words, then you shall delight yourself in the Lord; and I will cause you to ride on the high hills of the earth, and feed you with the heritage of Jacob, your father. The mouth of the Lord has spoken...

It was quite a promise. Clearly, the Lord would honor those who kept the Sabbath in accordance with His Word. But the only way one could know His will was by knowing His Word. With a smile, Julia anticipated the many lessons awaiting her in the precious scrolls so carefully tucked away at home.

Already, she knew bits and pieces pertaining to the biblical instructions regarding the Sabbath day. It was a day to refrain from ordinary work and to delight in the rest of God. A day to further establish sacred relationships between God and men. A day to gather together with other believers and study the ancient teachings. A day of praise. A day of worship.

With a soft smile, Julia decided that the Sabbath was indeed intended to be a delight! Why had she spent so many years resenting it, groaning when the sun set Friday evening as the Sabbath was ushered in? Rather than recognizing the day of rest and worship as a special gift from God, she had loathed the day, counting the hours until sunset Saturday night. After all, once the sun had set, she could resume her usual activities and carry on as always.

A sobering thought occurred to her as she traveled down a quiet dirt road toward home. How many opportunities had been lost in which she might have savored the joy of the Sabbath day? How many years had she wasted resenting something meant to be a priceless gift?

Sadly, Julia realized that this principle applied to many other areas of her life. The blessed Sabbath day was simply one of many.

Lord God, teach me to walk in Your ways and obey Your laws rather than simply accepting the word of man as divine revelation from You. Only by weighing each teaching against Your holy Word will I know if the teachings of men are true. Help me walk in Your will, Father. Grant me the wisdom to see Your many blessings for what they are. As the great psalmist once prayed, dear God, revive me according to Your Word.

CHAPTER 36

Malchus

Located on the eastern side of the temple structure, Solomon's Porch was an immensely impressive, breathtaking colonnade constructed of enormous pure white stones that glistened in the early afternoon sun, nearly blinding in its sheer radiance and intensity. The magnificent structure rested upon a Herodian retaining wall nearly four hundred cubits high, beckoning the harried citizens of Jerusalem to come forth and rest beneath the delicious shade of the sheltered colonnade. Unlike the inner courts of the prestigious temple compound, Solomon's Porch was accessible for Jews and Gentiles alike. Opening to the court of the Gentiles, curious Gentiles or converts to Judaism could glimpse the stunning temple structure from this inclusive court.

Like the entirety of the massive temple compound, Solomon's Porch was devastatingly beautiful. But Solomon's Porch was also revered by all who found refuge there, for it was the only section still standing after the Babylonians decimated the original temple compound over five hundred years earlier. Amazingly, the Babylonians had spared this elegant cloister with its magnificent rows of double pillars, sophisticated vaults, and fresco-splashed walls and archways.

To stand here in the midst of a great multitude of people, ensconced between layers of towering marble pillars that upheld an ancient structure established by the ridiculously famous King Solomon, Malchus felt a small shiver of awe and anticipation wrack his spine. Even so, he wondered why on earth his feet had carried him here. After dismissing Julia at the Pool of Bethesda with the promise to reconnect with Melina the following week, it was as if an unknown force had gently prodded him forward, prompting his feet to take him to this very location.

A confusing swirl of emotions battled for Malchus' attention as he tentatively leaned back against the cool surface of a shaded marble pillar. Crossing his arms, he tilted his head to one side and feigned disinterest as throngs of people piled beneath the shaded colonnade.

In the midst of a very great crowd stood Jesus. Several other men flanked closely about Him, and fleetingly Malchus wondered if the Man had wisely hired them as bodyguards. They possessed the rough looks and muscled forms of common laborers, and their eyes glistened with the passionate patriotism of the fiercest breed of Galileans. Malchus had heard that Jesus spent a great deal of time in Galilee. Perhaps He'd dredged them up from somewhere around there.

For the umpteenth time, Malchus wondered what on earth he was doing here. Why had he bothered to come? He despised large crowds even more than he disliked the solitary individual. He was far from a social creature. And here, the crowds pressed in so thickly that nervous sweat began to dot his brow.

What if these people instigated revolt? What if the crowd broke into a riotous frenzy? What if escape was necessary?

Intentionally, he had selected this location nearest the outskirts of the sheltered colonnade. He hoped he would be able to make a run for it without getting trampled or stampeded if the measure became necessary.

But aside from his immense discomfort in the presence of so many people, another thought assailed him, twisting his stomach into painful knots.

Malchus had not set foot within the graceful, pillared halls of Solomon's Porch in over a decade. Not since the last time his father had spoken here to a seething mass of angry people.

Days later, his father and mother were dead, their home burned to the ground and collapsed upon their charred forms. Upon that day, after his rescue at this exact temple compound, Malchus had sworn he would never visit the magnificent structure again. Here, his father's words had sealed his very own death sentence. Here, the people had hardened their hearts, stopped their ears, and refused to listen.

Disquieted, Malchus dared a glance at the humble

carpenter dressed in simple robes, surrounded by eager listeners.

Would His fate resemble that of Malchus' own father? How long would the people remain attentive? Already, the religious leaders were plotting against Him. It was only a matter of time before they turned the tide of the people against Him as well.

And this prompted yet another disturbing thought, one that sent his pulse racing and his palms sweating... What if Caiaphas discovered that his favored servant, Malchus, now stood beneath the shade of Solomon's Porch hungrily drinking in the words of this controversial Rabbi? He thought of Mara, and his pulse quickened all the more. She might be here even now, watching him from some unseen advantageous position! And she would be only too eager to report back to Lucius, the devil's advocate, who would in turn report to the devil himself – a devil of a man masquerading in priestly robes.

Truly, what would be the cost of following this new Teacher? It was a disturbing and sobering thought, indeed.

Taking a deep breath, Malchus forced himself to disregard the disconcerting thoughts violently battling for his attention. He was here now. He considered turning and fleeing for his life, but he couldn't decide if such an act would speak of cowardice, stupidity, or wisdom. Regardless, since his feet had carried him here – seemingly against his will – he might as well stick around long enough to hear what this enigmatic Stranger had to say.

Thousands upon thousands of religious teachers, doctors, and lawyers had instructed the crowds within these hallowed halls, but this Jesus was an entirely different breed. *Authority. Humility. Purpose.* These three words pounded a steady cadence within Malchus' mind as he watched the Rabbi teach the people. All three words could have been invented for the sole purpose of describing this Man, along with His words and His teaching.

Amazingly, the multitude gathered about Jesus remained shockingly, eerily silent. They drank in the words of the humble Teacher rather like the parched ground swelling beneath the pounding rain after years of painful, prolonged drought. And the words of Jesus rang out within the marble hall, reaching even those like Malchus who hovered tentatively at the outskirts of the enormous gathering. His voice, strong like the mighty waves of the churning seas, floated pleasantly upon the air, crossing the large distance as easily as a serrated knife slid through softened butter.

Attempting to remain cool and nonchalant, Malchus listened with veiled interest as Jesus continued to speak with gentle confidence and calm authority.

"...the Son can do nothing of Himself, but what He sees the Father do; for whatever He does, the Son also does in like manner. For the Father loves the Son, and shows Him all things that He Himself does; and He will show Him greater works than these, that you may marvel..."

Briefly, Malchus wondered to whom Jesus was referring. Clearly, the Father whom He regarded with such reverence and love was God the Father, Creator God. No observant Jew could argue that matter.

But the Son? Who was the Son? Was this the Messiah of whom Jesus spoke? Would Jesus reveal the identity of the Son of God, the One to whom the title *Messiah* would be assigned?

Perhaps Jesus had revealed the Messiah's identity in his absence. Perhaps he had not arrived soon enough! Malchus had overheard whispered speculation at the Pool of Bethesda. And it was no secret that some even considered Jesus to be the Messiah. But Malchus found it difficult to believe. The Jesus who stood preaching calmly before him was far too *ordinary* to fit the description of *the Messiah, Son of God.*

Though everything within his introverted being argued against it, Malchus turned to the woman at his elbow and asked quietly, "To whom is this Man referring to as the Son of God?"

Only after Malchus had asked the question did he notice the painted face, kohl-rimmed eyes, and bold, provocative clothing the woman wore. He winced, realizing he had just addressed a prostitute. How did she even get in here?

Clearly, the woman did not appreciate the interruption.

"He speaks of Himself," she responded in a practiced, seductive voice, her eyes glued to the humble Teacher.

Malchus recoiled, stunned. "*Himself?*"

"He claims to be the Son of God."

Malchus' stomach clenched. Unless such claims

were true, the Man spoke outright blasphemy! Why, to make Himself the Son of God would place Him on an equal footing with the God of the universe...

The woman's painted lips tipped up in a rueful smile. "You cannot accept it?"

"He is but a Man."

"And what do you suppose the Messiah will be? An elephant? Of course, He is a Man."

Malchus did not appreciate the woman's condescending tone. After all, who was *she* to cast judgment? Look at what she did for a living! He imagined the only reason she defiled Jerusalem with her presence now was in order to take advantage of the thousands of willing clients pouring into Jerusalem to celebrate the Passover. Such festivals had become excuses to partake in all manner of debauchery and licentious behavior!

Malchus raised a skeptical brow. "So you simply accept this great claim as fact?"

"I'm simply *listening*, as *you* should be," the woman hissed, turning her attention back to the simple carpenter.

Clenching his jaw in disgust, Malchus considered alerting the religious leaders about this woman's presence. She didn't belong in the temple! And who was *she* to reprimand *him*?

He colored slightly, considering the fact that the woman was probably right. He should be listening rather than distracting those who had gathered at Solomon's Porch to learn from the Teacher!

Setting his jaw in resignation, Malchus leaned against the pillar once more and attempted to focus on the words of Jesus. White light filtered through the layers of marble pillars, casting a slanted beam of light upon the new Teacher. It appeared as if the heavens themselves blessed Him, smiling down upon Him and bathing His form in a heavenly glow.

"...For as the Father raises the dead and gives life to them, even so the Son gives life to whom He will. For the Father judges no one, but has committed all judgment to the Son, that all should honor the Son just as they honor the Father..."

Honor the Son just as they honor the Father? Malchus shook his head in utter confusion. Was this Man demanding homage, worship? No wonder the chief priests were in a jealous frenzy! While they considered themselves the bridge between God and man, they knew they had no right to demand worship.

But this Man... Did He truly claim to be the holy Son of God?

Narrowing his eyes, Malchus studied the Man's every feature. Even as Jesus easily conversed with the people claiming to be divine, there was not the slightest trace of arrogance in His tone. His eyes were gentle and inviting. His movements were soft and graceful. Though He carried Himself with confidence, he bore not the slightest trace of pride. There was absolutely nothing self-gratifying about this Man!

"...He who does not honor the Son does not honor the Father who sent Him."

The final statement was like a punch in the gut. Malchus' head throbbed as he considered the gravity of such a truth, for this one statement completely invalidated his entire form of religion. After all, he had no issue whatsoever pledging allegiance to the God of the universe, the God of his forefathers. He believed that God existed – there was no doubt in his mind about that.

But now this Jesus claimed that there was another step to the process Malchus had been certain was already complete – a process that he was comfortable with.

Was it true that his respect for Almighty God meant absolutely nothing if he refused to accept this Jesus as the Son of God?

And how on earth was he to be certain that this Jesus was actually who He claimed to be?

Sacred words Malchus had long since forgotten whispered to his heart, weakening his knees and sending his pulse racing... *Then the eyes of the blind shall be opened, and the ears of the deaf shall be unstopped. Then the lame shall leap like a deer, and the tongue of the dumb sing...*

Malchus considered the paralyzed man who had been healed by the Pool of Bethesda. His head throbbed with tension as he recalled that withered old man dancing upon sturdy legs, overjoyed, tears streaming down his weathered cheeks...

For the waters shall burst forth in the wilderness, and streams in the desert. The parched ground shall become a pool, and the thirsty land springs of water...

Uncomfortable, Malchus glanced at the immoral woman still near his elbow. He had shied away the few inches permitted by the pressing crowds, but still she remained, her elegantly sandaled feet firmly rooted in place, her kohl-rimmed eyes wide with wonder and admiration. Tremendously curly black tresses spilled over her shoulders and down her back. Despite the great care she must have invested in her provocative appearance, she seemed completely unaware of herself in that moment. Hungrily, she drank in the words of the Teacher.

Malchus shifted uncomfortably when he noticed her eyes moist with tears. Her features were harsh and careworn, yet she absorbed every word Jesus spoke as a parched desert plant cried out for water.

"Most assuredly, I say to you, he who hears My word and believes in Him who sent Me has everlasting life, and shall not come into judgment, but has passed from death into life…"

Malchus was pulled from his troubled reverie by the calm instruction of Jesus.

Such a claim! *Everlasting life.* Caiaphas and those of his sect rejected this teaching of everlasting life. Malchus often wondered why they thought anyone would bother with religion if one's decisions had no lasting impact on their eternal state.

He shifted, further discomfited. The high priest would certainly not condone this teaching! Nor would he tolerate others who accepted it as fact…

"…the hour is coming, and now is, when the dead will hear the voice of the Son of God; and those who hear will live. For as the Father has life in Himself, so He has granted the Son to have life in Himself, and has given Him authority to execute judgment also, because He is the Son of Man."

At this, a murmur of confusion rippled through the crowd. Clearly, Malchus was not the only one among them who hesitated to believe everything this Man proclaimed.

"Do not marvel at this," Jesus said softly, His gentle features washed in an almost ethereal glow. "The hour is coming in which all who are in the graves will hear His voice and come forth – those who have done good, to the resurrection of life, and those who have done evil, to the resurrection of condemnation."

Malchus' spine tingled with unwelcome shivers of dread. The idea of eternal condemnation was not a particularly comforting one. And yet, Jesus had already explained that one must believe in Him in order to obtain everlasting life...

Conflicted, Malchus shook his head to clear the confusion.

"I can of Myself do nothing. As I hear, I judge; and My judgment is righteous, because I do not seek My own will but the will of the Father who sent Me."

The crowd was growing restless, and Malchus knew it wasn't a good sign. Even so, Jesus continued to speak, completely undaunted. He spoke about the prophet John – Malchus assumed He must be referring to the one called John the Baptizer, the one rumored to have baptized this Man in the River Jordan. In a calm and organized manner, Jesus explained how John had been sent to testify about Him, reminding the people that they had been receptive to John's teaching at the time.

"But I have a greater witness than John's," Jesus continued, His argument terribly practical, "for the works which the Father has given Me to finish – the very works that I do – bear witness of Me, that the Father has sent Me..."

Again, Malchus was reminded of the paralyzed man, dancing at the Pool of Bethesda like an exuberant schoolboy.

"...And the Father Himself, who sent Me, has testified of Me. You have neither heard His voice at any time, nor seen His form. But you do not have His word abiding in You, because whom He sent, Him you do not believe. You search the Scriptures, for in them you think you have eternal life; and these are they which testify of Me..."

Malchus stared at the Man in disbelief. It was simply too much to fathom. If this Man were truly who He claimed to be, He would have descended from the heavens, from the Throne Room of God Himself! Those eyes – so gentle and inviting – had possibly observed the wonders of heaven. Had He once conversed freely with the God of the universe, the Creator of all things?

Overwhelmed, Malchus attempted to organize the facts Jesus had presented. Jesus claimed that the Jews tore the Scriptures apart searching for clues about the Messiah, but to no avail. They twisted the Scriptures to fit their own expectations, completely missing the fact that the answer buried within those ancient texts now stood before them this very day! For Jesus claimed that the Scriptures pointed to *Him*!

Had anyone else made such a preposterous claim, Malchus would have laughed in their face! But there was something about this Man that gave him pause.

But there is absolutely nothing spectacular about him, Malchus argued inwardly. *Nothing whatsoever! How could He possibly be the Promised One, the One for whom we have waited for thousands of years?*

He has no form of comeliness; and when we see Him, there is no beauty that we should desire Him...

"*You search the Scriptures, for in them you think you have eternal life; and these are they which testify of Me...*" Jesus had said.

Malchus' entire body felt unpleasantly warm. Sweat dotted his brow. Were these the Scriptures of the Old Testament that Jesus referenced? Were they, in fact, pointing to Him?

Even as his heart responded to the teachings of this Man, rebellious thoughts rose unbidden within the dark recesses of Malchus' mind. It was as if an unsuspecting force had crept up on him, whispering reason to doubt.

His defenses rising, Malchus decided that some people – simple-minded and desperate individuals rather like the prostitute at his elbow – might be willing to simply accept the outlandish claims of a complete stranger after witnessing one miracle. But he himself preferred a bit more evidence. Proof. After all, anyone could state such claims.

Couldn't they?

Jesus spoke again, His words rocking Malchus to the very core. "But you are not willing to come to Me that you may have life."

That you may have *life*.

You are not willing.

Pierced to the heart, Malchus turned on his heel, ready to walk away. For he recognized the cold, hard reality and the simple truth of the situation: Deep in his heart of hearts, he did not doubt the spectacular claims of a simple carpenter. He had witnessed an act of God that very morning, and he knew only a fool would argue the miracle he had seen.

But what unsettled Malchus the most was the fact that trouble, danger, and absolute chaos seemed to follow this Man named Jesus wherever He went. Even now, powerful men highly trained in subterfuge and the art of killing plotted His certain demise.

Would the same fate await those who believed in His message and followed His teachings?

The one thing that mattered most to Malchus – more than anything else in the world – was *peace*. To pledge his allegiance to this extremely controversial new Teacher would surely rip his aspirations of peace apart, tearing them to shreds.

Several paces removed from the crowd, Malchus dared a glance over his shoulder.

Jesus' eyes were upon him, filled with pain and an overwhelming sadness that pierced Malchus to the very heart and twisted his soul in knots. Never had he seen such compassion and sorrow in the eyes of another person.

Heart racing, he picked up his pace, distancing himself from Solomon's Porch and the Man who spoke with such conviction beneath the ancient, pillared colonnade.

Unbeknownst to Malchus in his distracted state, a swarthy-skinned young man with dark eyes and striking features watched him go, a sardonic grin teasing his lips as he leaned easily against a marble pillar, far removed from the Teacher and the pressing crowd.

CHAPTER 37

Julia

The house was eerily silent when Julia pushed the splintered front door open. It creaked painfully upon ancient hinges, shattering the silence that had reigned moments earlier.

For one brief moment, Julia wondered if Barabbas had left her. Fear mingled with hope in the most disconcerting way. If Barabbas had abandoned her, she would be free to return to her father's villa!

Just as quickly, remorse followed. She knew that marriage was a sacred and binding oath. Despite the fact that her marriage was in shambles, she had made a vow before God. She must keep it to the best of her ability.

Shutting the door behind her, Julia gasped when a steely hand clamped down on her arm, pulling her roughly toward the hearth.

"Barabbas! What on earth –"

"Where have you been?"

Julia's hand flew to her mouth as her heart sank. She could smell the alcohol on her husband's breath.

"You've been drinking."

"As if that's any of your concern!" Angrily, Barabbas kicked an empty flask under the table. "I'll ask you again – where have you been?"

Frightened, Julia gazed into rabid eyes. Her husband was far from sober. How long had he been drinking? He exercised little restraint when he was sober. She had no desire to witness a fit of rage in his current condition.

"Answer me!"

Attempting to still her own violent trembling, Julia held her husband's gaze and prayed silently, beseeching God for wisdom. "To be completely honest," Julia said quietly, "I was afraid to come home."

"That's ridiculous!"

"Is it?" Julia met his gaze evenly, her unspoken challenge urging him to examine his own behavior.

Releasing her arm, Barabbas crumpled and dropped to the bench, defeated. Covering his face with his strong hands, he sat very still.

Gauging her distance to the door, Julia offered another silent prayer for guidance. *If I am in danger, Lord, show me. And if so, help me escape unharmed. Keep him calm, Lord. Help us. Please.*

Julia stared at her husband for what seemed like an eternity. Finally, Barabbas spoke. But his voice was so muffled she could scarcely discern the words.

"I thought you left me."

Compassion washed over Julia, unbidden. She did not want to feel compassionate toward this man. She did not want to feel anything at all. He was selfish. Foolish. Vindictive.

With a quiet sigh, Julia folded her hands before her and offered a small smile. "And I was just thinking that you had left me."

At this, Barabbas raised his head. "Why?"

"The house seemed empty and quiet when I arrived."

"I should have left. You would be better off without me."

Julia wished to voice her hearty agreement but held her tongue instead. Was this the first time Barabbas had ever voiced remorse?

"Well?" Barabbas slurred. He remained slumped and defeated upon the bench. "Would you not?"

Julia offered a pacifying smile. "Perhaps," she conceded, careful to keep her tone light. "But I'm sure there have been moments when you have felt the same about me."

"Every day." Again, Barabbas buried his face in his hands.

Attempting to curb her annoyance, Julia offered another desperate prayer. She wearied of Barabbas' endless verbal barbs. Quietly, she seated herself upon the bench beside her husband.

They remained seated silently for what seemed like a very long time – Barabbas lost in thought, Julia absorbed in prayer.

Eventually, Julia felt a gentle whisper in her spirit. It was time to speak.

"Barabbas, what happened that night?"

Barabbas remained very still.

"What happened to Dan?"

Julia was completely startled when a sob caught in her husband's throat. Covering his face with his hands, he attempted to still his own desperate weeping.

"Barabbas?"

"He took the blow for me," Barabbas managed, trembling in rage. "I was supposed to die that night."

Julia's blood ran cold. "What do you mean?"

Throwing himself off the bench, Barabbas rose and paced about like a caged animal.

"Barabbas?"

"In the past, we've pounced on caravans or raided remote flocks of sheep and goats. At first, we only targeted those who pledged allegiance to Rome. And always for a purpose. We needed sustenance."

Julia fought the urge to lift a skeptical brow. After all, there were many other ways to amass food and provisions. For heaven's sake, hadn't the men lounging about the hills ever considered getting a job and working for their own bread?

"The raids grew more frequent. Soon we were robbing our own people without even recognizing what we were doing. And now..." Barabbas' voice trailed off and he paused his endless pacing long enough to gaze bleakly toward his wife.

"And now?" Julia prompted softly.

"Amraphel has ordered violent ambushes. He wants to extract vengeance upon the Romans, uprooting them one by one. But we aren't equipped. Nor are we prepared. More of us will die."

Chilled to the core, Julia clasped her hands to

still their violent trembling. "Barabbas, you must leave them."

"I cannot!"

"Simon did."

Barabbas ran a nervous hand along the back of his neck. "And Simon will pay dearly for his error. I guarantee it."

Julia rose to her feet, frustration coursing through her. "But what if he doesn't? You must walk away while there is still time!"

"I can't!"

"And why can't you?"

"The blood of my family must be avenged, Julia!"

"And this is how you intend to do it? Vengeance belongs to the Lord, Barabbas."

"The Lord will do nothing!"

"That is not true."

"He has done nothing until now! When exactly do you expect Him to act?"

Julia went to her husband, tears streaming down her cheeks. "God has the power to redeem, Barabbas. He can redeem this situation. He can grant you a life worth living —"

"And why would He do that? He did not spare my family. What of their lives? What of their blood?"

Touching his arm, Julia gazed searchingly into her husband's fiery eyes. "What happened to them?" Not once had he opened up to her about this matter. Perhaps now, in his less than sober condition, he would speak more freely.

Barabbas stared down at her with alarming fury. "My father and older brothers were revolutionaries.

Father was zealous for the freedom of our people. But he and my brothers were crucified. One of my brothers was only thirteen years old, and yet he was crucified as well. The Romans sought to make an example of them."

Julia had never glimpsed such raw pain and suffering in the eyes of a man. Even as her own anger threatened to bubble over at her husband's stubbornness, her heart went out to him.

"Oh, Barabbas, if only you would allow the Lord to comfort you –"

"Why should I allow the One who wrenched my family away from me to then administer comfort?" His tone was fierce, challenging.

"He did not take your family away from you."

"He did not stop the Romans from murdering them. My mother was cut down like a common criminal as she scrambled after them, pleading for the lives of her sons."

"And yet you were spared?"

Barabbas stared at her, suspicion evident in his eyes. "I was too young to be considered a threat."

"Have you ever considered the fact that perhaps God spared your life because He has a plan for you?"

"To take my life would have been a mercy! Sparing it was an immeasurable cruelty."

"Oh, Barabbas –"

"The Romans must be vanquished. They have caused nothing but pain and suffering to our people."

"But the Lord will set it to rights in His own perfect timing. We must trust that."

"Spoken like a weak-willed child who has never experienced a day of suffering in her life."

Closing her eyes against the pain, Julia turned away.

Barabbas lowered his voice. "I'm sorry." His voice was flat, emotionless. "But you cannot understand."

"I have tried."

"But you never will. You have never experienced the pain of losing your entire family in one swift blow. You have never had to witness your beloved father and brothers suffer excruciating deaths upon a Roman cross. You were not at the base of the cross when their legs were broken, crushed by the Romans in cold blood. You were not forced to endure the unimaginable – watching your loved ones draw their final, agonizing breath."

Sickened by what she was hearing, Julia turned to her husband, her face pale. "I will never know, Barabbas," she whispered, her voice nearly inaudible in her own ears. "But one thing I do know: I do not wish that same fate upon my husband. And that is the path you are traveling upon at an alarming pace, Barabbas."

Barabbas tipped his mouth slightly, mocking her. "Only yesterday you sentenced me to my own cross without an ounce of remorse."

Julia despised the way he chronicled every word she ever said, only to throw it back in her face at an opportune time. "I should not have said that."

"But you did."

"And I regret that now. Barabbas, please. Choose a different path."

"What of my family? What of Dan?"

"They are in the hands of God."

"That's hardly comforting!"

"Others have placed their trust in Him, Barabbas, even if you have not. The Lord promises He will never leave us nor forsake us – not even in death. You know the Scriptures, which indicates that your parents knew them as well, for someone had to teach you."

"My mother trusted God. Her faith defied all reason. She attempted to win my father to her side, but clearly, she failed despite her efforts."

Julia's stomach turned. *Lord God, do not let their story become ours as well! Please, dear God, intervene!*

"As you can see, her faith did little to prevent her gruesome death."

"If she trusted the Lord, then she is secure and safe within His everlasting arms, Barabbas."

"And my father? My brothers? What of their poor, impenitent souls?"

"If they were crucified, there was time enough for them to repent, Barabbas. Perhaps the Lord knew all along what it would take in order for them to recognize their need for Him."

Barabbas turned away, the muscles in his jaw working angrily.

"Sometimes we fail to recognize God's greatest mercies. Those who die in the Lord will one day live forever. Don't you long to see them again?"

"Of course, I do!"

"Then why travel recklessly down a path that

guarantees you never will?"

Barabbas' only response was to eye her coldly.

"The wages of sin lead to eternal death, Barabbas. Please, I beg you, choose *life*! Choose the God who *loves* you! He wants to amaze you. He wants to do good things for you! He wants to transform your entire life, Barabbas."

"An excellent speech, by the way."

Tears coursed down Julia's cheeks. "It is not a speech, Barabbas. It's the *truth*! Why can't you see it?"

Crossing over to the window, Barabbas gazed out upon the empty central courtyard. A lone sparrow perched upon the well, chirping dismally.

Turning to face Julia, Barabbas' eyes softened in confusion. "The only thing that brings me comfort is knowing that Dan had peace when he died."

Julia recalled the expression on the dead man's face at the Pool of Bethesda. It had greatly puzzled her.

"What do you mean?"

"Dan heard a Man speak the day of the ambush. That is why he refused to participate. He believed this Man to be the Messiah, the Son of God. He withdrew his allegiance to Amraphel and pledged his life to this Man."

Julia's heart sprang into her throat, for she knew instinctively of whom Dan had spoken. "This Man," she managed, struggling to keep her tone even. "What was His name?"

Barabbas' eyes narrowed in suspicion. "What does that matter?"

"I would like to know."

"Dan was misguided, Julia. But at least he died

in peace."

"Did you not see the peace upon his face, Barabbas? He was not misguided."

"The Man of whom Dan spoke is not a revolutionary, Julia. Though He speaks endlessly about a *kingdom*, He refuses to take up arms. He never will."

Julia studied her husband, her heart hammering rapidly within her chest. "Perhaps," she dared to venture, her expression full of hope, "this battle is to be waged within the hearts of men, Barabbas."

"Spoken like a naïve child."

"What if the Kingdom of God begins in the individual hearts of men and women?"

"A poetic idea. But entirely unrealistic."

"The Scriptures point to a Messiah who will save the people from their *sin*. Though enslaved by Rome, we are even more hopelessly enslaved by our sins."

"Have you ever considered becoming a thespian or a poet?"

"You are not listening."

"Oh, I'm listening. Perhaps you should listen to yourself. You sound ridiculous."

"And is that how Dan sounded to you before he died from a wound intended for *you*? Did you laugh in his face and call him ridiculous?"

Barabbas' eyes narrowed dangerously. "You know I did not. I am thankful he found peace in the midst of his delusions."

"What Dan had was real, Barabbas. He found peace and fulfillment in Jesus – something he would never find seeking vengeance beneath the watchful eyes of Amraphel. Dan traded allegiance to a cruel taskmaster for the love of a Savior."

"How do you know about Jesus?"

"He healed our neighbor, Isaac. And today I witnessed Him perform a miracle at the Pool of Bethesda."

"I don't want you getting tangled up in this new sect."

Julia clenched her fists and silently begged God to still her wayward tongue. *May I speak truth to him, Lord...*

"I believe Jesus is the Messiah."

"You know nothing about what the Messiah entails. You haven't the wisdom, knowledge, or discernment to make such a judgment call."

"I know what the Scriptures clearly say. Is that not proof enough, or will you take issue with the holy texts as well?"

Barabbas stared at Julia, stunned. Even while her words gripped his heart, he forced himself to close his ears to the truth of them. After all, one could not serve two masters. And he needed Amraphel and his men to satiate his thirst for vengeance.

He possessed no inclination to walk in love. His blood cried out for vindication.

"Dan's last words to you, Barabbas." Julia spoke softly, but with great purpose. "What were they?"

"Why does it matter?"

"It mattered a great deal to Dan."

Barabbas' jaw twitched, and he remained silent for what seemed like an eternity. Finally, he met Julia's eyes. The fire seemed to have gone out of him. His hands hung limply by his sides, and he lowered his eyes in defeat.

"His last words," Julia prodded quietly, patiently. "What were they?"

When Barabbas lifted his head, tears swam in his eyes despite his flinty determination to hold them back.

"He invited me to surrender to the Commander of the armies of heaven and to join the battle for lost souls. He smiled at me. *I'm ready*, he said. Just like that. And then, when we returned to see him by the pool, he was already gone."

Tears sprang to Julia's eyes. "And will you do it?"

"Do what?"

"Surrender to the God of Heaven, the Commander of the heavenly hosts."

Curving his mouth derisively, Barabbas met her gaze. "If God Himself were to look me in the face and act on my behalf, proving His power and demonstrating His love for me, I might possibly consider it. But until that day comes – and I guarantee you, dear wife, it *never will* – I will fight my own battles, wage my own war, take my own plunder, and lead my own life."

"Barabbas, you speak of God with such bitterness, distrust. As if He alone is responsible for your misfortune. But God is not like that." Julia wasn't entirely sure where the words were coming from, but it was as if they bubbled up from the deepest depths of her soul. "We live in a fallen world. In the meantime, God is orchestrating events to bring about its redemption. But there is another force on this earth, Barabbas. An evil one."

Barabbas studied her drolly, interested but attempting not to show it.

"The devil prowls about like a roaring lion. It is he, not the Lord, who is responsible for the chaos and the tragedy and the pain in this world. And because God refuses to *force* men to choose Him, the Lord grants us the ability to choose which master we will serve. This is why evil abounds – there are men who refuse the Lord's goodness. Instead, they serve their own fleshly passions, bound to a wicked master."

"Like Amraphel?" Barabbas smirked.

"I spoke of the devil," Julia said with a wry smile. "But, yes, I can certainly see the correlation."

Barabbas shook his head in disgust.

"One day, the Lord will intervene, destroy the devil and his wicked works, and redeem mankind. But until that day, we must trust that He is working all of this for good to those who truly love Him. All the pain we have endured, all the tragedy – God can take all of it and transform it into something unimaginably glorious, Barabbas! And one day He will wipe every tear from our eyes. We will dwell in perfection with Him in a sinless universe, bathed in the glory of God and secure in the law of love. That day will come, Barabbas. Men will be judged. And those who refuse the Lord's way will not be permitted to enter paradise. After all, Heaven would not be Heaven if violent, wicked men were granted entrance. If that were the case, Heaven would be no different than this mess we're in now."

Barabbas studied her intently, the muscles in his jaw working in frustration.

"If you wish to find a fitting target for your rage, Barabbas, then look no further than the enemy of your soul, the devil. He is a cruel adversary, and terribly cunning. He has earned his title, the great deceiver. He is the one wreaking havoc on this earth while shrouding himself in mystery and lurking in the shadows. You are only hurting yourself by refusing the God who loves you."

"You speak with such conviction. It is amusing."

"Remember Dan, Barabbas. He protected you, shielding you with his own body. He came between you and the wicked one. God is like that, Barabbas. He stands between us and the wicked one. He is our shield, our Defender."

I am your shield, your exceedingly great reward... the verse whispered to Barabbas' heart, unbidden. The verse had once meant a great deal to him. Annoyed, he paced like a restless animal.

He did not wish to contemplate the depths of the Scriptures right now.

"God is *for you*, Barabbas. He wants to take the hits for you. He wants to be your shield."

"Then why hasn't He done so?"

"How could He? He stands at the door of your heart and knocks, Barabbas, but you must let Him in. Instead, you have barred the door to your heart and discarded the key."

"I've heard enough of this."

"Perhaps the Lord allowed Dan to make the ultimate sacrifice because He longed for you to understand the love He has for you, Barabbas."

"If He loves me so much, then let *Him* suffer for

me and take the hit Himself, rather than sending a convenient scapegoat." With a nod of finality, Barabbas turned on his heel and walked out the door.

Julia crumpled to the ground, her back pressed against the crumbling wall, her face buried in trembling hands.

But in that moment, the Lord gave Julia a new prayer for her husband. And she intended to pray faithfully, day after day, week after week, month after month, year after year... She determined that she would not cease her endless petitioning until her request was fulfilled beyond her wildest imaginings.

Almighty God, look him in the face. Act on his behalf. Prove Your awesome power and demonstrate Your love for him. Shake him to the very core and show Him who You are.

CHAPTER 38

Mara

The evening breezes filtered through the quiet, sequestered peristyle, ruffling Mara's soft curls and caressing her thoughtful features. As of late, she often found herself here, sitting upon a secluded bench sheltered within a peaceful garden alcove. Here, she could be alone with her thoughts. Perhaps she even hoped that Malchus would stumble upon her. She smiled sadly, remembering the secret laughter and camaraderie they had once shared.

Now, Malchus avoided her like the plague.

She had seen very little of Lucius as well. It seemed as if nothing she said or did ever pleased him. She wearied of his endless interrogations. He no longer sought her for the pleasure of her company. She couldn't fight the uneasy sensation that he simply endured her presence in order to gain information that would elevate him in the eyes of the high priest.

She could not deny that he had certainly risen above the ranks of soldiers granted for Caiaphas' personal protection. It was as if Caiaphas had singled him out, reserving special assignments for him, even confiding in him on occasion.

Mara recognized that Caiaphas indeed had a plan for Lucius. She just wasn't sure what that plan entailed. Her stomach churned uneasily as she considered the possibilities.

Caiaphas never groomed anyone without a very specific purpose. His sharp eyes were quick to recognize a useful instrument, and he never wearied of shaping and pruning individuals to carry out his own sinister deeds.

Shuddering, Mara stared down at her own hands folded in her lap. With every passing day, the events of her life grew more and more uncertain. She had lost her dearest friend. The man she loved did not betray the slightest desire to wed her. She was imprisoned within the imposing walls of Caiaphas' palatial villa, a lowly serving woman of no importance. She had no friends. No relatives. No financial means.

Would she die alone and childless, without a shekel to her name? The thought terrified her.

Mara longed for peace, for affirmation, for joy. And yet all her efforts to obtain such luxuries had proven futile, if not counterproductive.

Was it possible that, in her own desperate attempt to build a pleasing life for herself, she had dashed her own chances to pieces?

"Such a stormy countenance, sweet Mara. What I wouldn't give to see you smile."

Mara clenched her hands in her lap, unwilling to look up. Already, she knew who had intruded upon her private moment.

Alexander settled himself upon Mara's bench, which was far too small for two people to share. His handsome profile was shadowed by the slanted beams of moonlight washing over the garden peristyle.

Uncomfortable, Mara fixed her gaze upon her lap and licked dry lips.

"Troubled, lovely woman?"

"Why would I be troubled?"

"Your countenance is stormier than the Sea of Galilee in the midst of a squall."

Annoyed, Mara glanced up and was troubled by the tender interest reflected in Alexander's features. Though he had made his interest in her terribly apparent, she held her own curiosity in check. Despite his appeal and tender displays, there was a darkness about this man that troubled her. It was as if a dark presence lurked just beneath the smooth and polished surface. She wondered what cruelties were masked behind that striking smile.

"May I be of any assistance?"

"Yes," Mara responded, irritated by her own attraction. "You may leave me alone with my thoughts."

"I never weary of your warm welcomes, my sweet."

"I am not your *sweet*."

"True. You are terribly bitter."

"Go away."

"I can help you."

"Only God can help me. If He exists."

Alexander studied her, amused. "A devout Jewess

under the employ of the most revered high priest doubts the existence of God?"

Mara shook her head to clear the fog. "I don't know. I suppose He does indeed exist. But I haven't spoken with Him in quite some time."

"And you wish to?"

"I don't know."

"I think you do know."

Mara stared at him, miffed.

"Perhaps you are hesitant to speak with Him because you are afraid He would not approve of your lifestyle, your plans."

"You are rather perceptive...for a heathen."

Alexander could not suppress a surprised chuckle. "I suppose I should be insulted."

"Ah, for once you recognize an insult when it comes."

"Why should I be bothered by the fact that I am a heathen? After all, you seem to have a weakness for them. Perhaps I shall break through your walls yet."

Mara glanced at him, alarmed. "What weakness?"

"For pagan men."

"I love only one man."

"Yes, a pagan soldier of Rome, the city of abominations. I am curious, did you fall for him simply to irritate this God whom you are so reluctant to entreat?"

"I am disgusted by your insinuation."

"Not nearly as disgusted as the – what do you call us? *Gentiles*? – are by the haughtiness of your people. Like you, dear Mara, they claim to possess the secrets of the God of the universe even while leading lives completely contrary to His statutes."

"I doubt you know the first thing about His statutes."

"I am a curious individual. You might be surprised."

"Then why do you bend the knee to stone idols?"

"Oh, please. I no more bend the knee to worthless carvings of wood and stone than to any other god."

"You serve no god?"

"I live for pleasure. Like most, I take no issue paying homage to any deity that doesn't interfere with my lifestyle."

Mara stared at him, stunned.

"You, my dear, are the perfect image of your own people. Gaping at the sins of others, completely unaware of your own."

Mara bristled. "And which sins am I so unaware of?"

"By your own sacred text, it is unacceptable to marry someone of a different religion. And yet, that is exactly what you intend to do."

"And you think it would be any less a sin if I were to marry *you*?"

"My dear Mara, are you proposing?"

Mara blushed, furious. "Of course not! I would fling myself off a cliff before binding myself to you!"

"How noble."

"I detest you!"

"I believe you've said that before."

"And I meant it!"

"I have no doubt. Tell me, Mara. Why do the Jewish people insist on calling themselves believers when they refuse to do what their God commands? Doesn't this simply turn others away from the faith?"

It was a penetrating question, and Mara had no response. She had not considered religion of any importance for many years. Perhaps this was because she had once hoped to obtain all she desired by her faith. When her circumstances failed to improve, she had abandoned her religion. Or – even more troubling – perhaps Alexander was correct in his assessment. Perhaps she avoided a relationship with God because she feared He would not approve of her own desires.

For the first time in many years, Mara wondered about the Lord. Would He be interested in hearing from her?

Sensing Mara's quiet withdrawal, Alexander expertly changed his course. "I meant no disrespect, my dear. It is simply something to ponder."

Mara glanced at him sideways, irritated by his annoying logic. After all, wasn't she, too, sitting on the fence? She had not denied the existence of God, nor had she intentionally hardened her heart against Him. But she certainly did not bother to keep His laws.

She was no better than her own stiff-necked and stubborn people. The realization stung.

"Let me ask you another question," Alexander interrupted her thoughts.

"I weary of your questions."

"And my presence, as well, I imagine."

"My, aren't we intuitive."

"My question, dear Mara, is this: If you are so

determined to forsake your God for the love of a man, why continue chasing one who has absolutely no interest in you?"

Hurt and surprised, Mara looked away.

"There are others, Mara – believe me – who would not hesitate to make your wildest dreams come true." Taking her hand in his, Alexander met her gaze with disturbing ardor.

Trembling, Mara attempted to withdraw her hand, but Alexander held her captive. "He doesn't want you, Mara. I do."

Warning bells were going off in Mara's mind. Even as she doubted his sincerity, she longed to believe him. But why on earth would a strikingly handsome man like Alexander be interested in a plain woman like her? She couldn't understand it. And the uneasiness in the pit of her stomach was growing steadily.

Sensing her distress, Alexander released her hand.

Both relieved and disappointed, Mara exhaled slowly.

"You deny me because Malchus would not approve."

"What does Malchus have to do with this?"

"You care deeply for him – only God knows why."

"He is my friend. But he does not dictate my decisions."

"No?"

"Of course not. He doesn't approve of Lucius either, but his disapproval has not kept me from the man I love."

"An interesting thing, that."

Mara glanced up at Alexander in surprise. "What?"

"Well, we were just discussing the hypocrisy of the Jews, were we not? And I am afraid that – despite the vast number of hypocrites among the Jewish people – our dear Malchus is chief."

Temper kindling, Mara rose to her feet. "I don't have to listen to this."

"Your loyalty to him is touching, Mara, truly. Especially considering his own actions of late."

Alexander rose casually, and Mara turned to face him head on. "What do you mean?" she demanded, trembling.

"Well, clearly, he has condemned you because you love a Gentile. But he has no right to cast judgment. Did you know," his eyes narrowed, and he savored the words as he spoke them, "that our dear Malchus has taken a Gentile lover of his own?"

Mara stared at him in disbelief. "Malchus wouldn't know romance if it slapped him in the face."

"Well, I beg to differ. He is seeing a young woman, a Greek. I find it rather amusing that he would condemn you so swiftly even while he himself commits the same sin."

Insides churning, Mara's thoughts swirled maddeningly in her confusion. "You must be mistaken."

"Oh, no. I'm never mistaken." Alexander's eyes gleamed, for he knew he had succeeded in planting yet another seed of doubt and dissension. Alexander reveled in the distrust washing over Mara's features. After all, Malchus had turned Mara against him before he'd even had the chance to win her. Now Malchus would pay for his misdeeds. And Alexander savored the prospect of witnessing his downfall.

"I simply assumed you must already know, as you and my cousin are – or *were* – so close. But I suppose he did indeed keep his 'secret life' a secret— even from you."

Mara blinked, attempting to calm her beating heart.

"Well, I don't blame him. I can see why he kept it from you. After all, his deeds would reveal the depths of his hypocrisy. But – that aside – surely you are aware of the fact that he is a follower of that controversial Rabbi – the one they call Jesus?"

"You jest."

"On the contrary. I saw him hungrily absorbing the words of the Teacher myself at Solomon's Porch. Of course, if Caiaphas ever discovered Malchus' secret…" he allowed the sentence to hang menacingly in the air.

Mara turned sharply on her heel. "I don't believe you."

Gripping her elbow, Alexander pulled her back to him. "Why the fit of temper, my dear?"

"Let me go!"

"I wouldn't want to part on such troubling terms."

"Leave me alone and let me be!"

Catching her shoulders, Alexander held her captive. "I only spoke, Mara, because you need to know who you can trust. You have a terrible habit, my dear, of placing your heart in the hands of unworthy men."

"You should know, being chief of all unworthy men," Mara snapped through her tears.

"I'm not like them, Mara. I want you to trust me."

"Then why do you hurt me?"

"The truth is often painful but freeing."

"Speaking of freeing, I demand that you let me go!"

His mouth curving in a knowing smile, Alexander released her. "Think it over, sweet Mara. Consider my words. And when you finally come to your senses, I will be waiting for you. With open arms."

With an angry huff, Mara turned sharply on her heel and headed for the shelter of the pillared colonnades. She was eager for escape. Tears coursed down her cheeks as she considered all that Alexander had told her.

Malchus had taken a Gentile lover. He was following the Teacher that Caiaphas loathed and detested. One little word in the right ear, and she could make his life come crashing down around his ears.

But did she want to? Was his defection deserving of such punishment?

Alexander watched her go, arms crossed, mouth tipped in a sardonic grin. He had indeed accomplished his purpose. Mara would mull over the information he had presented, growing more and more resentful. Ruled by her emotions, she would eventually betray Malchus' secret. And Lucius would gladly convey the message to the high priest.

Alexander's father would have grandly proclaimed that the gods were smiling upon him once again.

He had found the woman he wanted.

He would ruin the cousin he despised.

And being a master of manipulation and deceit,

he was amassing an alarming amount of coin –
hush money he had received from multiple persons
after unearthing ruinous secrets. Clearly, his acute
powers of observation would take him far. It was a
gift he wielded like a double-edged sword. And he
imagined that gift would make him very rich. Soon,
he would have enough coin to forsake this detestable
place and strike out on his own again.

And when that time came, he intended to take
Mara with him.

CHAPTER 39

Melina

Serving the Lady Procula was a delight. When Chuza arrived to escort Melina back to Herod Antipas' palace wing, Melina could have easily wept at the prospect of leaving the stately woman and returning to serve Salome. But the Passover week had drawn to a close, and Procula's maid had made a full recovery. The girl was eager to serve her mistress again, and no doubt Procula would be delighted to be served by her own maid.

Struggling to match Chuza's swift strides, Melina glanced up nervously, noting his stormy countenance. "All is not well?"

Chuza's mouth formed a grim line. A muscle twitched in his firm, chiseled jaw. "Herod's house is in a state of upheaval."

Melina's stomach turned. "Perhaps Lady Procula would welcome my service for a few more weeks," she dared with a slight twinkle in her eye.

Chuza was not amused. "Your young mistress has instigated a great deal of turmoil in Herod's house. Perhaps your calming presence will help set things right again."

I doubt that, Melina thought, chilled to the core. Salome could be downright cruel when she was in one of her moods. "Do you know the cause?"

Chuza kept his gaze dead ahead as he continued to stride past rows and rows of stately marble pillars. "Her betrothal was finalized the week before Herod's birthday. Apparently, she resorted to histrionics when informed."

Remembering Salome's fierce countenance and bitter threats the last time they had discussed the prospect of her marriage to Philip, Melina knit her brow in deep concern. "There is nothing I can do for her, Chuza. She abhors the idea of wedding Philip, despite his success as a ruler."

"Your soothing presence is balm to her wounds. Be patient with her and pray for God's protection."

Nearly panting in her attempt to match Chuza's pace, Melina glanced up at him, a question in her eyes.

Pausing in the midst of the grand, colonnaded hall, Chuza touched Melina's shoulder and gazed upon her with a fatherly air of concern. "She has had two of her handmaidens lashed this week. One terribly beaten."

Melina wondered if her heart had dropped into the pit of her stomach. Frightened, she gazed imploringly at Chuza. "What was their offense?"

"She presented a vast array of complaints. Nothing deserving of the whip."

"God protect me," Melina murmured under her breath, trembling.

Daring a quick glance about the hall, Chuza placed two strong hands upon Melina's small shoulders. Bowing his head, he prayed in his deep, strong voice. "Almighty God, protect our sister, Melina. Keep her from the forces of evil."

"Amen," Melina agreed quietly. Taking Chuza's huge hand in her own, she gave it a quick squeeze. "Thank you, my brother."

"God will protect you, little sister. But no matter what you may face, He will be with you."

"This I know."

Resuming their purposeful walk toward Herod's tumultuous household, they continued forth in comfortable silence.

"I shall ask Elias to prepare that calming brew he makes for Salome, and I will take it to her upon my arrival," Melina decided aloud. "Perhaps that will help calm her frayed nerves."

Chuza smiled faintly. "A wise decision. But I advise you, do it quickly."

Parting ways, Melina hurried toward the kitchen, praying silently as she went.

"Elias!" she nearly gasped a moment later, bursting into the warm confines of the enormous kitchen.

"So she has returned." Elias drew a pan of golden loaves from the oven and set them aside to cool. "I daresay it would have been safer to remain with the prelate and his wife."

"I imagine so. Elias, I need a favor."

Elias rolled his eyes in mock frustration.

"Will you prepare one of your calming brews for Salome?"

"I know what I'd like to prepare for her –"

"Elias! Please," Melina nearly squeaked, gazing about the kitchen in fear. The other servants were far too absorbed in their tasks to pay any attention to her conversation with Elias.

"That girl has caused nothing but misery this week. We've all had quite enough."

"Perhaps the Lord will help me bring peace to her heart."

"I'd prefer He strike her dead."

"Elias!"

Elias held up two floury hands in surrender. "I know, I know. He does not work that way."

Melina grinned, wishing with all her heart that Elias would believe.

"Perhaps you have forgotten about Sodom and Gomorrah. Your God has been known to work with fire and brimstone on occasion."

"But it is His mercy that leads to repentance."

"There is not enough mercy in this wretched world to conform that wicked girl."

"God's grace can transform the most stubborn of hearts," Melina reminded him with a soft smile. *Even yours,* she thought wistfully. *Oh God, may it be so!*

Already, Elias was preparing the soothing brew. Melina watched with interest as he expertly mixed herbs and honey with wine. "Take this to your mistress. If your God is merciful, she will drink and then sleep. For a very long time."

Melina glanced nervously at the crusty old cook. "How long, exactly?"

"Don't worry. I didn't poison it. But the herbs will make her drowsy. Perhaps then she will sleep."

"Thank you, Elias, from the bottom of my heart."

"You can repay me the next time my worthless kitchen staff fails to perform."

"You know I will!" Touching his arm in appreciation, Melina accepted the brew he offered and steeled herself for the ordeal that was surely to come.

***

Melina was unprepared for Salome's reaction when she entered her palatial suite.

"Melina! You have returned!" Face crumpling, Salome covered her face in her hands and wept uncontrollably.

Stunned, Melina rushed to her mistress and took her hand. "My lady, I am here. What can I do? How can I help?"

Salome's entire body tensed, and she glared at Melina through make-up smeared, tear-stained eyes. "No one can help me! Certainly not someone of your impossible status!"

Melina would never understand Salome's split-second mood swings. Hadn't the girl been relieved to see her? For the first time, she noticed several nervous maids hovering nearby. Pale and trembling, they watched Salome with frightened eyes.

Sensing their perusal, Salome glared at them fiercely. "Leave me! Get out of here!"

The maidservants stared at their mistress in stunned question.

"Are you deaf? Dumb? I said, get out of here! You are of no possible use to me! Now *get out!*"

The maids scattered like frightened mice, relieved to be rid of Salome's contrary and demanding presence.

"The fools! They are ridiculously stupid, every single one of them. And slower than a lumbering ox!"

Melina assumed there was safety in silence.

"They don't know how to serve me like you do," Salome whined, her slender brows knit in disgust. "You know what I need without me having to order you about."

Wondering at Salome's stunning declaration, Melina offered the soothing brew. "May I help you lie down, my lady? This will help calm your nerves."

Salome's eyes narrowed in suspicion. "How did you know I would need it?"

"I learned about your betrothal, my lady."

Salome's emerald eyes glowed with suppressed fury.

"Come, let me serve you, my lady."

Wilting, Salome allowed Melina to guide her to the plush bed. Climbing beneath the luxurious sheets, Salome pulled the blankets close to her chin, her jaw quivering slightly.

"Why do you care what happens to me?"

"You are my mistress."

"So you simply serve me out of obligation?"

Salome was itching for a fight, and Melina determined she would not indulge the desire. She smiled.

"Of course not. I care about you, my lady."

"Why?"

Melina furrowed her brow. She doubted Salome would be gratified by a truthful response. After all, Melina harbored no warm feelings whatsoever toward her mistress. She chose to love and serve her because it honored the Lord. If God had placed her here with Salome, then surely, He had a purpose, a plan. And Melina knew she was called to love this difficult young woman, despite her own contrary feelings.

"See? You can't even think of a reason! Nobody loves me."

"That is not true, my lady. Your father and mother—"

"I haven't seen my father in years."

"Well, your stepfather –"

"Cares only about himself and bartering me off to form useful alliances! He is a beast and I hate him!"

"Oh, my lady –"

"I will hate him until the day I die!"

"You mustn't say such things, my lady."

"Perhaps I'll kill myself. That would be better than being forced to marry a disgusting old man!"

Alarmed, Melina took her hand. "Oh, my lady! You mustn't! Your life is far too precious –"

"See? You do care about me!" Salome squeezed Melina's hand, gratified. But her mood shifted just as quickly. "Why is it that the only person on this earth who cares about me has to be a worthless serving girl with no influence whatsoever? What good will that do me?"

Melina bit back a smile, despite the insulting nature of Salome's complaint. "I apologize, my lady. I wish there was more I could do for you."

"I hate everything. I hate my life. I want to die! No, I want *Herod* to die. And Philip, too. That's what I want!"

Sitting on the edge of Salome's bed, Melina stroked back her mistress's wayward raven black tendrils and offered her the steaming mug. "Drink, my lady. It will help."

"I don't need this. I need something stronger. Much stronger. I want to drink until I forget."

"But then you will awaken and remember again. And the headache that will surely follow will only make matters worse."

"I don't care."

"Please, my lady. This will help."

Salome accepted the mug with the air of an obstinate child. "You've served this before. It does help me relax."

"That is very good, my lady."

Salome emptied the mug, then leaned back against her fluffed pillows with a sigh of contentment.

Rising from the bed, Melina adjusted the blankets about her mistress and took the empty mug. "Now try to get some rest, my lady. I will awaken you in time to sup with your mother and stepfather."

Salome's eyelids fluttered heavily. "No, let me sleep. Besides, I lost my appetite when I heard the news last week and I've yet to find it again."

"I understand. Shall I have a tray sent up to you?"

"I don't want to eat anything."

"My lady, you must keep up your strength."

"Perhaps tomorrow." Closing her eyes, Salome sank further into the luxuriant pillows.

Preparing to make her exit, Melina trod softly toward the massive double doors that would lead her to safety.

"Melina?"

Melina turned to find Salome studying her intently. "I needed you last week." Her tone was plaintive, like that of a needy child.

"I am terribly sorry I could not serve you, my lady."

"By this time next year, I will be married against my will."

Melina offered a sympathetic smile. "Try not to fret, my lady. Perhaps you will learn to love him. It is a great honor to wed a successful ruler like Philip."

"I will never love him. I will find a way out, Melina. No matter what it takes. No matter what I must do. I will find a way out of this. Even if I have to kill him. Or Herod. Or anyone else."

Wishing she could dismiss Salome's disturbing musings as the meaningless babble of an exhausted, hysterical young woman, Melina hid a grimace. She knew better. Salome was determined to have her own way. And absolutely nothing Melina said or did would change that.

"Please, my lady, try to get some rest. I will check on you shortly." Mustering up what she hoped was a confident smile, Melina slipped out the door.

Releasing a deep breath, Melina paused in the hallway, thanking God for His protection and pleading for the salvation of her young mistress.

CHAPTER 40

Julia

"Praise God!" Deborah's eyes shone like two bright gems as Julia relayed all she had witnessed at the Pool of Bethesda – the death of her husband's friend after his decision for Jesus, the healing of the paralyzed man beside the pool, and her own faith in the One she believed to be the Son of God.

"I tremble inside each time I recall these miraculous happenings," Julia admitted, scooping freshly milled flour into her own sack.

"I have prayed without ceasing that you, too, would encounter the Messiah," Deborah declared, her face flushed after the difficult process of milling. "And yet again, God has answered an impossible prayer!"

"I prayed the same," Julia confided, preparing to tie her sack filled with the powdery substance. "I knew Jesus must possess great power, for He healed Isaac. And the testimony you shared about Him was enough to convince me that the impossible claims about Him are indeed true. Still, I longed to see Him for myself."

"Don't tie that knot yet, dear girl. Take more flour along with you."

"Oh, this is far more than I will need. Barabbas has already left with Father's caravan. He may not return for a month or more. I'll only need enough flour to bake loaves for myself." Even as she spoke, a familiar, nagging fear settled in the pit of her stomach. Though her marriage was far from blissful, she detested the long weeks of loneliness in a dark, empty house. Even more so, she worried about her husband as he traveled treacherous paths thick with bandits and cutthroats. Barabbas had hardened his heart against the Lord. He was not ready to perish.

"You may be needing a bit more, dear one. You see, Isaac intends for us to leave by this week's end." Her eyes lit up with eager anticipation. "He wants to return to Capernaum."

Julia's knees weakened. She attempted to keep her voice light and steady as she asked causally, "Capernaum again? So soon after your last journey?"

"It would seem Jesus has established His home base in Capernaum. There, He instructs the multitudes and teaches in the local synagogues. We are eager to learn all that we can. He is the Messiah, after all. Does He have orders for His people? What are we to do? Are we to watch and wait? Or is it time to act? We have so many questions – Isaac and I – and Jesus seems to be the only answer."

Struggling against tears of self-pity, Julia accepted the extra flour Deborah heaped generously into her sack. After all, Deborah was right. Following Jesus was surely a wise decision. If only she herself possessed the freedom to do so!

Wiping floury hands upon her apron, Deborah paused. "Julia! Why don't you come along?"

Julia's heart soared with hope but came crashing down just as quickly when she considered the harsh reality of her circumstance. "Barabbas would never allow it."

"He may come along as well!"

"He never would. He despises Jesus. And besides that, he must attend to Father's caravan."

"You yourself said he wouldn't return for quite some time. Perhaps he wouldn't mind if you came with us."

"He would certainly expect me to inform him, and I cannot. He has already departed."

Deborah sighed, disappointed. "I understand, dear one. But I will miss you."

Tears spilled over Julia's cheeks. "And I will miss you as well."

"Heavens, child! Don't cry. You'll get me going for sure. It's only for a time. Our plan is to return to Jerusalem for Pentecost."

Julia relaxed, relieved. Pentecost was just a few weeks hence! "I thought you were leaving for good," she admitted, her voice wavering.

Deborah reached for her and drew her closer. "You know I wouldn't leave you, child! We may do quite a bit of traveling until the Messiah's plans are revealed, but this is home. You are family. We love you, and God has brought us together. You needn't worry about losing us, Julia."

Swallowing tears of gratitude, Julia tied her sack of grain and heaved it over her shoulder, preparing to return home. "I will be praying for your safe travels."

"And we will be praying for you, too, dear girl."

"You must remember everything that Jesus says. I want to hear all of it when you return – everything! Down to the slightest detail!"

Deborah grinned, her face alight. "You needn't worry, my dear. Isaac has already packed piles of parchment and ink. He intends to chronicle every single word that proceeds from the mouth of Jesus. I hear others are already doing the same."

"Chronicling His words?"

"Keeping careful records. His words are precious. Those who believe in Him are doing all in their power to preserve His message. It's as if an unknown force has taken hold of them, compelling them to preserve the teachings of Jesus at all cost!"

Julia smiled. "I am thankful. Especially for those of us who will not have the privilege to hear His teaching in person."

When Julia returned to her own home, the silence hung heavily in the air, threatening to smother her joy. Setting aside the sack of flour, she refused to allow depression to take hold of her.

After all, today she had much cause for joy! She knew the enemy of her soul would love to shatter the delight she felt when pondering the possibilities of the day ahead. Well, she would not allow him to do so!

Before departing with her father's caravan, Barabbas had granted her permission to visit her parents under a few strict conditions. One – she was not to portray their marriage in a negative light. Two – she was to keep personal matters to herself. And three – she was only to stay for one afternoon. After all, he had reminded her, she had her own house to keep.

Despite his stringent conditions, Julia had been nearly giddy with excitement. And then terrified that he would change his mind before departing.

She planned to set off for her father's villa within the hour. It was still early morning, and that would allow her plenty of time for the trip. First, she must freshen up and attempt to look her best. Since she would travel alone, she decided against wearing anything expensive or eye catching, despite her great temptation to do so. Instead, she would don a simple robe belted at the waist with a common sash. She selected a modest head covering, for she had no desire to attract unwanted attention as she traveled the dizzying maze of streets that would take her from the Lower City to her father's grand villa in the wealthiest section of Jerusalem.

Chagrined, she knew she would appear sorely out of place once she reached the broad, fashionably col-onnaded marble avenues of the Upper City, but she preferred that over the prospect of being assaulted in her own poverty-stricken precinct along the way. She would not make herself a target if at all possible.

Every bit as exciting as the prospect of seeing her own family again was the fact that she would be meeting Malchus and Melina the following day. She could barely contain her excitement. She prayed that Melina would accept her humble apology. Perhaps then the Lord could restore their friendship.

Julia had done little to reach out to the servant girl after marrying Barabbas. Sadly, she recognized that she had been too caught up in her own personal woes to extend friendship to another.

Setting her shoulders in determination, Julia decided that her days of wallowing in self-pity during Barabbas' long absences were behind her. How many precious moments had she wasted in the past, drowning in her own tears and feeling sorry for herself? Despite the mental barriers she had unintentionally erected when she had allowed herself to sink into despair, Julia now recognized that the Lord had exciting plans for her every single day – even if she found herself alone in an empty house. She herself must decide whether or not she would walk in them.

After much prayer and self-examination, she could clearly see that she had two choices. One – she could remain barricaded at home, weeping and agonizing over her "hopeless" situation. Or two – she could cheerfully go about her household tasks, asking God to show her if there was someone He desired for her to reach. Today, she would minister to her beloved parents. She had already resolved that she would go in order to bless *them* – not to acquire personal gain or to gratify *herself*.

Tomorrow, she would ask the Lord to help her minister to her long-lost friends, Melina and Malchus. Another plan was also forming in her mind, and her eyes traveled to the bulging sack of excess flour she had propped near the front door.

Yes, in His graciousness, God was allowing her many opportunities to bless others. For the first time, Julia was ready to accept His call to love others more than herself. She knew she would not do it perfectly, but she also knew the Lord would walk beside her every step of the way, leading her, guiding her, and directing her steps.

According to popular rumor, Jesus had instructed the crowds that it was more blessed to give than to receive. And Julia intended to embrace this teaching with her entire being. God's commandments were *for her good*. The Lord was working mightily to teach her the power of this truth, and she longed to walk in His ways by His grace and to the best of her ability.

Help me to be a blessing to every single person I come into contact with today, Lord, was the prayer He had placed in her heart, and Julia was faithful to begin each day beseeching her faithful Creator in this way.

Somehow, beyond her wildest imaginings, the great God of the universe – the Lord of all Creation – was teaching her to deny herself and walk in love.

CHAPTER 41

"Lady Julia! Your father was not expecting you."

Julia's heart sank at the cautious reception she received from her father's trusty doorkeeper. He looked none too thrilled to see her.

Ashamed, Julia recalled her attitude toward her father's servants in recent years. She had paraded about the magnificent villa, impatiently making demands and seldom taking a moment to even recognize the staff as fellow human beings. She thought of Joanna, her nursemaid, and her cheeks grew warm. Did the faithful older woman still pray for her? Julia would not blame the woman in the least if she had completely given up on her haughty young mistress.

Now, as her father's doorkeeper gazed upon her with trained, expressionless features, Julia wondered what else she could have possibly expected. A warm reception from the people she had treated so haughtily?

A lump formed in her throat, but Julia had no desire to give in to tears before this steely servant. If anything, she detected a look of satisfaction lurking just behind his glazed eyes as he observed her worn garments and scuffed sandals.

Perhaps I should not have come, Julia thought, swallowing her tears. *Perhaps I should turn back –*

"My daughter? Could it possibly be my dear Julia?"

Julia heard a hasty rustling of fabric as the door swung open behind the doorkeeper. Before she was fully aware of what was happening, Julia found herself gazing into the kind, steady eyes of her father, Simon. And then she was in his arms, for he nearly swept her off her feet in his haste to gather his dear child close to his heart.

Her head covering had slipped about her shoulders, and her father's teardrops fell upon her head like sweet anointing oil. Then she realized that she, too, was weeping.

After a firm embrace, Simon held her at arm's length and studied her with the practiced eye of a concerned father. Much to her amazement, she didn't detect the slightest hint of the disdain she had witnessed on the doorkeeper's expression while observing her simple garments. Stunningly, it was not disdain or shock, but rather deep approval resonating within her father's gentle gray eyes.

"Welcome home, my precious daughter," Simon boomed in the kindly voice she had so dearly missed. "Welcome home."

***

"You've changed, my daughter."

Julia smiled at Simon's frank assessment, hoping it conveyed all the love she felt for her dear parents.

"I certainly hope I have."

Simon had arranged for a spread to be set up in the stunning garden courtyard, knowing this was Julia's favorite part of the stately villa. She had spent much time here, enjoying the sweet fragrance of lovely blossoming flowers, the cheerful chirping of tiny birds, and the soothing melody of falling water emanating from the beautiful marble fountain in the center of the courtyard.

Simon reclined near his wife, Iskah, on the opposite side of the table. The feast the servants had set before them was truly a wonder to behold. Julia marveled that she had once enjoyed such mouthwatering delicacies on a daily basis. At the time, she hadn't realized how remarkably blessed she had been to enjoy such fare prepared by her father's professional cooks. She ate sparingly, praying that the rich, exotic entrees would not dull her appreciation for the simple bread, vegetables, and water of which she partook at home.

"You look well." Iskah's dark eyes glistened with relief and thankfulness.

Julia thought her mother looked every bit as stately and elegant as she always had. Her dark hair was piled high in an ornate Roman style, curling tendrils framing her queenly features.

"I am well," Julia replied honestly. Though she might have felt differently several months earlier, she recognized that she possessed everything that truly mattered in life – a saving relationship with the God of the universe, a family that loved her, shelter, sustenance, the assurance of salvation.

Simon leaned comfortably on one elbow, his graying beard contrasting sharply with his leathery features. "Are you enjoying married life?"

Julia bit her lip, cornered. She knew she couldn't lie to her parents, but she also knew she must keep her promise to Barabbas. And she had agreed not to portray him or their marriage in a negative light. "I've certainly learned much," she answered safely and truthfully. "I had no idea what marriage was really going to be like."

"Few of us do," Simon responded drolly, a smile playing about the corners of his gray mustache.

"But we all learn rather quickly – out of necessity," Iskah amended with a gentle smile. "And I imagine you have learned more than you ever thought possible."

"I have," Julia replied honestly. "The Lord has been so patient with me. He has helped me to see that my behavior was unacceptable, Mother. I am truly sorry for all I put you both through in the years prior to my marriage. I was spoiled, willful, and selfish. Heaven knows I still have so much growing to do, but by the grace of God, I am learning a little bit more each day."

Tears glistened in Iskah's eyes. Reaching across the table, she took Julia's hand and squeezed it.

"Your faith and dependence on our merciful God is delightful to behold," Simon remarked, sitting up with a bit of effort. "I can see the effects of your faith written all over your features. And you no longer speak of our Lord as if He were some cold, distant deity uninterested in your plight – you speak of Him fondly, as a dear friend. And I'm proud of you, Julia. Truly proud of you."

Tears welled in Julia's eyes, but she determined not to dampen their lovely afternoon with tears. Instead, she smiled.

"Tell me," Iskah asked, drawing herself up gracefully beside her husband on the plush settee. "What is your new life like?"

Julia considered the question, her slender brows drawing together. What could she possibly tell them?

"Well," she said quietly, toying with the slender neck of a goblet overlaid in gold, "it's a very quiet life most of the time. I cook, I clean, I mend garments, and I attend to my husband's needs. I have even learned to make household repairs, tend the goats, and mill our own flour!"

Iskah's delicate brows lifted in calm delight. "My restless little Julia – cooking, cleaning, mending, and tending to her own house! I never thought I'd live to see the day."

Her tone was loving rather than condemning, and Julia couldn't help but smile.

"The Lord is teaching me to be content, whatever my circumstances. As you've seen once, Mother, my home is nothing like this one. But God has shown me how to be grateful for what I *do* have rather than despairing over the things I can no longer enjoy," she added, gazing about her familiar surroundings tenderly.

"A very important lesson, indeed," Simon agreed with a small smile.

"There is also a very kind woman who lives in the

house beside ours," Julia added, her eyes lighting up. "She is a wonderful woman and a very dear friend."

Iskah exhaled contentedly. "I am overjoyed to hear this, my daughter. I often worry about you, spending such long stretches alone while your husband travels with the caravan."

Simon placed his hand over his wife's. "But our Julia is faring very well," he reminded her gently. "She is in the Lord's hands, as we all are."

"Even so, I'm glad to hear it," Iskah put in certainly, her expression uncompromising.

Simon hid a small smile. "Tell us about this kindly woman, Julia."

"Her name is Deborah, and she is married to a wonderful man named Isaac. She was willing to teach me many things that I deemed unnecessary when you attempted to instruct me in the art of housekeeping, Mother. I can't quite explain how much I wish I had paid more attention to your instruction."

Iskah's eyes saddened, and Julia quickly changed the subject.

"Speaking of Deborah and Isaac..." Julia began cautiously, slightly hesitant. How would her parents respond to the story she was about to tell? Would they be interested? Skeptical? Dismissive? Offended?

Lord, give me the words to tell the story as it should be told...

"What about them?" Iskah prodded, her curiosity piqued.

"Well, Isaac was once a sailor. He suffered a life-threatening injury, which left him nearly immobilized. His two legs were withered and slack with disuse. Sadly, it used to disturb me to see them hanging lamely when he sat in his chair."

"The poor man." Iskah's dark eyes filled with sympathy.

"But then his sister passed away in Capernaum. They went to be with her for her final days. There, he met a Man named Jesus."

It was as if an invisible shock wave burst through the entire courtyard, rustling through flower-laden branches and whispering its way through the palm fronds. Simon and Iskah sat upright, both tensing in recognition. A knowing smile crossed over Simon's features.

Julia attempted to recover, her heart pounding rapidly. "You know of Him?"

"This is the same Man with whom Nicodemus arranged a meeting last year."

"Yes, it is."

"And how do *you* know of Him?" Simon prodded with a fatherly smile.

"Well, you did tell me a bit about Him at the time, Father. But when Isaac and Deborah returned from Capernaum, Isaac's legs were healed – whole, complete. I've never seen anything like it. He strides about on two sturdy legs, and one would never know he was once a cripple."

Simon stroked his beard thoughtfully, glancing casually at his wife.

"Though I didn't witness the healing myself, I believed Isaac's testimony. He is a good and honest man."

"And he claims this Jesus healed his legs?"

"He does."

"Praise God."

Julia's brows lifted in surprise. "You do not question his testimony? You have never met him, Father."

"I needn't question it. My dear friends and colleagues, Joseph and Nicodemus, have witnessed such healings themselves. And I myself have heard Jesus address the crowds at the Temple. My heart burns within my chest when He speaks with such authority, power, and humility. It's as if my very soul cries out for my Messiah, my Savior."

Julia's heart swelled with joy. "Oh, Father, I was afraid you and Mother might think I had lost my wits! I am so happy you believe!"

"We *hope*, but we must continue to watch and observe," Iskah cautioned in her usual, reserved manner. "One mustn't rush to a hasty conclusion about something as serious as this."

"But the evidence is here, before our eyes," Simon pointed out, his tone passionate. "We are the blessed ones – privileged to watch the events regarding the Messiah's coming unfold."

"There are many prophecies He must fulfill," Iskah reminded him.

"He has fulfilled many already."

Julia was terribly interested in learning. She had neglected to absorb her father's wisdom once, and she was loathe to do it again. "Which prophecies has He already fulfilled?"

Simon's eyes grew distant as ancient words emerged at the forefront of his mind. "The prophet

Micah declared, *But you, Bethlehem Ephrathah, though you are little among the thousands of Judah, yet out of you shall come forth to Me the One to be Ruler in Israel, whose goings forth are from of old, from everlasting."*

Julia smiled broadly as remembrance dawned. "Yes, the Messiah would be born in Bethlehem."

"And Jesus was. Some falsely claim He was born in Nazareth, but that is untrue. He was simply raised there. His parents were forced to travel to Bethlehem for the census during the reign of Augustus. He was born during their stay in Bethlehem."

"I've heard such talk. I believe the Pharisees and the Sadducees attempt to mislead the people by telling them such."

"This is sadly true," Simon conceded thoughtfully. "But there is more evidence, and it is becoming more and more difficult to refute."

"Such as?"

"Malachi prophesied boldly, *Behold, I send My messenger, and he will prepare the way before Me. And the Lord, whom you seek, will suddenly come to His Temple, even the Messenger of the covenant, in whom you delight. Behold, He is coming.* Clearly, a messenger would prepare the way for the Messiah. And Isaiah also spoke thus. We have seen this with John the Baptizer, whom Herod Antipas recently imprisoned."

Julia was saddened by the news. "But why?"

Simon shook his head in disgust. "Herod claims there were political reasons, but everyone in Palestine knows his illegitimate wife, Herodias, simply forced his hand. She despised John because he dared to speak against her unlawful union to Herod. It was no secret Herod respected John, and she must have felt threatened by him."

Julia remembered that Melina served both Herod Antipas and Herodias. Perhaps the servant girl could shed some light on the situation when they met the following day! A shiver of excitement wracked her entire frame as she anticipated their meeting.

"There is also the prophecy in Isaiah to consider: *Behold, the virgin shall conceive and bear a Son, and shall call His name Immanuel.* This too, came to pass, for Jesus was born of a virgin named Mary."

"At least, she claims this is the case," Iskah spoke up for the first time.

"Based on the woman's character, I tend to believe it," Simon mused thoughtfully. "I know an old priest who was born and raised in Nazareth. He instructed the people at the local synagogue. He knew Mary from the time she was born. He said he's never known a more honest, humble, obedient woman."

Julia nodded, absorbing every word.

"And there are other prophecies as well. For example, the Messiah would be called out of Egypt. This, too, happened when His parents were forced to flee from the wrath of Herod the Great."

"I am certainly not disagreeing with you," Iskah inserted firmly. "I hope and pray He is the One. But it is wise to keep our eyes open, for the Scriptures also warn us not to be deceived."

"True, and we will continue to watch and wait.

And pray. But as for me, I am convinced this is the One."

"I long for this to be true with all my heart," Iskah agreed quietly. "Come, Messiah, come."

Her heart burning within her, Julia prayed in silent agreement.

"The fact that these prophecies are being fulfilled in such rapid succession by one Man is beyond remarkable," Simon mused, appearing scholarly as he mentally reviewed the facts he had compiled after countless hours of intensive study. "Consider this, dear ones: There are many prophecies in the sacred Scriptures about the Messiah. But the chances of just one man fulfilling even eight of those prophecies is a mind-blowing one in one hundred quadrillion!"

Julia shook her head in disbelief. She supposed her untrained mind was incapable of even comprehending such a vast number.

"To put that in perspective," Simon continued, eyes alight with excitement, "that number is one with *sixteen zeros* trailing after it! And to think that we have already discussed four of the eight prophecies required to meet this astronomical probability! And that being said, imagine the chances of one man fulfilling every single Messianic prophecy in Scripture! The chances are far too remote for our human minds to comprehend. Could we possibly argue against a Man meeting such impossible requirements?"

"I imagine some will," Iskah stated, considering several of her husband's arrogant colleagues.

"This Jesus has created quite a stir among the

Sanhedrin," Simon remarked in amusement, seeming to read his wife's thoughts. "Even Joseph – a bold and fiery man by nature – has kept his allegiance to himself for fear of what the Sanhedrin may do."

"He is wise to bide his time before announcing his allegiance," Iskah mused. "He would be put out of the Sanhedrin if they knew he followed the Rabbi Jesus. At least this way, if he is misguided – and I certainly hope he isn't – he will not risk losing his influential position."

Julia remembered the hostile reaction of the religious leaders at the Pool of Bethesda, which prompted her to tell her parents all about the miraculous incident that occurred there. She left out a few key details – particularly the fact that she had spent the night at the pools after tending to the body of a dead Zealot.

Iskah's eyes were wide in amazement. "And you witnessed this healing with your own eyes?"

"I did. But even more miraculous than the healing was the Man Himself. I've never known anyone with such a commanding presence, Mother, and yet, so full of love. His voice, His eyes, His touch – it's as if His every move, His every motion, was an embodiment of that great love, the driving force behind His every deed. I wish I had Father's eloquence – perhaps then I could explain it better."

Simon smiled thoughtfully. "Your summation is correct, my daughter. I could not have explained it better myself."

"You must see Him, Mother. Father, you must take her to see Him!"

Simon chuckled in amusement. "We will attempt to do so as soon as possible. From what I've heard, He has already returned to Galilee."

"Before Pentecost?"

"I can only bide by hearsay. I'm not sure if anyone knows His true whereabouts."

Gazing beyond Julia and into the depths of the pillared porticoes sheltering the open-air courtyard, a small smile played about the corners of Iskah's delicate lips. "My dear Julia," she said with a knowing smile. "I do believe we have forgotten to alert a very important person about your arrival. And it appears she is quite eager to see you."

Julia wheeled around when a woman released a shriek of delight, rushing past rows of pillars and bursting into the courtyard, tears streaming down her rosy cheeks.

CHAPTER 42

"Julia, my dear girl! Is it really you?"

Julia rose upon shaky legs, her heart beating rapidly as her heavyset nursemaid approached with a speed that defied her large bearing.

Before Julia could utter a word, Joanna's soft arms had encircled her. The woman wept openly, unashamed.

Mercy. Forgiveness. The words whispered peace to Julia's heart. First, her father had lovingly accepted her into his home. No mention had been made of her deplorable behavior. Nor had her parents reprimanded her or stoutly declared *I told you so!* Instead, they had taken her into their arms and whispered words of love and assurance. And now Joanna – a woman whom she had treated with disdain – greeted her with the deepest love and genuine sincerity. She wondered at the level of mercy and forgiveness displayed by those she loved.

"How I've prayed for you!" Joanna gasped, studying her young mistress delightedly. "And how I've longed to see you! Look at you – you are beautiful! Just beautiful."

Julia swallowed the lump forming in her throat, recognizing her need to apologize to this woman but hesitant to do so. The elite of Simon's neighborhood would stoutly declare it was improper for a mistress to apologize to a servant.

But Julia no longer followed such manmade obligations. She now answered to a much higher power.

Swallowing her pride, Julia forced herself to meet Joanna's eager gaze. The woman had grasped both her hands in an iron grip. "Joanna, it is so very good to see you!"

"And you as well, dear girl, you as well!"

"You haven't changed a bit!"

"But you – you've changed." Joanna's sharp eyes studied the girl knowingly. Looking to Julia's parents, Joanna smiled broadly. "There's a glow that wasn't there before, a peace, a contentment. Now, pray tell – just where exactly did all that come from?"

From your faithful prayers, Julia thought, her heart constricting. "To be honest, Joanna, the Lord has had to teach me some hard lessons."

"You wouldn't be the first, I'm a-thinking, to learn a few hard lessons."

"I must apologize," Julia blurted out, before her pride could smother the apology in reasonable excuses. "I treated you so badly, Joanna. Thank you for serving me so diligently. And even more importantly, thank you for praying for me."

Tears sprang to Joanna's wise eyes, but she was quick to recover. "I've loved you since you were a tiny little sprout and I always will, you silly girl. But thank you for that beautiful apology, all the same. I know what it's like to be young and impetuous. You've learned your lessons far sooner than some."

Julia offered a self-deprecating smile. "If only it had been sooner."

"All in God's perfect timing. His ways are not our ways, to say the least."

Savoring Joanna's frank manner, Julia wondered why she had ever found such a pleasant woman to be irritating.

"And that incredibly good-looking man of yours – how is he?"

Julia wasn't entirely sure how to answer the question truthfully. She paused, searching for the right words.

Joanna nodded in sympathetic understanding. "I've been praying for that boy, I have. Every day. And I will not cease."

Julia's eyes grew moist, and she nodded her deep appreciation.

"Our good Lord has plans for that young man. Just give it time, beloved. Time and prayer – and lots of it."

Somehow, Julia felt a great sense of peace and comfort sweep over her entire being just knowing that Joanna prayed for Barabbas. After all, she herself was a living, breathing testimony to the power behind Joanna's fervent prayers.

"Would you just look at that sky," Joanna mused, interrupting Julia's thoughts. "All those pretty colors here to usher in another beautiful sunset."

Sunset! Julia gasped and clutched at her shawl.

"Oh, dear. I must be returning home."

Iskah's countenance fell as she and Simon rose from their settee. "I insist you stay the night, Julia."

Julia longed to defy her husband's orders and succumb to her mother's logic. After all, it was getting late, and she didn't relish the idea of venturing home alone. And even more than that, she gloried at the thought of soaking in the luxurious ritual baths, breathing in the heady scent of rich bath salts and fragrant oils. And to sink into her own plush, luxuriant canopy bed beneath the soft Egyptian sheets again…oh, it would be like Heaven after a year of sleeping on a hard-packed, earthen floor!

Julia could have wept when she considered the fact that she had given Barabbas her word to stay for one afternoon only. She did not wish to betray his trust, especially after he had extended this small olive branch. Even so, he had not forbidden her to visit her parents in the future. He had only insisted that her visits not interfere with her own housework; other than that, he had set no limits.

Breathing a silent prayer of gratitude, she chose to be thankful for this small slice of Heaven she had experienced coming home to her father, her mother, and her faithful nursemaid.

"I wish I could stay, Mother, but I promised my husband I would return home before nightfall."

It was obvious that Iskah wished to argue, but she clearly thought better of it and held her tongue. Instead, she said in a rather forced tone, "I understand."

"But I have spoken with Barabbas, Mother, and

he has consented to allow more frequent visits – especially when he is away."

Hope sprang to Iskah's eyes, and she offered a shaky smile. "I would like nothing better than to see more of my precious daughter."

"And you are always welcome at our house, small as it may be," Julia said with a teasing smile. "Please remember that."

Iskah and Simon exchanged knowing looks. "We would not want to intrude upon Barabbas' home, Julia," Simon explained gently. "But perhaps we can stop by occasionally if we are very careful not to overstay our welcome."

"I would love it if you would," Julia said, meaning it with all her heart. Gracefully adjusting her head covering, Julia prepared to leave despite the throbbing pain in her heart.

"I will be honest," she ventured tentatively, adoring the three glowing faces watching her intently. How different was their countenance from the last time she had stood in this courtyard, reciting vows to her betrothed! "I was reluctant to come. I hoped and prayed that I would not be a disappointment or an embarrassment to you, showing up on your doorstep in these old rags –"

"Nonsense," Simon interrupted her, taking her face gently in his weathered hand. "You are our cherished daughter. And, Julia, we could care less about the house that you live in or the clothes that you wear. The fact that you are seeking the Lord with all your heart and walking in His ways – that is what thrills us, my daughter, and brings the greatest joy to our hearts."

"Amen," Joanna breathed, dabbing at her eyes with the corner of her apron.

"Now you wait here and enjoy this beautiful evening while I arrange for a litter to take you home," Simon said with a warm smile.

A litter! How would her neighbors respond should she make a grand entrance upon a decorated litter like a self-important queen? Laughing softly, Julia said quickly, "I'm afraid I would draw much unwanted attention arriving home in that manner but thank you so very much for the extremely kind offer, Father."

"She's right, Simon," Iskah put in quickly, remembering the poverty-stricken precinct she had visited only once.

"Very well," Simon conceded, clearly apprehensive about the prospect of his daughter traveling Jerusalem's streets near nightfall, alone and unattended. "Then I shall send Jacob to accompany you home. That boy knows every street and alleyway in Jerusalem."

"That would be wonderful, Father. Traveling alone is rather daunting."

"Would you like to take some scrolls along with you? I have many copies you may find interesting."

"Oh, I would like nothing more!"

"Then you wait right here while I gather a few for you, and your mother will retrieve the care package she instructed the staff to put together for you."

Julia's eyes filled with thankful tears. "You all do too much for me."

Iskah smiled graciously. "You are our daughter. We love to do for you."

"I shall come along with you, Lady Iskah," Joanna put in stoutly. "I want to be sure they included the sweet rolls and fresh honey cakes in the care package."

Tears dimmed Julia's eyes as her loved ones disappeared beneath the pillared colonnades, bent on performing their respective tasks.

She was blessed. So very, very blessed.

Breathtaking streaks of pale pink, lavender, and gold swept across the early evening sky, and Julia was dazzled by the beauty of her surroundings. At peace, she paused before the striking marble fountain at the center of the courtyard, taking in the graceful lines of the carefully sculpted angel upon a marble pedestal, her hair falling about her shoulders in soft folds, her head thrown back as she held the marble trumpet to her still lips with graceful confidence. Cascades of crystal-clear water burst forth from the angel's trumpet, creating a soothing cadence as it splashed in glimmering sheets upon the cool waters of the fountain pool.

Julia had gazed upon this lovely statue many a time, pondering the meaning behind the angel's trumpet call.

Throughout history, the God of her fathers had wrought miracles, drawing the attention of a stubborn and contrary people by the blast of a mighty trumpet. By the trumpet, Jericho's impenetrable walls came crashing down upon its wicked occupants as Joshua led his men to a mighty victory. Later, Gideon's men defeated the Midianites when they heeded God's command to shout their battle cry, light their torches, and blast their trumpets. King David rejoiced before God, and his subjects gloried in the majesty of their Creator as the trumpet sounded its shrill cry, accompanied by a string of ancient instruments. For centuries, the trumpet ushered brave men to battle. The trumpet also famously announced the coming of the bridegroom for his bride.

Learned men who had studied the ancient Scriptures all their lives declared that their world would end with the blast of the mighty trumpet call of God. This not only declared the end but ushered in a brand-new beginning. Heaven and earth would one day pass away, but the Word of God would abide forever. And those who had given their lives to the Lord would abide with Him.

It was both a sobering and thrilling thought.

Tilting her head to one side, Julia observed the powerful stance of the lovely angel so skillfully wrought from the smooth pale marble, her eyes coming to rest upon that gleaming trumpet. The trumpet itself was a beacon to all – a call to...*something*. Before marrying Barabbas, the essence of the statue had troubled her spirit. At the time, she had known her bridegroom would come for her – but would she be ready? And even more importantly, she had instinctively known that – one day – the Messiah would also come. It had frightened her to consider that possibility, for she was entirely certain that she was far from ready for His coming.

But now, the trumpeting angel's powerful presence galvanized her spirit, calling her to action. The Messiah had indeed arrived, and His call went forth to all men: Will you love Me? Will you follow Me? Will you accept My instruction?

A peaceful smile touched Julia's lips as she considered the transformation that had taken place in her heart since the fateful day she had last stood here, binding herself in marriage to a man she scarcely knew.

The call she had once despised had now become her battle cry. And there was absolutely no doubt in her mind that she had fully accepted that clear clarion call to action. To obedience. Acceptance. Trust.

Another knowing smile graced her lips, and her heart pounded a steady drumbeat as it burned within her chest.

Let the trumpet blast its resounding battle cry!

This time, she would be ready.

CHAPTER 43

Julia glanced nervously at the loaves piled within the baskets she balanced delicately upon both arms. Despite the fact that she had feverishly baked pan after pan of bread until the wee hours of the morning, she knew the likelihood of satisfying the hunger of so many needy, pitiable invalids was infinitesimally small.

She had been no more prepared for the squalor, suffering, and misery that affronted her the moment she entered the pillared colonnades of the Pool of Bethesda than she had upon her first visit, when Barabbas had brought her to pray for Dan.

Now, as she stepped gingerly between moaning outcasts lying prostrate upon their mats, she wondered if she had made a mistake in coming.

No, she reminded herself firmly. *The Lord has called us to reach out to the needy, to feed the hungry. I have bread enough, but what of these poor souls? They have nothing.*

Confidence bolstered, Julia prayed silently as she knelt beside an aging man with cloudy, unseeing eyes. He gasped in fear when she took his hand.

"You needn't fear," Julia whispered, her heart bursting with sympathy for the blind man. "I have brought bread. Take and eat." Pressing a rounded loaf in his trembling hand, she closed her own hand over his and gave it a gentle squeeze. "May God be with you. May He bless you and keep you," she murmured softly as tears trickled from the man's uncooperative eyes. "He loves you. Put your trust in Him."

And so began Julia's ministry at the Pool of Bethesda. She knew she could not possibly feed all the hungry, but she could offer the little she did have and ask the Lord to multiply it. And she could offer hope. The sick and dying scattered about the healing pools were discarded by their own families and society, but Julia knew the Lord loved them with an everlasting love.

May I demonstrate Your love for them, Father. Move through my own feeble hands and feet. Supply Your words and speak through me. Take my pitiful supply and use it for Your glory!

Julia noticed a younger man propped against a marble pillar. He appeared healthy enough. An older woman – most likely his mother – sat beside him, her hand resting lightly upon his arm. Both wore ragged old garments that emphasized their bony shoulders and emaciated frames.

Julia wondered when they had last eaten.

Hurrying to their side, Julia knelt before them and offered her basket. "Please, take and eat," she encouraged with a warm smile.

The woman scrutinized her with suspicious eyes. "We have no coin."

"It is a gift – from the Lord," Julia tried to explain.

Tentatively, the woman reached for a golden loaf.

"Please, take one as well," Julia said, directing her speech toward the confused young man.

He opened his mouth, but the babble that spilled forth was garbled and unintelligible.

Attempting to hide her alarm, Julia looked to his mother.

"He's deaf. And dumb," the woman explained, her tone flat and unfeeling. "We come to the pool hoping the angel will stir the waters. He may be dumb, but he's nimble. We're hoping he'll make it to the pool first. You must be first in order to receive the healing."

Julia's heart went out to the woman and her son. "I see," she said quietly, touching the woman's shoulder in understanding. "May God grant the healing you seek."

The woman stared at her dumbly, but her eyes flickered slightly, betraying emotion.

"Here," Julia offered, removing several more loaves from the basket and placing them in the woman's shaking hands. "Please take them. And May God be with you."

The woman accepted the loaves with a slight nod, the faintest sheen of tears visible in her hopeless eyes.

Julia spoke to as many people as she could, passing out loaves of bread and whispering comfort from the Scriptures. Many people accepted the loaves with thanks. Others were too weak to understand. Still others responded with searing sarcasm when she assured them that God loved them.

Her work was interrupted when a strong hand landed heavily upon her shoulder. Turning around sharply, Julia looked up into the smiling eyes of the paralyzed man – the man whom Jesus had healed!

Stunned, Julia's hand went to her mouth, jostling the bread in the baskets she still balanced on each arm.

"The Lord has not forsaken us."

Tears sprang to her eyes when the man repeated the words she had spoken to him the night before his healing. Laughing joyously, she took his hand. "Look at you! You are healed!"

"By the grace of God! Heaven knows I don't deserve it."

"If any of us got what we deserved, we would be in deep, deep trouble."

The man laughed, his features relaxed and glowing. "I prayed to God that our paths would cross again. I sought you the day after my healing, but you were gone."

"I had to return home to my husband."

"I see. Your heart? Is your prognosis very bad?"

At first, Julia was puzzled. Then she remembered: the man had asked her what was ailing her. She had responded that it was her heart.

Blushing slightly, she admitted, "It isn't a weak heart, as you might have guessed. I meant my heart was broken, hurting. I sought healing in a different way than most gathered at this pool, I suppose."

The man nodded thoughtfully, stroking his long, wispy beard. "I doubt that, daughter. Many of us are prisoners of pain – not only in the physical sense. That night, you taught me an important lesson."

Julia studied him intently, captivated.

"That night, you spoke to me. And you were right, daughter. I had lost my faith. Once, God was my pillar of strength. But I had forsaken Him because He had not healed me. When you spoke to me with boldness, I realized that I had placed conditions upon my faith. I would honor God – as long as He performed as I wished."

"I understand," Julia said with great feeling. "I made the same mistake for many years. I had no desire to serve the Lord because I believed He interfered with my own plans for my life. He stood between me and the happiness I craved. Thankfully, our God is patient and He finally reached me. He taught me that I sabotaged my own happiness by forsaking the very principles He established to ensure our peace and security."

"You are a very wise young woman."

"Occasionally," Julia confessed with a weak smile. "I still have much to learn."

"Praise God you did not wait thirty-eight years as I did to recognize your folly."

"But you did see it – and our God is merciful! Look what He has done for you!"

"I sought you diligently because I wanted you to know that your words changed my life. The Lord used you to prepare my heart for Him. Had you not spoken, I would not have possessed the faith to believe in Jesus. The moment He laid eyes upon me, I knew Him. And in that moment, my desperate longing for healing no longer mattered. I realized I had wasted my entire life seeking after something that could not fulfill me. Healing and restoration had become my idol. I was convinced that I would never be happy in my current state. I was sure I would find joy if I could only be *healed*. But the joy I longed for was there all along – in His presence! I had simply turned away from it. And then, after I had surrendered my desires to God, Jesus touched me. He spoke to me. Power coursed through my entire being – and I was healed!"

Julia shook her head in wonder.

"It's as if the Lord already knew the very moment I would forsake my idol and return to Him. And the moment that I did, He was there – waiting for me with open arms."

Julia nodded, swallowing the lump in her throat. She understood all too well.

"This Jesus – He met me later, in the temple."

Julia's eyes widened in desperate interest. "What did He say?"

"He said, 'See, you have been made well. Sin no more, lest a worse thing come upon you.'"

Julia nodded in understanding. "I imagine it would be rather simple to fall into a sinful lifestyle after restoration – it's only natural to wish to feast on life when one has been confined for so long."

"I thank God for His mercy and truth. I will heed the words of Jesus and live according to His Word."

Julia hesitated but decided to plunge ahead anyway. After all, it was the boldness God had granted her that had changed this man's life. She would not cower now. "I believe Jesus is the Messiah," she whispered with great conviction.

The man's gray eyebrows rose in surprise. "You too?"

"There are others?"

"Many. We are watching, waiting. Who but the Messiah could perform the mighty works of this Man?"

Julia's entire being filled with warmth for this stranger she scarcely knew. It was as if those who believed in Jesus were tightly bound, joined together by invisible bonds of love, joy, and peace. The moment she stepped into the presence of another believer, she knew she was among family. It was a beautiful thing, a gift from God.

"I'm afraid I must go," Julia said, hating to leave but also eager for what was to come. "I am supposed to meet someone at the Upper Market."

"May I have your name, dear girl? I'd like to remember you in my prayers."

"My name is Julia, and I am honored that you wish to pray for me. And yours?"

"Matthias."

"I will be praying for you as well, Matthias," Julia assured him, meaning it with all her heart.

"Thank you truly, my daughter. Now go in peace, and may our Lord and Savior be with you always."

Julia took both his leathery hands in hers and squeezed them tight. "And may He be with you as well, dear friend."

Enveloped in a warmth she knew was from the Lord, Julia quickly distributed the remainder of her loaves, thanking God that so many had been fed and praying that others would be moved to help those she had been unable to reach.

She knew she must hurry in order to arrive at the Upper Market in time to meet Melina and Malchus. Her heart pounded furiously as she considered what it would be like to meet her closest friend after a year of separation. Would Melina be cold? Unfeeling? Cautious?

Julia certainly wouldn't blame her if she was.

Lord God, restore our friendship. Forgive my thoughtlessness. In Your great mercy, undo the damage I have done.

CHAPTER 44

Melina

"Are you sure you're up for this?" Malchus was agitated, concerned for Melina's tender heart and sensitive spirit. "After all, I never promised her that you would see her. I told her I would *try* to arrange a meeting."

Melina furrowed her delicate brows, attempting to curb her impatience. So many contrary emotions were battling for her attention. Anticipation. Fear. Excitement. Concern.

She longed to see Julia, but she wasn't sure what to expect. When last they had met, Julia was a head-strong, determined young woman fiercely in love with a forbidden man. Malchus had warned her that Julia was much changed. But how so? For the better? She certainly hoped so, for Julia's sake.

Malchus had also insinuated that Julia had finally discovered her common sense after enduring time in the "real world". What, exactly, had she endured? Had she been hardened by her trials, or simply enlightened?

"She has no right to feel upset should you wish not to see her," Malchus put in, drawing Melina from her silent reverie.

"Of course, I want to see her, Malchus! She is my dearest friend."

"She *was* your dearest friend."

"If friendship cannot survive when tried, then it is no friendship at all."

"Aptly stated. And a clear indication of the depth of Julia's dedication."

"You yourself have said she has endured much tragedy."

"Tragedy of her own making."

"Does that make it any easier to endure?"

"I wouldn't know. The blame for my own tragedies and misfortunes can be placed squarely at the feet of others more careless and cold-hearted than I. I myself am not at fault, of course." Though he intended to lighten the mood with his dry wit, Melina was further agitated by his callous words. Sighing, he took her by the arm and drew her closer to him. He wanted her to be near him.

While he tried to assure himself that his concern was solely for Melina's sake, he couldn't help but wonder if his motives were slightly self-driven. After all, he had come to depend upon his weekly rendezvous with Melina. He cherished that time alone with her. If Julia were to waltz back into the picture, he would be forced to share these treasured moments with a fickle friend who didn't deserve

Melina's loyalty in the first place.

It galled him just to consider it! Why, oh why, had he ever agreed to arrange this meeting?

Because you love this woman, Malchus reminded himself in annoyance, taking in Melina's silky black hair stirring gently in the wind, her soft green eyes, the curve of her smile. *And when you love someone, you do what is best for them – not for you.*

Still, that unwelcome bit of knowledge did little to make the trying ordeal any easier!

"I suppose," Malchus began drolly, attempting to mask the depth of his true feelings, "that once your friendship with Julia is restored, you will have little use for me."

Melina stared at him, stunned. "Malchus, why would you say that?"

"You began these lessons with Julia to discuss the Scriptures. I was simply a substitute after she deserted you – and now that she has returned, I'm clearly no longer needed."

Melina gazed up into his eyes. Seeing right through the mask of lighthearted humor he wore, she recognized his need, his concern. And nearly melted.

Reaching up, she touched the curve of his strong jaw. "Malchus, have I not told you that I love you? That will never change."

Malchus covered the gentle hand caressing his face with his own large, work roughened hand. "I'm going to hold you to that," he said huskily.

"Please do."

An easy smile crossed his face. He was relieved

to see her eyes glimmering with that familiar, playful shine.

Emboldened by her playfulness, Malchus cupped her face in one strong hand. "I want to be with you, Melina. When can we be together?"

Melina gripped his wrist as if it were a lifeline, her heart pounding steadily in her chest as heady, unfamiliar emotions soared. Praying for clarity and wisdom, she repeated softly, "Be together?" He hadn't asked *when can we marry*? There was a vast difference.

"I want to hold you. I want to kiss you. I want all of you, Melina."

It was no secret that nearly everyone in Roman society indulged in sensuous "relationships" before marriage – relationships in which they enjoyed the privileges of matrimonial bliss without the marital bond of commitment. There were even many here in Palestine claiming to be God-fearers who enjoyed the pleasures of marriage before entering into the sacred marriage covenant.

However, Melina knew the popular and widely accepted way of life was not for her. She had given herself to God, and she would not dishonor Him by forsaking purity and chastity.

Saddened, Melina gazed into the eyes of her beloved. "Intimacy is reserved for marriage, Malchus."

Malchus withdrew his hand, sensing the quiet reprimand. "You know I want to marry you."

"Then we have our answer."

"I'm not sure I even understand the question."

"The intimacy we long to share will happen one

day – if we marry."

"If?" Malchus' eyes narrowed suspiciously.

"If it is the Lord's will."

"Has He spoken to you about it at all? Has He even given you a *hint* about when we might fulfill our desires?"

Detecting the frustration in his tone, Melina looked away, disheartened. Didn't Malchus expect to hear from the Lord regarding this matter as well? After all, the Lord was *his* God, too! Why did he place the responsibility of spiritual leadership solely upon *her*?

It also disturbed her that Malchus' convictions did not mirror her own. Perhaps that was why the Lord had urged her to wait rather than acting upon her own raging feelings for Malchus.

"If you were any other woman," Malchus said ruefully, "I would think you were toying with my emotions."

"I'm sorry, Malchus. But I must wait on the Lord."

"I wouldn't mind so much if it didn't mean *I* had to wait too."

Melina smiled in understanding. "We must trust Him. His timing is always right, and His will is always best."

"You speak with such unwavering confidence. I admire it, really."

"You can possess the same confidence, Malchus. God loves us. He wants what is best for us."

"How could having you be anything other than absolutely *best* for me?" he inquired with a teasing grin.

Because the Lord has both of our interests to consider, Melina wished to say, exasperated. *And at this point, you are more interested in serving yourself than serving Him.*

Why, oh why, didn't Malchus understand? The Lord guided His followers by His Word! He spoke to her heart in a still small voice. Didn't He speak to Malchus as well? Was Malchus simply deaf to His voice? Had he no ability to recognize the Lord's voice for himself?

"Have you sought the Lord about this matter yourself, Malchus?"

Malchus ran a nervous hand through thick dark hair. "He doesn't speak to me the same way He speaks to you."

"Oh, but Malchus, He would – if you would *listen*!"

"Are you implying that I don't know how to pray?"

"Of course not. But praying is the simple part. The hardest part is listening to God's voice and acting in obedience."

"So now I'm disobedient, too?" Though Malchus' voice teased, Melina sensed an edge to his tone that hadn't been there before.

"I have offended you." Tears welled in her large green eyes.

Malchus could have kicked himself for hurting her. Gathering her hands, he pulled her closer. "Melina, I love you. I don't ever want to hurt you."

She gazed up at him with glistening eyes.

"I will wait for you as long as it takes – even if it kills me. I promise."

Melina offered a weak smile, her spirit strangely unsettled.

"God will show you when the time is right. And the moment He grants you peace or permission – or whatever it is you seek from Him – I will be waiting with open arms to scoop you up and carry you home!"

"But will *you* seek the Lord diligently about this, Malchus? God will speak to you, too."

"Anything to make you happy, my love."

"Not for *me*, Malchus. For *you*! The Lord will speak to you and give you guidance in this situation if you earnestly seek Him. Is it not the man who is accountable to God for providing spiritual leadership?"

Malchus attempted to hide his grimace.

"Is it not so?" Melina asked innocently.

"It is," Malchus managed, breaking out in a cold sweat. What exactly did she expect of him? He was no Moses or King David! He was a simple, ordinary manservant, for Heaven's sake! Did she expect him to part the Red Sea or to write a hundred psalms? If so, she was to be sorely disappointed.

"Promise me you will pray about this."

Lifting her hands to his lips, he kissed them gently. "I promise." He would have agreed to anything in order to abandon this uncomfortable topic of conversation!

"Oh, thank you, Malchus! The Lord will not disappoint you."

Malchus didn't mention that *that* was exactly what he was afraid of! What if the Lord's will didn't line up with his own? He couldn't bear to live without this woman! He knew he would never get over her – never! Melina was the embodiment of the peace he so desperately craved. He had never met anyone who possessed such depths of peace and tranquility. She was a gift from God, a bright light burning in a world encompassed in darkness.

He needed her. He needed that light.

"Malchus!" Melina reached for his hand, her body stiffening.

Instinctively, Malchus' eyes scanned their bustling surroundings. A young woman had broken through the crowd of haggling shoppers on the market floor and was rushing toward them, tears streaming down her cheeks, her simple robe fluttering in the breeze, her modest head covering slipping over one shoulder.

"It's her," Melina gasped, her face blooming with excitement. "It's Julia!"

Malchus' stomach clenched along with his fists. Working his jaw back and forth, he took a deep breath and determined to be there for Melina, regardless of the outcome.

If Julia was the same spoiled girl she'd always been, Melina would need him now more than ever.

CHAPTER 45

Julia

A torrent of distressing thoughts flooded Julia's mind as she approached Melina and Malchus. Sheltered beneath the stately pillared colonnade, they appeared deep in discussion. When Melina turned gracefully and met her gaze, Julia's heart constricted, and tears sprang to her eyes.

What on earth must Melina be thinking? When they had met, Julia had been a stunning, vibrant young woman dressed in extravagant, imported finery, arrayed in exquisite jewels and doused in expensive perfume. She winced when she considered her appearance now. Face devoid of cosmetics and donning a simple, worn robe and shawl, Julia imagined Melina's surprise at the shocking change in her appearance.

Would Melina secretly condemn her for her foolish choices and lack of restraint? Melina had faithfully served God, unwavering in her devotion to Him. She, Julia, had abandoned Him the moment His will had interfered with her own. And in her time of trouble, she had neglected her friendship with Melina, drowning in a flood of self-pity and despair.

What must Melina think of her now? Would she even wish to continue their friendship?

Humiliation stained her cheeks as she picked up her pace and rushed toward the two servants, her heart racing, her empty baskets bouncing gracelessly up against her as she attempted to balance them on her arms.

Oh Lord, I'm so ashamed. If I were Melina, I would want absolutely nothing to do with me –

"Julia!" Tears streamed down Melina's cheeks as she burst toward her friend, running to her with both arms held open, beckoning, welcoming.

"Melina!" Julia's heart nearly burst with relief as warmth washed over her entire being. Dropping her baskets, she ran into Melina's open arms, overjoyed.

Finally pulling away from their embrace, the two young women studied each other's glowing faces, tears streaming down their cheeks and joyous laughter bubbling up from deep inside.

"Oh, Julia! I can't begin to tell you how much I have missed you!"

"And I have missed you!"

"I have not ceased to pray for you. How I have worried for you!"

Julia shook her head in disbelief. "Oh, Melina, you are too good – too merciful!"

"I would agree wholeheartedly with that assessment."

Both women turned in surprise, unaware that Malchus stood beside them. He had retrieved Julia's discarded baskets, for she had neglected them in her haste to reach Melina.

Julia offered him a broad smile. "Malchus, I am in your debt. Thank you for arranging this meeting."

"You are most welcome, as long as you conduct yourself in such a way that I don't regret it."

"Malchus!" Melina stared at him, horrified. "How can you say that?"

"She has abandoned you once. I don't want to see you suffer like that again."

Melina gaped at him with great displeasure, but Julia quickly touched her arm and intervened. "No, Melina, he's right. After I married Barabbas, my entire life fell apart. Rather than reaching out to you, I withdrew into myself like a turtle in its shell, wallowing in my own misery. It was a selfish thing to do. And I beg your forgiveness –"

"You already have it!" Melina declared forcefully, taking Julia by the arm and drawing her beneath the cool shade of the colonnade. "Come! Sit! We have so much to discuss, and so little time to do so."

The three seated themselves comfortably upon cool stones, ignoring the milling throngs of harried shoppers and the heated debates ensuing all around them as bored men gathered in the shade of the colonnades, restlessly biding their time until the arrival of Pentecost.

"Now tell me everything that has happened

since last we met!"

"Melina, we have less than an hour – not two weeks," Malchus remarked dryly.

Melina ignored him and turned to Julia. "I want to hear everything."

Julia swallowed the lump in her throat, determined not to shed any more tears today. She was touched by Melina's kindness, overwhelmed by her mercy, and so thankful to be among friends again. Tremulously, she filled them in on all the details – her marriage to Barabbas, her high hopes for happiness, and then the searing disappointment she experienced after marrying him. Knowing that both could be trusted to keep silent, she revealed her fear over her husband's involvement with the Zealots, his refusal to turn to God, and his determination to extract vengeance upon the Romans at any cost.

"This is how – by the grace of God – I stumbled upon Malchus that day at the Pool of Bethesda," she explained, taking a deep breath. "Barabbas hoped God would answer my prayers on behalf of his dying friend."

Melina placed a loving hand over her dear friend's. "Malchus told me all about it. Julia, I'm so terribly sorry. I can't imagine what you must have gone through."

"My heart aches for Dan. I have been unable to discover if he has any family to notify. My husband refuses to speak of it."

"I will pray the Lord opens his heart then," Melina said decidedly. "If Dan has a family, they must be hurting wondering what has happened to him."

"It pains me terribly when I think of it."

"But the wonderful news is that he made a decision to follow Jesus and gave his life to the Lord before his death," Melina assured her. "We will see him again, Julia! His troubles are behind him forever, and his future is sealed - He will spend eternity in paradise with the Lord!"

"Praise God," Julia said with great feeling. "And despite the fact that it was a dreadful ordeal, I am so thankful it happened because God used it for His own good purpose. Had Barabbas not dragged me there against my will, I would have been unable to encourage Matthias – the man who was healed that day. Nor would I have met Jesus, witnessed a miracle, or learned of the great need of those who suffer by the healing pools."

Melina shook her head in wonder. "How I envy you, Julia! I would give anything to see Jesus. Oh, how I long to see Him, to hear Him speak!"

"Disaster and turmoil trail behind this Jesus wherever He goes," Malchus put in dryly. "I imagine you are far safer within the secure walls of Herod's fortress."

"Perhaps from a mere human standpoint," Melina countered softly. "But men who trust in horses, chariots, and fortresses for protection have often come to ruin. Don't the Scriptures say, *The fortress of the high fort of your walls He will bring down, lay low, and bring to the ground, down to dust*? But David declared, *The Lord is my rock and my fortress and my deliverer; my*

God, my strength, in whom I will trust; my shield and the horn of my salvation, my stronghold. God will protect those who put their trust in Him and accept His chosen One."

"Let's hope the Lord will also protect His chosen One. Even now, Caiaphas and his underlings plot His demise."

"He has committed no crime," Melina stated firmly. "What can they do to Him?"

"Ah, my innocent friends. So much to learn, though I daresay Julia sampled a bit of their venom that day by the pool."

"I have never known men who possess such cold eyes." Fleetingly, Julia's thoughts drifted to Amraphel. His eyes possessed the same fierceness and restlessness she had glimpsed upon the faces of the Pharisees, scribes, and Sadducees that day, and yet the ferocious Zealots and stately religious leaders hailed from entirely different worlds. Even so, they possessed the same insatiable hunger to gratify their own desires. Perhaps their common ground was the fact that they unknowingly bowed to the same dark master in their unbending determination to serve themselves and their own purposes.

"But Jesus cannot be arrested without a charge," Melina said hopefully, drawing Julia's attention back to the present.

"The Sanhedrin can fabricate a charge out of thin air," Malchus reminded her grimly. "I've seen them do it more times than I care to recount."

Melina stared at him, wide-eyed. "They would lie about an innocent Man?"

"Of course, they would, if it served their purposes. All they need are two or three witnesses, and bribes are most effective – as long as the perjurers recite their lines accurately so the testimonies agree."

Julia shook her head in disgust. "*They* should be the ones imprisoned, operating in such a disgraceful and unlawful manner!"

"Unfortunately, Caiaphas has grander plans for this Jesus than a simple prison sentence."

Melina turned fearful eyes toward Malchus. "What do you mean?"

"Caiaphas won't rest until this Man is buried in a fresh tomb. I've seen him like this before. Jesus has threatened everything Caiaphas stands for. He won't allow it to continue long."

"But by Roman law, the high priest no longer possesses the power of execution. A Roman authority would have to condemn Jesus, and He has done nothing worthy of condemnation."

"A trifling detail. Caiaphas is a master at manipulation. He will string the people along like little puppets, and they will dance right along to his tune, completely unaware that they're walking directly into his trap. And, unfortunately, Jesus Himself will bear the brunt of it."

"But how?" Melina asked with pleading eyes.

"I haven't the slightest idea. But Caiaphas will do it. I've served the high priest for many years, and I know when he is biding his time."

The two women remained tragically, thoughtfully silent.

"Now I've seen Caiaphas buck the Roman system

numerous times, condemning men and women to death when he had no right. I've seen him orchestrate events like a trained puppeteer, turning the people against a victim in a split second. I've witnessed angry crowds doing the dirty work for him, stoning an innocent man to death after Caiaphas fanned the flames of the people's envy or animosity. But those victims were all nobodies, all unknown men. This Jesus – He has accumulated an impressive following. The people love Him – for now. Caiaphas will have to wait for the perfect opening, or risk revolt – which He will never do, for then his power and his precious title would be at stake."

Melina knit her slender brows thoughtfully. "Perhaps it is all part of God's plan. Isaiah prophesied that the Messiah would be put to death for the sins of the people. Men often collide headfirst with the will of God in their own violent attempts to avoid it."

"Would you please clarify that lofty statement for the sake of uneducated mortals like us?" Malchus asked wryly.

"Speak for yourself, uneducated mortal," Julia grinned impishly.

"Malchus, you say that Caiaphas wishes to turn the people against Jesus. But isn't this exactly what the Scriptures predict? *He is despised and rejected by men*, according to the prophet Isaiah. Perhaps in his desire to squelch the will of God, Caiaphas will unwittingly accomplish the Lord's purposes."

"Well, that would be the first time in his life that Caiaphas was actually in step with the Almighty,"

Malchus disclosed dryly. "But all that aside – have either of you even considered the possibility that this Jesus could simply be another gifted Teacher who has aroused the jealousy of the Sanhedrin? The prospect of the Messiah's coming is titillating, yes, but is it realistic?"

"The Scriptures themselves bear witness of His coming, unless you deem them unrealistic as well," Melina said quietly, a hint of accusation in her tone.

"If one decides to pledge his allegiance to any so-called Messiah, he risks the wrath of the greatest religious and political superpowers on this earth – both Rome and the Jewish Sanhedrin," Malchus argued vehemently.

"But one cannot make himself an enemy of God for fear of making an enemy of man," Melina said with quiet conviction. "Running from the truth will not make it any less true, Malchus."

He who does not honor the Son does not honor the Father who sent Him... The jolting words Jesus had spoken at Solomon's Porch came rushing back, and Malchus hid a grimace. In his opinion, Jesus simply made life more complicated and peace more elusive. Malchus had discovered such joy and peace when he had chosen the God of his fathers, but now Jesus was here, rocking the boat. His forefathers had worshipped only God the Father before the appearance of this Man claiming the lofty title of Son of God. Why must *he* now honor a man who tempted death at every turn?

One look at Melina's glowing features was enough to convince him that she had already made up her mind. As far as she was concerned, Jesus was the Messiah. Period. And that realization greatly disturbed him.

He dared a cautious glance at Julia and deduced that he would gain no help or support from her in swaying Melina's stubborn opinion. Julia, too, had made her decision for the Man claiming to be God's Son.

Had they not the slightest idea about the trouble that was about to come upon those who followed this Jesus and His controversial teachings? Had they completely disregarded the prospect of a peaceful, pleasant future?

The thought that disturbed him far more than he cared to admit was the fact that Melina had chosen to embrace a new religious sect that invited turmoil, uncertainty, and violence – regardless of the impact it might have upon their life together.

Briefly, he considered arguing that the great men of old hadn't even known about this Jesus, and surely God had accepted them! Perhaps then Melina would listen to reason –

"The time the Scriptures foretold is finally upon us," Melina was saying, her voice drawing him back to reality. "Just think – even the mighty men of ancient times – men like Abraham and Moses and David – foresaw the Messiah's coming! They believed in Him and tried to prepare us for His coming through their writings and prophecies!"

Malchus hid his annoyance, wondering if Melina had somehow managed to detect the direction of his rebellious thoughts. How could she possibly refute his arguments before he even voiced them?

"Moses had no idea that a Man named Jesus would appear centuries later claiming to be the Son of God," he dared to argue. "Nor did Abraham or David or any of the rest."

"Moses did indeed know that Jesus would come, though he may not have known Him by name," Melina said, her eyes alight with excitement. "Remember, Malchus? Moses said, *The Lord your God will raise up for you a Prophet like me from your midst, from your brethren. Him you shall hear*...for the Lord had said to Moses, *I will raise up for them a Prophet like you from among their brethren, and will put My words in His mouth, and He shall speak to them all that I command Him. And it shall be that whoever will not hear My words, which He speaks in My name, I will require it of him.*"

Malchus had fled from Jesus' presence the day He had spoken at Solomon's Porch. But Jesus' mighty words had drifted upon the wind, chasing after him even as he fled. Those words returned to him now, piercing him as they had that day, urging him to heed the quiet voice beseeching his spirit...

You do not have His word abiding in you, because whom He sent, Him you do not believe. You search the Scriptures, for in them you think you have eternal life; and these are they which testify of Me. But you are not willing to come to Me, that you may have life... Do not think that I shall accuse you to the Father; there is one who accuses you – Moses, in whom you trust. For if you believed Moses, you would believe Me; for he wrote about Me...

"And Jeremiah also prophesied that God would raise the Messiah from the line of David!" Julia added, affected by Melina's enthusiasm.

Malchus attempted to follow Julia's excited chatter, but his soul was strangely troubled.

"*'Behold, the days are coming,' says the Lord, 'that I will raise to David a Branch of righteousness; a King shall reign and prosper and execute judgment and righteousness in the earth. In His days Judah will be saved, and Israel will dwell safely; now this is His name by which He will be called: The Lord our righteousness.'*" Julia smiled broadly, pleased that she had succeeded in committing parts of Simon's scrolls to memory.

"And the Lord must have revealed this to David himself, for he said: *The Lord said to my Lord, 'Sit at My right hand, till I make Your enemies Your footstool.'* David must have known that the Messiah would descend from his bloodline!" Melina added excitedly. "See, Malchus? The Messiah is mentioned in nearly every book of the Old Testament! He's there, biding His time, waiting for the moment when He would step into the world He created and turn it upside down!"

"And Abraham must have known as well, because God promised that all the earth would be blessed through his seed. From the very beginning, God handpicked the men who would carry the seed of the promised Messiah," Julia mused thoughtfully.

"That was the verse that Joanna pointed out to me when I grew discouraged," Melina explained with a soft smile.

"Joanna?"

"Yes, the wife of Herod's overseer, Chuza. She is a wonderful woman, committed to the Lord."

"It must be such a joy to work alongside a fellow believer!"

"It is! She has begun following Jesus and supporting His ministry financially. She and her husband are rather well off, due to his incredibly prestigious position in Herod's household. When she returns, she tells me wonderful things about Jesus. I would give anything to travel with her."

Ah, the regal Joanna – Melina's self-appointed guardian and chaperone. Malchus hid his annoyance as the women discussed Melina's newest friend. He imagined the severe woman had greatly influenced Melina in her decision for Jesus – yet another mark against the austere woman.

"My neighbor, Deborah, has decided to do the same!" Julia explained, interrupting Malchus' line of thinking. "She and her husband have left for Capernaum to follow Him and hear more of His teaching."

"Perhaps they will meet then – my Joanna and your Deborah – and they will become friends," Melina said with a whimsical smile. "I was afraid that perhaps the Messiah was only for the Jewish people. But it was Joanna who reminded me that God promised *all* nations would be blessed by the Messiah – and that includes the Gentiles. I began to study the Scriptures for myself, and I discovered many other verses that supported this. For example, Isaiah claimed: *In that day there shall be a root of Jesse, who shall stand as a banner to the people;*

for the Gentiles shall seek Him, and His resting place shall be glorious."

"It's a beautiful promise, Melina," Julia agreed with a warm smile.

"I long to share this news with others, to shout it from the rooftops!" Melina said, her eyes distant. "I remember what it was like to have no hope. There are others out there – Gentiles who long for the assurance of salvation."

"You have already impacted many by your testimony, Melina," Julia said forcefully, "and I am among those who have learned a great deal from you. I know the Lord will continue to use you for His glory."

"May it be so," Melina agreed softly.

"As much as I hate to be the bearer of bad news, dear ladies, I imagine the three of us ought to consider returning to our respective taskmasters."

Both women were drawn back to the present, and they smiled at Malchus' dry wit.

"I suppose Malchus is right," Melina said sadly. "Julia, I praise God that he brought us together again. I have missed your friendship."

"And I have missed your company more than you know," Julia agreed.

"Shall we meet again next week?" Melina asked, her eyes full of hope.

"I will do everything in my power to be here, Melina."

Well, of course you will! Malchus gritted his teeth in frustration.

"Please be praying for my mistress, Salome. She

is in a terrible state. I fear for her – and for myself, to be honest, when I am in her presence."

"Of course, I will pray for her, Melina, and for you too," Julia promised.

"I have never ceased praying for you – or for Barabbas, Julia," Melina assured her, touching her shoulder. "I will continue do so with fervor."

"I see how quickly I have been forgotten," Malchus mused, a wry grin tipping his lips. "Yes," he stated to no one in particular, "I would greatly appreciate your prayers for me as well, thank you so much for asking."

"Oh, Malchus, you know I pray for you," Melina said, touching his arm.

"Well, then, pray specifically for the demise of my dear cousin, who continues to derive the greatest joy and pleasure plaguing me unto death."

Julia's eyes twinkled with mischief. "This sounds rather interesting. Perhaps I'd like to meet this cousin of yours."

"The devil would prove more gracious."

Melina smiled her understanding. "Malchus, from what you've shared about your cousin, he is a born leader of men with his kingly bearing, charisma, and powerful presence. Perhaps you should be praying for him purposefully, fervently, without ceasing."

"Oh, I do pray fervently – that he would step off a cliff."

Julia erupted in delightful laughter.

"Please, Julia, don't encourage him," Melina entreated with a teasing smile. She turned serious eyes to Malchus. "Truly, Malchus, your cousin is a menace because he serves himself. But a man like that – he will always lead other men, be it for evil or for good. But with his magnetic personality and determination, imagine what he could accomplish if he were won?"

"The devil himself will recant before he does!"

"I wouldn't be so sure, Malchus. Is anything too hard for God?"

"Woman, how great your faith."

After exchanging several additional last minute prayer requests, teary farewells, and embraces, the three friends reluctantly parted ways. Melina and Julia departed restored, edified, and encouraged, but a dark cloud had settled over Malchus. As he strode unhappily toward Caiaphas' estate, brooding, he wondered what had happened to shatter his serenity. Was it the fact that he and Melina couldn't see eye to eye where this debatable new Rabbi was concerned? Or was it the fact that Melina had rallied in favor of his detestable cousin, urging him to pray for Alexander when he would much rather witness his swift demise?

You are not willing to come to Me, that you may have life...

Life! He sighed, dismal. What quality of life could one possibly hope to possess while committed to a Man who was wanted by the Sanhedrin, bore a price on His head, and made preposterous claims that infuriated those with the power to annihilate any threat?

CHAPTER 46

Malchus

Pentecost swept into Jerusalem like an early summer storm. Bored and listless after seven weeks of monotony and inactivity following the Passover celebration, the city's occupants partook of the feasting, festivities, and camaraderie with reckless abandon.

Malchus could have easily wept for joy when the festival finally ended. It had been a maddening week in Caiaphas' household. Caiaphas was ridiculously particular under *normal* circumstances – the feasts and holy days simply intensified his determination to attain perfection in the eyes of his adoring public.

Malchus was exhausted. He was convinced he hadn't been off his feet in days, nor had he partaken of a decent meal since the festival began. While the family and the guests of the high priest enjoyed festive banquets, long, relaxing evenings of storytelling and musical entertainment, delicious soaks in the elaborate ceremonial baths, and the tranquility of

Caiaphas' pristine gardens, the household servants nearly ran themselves ragged attempting to meet the countless demands.

In fact, Malchus had been so consumed in the preparations and execution of the religious feast that he had missed several meetings with Melina and Julia. Though he had left a note explaining his actions, he knew Melina would be disappointed. At least, he hoped she would be.

They hadn't parted on the best of terms. Melina seemed convinced that Jesus was the long-awaited Messiah, but he wasn't ready to jump to any conclusions. Fortunately, the ensuing chaos had distracted him from dwelling on the widening rift between him and his beloved. Otherwise, just thinking about it would have driven him mad.

The only positive thing that could be said about the last two weeks was the fact that every servant in the great house had been so overwhelmed that Malchus was spared Alexander's endless plaguing and Mara's weepy entreaties. Thankfully, they too had been completely absorbed in household tasks.

Pausing before Caiaphas' impressive Roman-style bibliotheca, Malchus rapped twice upon the door before entering. Receiving no response, he breathed a prayer of gratitude and entered the luxurious chamber. Abisha had ordered him to see to the scrolls scattered about the marble-topped tables and the monumental work desk within the impressive library.

Eager to complete the task so he could retire for the evening, Malchus scooped up several scrolls scattered atop the first table. Carrying them toward the massive floor-to-ceiling shelves lining the walls, Malchus girded himself for the impossible task of locating the proper slot for each scroll. In the dim, flickering lamplight of early evening, the task proved even more trying than usual.

With an amused smile, Malchus supposed he should be interested in whichever scrolls the high priest had been studying so intently. All throughout the festival week, Caiaphas had closeted himself within this library – sometimes alone, other times with carefully selected associates – and remained buried beneath piles of ancient texts for hours and hours on end.

What exactly had he been looking for?

Probably desperately searching for grounds to condemn his favorite Rabbi, Malchus thought drolly, weary of the entire ordeal. He didn't want to think about it.

At the farthest end the bibliotheca, stately Babylonian curtains swayed and flapped gently in the early evening breezes. The curtains sectioned off an elegant balcony overlooking another stretch of neatly manicured gardens.

Malchus' ears pricked uneasily when he recognized the sound of hushed voices floating upon the evening breeze.

Good heavens! Malchus' face paled when he realized Caiaphas was sequestered with someone on the balcony hidden behind those impressive hanging curtains.

Instinctively, he lowered the scrolls quietly upon

the nearest tabletop and prepared to make haste. He had no desire to be accused of eavesdropping upon the priest's private conversation. The consequences might prove dire indeed.

"You needn't be alarmed, nor look at me with that ridiculous expression."

It was Caiaphas speaking. Malchus paused as he neared the enormous arched entryway by which he had planned to escape, consumed with curiosity.

"I am simply reminding you that – in some cases – marriage can prove rather advantageous."

"I've never considered myself the marrying type."

Lucius! Malchus' blood boiled. He should have known. Caiaphas had grown more and more dependent upon the vile soldier, even promoting the man to captain of his guard. Caiaphas' most crucial – and unethical – cases always fell to Lucius, for the guard obeyed blindly at the mere mention of gold coin.

"I don't care what you 'consider' yourself, and neither should you, for that matter." The irritation was evident in Caiaphas' tone. "You should be interested in pursuing the path that proves the most advantageous. And marriage to this serving wench will, in fact, prove quite advantageous to you, as well as to the advancement of your career."

"I'm listening."

I wish I wasn't, Malchus thought grimly. He had to strain to hear the following sentence, for Caiaphas had lowered his voice considerably.

"We have constructed the perfect trap, but we must incorporate the process immediately. It will take a bit of time to carry out, and as you know, time is of the essence. We must act now, for we are losing precious time."

"And how will a union with the serving woman, Mara, further your plans to trap the pestilent Rabbi?"

"In time, you shall see. For now, I simply ask you to wed the maiden. She's plain, but it is no secret she has been pining for you for years. Use this situation to your advantage. Revel in her worship and feast upon her desire."

A soft chuckle escaped Lucius' lips, and Malchus' hands balled into fists.

"The wedding needn't be a traditional Jewish affair. After all, a Roman union is only as sacred and binding as you wish it to be. And you, my good man, are every inch a Roman. According to the Roman way, you possess the option of marriage by *confarreatio* which would result in union until death, *coemptio*, or *usus*. I would recommend marriage by *usus*, as it is easily absolved. Once our plan has come to fruition, I myself will personally see to the abolition of your 'marriage', if you wish."

"And in the meantime?"

"Make an elaborate proposal. Marry the girl. Convince her that her wildest dreams have come true. Then, within a few weeks, we will carry out the next phase of the plan. You are not averse to travel?"

"I never have been."

"You needn't worry about your lovely 'wife' accompanying you, as she will be needed here in the kitchen."

"Based on your tone, I imagine my assignment would prove distasteful to a young bride?"

Caiaphas chuckled darkly. "It certainly would. I cannot disclose the information yet, but soon you will know."

"I welcome the opportunity."

"Then I imagine it is safe to assume you will participate in this affair? It is of the utmost importance. This will prove to be your most crucial assignment yet, and I do not want to be disappointed, nor can we afford to fail in this attempt."

"I live to do your bidding, my lord."

"Ah, my young friend. I am pleased to hear it. And I assure you, you will receive your weight in gold for your service."

Sensing that the morbid conversation had drawn to a close, Malchus disappeared around the corner, sickened.

How on earth could a marriage between two unimportant people possibly prove advantageous to the high priest? A trap, he had said. And Lucius' words indicated that the trap was intended for Jesus, the famous carpenter-turned-Teacher.

Just what did Caiaphas intend to do?

Shaking his head in frustration, Malchus strode angrily down the long, frescoed corridor, making a sharp turn and then jogging down a flight of broad marble steps two at a time.

Clearly, Caiaphas had a plan. And he didn't care in the least if his cruel scheme demolished Mara's heart and shattered her world – as long as his plans succeeded.

For a brief instant, Malchus considered warning Mara. Shaking his head to clear the confusion and remembering the last time he had attempted to warn her about Lucius' intentions, he thought better of it.

No, the woman was stubborn as an ox and blind as a bat. She was going to believe whatever she wanted to believe, anyway. She would simply resent him all the more, making preposterous claims about his determination to squelch her happiness! Unfortunately, Mara was going to have to discover the truth for herself. Nothing he said or did would convince her of Lucius' wicked intent.

To warn her would only further strain an already unbearably tenuous relationship.

CHAPTER 47

Julia

Barabbas swung into the small house, slamming the door with such fury that the entire structure shuddered in response.

Alarmed, Julia glanced up from the fire she tended, her eyes round with fright.

"By the gods, I'll kill him. *I'll kill him*!"

"Barabbas! What has happened?"

"I would have murdered him in the streets in cold blood, had there not been a hundred witnesses milling about to guarantee my crucifixion!"

Frightened, Julia backed against the wall nearest the hearth, her eyes following her husband as he paced about the small house like a confined predator. His fierce eyes kindled with angry fire, and the set of his jaw was dangerous.

From across the room, Barabbas faced her head on, his eyes alive and blazing with scarcely contained fury. His broad shoulders were thrown back, his wide chest heaving with every breath. "I saw him."

Heart hammering loudly in her own ears, Julia dared shakily, "Who?"

"I saw him! The man who murdered Dan. The wretch is *alive. By the gods*!"

"You said you saw him die –"

"I saw him pitch headlong over the edge of a cliff. No man could have survived that fall. Unless by some bloody miracle the devil landed on an extremely narrow ledge or shelf protruding from the cliff face! Even so, he should have been crushed by the shower of rocks and boulders the men were heaving over the edge of the highest peaks."

Julia's body grew cold as she imagined the violence involved in her husband's work. "Perhaps you saw another who simply looks like him," she offered weakly. It frightened her to consider what Barabbas might do if he knew the man responsible for the death of his closest friend was within his grasp.

"I know it was him. I looked him in the eyes, and he recognized me. I know he did. His eyes lit like fire and the coward whispered to the legionnaires nearest him. I hightailed it out of there and led them on a merry chase through the winding streets and alleyways of this pestilent city. They couldn't keep up, but they know I'm still on the streets."

The blood drained from Julia's face. "Oh, Barabbas. Will they come after you?"

"They won't find me. Nor will that worthless wretch see me when I come for him."

"Barabbas, please –"

"He will pay for what he did to Dan. The last

thing on this earth he will see is the face of the man he meant to kill. But he will pay the price."

"Barabbas, sit down and calm yourself. You mustn't say such things!"

Ignoring her, Barabbas gathered up his leather satchel and began furiously packing his belongings.

Julia watched him, pale and troubled. "What are you doing?"

"I have to go."

"Where are you going?" she asked faintly, reading the rage upon his face.

"I need to find Amraphel. He is in Galilee. I'll return after I find him."

"Barabbas, please, leave him out of this! Amraphel is a wicked man!"

"More so than the man who murdered Dan in cold blood?"

"Have you so swiftly forgotten your own intent? You were there to murder and pillage as well! What right have you to judge another?"

Barabbas turned on her, grabbing her arm and drawing her close to his face. "That man is a blood-thirsty coward, trained to take the lives of innocent men by force. I bear the sword of retribution. Don't you ever compare me to bloody Roman swine again, or you will have great cause to regret it." Releasing her, Barabbas slung his satchel over his shoulder and headed for the door.

Julia rushed ahead of him, shielding the exit with her own body. Tears coursed down her cheeks as she beseeched him. "Barabbas, don't do this. I beg you, consider the consequences of your actions!"

"Step aside, Julia." His menacing tone chilled her to the very core.

"Leave vengeance in the hands of God! He alone can recompense and redeem your life in the process!"

Drawing his face close to hers, Barabbas' lips curved in a ferocious sneer. Julia scarcely recognized him and drew back at the black fire glowing within his eyes. It was almost as if a dark presence had settled there and now peered out from Barabbas' own eyes, gloating as it dug its talons deeper into the soul of her husband.

"You listen to me, Julia, and listen well," Barabbas ground out, his tone low and increasingly menacing. "I swear by all the gods in the universe that I will take the life of that wretched man, and if I rot in Hades for avenging the life of my dearest friend, so be it."

Staring into the eyes of her husband and whatever dark presence had chosen to reside within him, Julia's strength was suddenly bolstered as she placed her battle into the strong hands of the God of Heaven's armies. Unflinching, she spoke clearly.

"There is but one God, Barabbas, and He is the only God. He will hold you accountable for your deeds. To swear by the gods of the universe means absolutely nothing, for the god of this world, the devil, will not be victorious in the end. And if you choose to rot in Hades as you have so flippantly suggested, it will be by your own choice and deeds. For the true God of the universe has called you, but you have closed your ears to Him."

The fury that crossed her husband's features was frightful to behold. Shoving her roughly aside,

Barabbas pushed his way out the door, slamming it behind him with a resounding *thud*.

Falling to her knees, Julia lifted her hands heavenward, offering everything to God. The battle had been waged; the plans had been drawn up.

As from the beginning of time, the prince of darkness continued to wage war against the children of the light.

"Oh, God, this battle belongs to you."

The Lord will fight for you, and you shall hold your peace.

"I don't know what to do, Lord God, but You do. Pave the way. Grab the enemy by the throat and cast him far from this house, our home. Trample him under Your feet."

The Lord your God, who goes before you, He will fight for you...to fight for you against your enemies, to save you.

"You promise to go before and behind us, Lord. Do so now with Barabbas, Father. Stagger him with Your awesome power and bring him to his knees." Rising to her feet, Julia lifted her hands heavenward, reaching for the only One who could intervene. "Do so, Lord, whatever it takes."

Barabbas' soul hung in the balance. The enemy would like nothing more than to topple him over the edge, straight into the abyss.

"By Your mercy, God, intervene and save my husband." Drawing strength from the inspired words of Nehemiah, she raised her hands higher and spoke the word of God over her home, herself, her husband.

"Our God will fight for us!"

CHAPTER 48

Mara

"God, help me!" Mara sat bolt upright upon her thin sleeping pallet, her body tense, trembling, and drenched in sweat.

Disoriented, she glanced frantically about her surroundings, suddenly remembering that she had bedded down before the enormous hearth in the kitchen the night before. The prospect of sharing a dark room in the servants' quarters had frightened her. And besides, in the last few weeks she had garnered several enemies, awakening the female servants as she cried out in her sleep and struggled against the imaginary adversaries of her nightmares. Consumed with fear and embarrassment, Mara had opted to sleep in the kitchen, where she felt the most welcome and at ease. Besides, she always awakened long before the kitchen help arrived. Here, she could light the hearth and warm her chilled bones. It seemed as if a permanent chill had taken hold of her – a chill that not even the rumbling hearth could dispel.

Pressing shaky hands against her throbbing temples, Mara attempted to slow her rapid breathing and pounding heart.

The nightmares had taken hold of her again.

Distraught, she wondered if they held any significance. Her ancestors had believed dreams to be a source of divine revelation.

Was God Himself attempting to speak to her? And if so, what was He trying to tell her? The thought was disturbing at best, and downright terrifying at worst.

The nightmares had begun several weeks ago, the night she had agreed to marry Lucius. Every single time, she stood alone in an empty room, preparing for her wedding. In her dream, she knew the guests were already seated and impatiently awaiting the bride's arrival. But to her horror, each time the dream recurred, she found herself lacking pieces of her wedding apparel. In the first dream, it had been her shoes. Clad in her finest gown and preparing to step out of the empty room to meet her beloved, Mara had realized she was barefoot. Not only was she barefoot, but her feet were smudged and dirty, caked with mud and filth. Humiliated, she had thrown open closets and peered behind doors, desperately seeking a pair of shoes to wear for her wedding, but to no avail. Then the trumpet had blasted, announcing the arrival of her bridegroom. Cheeks flaming in embarrassment, she had adjusted her robe, hoping the long hem would cover her bare feet, and stepped out into the open, fully aware of the fact that she was not prepared to meet her bridegroom.

The following night, the dream had occurred again. This time, she had forgotten to do her hair. Embarrassed, she had flown to a mirror to find her hair a tangled, snarled mess. Dead leaves and brambles clung to the knotty tresses, as if she had just run through a thick, tangled forest. Frantically, she had attempted to rake her fingers through her hair to loosen the tangles, but the trumpet had blasted again, announcing the arrival of her bridegroom.

Again, she hadn't been ready.

The dream occurred again and again, deepening in intensity with each passing night. And every single time, she was lacking in some way. She had forgotten her jewelry. Her dress was stained or torn. Her veil was missing. And with maddening regularity, the trumpet had shrieked in unwelcome announcement, reminding her that she was not fit nor ready to meet her bridegroom.

But this most recent dream had been the most disturbing, for in it, Mara had stood before a mirror, basking in the reflection of her own lovely face graced with Roman makeup, her hair elaborately styled in an elegant design. She had been awed by her own beauty, for she had never considered herself beautiful.

But then the trumpet had sounded, the blasting cry announcing the arrival of her long-awaited bridegroom. In her dream, she had reached for the door. Recoiling, she had drawn back at the sight of her own bare arm. Horrified, she had glanced down and realized she had donned a short, simple, sleeveless slip. Why, she was practically naked! How could she step outside and face the crowds and her bridegroom in such a shameful state?

Desperately, she sought an acceptable wedding garment, but the enormous room was empty. She had known she could not present herself in such a state, for she would never be accepted! Instead, she would be mocked, ridiculed, and cast out.

Another trumpet blast had rent the air, sending her heart hammering unbearably in her chest. In one last frantic attempt, she had torn down the curtains hanging from one of the towering windows lining the walls of the vast chamber. Wrapping herself in the tattered curtain, she rushed back to the mirror. Tears welled in her eyes as she examined herself. The curtain was rough and worn, dingy, and even torn in some places. This would never suffice as a wedding garment. The whole idea was a mockery, a sham, a farce. Her own desperate efforts had accomplished nothing. She had no garment worthy to be worn upon her presentation to the bridegroom.

Eyes spilling with tears, she had given in to her grief. For yet again, she had not been prepared for her bridegroom's coming.

Now, as Mara sat shakily upon her sleeping pallet, the power of the emotions she had experienced in her dream tore at her heart. Why must she be plagued by endless nightmares when she longed to celebrate her betrothal to the man she loved? Dark circles were beginning to appear under her eyes, and she had no desire to look like a miserable wraith for her wedding day. The day was fast approaching, and within a week, she would be a married woman.

"Don't do it, Mara."

Alarmed, Mara drew her thin bed sheet to her shoulders, aware of the fact that she still wore the dingy, sleeveless robe she slept in. Heart pounding, she wondered fleetingly if it was the voice of God she heard.

"Who is there?" she dared tremulously.

Alexander stepped out of the shadows, the faintly flickering flames of the hearth casting eerie shapes that danced across his striking features.

Tears of anger and humiliation sprang to Mara's eyes. How long had he been crouching in the shadows, watching her moan in agony as nightmares gripped her? He had no right to be here, to intrude upon her privacy in such a blatant manner!

"Why are you here?" She drew the bed sheet to her chin, her eyes cold and uncompromising.

"Have I mentioned the way I adore your warm welcomes?"

"Only every time we meet."

"Ah, good. So you know how I feel."

"I doubt even *you* know what you really feel, Alexander."

Recognizing her discomfort at his powerful presence, Alexander reached for the robe she had slung carelessly over the back of a wooden chair the night before. After dropping it in her lap, he seated himself in the chair, leaning forward with both elbows upon his knees, his strong hands clasped patiently.

Surprised by the uncharacteristically thoughtful gesture, Mara gratefully slipped the robe over her head and adjusted the billowing folds.

"I'll state my case once more," Alexander said in a low tone, his expression grim. "Don't do it."

Annoyed by her own interest in him, Mara hardened her gaze. "Don't do *what*, Alexander?"

"Don't marry that man. He doesn't love you."

"And *you* do?" She had blurted the angry words before she could stop herself, and now she dropped her gaze in embarrassment.

"I don't know," he answered honestly, gazing intently into the rapidly diminishing flames of the hearth. "To be frank, I never thought myself capable of love."

"I'm sure your cousin would agree with you."

"But now I'm beginning to wonder," he finished calmly, ignoring Mara's insult. "I won't lie, Mara. I am drawn to you in a way I cannot describe. It's not your looks nor form –"

"Because I am not beautiful enough to captivate the attention of an attractive man like *you*?" she interrupted bitterly.

"Thank you for calling me attractive," Alexander conceded with a wry, self-deprecating grin. "But, no, that's not the case at all. You *are* attractive, Mara. Why you fail to see that is beyond me. Perhaps if you didn't consider yourself so unworthy, you wouldn't be selling yourself short."

Mara tilted her head to one side, studying the swarthy young man with cautious interest. When he laid aside his weapons of sarcasm and his sardonic shield, he reminded her of his cousin, Malchus. Tall. Confident. Endearing. Possessing a dry wit and an unexpected dose of humor.

Thinking of Malchus saddened her even further. They had shared such a special friendship. On more than one occasion, she had wished Malchus were a decade older. She would have happily married a man with his traditional values and likable disposition, but their age difference rendered it impossible, in her opinion. And she considered him more like a son or a younger brother than a prospective suitor. No doubt he felt the same way.

"What I am trying to tell you," Alexander said quietly, interrupting her straying thoughts, "is that I feel drawn to you in a way that defies all logic, all understanding. It's as if some powerful force beyond myself is moving me in this direction, guiding me, directing me to you even against my will. Can you understand that?"

Mara cocked her head to one side, her defenses rising. "Ah, so you're saying I should reject a proposal from the man I've loved for ten years because a man I scarcely know is being drawn to me against his will?"

"That's not what I'm saying, Mara –"

"Perhaps you've been struck by one of Cupid's arrows. I've heard the Romans say he is mischievous by nature and has even been known to strike the wrong target on occasion."

"You speak of Cupid," Alexander grinned wryly, "but my ancestors were Greek, and they worshiped Eros."

"Why does that not surprise me?"

"Should I be flattered or insulted?"

"Take your pick. You will believe as you wish, anyway."

"The Greeks worshiped their own gods long before Rome stole their identities and assigned them Roman titles."

"Why should you care? You have no god at all."

Why should that statement bring a pang to his heart? Alexander's mouth hardened as he contemplated the seriousness of her assessment. This past year in Judea had certainly given him much to think about. These Jews were zealously religious, constantly emphasizing the dire consequences of turning away from God.

In Tiberias, the gods had dwelt in elegant shrines that served as houses of revelry and entertainment rather than houses of worship. One could enter and partake of the pleasures Rome had to offer while pledging service to whichever god the shrine represented.

Here in Judea, it was different. The God of the Jews was revered, even feared. And now a new Teacher had arrived upon the scene, claiming to be the Son of this powerful God. Alexander had stumbled upon this Man and His controversial teachings in an attempt to blackmail his cousin and cause his downfall. He hadn't expected to be haunted by the words of the Man speaking with such authority at Solomon's Porch.

*"Most assuredly, I say to you, he who hears My word and believes in Him who sent Me has **ever-***

lasting life, and shall not come into judgment, but has passed from death into life. Most assuredly, I say to you, the hour is coming, and now is, when the dead will hear the Son of God; and those who hear will live. For as the Father has life in Himself, so He has granted the Son to have life in Himself, and has given Him authority to **execute judgment** *also, because He is the Son of Man. Do not marvel at this; for the hour is coming in which all who are in the graves will hear His voice and come forth – those who have done good, to the* **resurrection of life***, and those who have done evil, to the* **resurrection of condemnation***..."*

The words themselves had raised the hairs on the back of Alexander's neck, but even more eerie and disturbing was the fact that Jesus had turned and looked directly into his eyes that day after uttering this troubling statement. It was as if the Teacher had gazed into his soul, stripping away his carefully preened exterior and revealing the rotting stench of his true motives deep within – as if Jesus had known why he was at the temple. Outwardly, it appeared as if he were interested in worship at the temple grounds. But inwardly, Alexander had set foot within the compound to trap another – and his own flesh and blood, at that!

How had Jesus known that? How could He have possibly interpreted Alexander's deepest thoughts, detecting his hidden motives? Most people were charmed by his good looks and confident nature.

But Jesus had not been the least bit impressed, and certainly not fooled. If anything, Alexander had detected the deepest kind of sorrow reflected in His compassionate eyes.

Annoyed by the long lull in conversation, Mara rose to her feet and began to rekindle the fire in the hearth. "Well, I suppose this conversation is over."

Alexander looked at her, unsettled. "It has scarcely begun."

"It's over, in my opinion."

"Do you believe there is a God who controls the universe? Or, like the gods of Greece and Rome, have they all simply been penned by men with overactive imaginations and a desire to both shock and entertain?"

Mara turned and studied Alexander as he stood across the room looking strangely vulnerable. "My upbringing requires me to state that the God of Abraham, Isaac, and Jacob is indeed the one true God who both created and controls the universe."

"But do you believe it?"

Mara sighed, adjusting an extremely heavy cooking pot over the licking flames. Sensing her struggle, Alexander came to her aid, steadying the heavy pottery as if it were a lightweight kettle of little consequence.

Caught off guard by his assistance and surprising strength, Mara hesitated.

"Well?" Alexander asked, aware of their close proximity and the way Mara flushed beneath his scrutiny.

With another wistful sigh, Mara turned from him and prepared to begin her daily chores. "I don't know what I believe."

"You certainly don't believe in *me*."

Mara turned sharply. "What is that supposed to mean?"

"You haven't the slightest bit of faith in me, in my intentions."

"Why should I? I hardly know you, and your reputation is far from commendable."

"People change."

"Rarely, and it requires a total transformation and nothing short of a miracle from God."

"By your speech, I would assume you believe in Him, despite your misgivings."

Mara hesitated. Perhaps she did. Why this sudden longing to know God, to hear from Him?

"Another worthy question, Mara: If your soldier loves you so very much, then why does he insist upon marriage by *usus* rather than a binding union or even a traditional Jewish ceremony?"

Mara blinked, confused by the sudden twist in conversation. Did Alexander know *everything* about her life?

"Lucius wishes to protect my rights," Mara maintained stoutly, peeved by Alexander's annoying logic. She recognized that she offered a flimsy excuse, which irritated her even further. "Marriage by *usus* preserves a woman's rights and does not allow the husband to exert legal control over her."

"Yes, and if either one of you tires of the other, you simply walk out the door and never look back."

"That's not why he suggested it!"

"Isn't it?"

"Of course not. He was simply considering my

rights and my feelings."

"That man has never considered your feelings."

"You don't know what you're talking about."

"For Heaven's sake, Mara, are you really so naïve?"

"If I were, I would have fallen prey to your charms long ago. But that certainly hasn't happened, has it?"

With a sly smile, Alexander retreated toward the door. "Only time will tell, dear Mara. In the meantime, I will leave you to consider my words."

"There is nothing to consider!" Mara shouted after him, annoyed by his dramatic exit.

Alexander paused in the doorway, a teasing smile playing about the corners of his mouth. "We'll talk later."

He disappeared around the corner, his soft chuckle floating upon the air like an ill omen.

Distressed, Mara wept softly as she went about her chores.

CHAPTER 49

Melina

It had been weeks since Malchus had attended a meeting, and Melina experienced both delight and trepidation at the sight of him.

He arrived beneath the sheltered colonnade before Julia, and Melina's face flushed as he jogged toward her with a wide grin splitting his handsome features. Once he reached her, he caught her up in his arms in a warm embrace.

Melina withdrew from his arms, slightly disturbed by the warmth of his touch. She forced a smile that she hoped appeared genuine. "If not for this warm welcome, I might have thought you were avoiding me."

Malchus touched her face tenderly. "I could never do that. But I do have some bad news."

Melina stiffened. "What is it?"

"I cannot stay. You remember Mara, the woman I've told you about?"

"The girl who is in love with the Roman soldier?"

"Yes, that would be the one. She will be marrying the miscreant upon the morrow, and unfortunately, I am to supervise many of the preparations."

Melina was saddened to hear the news. "Then she has not returned to her faith?"

"I'm not sure she ever had one."

"We must continue to pray for her, Malchus. Julia can attest to the dire consequences of marrying an unbeliever." Even as she spoke, warning bells went off in her mind. But surely Malchus could not be considered an unbeliever! He was committed to the God of his fathers, the God of the universe. So why did she feel uneasy when she considered a future with him?

"I doubt it will do any good, Melina. She's made up her mind."

"But God can change a heart."

"Her heart is as cold and hard as stone."

"I find that rather hard to believe, considering the fact that she cared for you when you became a servant as a young boy."

Annoyed by the guilt her statement provoked, Malchus changed the subject. "How have you been faring, Melina? I've missed you."

"I have missed Joanna's serene presence within the palace. She continues to follow Jesus in His travels, ministering financially and helping with food and travel preparations. Oh, Malchus, how I long to meet Him."

Briefly, he wondered why their every conversation had to center around the Rabbi that made him so uneasy. Eager to change the subject, he remarked sincerely, "You look well." *Better than well,* he silently amended with a mischievous grin.

"My faith is strengthened every day," Melina said with a sweet smile. "God is gracious. How can I not be well?"

Julia arrived at that moment, flushed and breathless. As usual, empty baskets dangled carelessly from both arms.

"Julia!" Melina gathered her friend in a joyful embrace, sending her baskets bouncing upon the stone floor. "I see you've been serving again at the Pool of Bethesda."

"It's such a joy!" Julia confided with a broad smile. "Mary and Bartholomew are beginning to open up when I share the Scriptures, and Matthias was there preaching the Word today."

"Mary and Bartholomew? That is the deaf young man with his mother, is it not?"

"It is."

"I continue to pray for them, Julia."

"God is opening their hearts to His Word. It's very exciting!"

"How I wish I could go with you!"

Malchus cleared his throat loudly when Julia failed to acknowledge his presence.

Smiling sheepishly, Julia grinned at him and said rather impishly, "Always a pleasure to see you, Malchus."

"Well, as much as I hate to cut short this delightful pleasure, I must return to the estate. Unfortunately, there is much to be done, and those under my supervision are in no hurry whatsoever."

Melina took his arm and offered him a smile that she hoped conveyed the tenderness she felt for him. It was as if a small rift was widening between them, and she didn't know what to do about it. She knew Malchus was impatient to marry her, but she couldn't do such a thing without the Lord's approval.

She prayed that Malchus would understand, and that his heart would be softened toward the teachings of Jesus. The Rabbi's controversial presence and teachings seemed to be the root of the tension between her and her beloved.

Sensing her unease, Malchus stooped and kissed her forehead tenderly.

Melina gazed up into his eyes, her own misty. "You know I love you, don't you, Malchus?"

"I know you do. I love you, too, Melina."

"Perhaps soon the Lord will answer my prayers and we –"

With a pained smile, Malchus placed a finger upon her lips to silence her. "It's alright, Melina. I love you. I'm not going anywhere...well, except back to Caiaphas' estate," he added with a mischievous smile.

Her peace restored, Melina laughed through her tears. "I will continue to pray for your friend, Malchus. And I'll update Julia about her situation now. All hope is not lost."

Malchus offered a dry smile. "We'll see about that."

Squeezing Melina's hand, he offered Julia an exaggerated bow before departing, tossing a good-natured wink over his shoulder at Melina.

Melina watched him go, her heart aching. How

she longed to marry that man! Why, then, did God remain silent?

I must continue to trust Him, she reminded herself, dismissing the dull ache in her chest. *His will be done, not mine.*

"Well, that was a tender and gripping scene," Julia teased with a toss of her lovely chestnut-colored hair.

Drawn back to the present by Julia's unexpected commentary, Melina glanced into her friend's playful eyes and blushed prettily.

"It appears your feelings are deepening for each other," Julia added, giving her friend's shoulder a playful tweak.

Melina sighed, still blushing in embarrassment. "We wish to marry, Julia, but the Lord has not given me peace about it…at least, not yet."

Julia sobered after glimpsing the agony reflected in the eyes of her dearest friend. "Then you possess great wisdom to wait on the Lord, Melina. I can tell you by experience, to go against the Lord and marry despite your misgivings is a grave mistake. It brings about nothing but pain."

Now it was Melina's turn to grow reflective. "Has it been terribly difficult at home?" she asked after a long pause.

Julia sighed, her gaze drifting to her own sandaled feet in defeat. "Worse than difficult. Barabbas has departed for Galilee. He seeks Amraphel, their leader. The man is evil incarnate."

Melina nodded her understanding. "You have mentioned him. I pray for him as well."

Julia arched a slender brow. "Do you pray for

everyone?"

"I certainly try!" Melina laughed in her pleasant, silvery tone.

"Well, then, can you pray specifically that he will be eaten by a lion or mauled to death by an angry bear?"

Melina laughed before she could stop herself. "I'm sorry," she gasped, covering her mouth with her hand. "I cannot pray for such things. But I *have* been praying for his salvation."

Julia's mouth hardened. "There's a real laugh."

"It can happen, Julia."

"You haven't met him."

"But God knows him by name. The Lord will stop at nothing to reach him. But Amraphel will have to choose for himself – the Lord will not force him."

"This is what I fear most when I pray for Barabbas. I see the Lord reaching out to him in a thousand different ways, and yet he hardens his heart every single time. I don't know what else to do."

"You must continue to pray for him – that is your role. The Spirit of the living God will accomplish the rest."

"Oh, you make it sound so easy."

Melina smiled. "I suppose we make it much harder than it ought to be."

"But this time I'm truly frightened, Melina. Barabbas saw the soldier who murdered Dan. Until now, he thought the man was dead." Julia met Melina's gaze, her hazel eyes burning with intensity. "He has vowed to kill him."

Melina drew in a shaky breath. "Dear God, help

us. Intercede on our brother's behalf."

"Pray without ceasing, Melina. I fear the real battle has already begun."

"I will not cease to pray for him, Julia, nor for you."

Sweet assurance filled Julia, for she knew Melina was faithful. Earnestly, the lovely young servant girl would beseech the very throne room of Heaven on Julia's behalf.

"Speaking of prayer requests, who did you agree to pray for while speaking with Malchus a moment ago?"

"A woman named Mara. She serves in Caiaphas' house as well. Apparently, she has lost her way. She is about to marry a Roman soldier, and Malchus is convinced the man is simply using her."

Julia shook her head sadly. "How I wish I could warn her against such a foolish decision. She may have her entire life to regret it."

"We must pray for her, Julia, fervently. The Lord will hear, and He will act."

"Why on earth would *you* pray for *me*?"

Stunned to silence, both Melina and Julia stared open-mouthed as a tall woman dressed in simple garments and a modest head covering strolled deliberately beneath the colonnade, facing them head on.

Melina needn't have met the woman to know exactly who she was.

Looking to Julia in surprise, Melina mustered her most inviting smile and held out her hand in welcome. "You must be Mara. There aren't words enough to describe my joy in finally meeting you, dear sister!"

CHAPTER 50

Mara

Malchus' beloved was a lovely young woman with waist-length black hair, luminous green eyes, and a gentle smile that invited both secrets and confidences. Mara could see exactly why Malchus had fallen for her. The young woman possessed a tranquility and a calm delight that was absolutely lovely to behold.

Mara noted the exotic young woman who stood beside the peaceful servant girl. She was exquisitely beautiful with slanted, hazel-colored eyes framed by dramatic lashes, smooth olive-toned skin, a soft, full mouth, and an impressive figure. Golden brown curls spilled down the girl's back like a gently cascading waterfall. She stood out like a beacon among the other women milling about the Upper Market despite her simple dress.

A rose among thorns, Mara thought dejectedly. Why were some women granted exquisite beauty while others bore none at all? Life was unfair. Mara detected a hint of fire in the attractive woman's eyes and assumed she must be very passionate.

Suddenly remembering her manners, Mara stuttered in embarrassment and managed a shaky response. "You are correct in your assumption. I am Mara. I followed Malchus because I suspected he was seeing someone and…well, I just felt led to follow him. It sounds absurd, I know."

Melina smiled warmly. "Not at all. I imagine it was the Spirit of our God that led you."

Mara looked up at her, curiosity written all over her features. "Well, it was my own two feet that brought me here."

"*A man's heart plans his way, but the Lord directs his steps*," Melina explained with a luminous smile. "My name is Melina. Malchus is a dear friend of mine."

"I imagine he's a bit more than that," Mara stated pointedly.

Defenses rising, Julia studied the woman sharply. "Have you come all this way just to insult a woman who has done you no harm?"

Reaching out, Melina touched Julia's arm. "It's alright. She hasn't insulted me at all." Turning her attention back to Mara, Melina added calmly, "Julia and I are so pleased to meet you. Malchus has told us so much about you."

"Oh, I'm sure he has."

"Many wonderful things," Melina clarified with an encouraging smile. "It was so kind of you to care for him when he joined the high priest's staff as a small boy."

Mara nodded once, blinking back tears.

"Have you come with a specific purpose in mind?"

Biting her lower lip, Mara looked away from Melina's compelling gaze. "Frankly, I'm so afraid. I don't know what to do, Melina. But I felt led to come here and perhaps…perhaps the Lord really did have something to do with it. I just don't know."

Melina took the woman's hand in her own, compassion sweeping through her. "How can we help you?"

Blinking back tears, Mara studied her own two feet uncomfortably. "I'm not sure if anyone can help me."

"God can help you," Melina said with great feeling. "He loves you, Mara, and He waits for you to turn to Him. His arms are open wide."

Mara glanced about her bustling surroundings uneasily. "Malchus doesn't know I followed him."

Julia's eyes gleamed conspiratorially. "We won't say a word," she winked, her initial dislike for the woman swallowed up in sympathy for her.

"I am to marry tomorrow at sunrise."

Neither woman spoke, and Mara sensed both were searching for the proper words. Perhaps there weren't any.

"I've been having dreams. They trouble me so."

"What kind of dreams?" Julia asked with great interest.

"Dreams about my wedding day." Mara looked to Melina, her eyes full of hope. "The moment I laid eyes upon you, Melina, I knew you could tell me what they meant."

Melina attempted to conceal her surprise. "I am not a prophetess like Huldah, nor a seer of dreams like Joseph or Daniel –"

Mara was not dissuaded. "Something urged me to follow Malchus – perhaps it was the Lord, although I can't imagine why He would be interested in my plight after I abandoned my faith in Him. Then I saw your face, Melina. It's as if a small voice whispered into my ear: *Ask this one about your dreams.*" Mara covered her face with her hands, overcome. "You must both think I have lost my mind."

Taking Mara by the hand, Melina led her further into the pleasant shade. "Come, sit with us. And tell me about your dream. I will listen."

After the three women were settled comfortably in the shade, Mara looked to Melina, her eyes full of tears. "Every night, it's the same. I am haunted by a recurring dream. I am standing in an enormous, empty room. I don't know where I am, and I'm filled with confusion. But somehow, I know the bridegroom is coming. I must be ready for him. As I am about to step outside, I realize I am not prepared. In one of my first dreams, I had no shoes. I glanced down to see dirty bare feet peeking out from beneath my gown. In another dream, my hair was a snarled, tangled mess. And in last night's dream, I had no wedding garment. I was about to step out to meet my bridegroom when I realized I was barely clothed in a flimsy slip. You can imagine my shame and embarrassment. I rushed about the empty room, looking for an appropriate wedding garment. When nothing could be found, I ripped down a dingy old curtain filled with holes and wrapped it around my body. But when I gazed into the mirror, I knew it would not do. My bridegroom would see my nakedness and recognize I was completely unprepared for him. At that moment, the trumpet had sounded, announcing his arrival. I cannot explain the agony that swept over me in that moment."

Melina nodded slowly, thanking God as recognition dawned and sacred Scriptures surfaced in her mind in answer to Mara's plight. Taking Mara's hand, she smiled. "God is truly gracious. I believe He has given me the interpretation."

Mara stared at her, wide-eyed and astounded. Even while relief washed over her, her spirit was filled with alarm and trepidation. Intuitively, she sensed that what she was about to hear would turn her life upside down.

"Throughout the Scriptures, the Lord has referred to Himself as the bridegroom, and to those who follow Him as His bride." Melina spoke carefully, her delicate brows furrowed. "God's intent is to mold and shape us into a pure and lovely bride in whom He takes delight, and we also delight in Him, our bridegroom."

Julia's eyes brightened with recollection. "It is so!"

"In your dream, Mara, you dwelt in a state of fear and confusion, as you do now. You knew your bridegroom approached, but you were unprepared. When you realized you had no wedding garment, you were paralyzed with fear because you recognized that you would not be accepted by the bridegroom in such a state. When the trumpet sounded, you knew you had run out of time."

Mara nodded, her eyes wet with tears. The terror of last night's dream returned to her full force.

Sensing Mara's struggle and filled with compassion for her, Melina squeezed her hand. "Do you know Jesus, Mara?"

Mara nodded, her face flushing with shame. Of course, she knew of Him – everyone in Judea and Galilee knew of Him!

But not everyone in Judea and Galilee has agreed to betray His followers, she thought, consumed with shame.

"Jesus is our bridegroom, Mara," Melina said softly, her eyes aglow. "Your dreams haunt you because you know He is coming, and you must be ready for Him. But you are not. This is why you attempted to cover your own nakedness in your dream. But, Mara, only Jesus can cover and cleanse us. Only Jesus can provide the robe of righteousness that covers our shame and nakedness."

"How can you know this?" Mara whispered, visibly trembling.

"Because the prophet Isaiah said, *I will greatly rejoice in the Lord, my soul shall be joyful in my God; for He has clothed me with **the garments of salvation**, He has covered me with **the robe of righteousness**, as a bridegroom decks himself with ornaments, and as a bride adorns herself with jewels.*"

Mara shook her head, amazed by the correlation between her own dream and the prophecies buried within the ancient Scriptures. "But how can you know that *Jesus* is our bridegroom, when the Scriptures say the bridegroom is God Himself?"

"Jesus is God's Son, and the Scriptures tell us that God will send His Son into the world to cleanse us of our unrighteousness. Chuza, my overseer, told me that Jesus Himself confirmed this when He spoke at a synagogue in Nazareth, for He quoted the prophet Isaiah – the very same section I've just shared with you concerning the garment of salvation and the robe of righteousness which He will bestow upon you! Jesus said, *The Spirit of the Lord is upon Me, because He has anointed Me to preach the Gospel to the poor; He has sent Me to heal the brokenhearted, to proclaim liberty to the captives and recovery of sight to the blind, to set at liberty those who are oppressed; to proclaim the acceptable year of the Lord.* If you continue to read the scroll from which Jesus read that day, proclaiming Himself the Anointed One whom God has sent to save us, you would find many other beautiful things Jesus has promised to do. He has come *to comfort all who mourn…to give them beauty for ashes, the oil of joy for mourning, the garment of praise for the spirit of heaviness; that they may be called trees of righteousness, the planting of the Lord, that He might be glorified.* The prophet then reminds us that it is He – Jesus now revealed to us – who will cover us in a blessed robe of righteousness. He will adorn us as a lovely bride, pure and chaste, eager and prepared to meet her bridegroom – the Messiah, the Christ!"

"Amen," Julia breathed softly, overwhelmed by

the powerful presence enveloping the three women huddled in the shade.

"I was certain my dreams pertained to my upcoming wedding rather than some mystical ancient prophecy which I know nothing about."

"In a way, it does," Melina answered gently. "This is not a vague prophecy veiled in mystery, Mara. The Scriptures are clear: God's Son will come as a bridegroom. He will pursue us, drawing us to Him. He will come first not to condemn the world, but to save it. Then He will return to Heaven. But He will come again, Mara. The Scriptures are quite clear: Upon His second return, when the trumpet sounds – just as the trumpet sounded in your dream – He will gather His bride and carry her to a perfect home, where she will dwell with Him in perfection for all eternity. There, as Isaiah predicted, *He will swallow up death forever, and the Lord God will wipe away tears from all faces.* But we must be ready for Him, our bridegroom. When the trumpet sounds, our time runs out. We must make a decision to follow Him *now*, while there is still time."

"And how does this concern my upcoming union with Lucius?"

"We must seek the Lord for guidance concerning every decision of our lives. You are about to enter a sacred and binding union, Mara. Will this man ready you for the coming of your Savior, or will he stand like a stumbling block between you and your true Bridegroom?"

Troubled, Mara looked away.

"Only God can save us, Mara. Nothing on this

earth can satisfy the aching desire in our hearts. We long for our Savior, and only by accepting Him can we find true peace."

"But I don't even know Him," Mara whispered, tears streaming down her face.

Melina and Julia exchanged knowing smiles.

"But you *can*," Julia assured her with confidence.

"How?"

"Repent of your sins and turn to God," Melina said softly. "A very famous man, John the Baptist, exhorted us to bear fruits worthy of repentance. Ask God to forgive your sins and trust Him to lead and guide you. He will do what is best for you, Mara, no matter what."

"What of my betrothed?"

"Does he love the Lord?"

"He is a Roman soldier, recently promoted to Caiaphas' captain of the guard. He is very successful, a powerful man."

"But does he love the Lord?" Melina repeated gently.

Mara's eyes filled with tears of trepidation. "I think you already know the answer to that."

"Turn to God, Mara, while there is still time."

"But I love Lucius. How can I bear to see him about the palace knowing what could have been?"

"God has good plans for you, Mara – better plans than you have for yourself!" Melina insisted. "Can you trust Him?"

"But there is the possibility that Lucius might accept the God of my fathers someday, is there not?"

"Mara, I thought the same when I married my

husband," Julia said with great feeling. "I was certain I could soften his heart. Please, don't make the same mistake I did."

Mara stared at Julia, surprised. "You married an unbeliever?"

"I did. I tell you, disobedience to God results in great pain and suffering. Only God can change a heart, Mara, and it is terribly dangerous to marry someone, imagining that you can change them. We can change no one – not even ourselves. Only God can do that."

"I'm so afraid."

"I know," Melina said, her eyes filled with sympathy. "And God knows. He will take you by the hand and lead you through this, if you will trust Him."

Considering her dreams of recent nights, Mara held back tears. Twisting her hands nervously in her lap, she wondered if the weight of her contrary emotions would crush her spirit. "I don't know what to do."

Melina offered another sympathetic smile. "I think you do, Mara. The Lord may be calling you to walk away from this potential husband, but He will fill that hollow void and heal your aching heart. Though it may be hard to believe right now, no man on this earth is capable of fulfilling your deepest desires. Only your heavenly Bridegroom can do that."

"Consider another of God's awesome promises," Julia added, her eyes alight with joy and peace. "*For Your Maker is your husband, the Lord of hosts is His name; and your Redeemer is the Holy One of Israel; He is called the God of the whole earth...*"

"*For the Lord has called you like a woman forsaken and grieved in spirit,*" Melina said softly, picking up where Julia had left off, "*like a youthful wife when you were refused, says your God.*"

"It's as if it were written for me!" Burying her face in her hands, Mara wept. "I *am* grieved in spirit, I *am* forsaken!"

"You may be grieved, but you are never forsaken," Melina reminded the sobbing woman. "The Lord your God has called you, Mara. He calls you still. *The Lord has called you like a woman forsaken and grieved in spirit.* He will never stop pursuing you, but you must respond to His entreaties. Will you accept the call?"

"I so desperately want to…" Shoulders shaking, Mara wept as only a broken woman can. "But, unfortunately, I cannot."

CHAPTER 51

Malchus

Grimly, Malchus observed from the sidelines as Mara and Lucius exchanged sacred vows beneath a flower-clad arch in one of Caiaphas' spectacular gardens. Lucius appeared rigid and ill at ease, though he attempted to mask it beneath a forced smile.

Mara appeared equally uneasy, though it was apparent she had taken great care to style her hair and select a worthy garment to wear for her groom. She was very attractive, in Malchus' opinion, despite the fact that she lacked the glowing luster of a new bride.

Malchus' heart clenched as he watched an elegantly clad priest presiding over the ceremony. A few of the household servants were in attendance, but the affair boasted a rather pathetic turnout. The women who served with Mara did not approve of Lucius. His greed and inclination to intimidate were rather famous within Caiaphas' household.

Saddened, Malchus struggled to dismiss his own guilt and his battling thoughts. Perhaps he should have made a greater effort to dissuade Mara from making the greatest mistake of her life. Had his own bruised pride influenced his decision to remain silent?

Why did it feel like *he* was participating in sealing Mara's cruel, unfortunate fate?

Guilt gnawing relentlessly at his conscience, Malchus looked away...directly into the eyes of his cousin, Alexander. The man leaned against an elegant marble pillar beneath the long portico at the fringe of the garden, his body tense, his eyes burning with angry fire.

What on earth was he doing here?

***

Mara

Even as she stood before her lover of over a decade, pronouncing sacred vows to him, Mara's thoughts were elsewhere.

She couldn't shake the image of a gentle, soft-spoken servant girl, her eyes aglow with true contentment, the sacred Scriptures upon her tongue.

For your Maker is your husband...the Lord has called you... Will you accept the call?

Numbly, Mara repeated the words of the priest, wondering fleetingly if the man dressed in elaborate garments was Jewish or Roman. After all, this ceremony was Roman by nature. She found it troubling that Caiaphas had approved such an inherently non-Jewish ceremony, even hosting the simple affair in his own gardens… She found it even more troubling that Lucius had insisted upon marriage by *usus*. She knew prominent Roman women possessing property and fortunes often consented to marriage by *usus* because they didn't want their husbands exerting legal control over their assets… but she hadn't a penny to her name! What protection was Lucius actually offering her by this most informal version of marriage according to Roman law? Even this *ceremony* was unnecessary! *Usus* did not involve a ceremony or a marriage contract – the man and the woman simply moved into the same house and began a life of mutual consent under one roof.

Was this marriage even legally binding? What would the Lord have to say about her decision, her capitulation to Lucius' demands?

Doubts gnawed at Mara's spirit as she gazed into the eyes of her beloved.

He was uneasy, she could tell.

After all these years, why was he marrying her *now*?

The priest pronounced a few magnanimous words accompanied by several animated gestures, and Mara realized it was finished.

The ceremony had ended. She was now a married woman. For the first time in her life, her existence held some meaning, some purpose! She would be a loving, doting wife. Her husband would bless her with children. She would not be alone in her feeble old age.

She had done the right thing, the advantageous thing. She had done what any other woman in her position would have done.

Hadn't she?

She offered her new husband a tremulous smile. He appeared to return the gesture with great effort.

Troubled, Mara's eyes wandered toward the edge of the garden. She saw Malchus, watching grimly from the shade of a covered balcony. His stance and posture grated upon her raw nerves, and she quickly looked away. She was fed up with his self-righteous airs and archaic values. If only he knew what she knew about him! Perhaps then he would save his criticisms for someone else! One little word in the right ear about his secret excursions to see the forbidden Rabbi and he would be ruined...

Suddenly overwhelmed with guilt, Mara averted her gaze. Her eyes locked with a pair of dark eyes, smoldering like two burning coals.

Her heart leaped into her throat at the sight of Alexander leaning stiffly against a tall pillar, his lean body tensed like a wary animal, his arms crossed over his broad chest, his eyes glittering a clear warning.

She remembered his admonition earlier that week: *Don't do it, Mara*.

Tearing her gaze away from the swarthy young man at the garden's edge, she took her husband's hand and prepared to leave. She needed to get away from here. She needed to escape.

Jaw tensed and hands clenched, Alexander turned and left the garden.

CHAPTER 52

Julia

The Feast of Trumpets dawned with a mighty blast
of a thousand blaring instruments upon the first day
of the seventh month, the sacred month of Tishri.
This feast would not only prepare the people for the
holiest day of the entire year – the Day of Atonement,
which would occur on the tenth day of the same
month – but was also celebrated as the first day of the
civil year, despite the fact that God had established
the venerated month of Nisan – the esteemed month
of the sacred Passover – as the first month of the year
for His people at the time of the Exodus.

Startled by the mighty trumpet blasts, Julia sat
bolt upright upon her sleeping pallet, her bed sheets
sliding into her lap. For one brief moment, she wondered if that long-awaited trumpet had sounded,
signaling God's chosen ones to the eternal Promised
Land! Just as quickly, she remembered the day and
realized that the sacred feast had begun.

Pressing trembling hands against her ears, Julia attempted to adjust to the deafening sound of countless trumpets blasting the cry of victory from the distant temple compound. The trumpets would sound from the temple from dawn until dusk, ushering in the civil New Year and stirring the hearts of Jerusalem's lethargic residents. This would be a sacred day of rest, a day to offer sacrifices to God, a day to contemplate the mighty works He had done for His chosen people. The ten days following the Feast of Trumpets and leading up to the fearsome Day of Atonement were considered the Days of Awe, in which all in Judea and Galilee would contemplate their need for repentance and atonement – their need for a Savior.

Blood stirring with excitement, Julia rose from her sleeping pallet and threw open the front door. Leaning out, she feasted upon the sound of the mighty trumpets.

Throughout the holy Scriptures, the trumpet symbolized many things, particularly the call to action. It was the trumpet call that urged the Israelites to pack their belongings and move forward on their weary desert trek as they neared the Promised Land. The trumpet marked the sacred feast days and the holy sacrifices. Its strong, dependable cry had called men to action in times of strife and sounded the song of celebration during times of peace. The trumpet called the people to gather together to partake of worship and holy assembly before God. It was a call to praise, to worship. A summons of peace. The trumpet also warned of coming danger. It was the trumpet that summoned the troops to battle and, after, boldly proclaimed the song of victory.

Julia considered the thousands of people that would flock to the temple to celebrate the sacred ordinances of this special day, eager to hear the Law proclaimed aloud with great pomp, ceremony, and rejoicing.

In that moment, she made up her mind to join them.

Last month, Barabbas had left on another important assignment from her father. This time, she had been terribly grateful for his absence. While traveling with her father's caravan, he would be unable to extract the vengeance he had purposed against the Roman soldier he despised. She knew he had been actively seeking information about the legionnaire. Even now, she was unable to forget the livid expression twisting his features when he had learned that the murderer had set sail for Rome and would not return for many months. Silently, Julia had thanked God for His mercy. Perhaps in the following months, Barabbas would respond to the consistent calling of the Lord upon his life.

Fervently, Julia prayed it would be so.

But with Barabbas away on business, she could easily slip to the temple compound and bask in the glory of God within the Court of Women. Her husband was not present to shame or forbid her.

Stepping back inside and closing the front door, Julia tenderly traced the Hebrew writing etched into the ancient doorposts of her home. She wondered if the original owners of this home had considered that, perhaps centuries later, these sacred words would comfort the heart of a frightened young bride.

She remembered the night she had discovered them. Now, it seemed so long ago. The ancient letters read: *Hear O Israel: The Lord our God, the Lord is one! You shall love the Lord your God with all your heart, with all your soul, and with all your strength...*

She had drawn strength from that command, finally realizing what it was that the Lord required of her: *love.*

Love for Him. Love for others. And love did no harm to its neighbor.

How simple was that? Why did she often attempt to make it so complicated?

After quickly washing her face and brushing her long tresses with quick, purposeful strokes, Julia slipped into a simple, comfortable gown, smoothed a head covering over her shining hair, and slipped out the door.

Her heart beat in time to the sounding of the trumpets; she reveled in the glory of the day.

***

"Melina?"

The lovely young servant spun around, a look of pure relief washing over her gentle features.

Laughing joyfully, Julia ran into the arms of her friend. "What are you doing here at the temple compound?"

"I was beginning to wonder about that my-self," Melina laughed melodiously, gazing about her surroundings in absolute astonishment and awe. "Julia, I've never seen anything like this. I am overwhelmed."

"The temple is rather stunning, isn't it?"

"Many times, I have seen it from a distance. But I had no idea it was so enormous, so magnificent! Julia, I felt completely lost, tossed about in this raging sea of humanity. I was praying, asking God for help, the moment you arrived."

"That would be the first time I was anyone's answer to prayer," Julia laughed, nearly giddy at the prospect of sharing this special day with her dearest friend. "How did you come to be here? I thought we agreed with Malchus not to meet today."

"Yes, he's far too busy trying to keep up with the high priest's demands," Melina laughed, amused. "But Herod dismissed several of his most trusted servants to partake of the festivities, and I was among them. I couldn't resist coming here, Julia. For so long, I've wondered what it would be like."

"It's beautiful, isn't it?"

"Beautiful…and frightening…and awe-inspiring!"

The trumpets continued their marvelous, never-ending song, filling the air with crackling excitement. Far beyond the Court of the Gentiles, the magnificent temple face towered into the heavens like a shining beacon of marble and gold. Encased by impressive Roman-pillared porticoes on all sides, the temple compound seemed to stretch on for eternity. Even filled to the brim with worshipers and revelers, the compound appeared absolutely enormous.

Moments earlier, Melina had feared she would be swallowed up in the madness.

Taking Melina's hand, Julia led her through the suffocating throngs of people milling about the Court of the Gentiles.

"Where are we going?" Melina asked, her blood tingling with excitement.

"I want to take you closer to the temple sanctuary," Julia explained, her voice tinged with enthusiasm. "You gain a better view from the Court of Women. It's absolutely spectacular!"

"It looks rather spectacular from here, too," Melina chimed, her heart pounding in her eagerness and anticipation.

Nearing the edge of the Court of the Gentiles, Julia paused suddenly, uncertain.

Melina sensed her friend's unease. "What is it?"

Cheeks flaming with embarrassment, Julia scanned the imposing row of temple guards flanking the wall that separated the Court of Women from the Court of the Gentiles. Each guard bore an intimidating pointed spear. Tall, immovable, and ever watchful, their eyes scanned the milling crowds, always on the alert for any threat.

"Perhaps we should enjoy the view from here," Julia faltered, embarrassed that she hadn't had the foresight to consider what she was doing.

Confused, Melina's eyes flitted to the guards, then to the warnings posted beyond them. Her heart sank as she read the bold Greek inscriptions posted conspicuously and equally spaced, stretching across the entire span of the dividing wall:

No foreigner
Is to go beyond this balustrade
And the plaza of the Temple zone.
Whoever is caught doing so
Will have himself to blame
For his death
Which will follow.

Fleetingly, Melina's eyes traveled to the deadly looking spears in the hands of the armed guards, the dangerously sharp iron tips glistening in the sunlight.

Julia looked embarrassed. "I'm sorry, Melina. I forgot that the Gentiles –" she winced. Why did the term sound so harsh and unfeeling upon her lips? "I forgot that only Jews are permitted past this point."

Melina smiled graciously, recovering from her initial surprise. "You go on ahead, Julia. I can enjoy the festivities from here!"

Indignation welled up inside of Julia. Wasn't the Lord God the Creator of *all* men? Why, then, were some barred from His presence?

"No," Julia stated firmly. "I will remain with you."

"Oh, Julia, I'm simply holding you back. Please, do go on."

"I will not."

Melina's expression was pained. "I should not have come. I have hindered your ability to celebrate with the other women."

"Melina, I would rather celebrate with you than with anyone else."

Suddenly feeling terribly conspicuous, Melina studied Julia's uncompromising features and smiled warmly. It appeared the matter was settled.

"The teachers of the law often read from the sacred texts beneath Solomon's Porch. All are permitted to gather there," Julia explained, her eyes resting upon the impressive double-pillared colonnade on the eastern side of the compound. "Shall we go listen?"

"Malchus heard Jesus speak at Solomon's Porch!"

"I must admit, I went there first – hoping to catch a glimpse of Him."

Melina smiled sheepishly. "I did as well, but He was nowhere to be seen."

"Perhaps another time. For now, we must content ourselves with whatever we discover at Solomon's Porch. The speakers are often rather entertaining."

Melina nodded in agreement, feeling bereft and discomfited. She couldn't dismiss the image of the long row of guards with pointed spears shielding the way to God, standing uncompromisingly in the path of atonement.

Why am I shunned from Your presence, Lord? Isn't salvation for the Gentiles also? Surely, I have not been mistaken, Lord...

A large crowd had gathered at Solomon's Porch. A rather unimpressive man dressed in simple attire held a scroll before him, proclaiming the message to the listening crowds.

"*And it shall come to pass afterward,*" the man loudly declared, "*that I will pour out My Spirit on all flesh.*"

Tears sprang to Melina's eyes, for *already* the Lord had answered her unspoken prayer. *All flesh*, the Scriptures said! God would pour out His Spirit on *all* flesh, and that included the Gentiles.

"*Your sons and your daughters shall prophesy, your old men shall dream dreams, your young men shall see visions. And also on My menservants and on My maidservants I will pour out My Spirit in those days. And I will show wonders in the heavens and in the earth: blood and fire and pillars of smoke. The sun shall be turned into darkness, and the moon into blood, before the coming of the great and awesome day of the Lord. And it shall come to pass that whoever calls on the name of the Lord shall be saved.*"

Strengthened, Melina basked in the sweet presence of her Maker.

Whoever calls on the name of the Lord shall be saved.

Whoever meant anyone, everyone! And *whoever* most certainly included *her*! One day, she would shout this message from the rooftops! How she longed to proclaim the Gospel of God's salvation for all people to the very ends of the earth!

CHAPTER 53

Malchus

A hush fell over Jerusalem on the sacred Day of Atonement.

Today, the lot would be cast. Today, the scapegoat would be chosen. Today, blood sacrifice would atone for the sins of all mankind within the hidden chambers of the Most Holy Place.

The venerable high priest, Joseph Caiaphas, was resplendent in garments of pure white linen worn on the Day of Atonement rather than his magnificent golden vestments. Malchus knew it galled his arrogant master to "borrow" the magnificent golden vestments from the Roman powers, which were secreted away from the sealed chambers of the Antonia Fortress and presented to the high priest. But on the Day of Atonement, the priest donned simple white linen garments once rendered ceremonially clean. He would then perform the ritual sacrifices that would result in the cleansing of the sins of the priestly family and the nation. The blood sacrifices would wipe out the record of sins committed the previous year.

All of Judea held its collective breath as Joseph Caiaphas climbed the marble steps that would take him to the temple sanctuary. On this day alone – the consecrated Day of Atonement – was the high priest permitted to enter the Holy of Holies, the Most Holy Place. There, he would sprinkle the blood of the sacrifice upon the place where the mercy seat once resided.

After the sin offerings had been presented, Caiaphas proceeded to the next ceremonial ritual – casting lots to determine the scapegoat. Once the lot was cast, two scarlet ribbons were presented and fastened to both the scapegoat and the sacrificial animal.

The temple compound sprawled before Malchus from his vantage point at the Royal Colonnade. Though he was too far away to witness the symbolic rituals, Malchus knew exactly what Caiaphas would be doing. He imagined the man regally examining the goats presented to him. One would be placed upon his right hand, the other at his left. Two golden lots would be placed in an urn, and Caiaphas would solemnly place his hand within. Once the lots were drawn, they would indicate which goat would become the scapegoat to be released into the wilderness. The remaining goat would then be sacrificed for the sins of the people.

Scarlet ribbons would be fastened to both animals. The high priest would place his hands upon the scapegoat's head, softly murmuring a disturbing chant as he transferred the sins of the nation to the animal. A trusted servant would then lead the scapegoat out into the wilderness to die. Malchus understood the symbolism: Once the sins of the people were transferred to the scapegoat, he carried them into the wilderness, where they perished with him. Like the scapegoat, the sins of the people would be no more.

The second goat was offered as a sacrifice, and the scarlet cord that had been fastened to it was tied to the Temple door. When God accepted the sacrifice, the scarlet thread fastened upon the door turned white as snow, indicating that God had removed the sins of the people.

Within the Temple compound, Caiaphas watched, solemn and stern, as a young man took the rope bound to the scapegoat and led him away. The second goat was slaughtered, its blood offered in atonement for the sins of the people.

When Caiaphas returned from the Most Holy Place, he paused with his hand upon the Temple door. His practiced eye traveled downward and came to rest upon the ribbon bound to the door.

The ribbon flapped and flickered as a chill wind swept through the temple compound. Stretching forth his arm, Caiaphas lifted the ribbon, once the deepest shade of scarlet.

It was white as freshly fallen snow.

A slow, mordacious smile curved his thin lips, his body trembling at the power he possessed. He – Joseph Caiaphas, high priest of Israel – stood between an entire nation and the God they served.

Life, death, mercy, and condemnation were his. As long as he drew breath, he would wield this power like a sword. The power was his to bear.

Releasing the snowy white ribbon, Caiaphas watched as it flapped helplessly in the breeze.

It was finished.

***

Caiaphas appeared pensive and brooding when Malchus served him wine upon his own private terrace later that evening.

Malchus would've liked to assume it was due to the fact that the priest had spent a grueling day at the Temple, his hands immersed in the blood of innocent animals. Unfortunately, Malchus knew better. Innocent blood had never weighed heavily upon his master's conscience.

Outwardly, the high priest appeared comfortable and relaxed, stretched upon an elegantly upholstered settee, a full golden goblet balanced delicately in one hand.

Inwardly, the man was a seething mass of tension. His shrewd gray eyes were alert, his body taut.

Malchus could almost feel the tension crackling in the air.

"Abisha!" Caiaphas' unexpected command startled Malchus, but he quickly regained his composure.

Abisha passed beneath an enormous archway and bowed before his master.

"Summon Lucius. Do it now."

"As you wish, my lord." With another slight bow,

Abisha hurried away as quickly as his old bones would permit.

Malchus hid his annoyance. Lucius was the last person he wanted to see. Marriage had certainly done little to soften the man's rough exterior nor dampen his thirst for violence. Fleetingly, Malchus wondered how Mara fared after her first few months of marriage. They seldom spoke anymore, but he often noticed her weeping as she went about her chores in the kitchen.

Lucius appeared with surprising speed, causing Malchus to wonder if he had been expecting the summons.

"My lord?"

"The problem we discussed last night?"

"Remains unresolved, my lord."

"Then it is a problem."

"Nothing that cannot be easily amended."

Caiaphas released a longsuffering sigh. "I hadn't a solitary moment to weigh our options until now," he admitted, as if the single most important religious day of the entire year was a terrible inconvenience.

Malchus stood, silent and rigid, disturbed by the course the conversation was taking.

"How much does he know?" Caiaphas asked after a long, uncomfortable pause.

"Enough to prove problematic, my lord."

Caiaphas' mouth formed a grim line. "This won't do."

Lucius stood at the alert, awaiting his orders.

"Take care of it."

Hand resting lightly upon the hilt of his gladius,

Lucius nodded his consent. "It will be as you say." Clicking his heels sharply, Lucius left the room to perform the master's cruel bidding.

Malchus' mouth went dry. He had overheard enough of these whispered discussions to recognize that some unfortunate soul was about to be eliminated. He was slightly relieved when he considered the fact that the victim could not possibly be the Rabbi Melina esteemed so highly. Caiaphas wouldn't lay a finger on Him – at least not yet. The people adored Him, and Caiaphas couldn't risk inciting a rebellion.

No, whoever had erred was clearly too unimportant to create any harmful repercussions.

Caiaphas had proven more and more secretive as of late. Unsettled, Malchus made a conscious decision to keep his eyes and ears shut. He had no desire to stumble upon the wrong information. He'd surely become Lucius' next target, buried beside a long row of unfortunate souls who knew too much about Caiaphas' secret endeavors.

Sickened, Malchus wondered if the sacrifices the priest had offered that afternoon would cover his murderous deeds of this evening. He attempted to hide his grimace, but not in time.

"You object?"

For one terrible moment, Malchus gazed into the coldest gray eyes he had ever seen. Swallowing the gall that had risen in his throat, Malchus managed mechanically, "I live to do your bidding, my lord." Even as he spoke, he hated his capitulation, his inexcusable cowardice.

"Do you?" Caiaphas' eyes never left his as he took

a slow sip of wine. Lowering the goblet, he swished the ruby liquid slightly back and forth in the cup.

Malchus' body broke out in a cold sweat. He prayed unlike he ever had before. "Yes, my lord."

"Yes, what?"

Gritting his teeth, Malchus ground out stiffly, "I live to do your bidding."

Caiaphas studied him with an air of challenge, daring the servant to defy him. "You'd best remember that."

Malchus breathed a silent prayer of thanksgiving when Caiaphas finally tore his gaze away from him and dully surveyed the spectacular view the terrace offered of the Temple compound.

Malchus attempted to mask his fear as he continued to serve the brooding priest. Even so, his hands shook, and his stomach clenched in the most unpleasant way. For the first time, it occurred to him that he stood alone on an empty terrace with a ruthless killer.

Had it always been this way?

It would seem the darker presence had finally won its battle for the soul of his master.

CHAPTER 54

Julia

It was as if her last shred of hope disintegrated before her eyes.

Barabbas returned from his journey a hardened man. Something was eating at him, tearing him apart, gnawing at his spirit. It was as if his bitterness, fury, and thirst for revenge had taken root in his soul, and now the branches spread throughout his entire being, wrapping their relentless tendrils about his heart and mind, numbing his conscience, and threatening to choke all that was good.

Julia watched in horror as her husband threw himself into the cause of vengeance with untamed and unmatched fury. The fact that his intended victim had sailed for Rome infuriated him. He was seething inside, lashing out at a future that he could not control.

After immersing herself in the Word of God and meditating upon the teachings of Jesus, Julia found herself more and more appalled, for her husband's actions stood in stark contrast to the Lord's way. Alarmed and helpless, she prayed without ceasing as a dark presence settled over her husband like a raging storm.

Had Barabbas silenced his conscience so frequently that his deeds no longer mattered to him? Had he reached the point of no return? Would God continue to reach for him?

As she went about her chores, Julia prayed fervently for the soul of her husband. She prayed for God to intervene.

She sensed that something was about to happen... something earth-shattering, possibly even life-threatening...and whatever it was, it involved her husband.

***

Floating upon a dark, vast sea of nothingness, Julia shrank back at the deafening sound of fierce waves crashing upon coastal rocks. The waters roared ominously like a raging beast, churning and foaming madly as they smashed upon the rocky shore.

Horrified, Julia realized she stood alone in the darkness, facing the fury of the sea. Her bare feet sunk into the coolness of the soft sand. She shivered in the icy breeze, wrapping her arms about her own frail body in an attempt to warm herself.

Suddenly, a voice even mightier than the crashing ocean waves boomed across the expanse of the sea...

"Fear not, for I have redeemed you; I have called you by your name; you are Mine."

As if in response, a tremendous wave crashed against the shoreline, churning and foaming angrily as the receding waters swirled momentarily about her bare feet. The water was so cold she sucked in her breath. Even so, the powerful voice that called to her drowned out the fury of the raging sea.

Unafraid, Julia stepped into the churning water.

"When you pass through the waters, I will be with you; and through the rivers, they shall not overflow you."

Gingerly, Julia took another step into the sea. The water swirled about her calves for one brief moment before slowly receding. Then, miraculously, the waters parted.

Delighted and amazed, Julia walked through the raging sea upon a path of dry ground. A firm hand took hold of her own. She needn't look to know who held her. She knew the tender Shepherd walked beside her, guiding her through this dark and harrowing experience.

Julia's delight evaporated when searing heat coursed through her entire body. A fear unlike anything she had ever known washed over her. Frantic, she realized that the raging waves had transformed into towering pillars of flame on either side. With alarming speed, those flaming pillars closed in on her, threatening to smother her in their intense heat. Tears coursed down her cheeks as billowing smoke assaulted her senses and seeped into her garments. The putrid smell of fire and smoke filled her nostrils. She could feel the heat upon her skin, and she knew in that moment that her life was about to end.

But then the powerful voice returned. "*When you walk through the fire, you shall not be burned, nor shall the flame scorch you.*"

Instantly, the pillars of flame drew back. For the first time, Julia realized her hand was still firmly clasped by One with a grip as gentle as a newborn's yet relentless as forged steel. She was still being led, guided through the fire by the One who possessed all power over the deadly, devouring flames.

"*For I am the Lord your God, the Holy One of Israel, your Savior.*" The words resounded with the might and power of an avalanche, relentless as a raging flood. In that moment, Julia knew she would be held securely in the arms of her Savior.

No matter what happened.

Julia awoke with a start as a sharp cry escaped her lips, her entire body drenched in sweat. Clasping her hands over her heart, she attempted to slow her rapidly beating heart.

As the fog began to clear, she gazed about her surroundings. One lone oil lamp continued to sputter and burn pitifully from its perch on the table, a faint ring of yellow light hovering like a halo above it. Other than that, the house remained dark. Quiet.

She wasn't surprised to find that Barabbas had not yet returned. Emotionally exhausted, she had succumbed to her weariness and retired early, doubtful that her husband would appear before morning. He was probably still in the hills with Amraphel, sipping stolen wine and feasting upon the fruit of another's labor.

Rising slowly to her feet, Julia crossed over to

the window and gazed longingly at the full moon casting silvery beams of light upon the open street. Resting her arms upon the windowsill, she tried to dismiss the fear that clutched at her heart.

Her dream had been so frightening...and so very *real.* So real, in fact, that she had no doubt whatsoever that the Lord had spoken to her. She supposed that she should be comforted, for the Lord had promised to walk beside her. She knew her tender Shepherd would take her by the hand, lovingly guiding her through the difficulties ahead.

Even so, that did not change the chilling facts the Lord had revealed to her. For soon, she must face the deep waters.

Soon, she would go through the fire.

CHAPTER 55

Barabbas

Barabbas stood before a long row of freshly dug graves. Amraphel's ambushes and raids were growing even more brazen, more daring.

And as a result, more of his men were perishing.

Tears wet his eyes, mingling with the sweat upon his brow. He had lost many friends today. And he couldn't help but wonder...

Was it even worth it? What were they really accomplishing?

And when would *he* be next?

Heart pounding, blood afire, consumed with pain and fierce emotion, Barabbas fell to his knees and, gripping the front of his garment, rent the rough fabric with a savage cry. The garment groaned in protest as his strong hands ripped the tattered pieces until they hung pathetically, fluttering gently in the desert breeze. He knelt before the unmarked graves, grieved, wondering if anyone would care that these men were lost forever.

I care.

Barabbas froze.

More than you will ever know.

The hairs on the back of his neck stood on end. Lifting his eyes, he was startled to see another pair of eyes gazing steadily back at him.

An older man dressed in simple desert garb stood behind the row of graves, watching him with solemn eyes. There was nothing remarkable about him, and yet his old eyes possessed an air of mystery that raised the gooseflesh on the back of Barabbas' neck.

Shocked that he had actually been caught off guard, Barabbas reached for the hilt of his dagger.

The man held up a hand. Somehow, the simple gesture was enough to halt Barabbas in his action. Tense, Barabbas remained upon his knees, hand resting upon the hilt of his dagger, strangely unsettled.

Where had this desert nomad even come from? Surely, he hadn't materialized out of thin, dry desert air! Barabbas knelt in a vast wilderness, far from the nearest settlement, far from civilization. Like the endless sky above it, the rocky desert expanse was wide open. From where had this stranger come?

And then the curious man of the desert spoke.

" 'Now therefore,' says the Lord, 'Turn to Me with all your heart, with fasting, with weeping, and with mourning. So rend your heart, and not your garments.'"

Ashamed, Barabbas gazed down at his own tunic, torn and hanging limply from his heaving chest.

"*Return to the Lord your God, for He is gracious and merciful, slow to anger, and of great kindness; and He relents from doing harm.*"

Barabbas stared at the strange desert nomad, the hairs on the back of his neck prickling, a chill skittering down his spine, a strange longing tugging at his calloused heart.

"*Who knows if He will turn and relent and leave a blessing behind Him.*"

Lowering his gaze, Barabbas shook his head in awe. "A blessing," he rasped bitterly. "I am the least deserving of all men."

He had lowered his gaze for but a moment. When he glanced up again, the man of the desert was gone.

***

The haunting cry of the shofar drifted upon the cool night air after a lone priest lifted the ancient horn to his lips from the Pinnacle Corner, ushering in the new moon and inviting the inhabitants of Jerusalem to remember the Lord their God, their Deliverer.

From her perch at the Royal Colonnade, Melina was provided a stunning, panoramic view of the entire city and the sprawling temple compound below. It was a spectacular sight. Beyond the towering walls enclosing the ancient city, gently rolling hills welcomed the setting sun. Jesus had been known to frequent those hills, particularly the Mount of Olives. What she wouldn't give to freely roam those sloping hills, gold-tinged in the setting sun, until she stumbled upon the Man she so desperately longed to meet.

Malchus had seen Him. So had Julia. And her dear friends, Joanna and Chuza.

She alone had missed the opportunity to bask in the glory of the Son of God.

Blessed are those who have not seen and yet have believed...

Warmed by the still small voice that continued to minister to her heart, Melina lifted her hands in worship, savoring the shofar's melancholy song.

Though she hadn't yet laid eyes upon the miracle-worker who fulfilled thousands of years of ancient prophecies, she believed in Him. These were remarkable and mysterious times. She knew she was privileged to experience them, and she intended to hide these moments in her heart, to cherish and ponder them.

And now, she would gladly embrace this sacred opportunity to commune with the true lover of her soul. Certainly, there were times when God felt rather distant. In those moments, she had learned to lean upon her faith rather than succumbing to her wayward emotions. But there were also times – like this – when the Lord's presence was so astoundingly clear she felt as if she were enveloped in a warm spiritual blanket, cloaked in His tenderness, mercy, and love.

"Oh Lord my God, You are so good. I am in awe of You – and I am amazed to see Your hand at work." Smiling, she considered the words of the prophet Isaiah. He had so perfectly captured the essence, might, and power of her God that she couldn't resist borrowing his fitting words as she conversed with her Creator.

"*O Lord, You are my God. I will exalt You, I will praise Your name, for You have done wonderful things; Your counsels of old are faithfulness and truth… For You have been a strength to the poor, a strength to the needy in his distress, a refuge from the storm, a shade from the heat…*"

Several minutes later than the time they had arranged, Julia drew up alongside Melina and smiled at the joy upon her friend's face. "This is a beautiful meeting place."

"I feel so close to the Lord here – like I could reach out and touch Him."

"You can! He is always near."

"He is working mighty miracles. It thrills me to see it. And I simply cannot help but wonder…what will be next?"

Julia's eyes danced with delightful anticipation. "Only God knows, but we *do* know it will be spectacular."

The two women fell into a comfortable, reflective silence. Far below, in the temple compound, the priests bustled about, performing their final tasks before the day drew to a close. The entire compound was bathed in the warm pink and golden tones of sunset. Magnificent white stones and gold accents gleamed brilliantly in the ebbing light.

Melina's eyes drifted from the priests working busily below, to the vast expanse of the city beyond. Just south of their glorious location at the Temple compound swept the Lower City, its tightly clustered houses washed in the fading light. In stark contrast to the crowded precinct of the poor, the magnificent Upper City towered upward toward the west like a stairway to Heaven, breathtaking marble villas dotting the broad avenues and fashionable vistas. Enclosed by thick, intimidating walls, Jerusalem appeared nestled in comfortably for the night, bathed in a glorious, otherworldly light.

The city was indeed magnificent. Herod the Great hadn't spared a single coin in his ambitions to cultivate Jerusalem into a great city rivaling the powerful cities of prestigious Italy or Greece. In the great distance, his own palace rose like an imposing fortress, keeping watch over the entire city. Scattered throughout the winding streets and alleys, Herod had erected impressive secularized buildings as well. The great theatre rose grandly in the distance, beckoning the residents to enter and revel in the obscene and graphic dramas brazenly enacted upon its massive stage. How many citizens lived for the plethora of base entertainment for which Rome was becoming famous? Did these people fail to recognize that their sinful pastimes only whetted their desire for further shocking obscenities rather than sating it?

High upon a hilltop perched the house of Joseph Caiaphas, the ruthless high priest. Melina furrowed her brow, deep in thought, when she considered Malchus' dark master. If Malchus' observations were accurate, Caiaphas had much in common with her own master, Herod Antipas.

"God is at work," Melina observed quietly, "But there are men who desire to silence the clear call to action, to obedience. They would like nothing more than to smother the message of hope before it reaches the waiting world."

"But what does God promise?" Julia reminded her with a knowing look. "*Surely*, God says, *as I have thought, so it shall come to pass, and as I have purposed, so it shall stand.*"

"Amen." Melina's eyes rested upon the vast expanse of ridges and valleys surrounding their ancient city. "No man can alter the will of God."

"God's will prevails."

Melina's gaze swept across the ancient city, considering the many mountains and valleys, the magnificent structures, the beauty of the setting sun upon the eastern hills. On the southwestern side of the city was the abhorred Valley of Hinnom, and on the eastern side was the Kidron Valley. Melina marveled, imagining the great men and women of old who had gazed upon these same hills and valleys with majestic mountains roundabout.

"The prophesy of Ezekiel weighs heavily on my mind," Melina mused thoughtfully. "*The hand of the Lord came upon me and brought me out in the Spirit of the Lord and set me down in the midst of the valley, and it was full of bones.*"

"The Valley of Dry Bones!" Julia confirmed. It had been a childhood favorite of hers. "My father used to chase me about the house, crying out, 'Dry bones, dry bones, come alive!' And I would squeal and jump upon his back, proclaiming to be the dry bones brought forth!"

"Yes! I recently learned of it, and I was intrigued."

"Who wouldn't be?"

"I like to imagine the ancient prophet standing upon a rocky ledge, defeated as he stares upon a vast valley filled with the bones of dead men – filled with the bones of his people. And Ezekiel said, *He caused me to pass by them all around, and behold, there were very many in the open valley; and indeed they were very dry."*

"Like us," Julia mused, imagining the valleys beyond the city walls scattered with corpses, their dry bones decaying in the sun. "Hopeless, dry, and lifeless."

"But what did God ask of Ezekiel?"

Julia smiled faintly. *"Son of man, can these bones live again?"*

"So I answered, 'O Lord God, You know.'"

"He alone knows!" Julia enthused. "He knows our past, present, and future. He knows what He wants to do for us, and He also knows what our stubborn hearts will allow."

"And God said to Ezekiel, *'Prophesy to these bones, and say to them, **O dry bones, hear the word of the Lord!**'"*

A broad smile stretched across Julia's radiant face. "Even now, we are called to the same: *Hear the word of the Lord!* God's Word is life. Will we accept the life God offers us?"

Closing her eyes, Melina lost herself in her own gentle recitation of an ancient, powerful story.

"So I prophesied as I was commanded, and as I prophesied, there was a noise and suddenly, a rattling; and the bones came together, bone to bone.

Indeed, as I looked, the sinews and the flesh came upon them and the skin covered them over, but there was no breath in them."

"I can just see it," Julia breathed, her cheeks flushed with excitement. "An endless valley, stretching on as far as the eye can see. And filling it, piles of dried out human bones – once a powerful army, now dead. Gone. Defeated. A fiery prophet stands above the gruesome scene, stern-faced and solemn. In obedience, he begins to speak the word of the Lord, and then there is a great rattling as those old bones rise – seemingly of their own accord – and meld together, piece by piece. A mighty wind blows through the ancient camp as muscles and sinews appear upon the bones, and then flesh wraps around those fearsome forms. Imagine the mighty rattling as the armor of a thousand warriors appears and locks into place! And there stands an impenetrable army, lifeless and still, awaiting the command of God."

"God said, *'Prophesy to the breath, prophesy, son of man... Come from the four winds, O breath, and breathe on these slain, that they may live.' So I prophesied as He commanded me, and breath came into them, and they lived, and stood upon their feet, an exceedingly great army."*

"And like those dead, dry bones, we are completely dead in our sins, oblivious to the powerful life God wants to grant us. But when we heed the word of the Lord, our lives are transformed."

"And God is doing so even now," Melina added with an awed smile. "One by one, He is raising up an army of men and women who will follow Him, live for Him, possibly even die for Him. The great question is – who will accept the call?"

"God, grant us the faith and the strength to accept this mighty calling," Julia prayed softly. "There are so many lost." Tears stung her eyes as she considered her own husband.

Sensing her friend's distress, Melina took Julia's hand in her own. "*The Lord is gracious and full of compassion, slow to anger and great in mercy.* He will continue to reach for us, to call us by name. It is not His will for any to perish."

"Lord God, may it be so."

Sadly, Melina considered the people God had placed in her own life. So many lost. So many grasping for joy and fulfillment in every single place – except where they would actually find it. And yet the call went out to each and every one of them. The opportunity was graciously extended to *everyone*.

Why, then, did each respond to the call in vastly different ways?

She thought of Barabbas, madly pursuing the path of vengeance as he sought to silence the voice of God.

Malchus, and his hesitance to accept the Savior, apprehensive about the turmoil and persecution that would surely follow.

Mara, and her paralyzing fear of being alone.

Alexander, and his determination to pursue pleasure above all else.

Elias, and his stubborn self-dependence.

Salome, and her desperation to make her own way, choose her own path.

Herod Antipas, and his longing for power and recognition.

Caiaphas, and his thirst for absolute control.

All of these clung desperately to the very things that prevented their complete surrender to the only One who could heal them.

But then there were others... Julia, for example, had completely surrendered her life to the Lord. Joanna and Chuza were committed to God, whatever the cost. Julia's neighbors, Isaac and Deborah, had left all to follow Jesus. And she, Melina, had whole-heartedly embraced the message of hope and redemption found in God alone.

Why couldn't the others see that in their desperate attempts to capture happiness and experience true fulfillment they were destroying their own chances of ever actually finding it?

Only God could provide lasting joy, peace, and fulfillment. And one must accept His call to faith in order to experience the miracle of everlasting life.

Stretching out her arms over the ancient city of Jerusalem, the beloved city, the bride of kings, the city of peace, Melina clung to the promises of God and spoke the word of life over its inhabitants. For not only did the Lord God call His children to faith, to action, to obedience, but He also commanded them to sound the alarm, to spread the word, and to continue boldly in prayer.

"O dry bones, hear the word of the Lord! *In that day this song will be sung in the land of Judah: We have a strong city; God will appoint salvation for walls and bulwarks.* Oh sleepy Jerusalem, will you be ready for the salvation of our God?"

"Heed the word of the Lord, Jerusalem. Heed the call of our God," Julia whispered in agreement.

"For God Himself has commanded, '*LIFT UP YOUR VOICE LIKE A TRUMPET*!' And so we shall. *For God so loved the world that He gave His only begotten Son, that whoever believes in Him shall not perish but have everlasting life*! Believe, O Jerusalem! Believe upon the Lord and His Son, Jesus, that you may be saved!"

As if in response to their mighty clarion call to action, another blast of the shofar rent the air, floating upon the early evening breezes like a gentle beacon, an invitation, to accept the Word of the Lord, the Word of Life, the trumpet call of God.

Lifting her hands and eyes heavenward, Melina drew in a lusty breath, thanking God for His mercy and His goodness. "Precious Lord, Your wonders are awesome to behold. Surely the time for salvation draweth nigh! And it is nearer now than when we first believed!"

"Amen," Julia agreed softly, her eyes bright, her features awash with hope.

Melina's luminous emerald eyes mirrored that same blessed hope. For, like Julia, she had made up her mind long ago, and instinctively, she knew there would be no turning back.

Jesus was calling men and women to become His followers, His disciples. Yes, there was danger. Such a decision involved great risk. But even the greatest risk on earth could not compare with the all-encompassing peace and power made available to the saints by the Spirit of Almighty God abiding within His only Son.

Without the slightest hesitation, Melina accepted the call.

It was time to show the world what it meant to follow Jesus.

A LOOK AT: REDEEMED
BY RACHAEL C. DUNCAN

One of History's First Love Stories Ever Told.

Set in a land of ancient mysteries and unexpected miracles - the Promised Land - this is the powerful love story not only of Ruth and Boaz, but also of Adara and Kemuel - a young, childless couple struggling to survive the curse of barrenness in a culture convinced the lack of children equates the presence of sin. Together, as their lives intertwine by the mighty hand of God, these two couples experience both the magnitude of God's redemption and the marvel of His grace.

Be swept away in this Biblically-based narrative of hope, as you discover the relentless power of faith and redemption.

Racheal interweaves a Biblical romance with a fictional romance that readers are loving!

ABOUT THE AUTHOR

Rachael Duncan is a passionate follower of Christ. Her goal is to reach as many people as possible for the sake of Christ and His kingdom. She believes that God has gifted each of His children with different gifts to be used to strengthen the body of Christ and fulfill the Great Commission. (Matt. 28:19-20; 1 Cor. 12)

Rachael was blessed to be raised in a strong Christian home, and she accepted Jesus Christ as her Lord and Savior at a very early age. Since then, she has determined to live her life in accordance to His Word and to share the love of Christ through the gift of writing.

Rachael has been passionate about writing since she was a small child. She especially loved writing plays and short stories. At the age of fourteen, she wrote her first play, which was performed as a dinner theatre production by a local school.

She has been actively involved in both women's and children's ministries for over a decade. Currently, she enjoys teaching a weekly girls' Bible study, writing plays for a local homeschool group, and participating in local ministry outreaches for women and children.

Rachael currently resides in Texas with her husband and their first "child" – a playful rescue puppy named Riley! In addition to her writing, she is an enthusiastic "keeper of the home" and "helpmeet", as well as being actively involved in ministering to the women and children God has placed in her life. (Titus 2:3-5; Gen. 2:20-23)